THE IRON SLEEP

THE IRON SLEEP

RONALD PEARSALL

LONDON
MICHAEL JOSEPH

First published in Great Britain by Michael Joseph Ltd
52 Bedford Square, London WC1B 3EF
1979

© 1979 by Ronald Pearsall

ISBN 0 7181 1761 1

Filmset in Great Britain by
D.P. Media Limited, Hitchin, Herts
and printed and bound by
Billing & Sons Limited, Guildford, London and Worcester

1

A soldier without a war, thought George Oakwood, sergeant-major in the Royal Warwickshire Regiment, that was what he was. At one time, it would not have mattered. He would have bided his time, waiting for the next call, the next adventure, the next expedition into foreign parts. But he was now fifty. He had done all that was expected of him in the Boer War. And more. But time was taking its toll.

Now here he was back in the city of his birth, no longer certain whether he had a home. His wife had left Aldershot while he was away, and taken up work as manageress of a shoe shop in Birmingham. Jane's letter had been friendly, but slightly remote. If she had a mind to it, she could tell him to find his own way, fill in time in the Warwickshires' barracks until his discharge came through.

He recoiled as he stepped outside New Street station. Motor-cars, horse-drawn omnibuses, sturdy waggons, bicycles, and carriages, all vied for road space. Huge posters stated the merits of the music-hall programme at the Hippodrome. He looked down Corporation Street, remembering that he had seen it being built. He took a cab, hoping that Jane had received the telegram, and stared out of the window at a people who had already forgotten the war. The army wanted to forget the war, too: it had been fought by too many old men with fond memories of the Zulu Wars and easy annihilation.

So this was what he must consider as home. He paid off the cab-driver, and counted the upstairs windows. Three bedrooms: one for him and Jane, one for the boys, and one for little Mary, though of course she would not be so little now. How old was she? Twelve? Certainly he was taken aback by the young man who answered the door.

'Hullo, Dad,' said Harry, 'come on in.' George took off his cap, as if he were visiting unfamiliar relations rather than coming home from the wars. Harry must be eighteen—about time he enlisted. He thought he would wait a while before touching on the subject.

'Where's Leonard?' he asked, as he sat down while Harry bustled about making him a cup of tea.

'Oh, Leonard's at the library,' Harry replied, 'he reads a lot. He'll ask you all about the war.'

Harry looked at his father from the kitchen doorway. It was like looking at a stranger. And so it seemed to Jane when she came in from work. Her heart thumped. Was it George? Her mind went back to that day more than twenty years before when she had found him sitting in that poky little hovel in Hockley.

'Hullo, Jane,' said George, getting up and giving her a peck on the cheek.

She had a moment of panic, reminded of the hated foreman of the factory where she once worked making pins, but George was equally nonplussed. Jane was no longer a soldier's wife but something near a lady in her long black dress with neat lace at the neck, a becoming jacket trimmed with velvet, and a hat high on her hair. *Her* hair? No, she must be wearing a kind of wig, what they called a chignon. Her eyes were as blue as ever, but the face was more finely chiselled, the mouth firmer, the voice more authoritative.

She took him round the house. There were two big bedrooms and a box room. 'I sleep in one of the big rooms with Mary,' explained Jane, 'and the boys have the other big one.' She pushed open the door of the small box room, and George looked inside. There was a single bed, a chest of drawers, a marble-topped washstand, and a wardrobe. On top of the chest of drawers were his books, a couple of regimental photographs and a few odds and ends—an old pocket-watch, a sovereign case, a pocket-book and a fountain pen.

For want of something to do he picked up the pen. 'I don't think I want that,' he said, 'it always leaked.'

Jane sat on the bed, making up her mind. 'I'll be straight with you, George. I've managed perfectly well without a man for two and a half years and I don't want to start again. We're

2

both too old for those sort of games. I've thought about it a good deal, even when I was in Aldershot. I'm a breadwinner now.'

'I was never mean with you,' said George uncomfortably.

'Of course you weren't, George,' Jane said, touching his hand, 'but things have changed. I'm still fond of you, but we have to sort this out from the start. What you have done in South Africa is your own affair. I know what soldiers are like, none better.'

At one time she could have visualized George going red in the face, hair bristling, mouth tight. But George looked at his hands. 'Yes,' he said quietly, 'things have changed. I'm finished in the army, Jane, pretty sure I'm finished. "You can go on the reserve," the adjutant said, "but you won't be needed." Re-enlistment? "It's a young army now", he said, "none of your old soldiers." I'll have to find something to do, that's for sure. I won't sponge on you.'

'We can talk about that later,' said Jane, 'but the boys need a father to keep them on the straight and narrow. Mind, Harry's a good boy. He didn't have to do a newspaper round. He decided that for himself. He's up at five every morning, then back to take the children to school, then fetches them at mid-day.'

They went downstairs, and Harry poured out tea for his mother. He had read that when man and wife were reunited after a long separation they fell into each other's arms, kissing and cuddling, but mum and dad didn't. They sat at opposite ends of the table talking about the weather, the trip home, the shop, the new fashions in shoes and how they had changed. While they were chatting, Leonard came in.

'Where's your rifle, Dad?'

George patted him on the head. 'Had to hand it in, son,' he said.

'Were the Boers hard to beat?' the boy demanded.

'Hush, Leonard,' reproved his mother, 'your father doesn't want to talk about the war. It's all over now.'

'It's all right, Jane,' said George, pleased that the boy was interested. 'It's like this, Leonard. They fought a different kind of war to the one we were trained to fight. They didn't have big slow-moving armies like us. They fought from horses. . . .'

'I know that, Dad,' broke in the boy impatiently, 'I've read

3

all about that in the *Strand* magazine. But were they good shots? They don't tell you that. And what sort of rifles did they have?'

George and his eight-year-old son were still talking about the war, about General Roberts and General French, when Harry slid away, went into the cycle shed, removed a brick from the wall and took out some cigarettes. He pulled out the cycle, opened the door again and headed for freedom, represented by Roy.

A year older than Harry, Roy lived in one of those middle-class houses that George had seen from the cab. The gateposts were cracked and peeling and the iron gates had long since disappeared. The garden was overgrown, and old zinc baths and perambulators poked up above the long grass, serving as fortresses and castles for children and love-nests for alley cats. The front door was barricaded with planks, and entrance to the house was effected through a basement door at the side.

As Harry pushed his way into the house, he could hear the gramophone squeaking out its music hall tune:

> I'm very fond of pickin'
> A little bit of chicken,
> A little bit of mutton or a little bit of ham.
> It's just a very little
> Of any sort of victual,
> A little bit of pie, or raspberry jam.

Roy looked out over the rails at the head of the basement stairs. 'Bit late, aren't you, cocky?' he inquired.

Roy Abbott was a thin young man with sleek hair and a small moustache which he darkened with a black pencil. He was dressed in dapper trousers and a tight-fitting coloured waist-coat.

'Don't matter, anyway. We can catch the second house at the Hippodrome.'

'Is your sister coming?'

Roy nudged his friend in the ribs. 'You fancy her, don't you, pal? I've seen the twinkle in your eye. What kept you so long?'

'Dad came back,' said Harry, going into the room and winding up the gramophone.

4

Roy did a parody of a march, pursing his lips and imitating the sound of a bugle, his arms pivoting up and down like those of a long-distance walker.

'Got a smoke?' he asked suddenly, and Harry took out his packet of Gold Flake. 'Ta,' said Roy, taking one, lighting it by flicking a match on his thumbnail, a trick Harry had tried to copy more than once without success.

'Your mum's out?' asked Harry.

'In the pub,' answered Roy negligently. 'She'll be back with a bloke soon, I'll be bound.'

'I've never seen your mum,' said Harry.

'The only time you're likely to see her is lying on her back with her legs open,' said Roy. 'Still, she makes a living at it, give the old bag that.'

He put his foot on one of the over-stuffed chairs and gave his patent-leather shoes a shine with the chintz cover. Harry picked up the ornaments on the dusty mantelpiece and read the inscriptions: a present from Ilfracombe, a present from Weston-super-Mare, a present from Minehead.

'We used to go to the seaside every year,' said Roy, putting on his jacket. 'She used to pick up a fair amount of men, and they'd have to pay me to keep out of the way. She took it off me, though. Part of her wages, she said, the old cow. She did it everywhere, behind rocks, in bathing-huts, you name it, the old cow, she's had it every place under the sun. Dotty Abbott, known everywhere from Land's End to John o'Groats. Before I was born she used to have a crib down in Cherry Street in town. Then she took up with old Abbott. He was old then, now he's ancient. Seventy or thereabouts.'

'Is he your dad?' asked Harry.

Roy snorted. 'Do you mind?' he asked indignantly. 'I draw the line somewhere. Funny, I think he was in the army once. Must have been, mustn't he, if he was a recruiting sergeant in Dale End?'

The two men went off to catch the bus to the Hippodrome, Harry aware that Roy's clothes made him look old-fashioned and a bit shabby. But the girls looked at Harry and not Roy when they got off the bus and walked round the side street to the gallery paybox. Harry found the Hippodrome a romantic place at night, with its tall mock-Persian tower probing into the foggy

5

sky, the twinkling lights around the entrance, the chocolate girl giving him the eye as she loaded up from the kiosk.

They clambered up the stairs after paying their threepence each. 'Who's the first on?' Roy asked.

Harry looked at the programme. 'A bloke named Vince,' he replied.

Roy spat on the stone steps with disgust. 'I've seen him before,' he said. 'He's only got two songs really, "Come into the garden, Maud" sung like a woman, and "Chickaleary, one, two, three". If you think Abbott's old, you ought to see *him*.'

As if on cue, the banal words of 'Chickaleary' floated down the steps. Jane Oakwood would have recognized them. For she had heard them on her first (and only) visit to the music hall when she was seventeen, when she had gone to the Hockley Palace with the Oakwoods' lodger, Sam. She would not have recognized the singer, for Vince was now an old man. He knew the audience laughed at him instead of with him. They did think he was comical dressed up as a woman, but daft as well.

Roy ignored the stage as they came up at the top of the gallery and plunged into the tiny bar.

'Ah,' said the fat barmaid, her glass necklace shimmering over her bulging bosom, 'the stage-door johnny himself, his very self.'

'Less of the lip, Sal,' said Roy, 'and a bit more service. Usual, Sal.'

'How are you keeping yourself?' asked Sal.

'Mustn't grumble,' replied Roy, 'up and down you know, like a bishop's dangler.'

'What would you know about that, you dirty little heathen?' Sal asked coyly.

The men drank their bitter.

'Poor old sod,' said Roy, 'I really don't know how he gets a booking.'

'Old time's sake mainly,' said Sal. 'I remember when he first came to Brum, when you wasn't even a twinkle in your old man's eye. I was in the pay box at the Hockley. Always full of soldiers from the barracks feeling you up. Threepence for the gallery and a penny to put your hand up Sal's drawers they used to say. Cheek!'

'That was the Warwickshires,' said Harry suddenly.

'Gawd, he can speak!' said Sal in mock surprise. 'That's right, love.'

'Dad was at those barracks,' said Harry, 'he used to gab on about them and an old bloke called Stryker, Sergeant Stryker. Sounded a real bastard.'

'Old Stryker?' Sal burst into laughter, filling the men's glasses again and pouring herself a gin. 'Gawd's struth, I remember old Stryker. He wasn't above a bit of four-legged frolicking I can tell you. Ah, those were the days I can tell you. Them young men from the barracks, they didn't need to pay me no penny.'

'Still', said Roy, bored with these reminiscences, 'you kept yourself to yourself I'll be bound, eh, Sal?'

Sal did not like sarcasm, and said nothing, and the two young men went and found themselves seats, putting their feet on the chairs in front to the annoyance of other patrons.

A comic came on doing a pale reflection of Albert Chevalier, and a troupe of acrobats swarmed on after him.

'Look at them thighs, mate,' said Roy, licking his lips, 'look at all them bleeding thighs. I'll go down and chat up to them in the interval.'

Marco the magician did not come up to expectations, and the smashing of the watch did not go down well.

'Let's see that bleeding watch!' yelled a man in the stalls, and there was a fight between him and the accomplice who had handed up the watch.

Roy and Harry bent over the guard rail to see what was happening.

'There's Judy,' said Roy. 'The little cow's on to the game young. That's a real old codger she's got with her.'

Harry felt disappointed, and he was still brooding on Judy when the lights came up for the end of the first half, the safety curtain covered with advertisements fell with a clang, and the audience made a run for the bars.

Deciding that he would nip down to the stage door to see if he could sneak in to have a word with the female acrobats, Roy was gone before Harry could turn round. Harry decided to hang around outside to see if he could see Roy's sister, Judy. He had just turned the corner into Hurst Street when he saw the girl come out, looking petulant. His heart beat as he saw that she was alone.

'Hullo, Judy,' he said, sidling up.

The girl's face cleared as she saw who it was. Her hair was frizzy in the modern style and framed a face that was pert and attractive. Her best features were her brown eyes and her cupid's bow lips, delicately outlined in carmine as her mother had taught her. The eyes, too, had help from a stick of mascara. She looked, thought Harry, like something off a picture post-card, and that, in his book, was a compliment. She wore a long dress, nipped in sharply at the waist.

She took Harry's arm and led him round the corner.

'The dirty beast,' she said, her large eyes flashing, 'he pinched my thigh. Look!'

She pulled Harry into the entry and lifted up her dress and the froth of white petticoat. Above the stockings and below her purple garter was a small bruise. Harry's mouth felt dry as he eyed her slender leg.

'I'll kiss it better,' he said boldly, and he bent down and placed his mouth about the bruise, moving it slowly towards the hidden regions.

'Saucy,' said Judy moving backwards.

'Where are you, Judy?' shouted a voice, and Harry peeped out. A very elegant gentleman in a fur-collared coat and sporting a monocle was standing under the gas lamp, unconcerned by the manner in which passers-by were staring at him.

'Come on, Judy,' shouted the man.

'I must go,' whispered Judy, and before Harry could stop her she had flitted out.

He watched her slip her arm under the man's and disappear into the theatre. Women! he thought. They get you going and then they drop you like a hot brick. It was the first time he had seen a girl's leg, and the thought of that garter kept him going through the second half, and he even encored the second appearance of Mr Vince.

2

It was not really a barracks, thought George Oakwood as he walked down Thorpe Street. It looked more like a school, a great red-brick building with narrow barred windows, a pointed archway cluttered with ornament, with a date on the keystone. 1884, he read. Then he was still a youngster at Aldershot making his mark. Just before Harry was born. He was not too sure about Harry. He did not like the way he sloped off at night to meet this fellow Roy, and he had caught Harry looking at him and Jane with pursed lips. He had seen that look on the face of recruits; it meant, 'How much can I get away with?'

His uniform was spick and span, the brasses were burnished, his boots were a pleasure to look at. The belt was drawn in an extra notch so that the waist bulge was hidden and his hair, slightly longer than it had been in his days as a drill sergeant, was combed to cover the incipient bald patch. 'Sergeant-Major Oakwood to see Colonel Ludlow,' he said to the corporal curtly. If he was going out, damn it, he was going out in a soldierly manner, not whining to come back like a whipped cur.

'Colonel Ludlow is not available, Sergeant-Major,' said the corporal uneasily and looked thankful when a sergeant took over.

'Morning, Sergeant-Major,' he said cheerfully, 'anything I can do?'

'Morning, Sergeant. I was told to look in at my leisure to see Colonel Ludlow about re-enlistment.'

'Colonel Ludlow's on sick leave,' said the sergeant, then turned and asked the corporal: 'Who have we got in in the way of officers, Corporal?'

The corporal said something that George Oakwood did not hear, but it seemed satisfactory, for the sergeant nodded and trotted off, returning shortly with the message to let the sergeant-major through.

Oakwood was used to surprises—his wife getting a job, the house in Birmingham, being put in the spare bedroom by himself without kicking up merry hell—but this was one that took him by the throat. His old company commander, Captain Griffen, was sitting in the office. Last time he had seen him was after the Battle of Omdurman, and then Griffen had been a major. He was now back to captain.

The sergeant-major saluted but the officer ignored the salute, came round the table and gripped Oakwood warmly by the hand. 'Sergeant-Major Oakwood, it's good to see you. What brings you here?'

'They said at Warwick that they were sending the papers to you, sir,' said Oakwood, sitting down.

'Haven't had time to get straight yet,' admitted Griffen, the old scar on his cheek livid against the pale face, 'the colonel has just gone into dock for an operation. Ah, here we are. My word, you've been at it again, you got another war in.'

'It doesn't seem to make much difference when you want to re-enlist, sir,' said Oakwood.

'I suppose not,' said Griffen. Oakwood looked old, there was no doubt about it. Fifty *was* old for a serving soldier, especially one come up from the ranks. Officers were different, of course. He himself didn't feel a day over forty.

'I'm glad you're here,' Oakwood continued, 'they were damned toffee-nosed at Warwick.'

'Colonel Ludlow would have been, too,' warned Griffen. 'His son was killed at Spion Kop and he blamed it all on poor leadership. He wants a clean sweep.'

'What's to be done, sir?' asked Oakwood, feeling depressed.

The captain leaned back and chewed his pencil. 'Officially, nothing,' he said, 'but I'm not seeing one of my old soldiers go down the drain. I've seen 'em, Sergeant-Major, I've seen 'em, and the sergeants are the worst hit. They go from something to nothing. Would you do a sergeant's job on a sergeant's pay?'

It was a question that admitted of only one answer. There was a vacancy for a recruiting sergeant at Dale End, in Birmingham, and George jumped at the opportunity.

So Sergeant Oakwood took on a new lease of life. It was he on Sunday who went down to the office in Dale End, stripped off his jacket with the three stripes newly sewn on and cleaned the plate-glass windows, scrubbed the floors, polished the counter, and pinned up recruiting posters on the woodwork. On the Monday he was open for business, on Tuesday he had his first caller. It was a shy timid boy who wanted to join the Royal Engineers.

'My dad was in them, Sergeant,' he said.

'It's a great life, lad,' said Sergeant Oakwood, 'you see the world. When I was in Africa you could see the horizon stretching sixty, seventy miles into the distance. And the animals. Antelopes bounding along, queer beasts I never got to know the name of . . .' He found himself telling the boy about the first war he was involved in, the Ashanti War of thirty years before. 'I remember as if it was yesterday those forests. Like being in a huge green cathedral. And butterflies as big as bats. Orchids, well, as big as a dinner plate and then some . . .'

The recruit listened spellbound. And signed on the dotted line. The day after another boy came, a burly lad with hair brushed low over his eyes.

'My friend joined up yesterday', he began, 'and he was telling me about butterflies as big as bats, and blackies who used to climb up the trees and throw spears at you. I want to get there, Sir.'

'Do you want to be a fighting soldier, lad?' asked Oakwood breezily.

'That I do, sir,' said the boy, 'and my ma said I can and she's written it down. I know I'm too late for them Boers, but they weren't blackies anyway. Still, I don't mind who I fight . . .'

Jane was as gratified as her husband was by his happiness and pleasure in his work, and when the further period of enlistment was approved they went into town and had a meal at a restaurant. They ordered roast beef and Yorkshire pudding, fresh peas and new potatoes, followed by ice-cream with chocolate sauce. A string band played the latest tunes from the musical comedy *A Chinese Honeymoon*. 'It's good to be alive,' said George smiling. 'I don't remember a time when I've been so contented.'

Jane put her hand over his. 'I'm happy, too,' she said.

When they got back he moved into the big bedroom with his wife. Mary was asleep. 'If we're quiet she won't know', said Jane, giggling slightly, 'and she won't understand anyway.'

He had forgotten, or had repressed the memory of what a smooth body Jane had and, careful not to let the bed springs sound too much, they made love. But Harry had heard. It

11

wasn't fair, he thought indignantly, they should be too old for that kind of thing. And, damn it, he'd have to tell the old man to oil the bloody springs else he would never be able to get up in time to deliver the flaming newspapers in the morning.

George and Jane went out in the mornings, caught the bus together at the bottom of the road, and sometimes came back together in the evening. There was plenty of money going into the house and George had saved a considerable amount of money from his back pay. They invested in a gramophone, and bought a piano which was put in the parlour so that Leonard could learn to play. They bought two new Triumph cycles at ten guineas each and on Sundays went out into the countryside, leaving Leonard and Mary at home. Leonard was perfectly happy to sit reading. No one took Mary into account.

As for Harry, no one knew what he did. He seemed always to have money, more than would come from a delivery round. George thought that he smoked; he mentioned this once to Jane, but she did not seem particularly worried or, indeed, interested.

Had George frequented the football match at the Birmingham ground he might have had an inkling of the truth, for Harry never failed to turn up, fair weather or foul, with his tray of 'official' programmes printed by a shady back street printer and 'favours', cheap rosettes made from crinkly paper and put together in Roy's house. Harry took one corner of the street, Roy the other. They dressed in old mackintoshes and Wellington boots to make themselves as much a part of the background as possible.

'Get your rosettes here,' shouted Harry, 'twopence each. Penny cheaper than them down the road.'

'They ain't so good, though,' grunted one man, paying his twopence and inspecting his rosette.

'You only throw them away, mate, after the match,' said Harry, 'so what's the odds?'

'That's true enough,' said the purchaser, convinced.

'Official programmes, a ha'penny!' screamed Roy. 'Know who's playing. All the names.'

The club officials did not like it; occasionally they sent out a policeman but the hawkers soon vanished. Harry and Roy had a small but profitable little business, and when Birmingham were playing away from home they would change the colours of the rosettes and sell them at the Aston Villa ground a few miles away.

One Saturday, Harry was approached by a man dressed in a close-fitting cloth cap, a muffler and an ankle-length overcoat. He had a couple of campaign medals pinned to the breast of the coat. An old soldier, thought Harry, not done so well as his dad. 'What you in this game for, lad?' the man asked. 'There's better pickings elsewhere.'

'Rosettes twopence each. Penny cheaper than down the road,' repeated Harry scornfully, 'two for threepence for you, mate, match your medals.' He put on the old-time bark of his father, and the little man recoiled.

'Blimey!' he muttered, 'you reminded me of me old sergeant. No, seriously, I got a proposition. Meet me in that corner coffee shop after the match, with your mate.'

'Nothing to lose,' said Roy when he was told, so they went.

The man was sitting in the corner drinking tea. 'Listen,' he said, 'do you know what pirated music is?'

'No,' said Harry sitting down. 'What is it?'

'It's like this, you see,' said the man, still wearing his cap, but pushed up from his eyes, sharp weasel-like eyes, 'the proper music publishers do a song, a musical comedy song, say, for three shillings, sometimes four. We sell the same song for threepence. We knock 'em out, give 'em to blokes like you, at a penny-ha' penny a sheet.'

'We can make a couple of quid on a good Saturday,' said Roy curtly.

'Ah, mateys, but there's only one football match a week whichever way you look at it. This is all the week. And it's not just one at a time. Newsagents, they sometimes take half a gross of a really topical song. You've got nothing to lose by trying it out, and to prove I trust you I'll give you a batch of the latest musical comedy success, from *Chinese Honeymoon*.'

'All right,' agreed Roy, 'we'll give it a go. Where do we get this stuff?'

'We've got a printing press in Bradford Street,' said the man. 'Just give it a go and see how you do.'

So on Monday Roy and Harry took the bus to the address, a small hut behind a factory smelling of oil. A middle-aged man

13

with a muffler tied round his throat was operating an old Columbia press and by his side was a pile of the song 'Martha Thumps the Grand Pianner', which had caught on amongst the general public. There seemed an uncanny resemblance between the printer and the man the boys had seen in the café, but after a short conversation, concerning mainly how much money could be made and how best to sell the merchandise, Harry and Roy realized that the two men were brothers.

'If you fancy it,' said the printer casually, 'I've got another best-selling line. Dirty songs.'

'Let's see one,' said Roy. The man handed him a specimen. On the cover was a crude wood-engraving of a woman and man copulating, and Roy read out the first verse:

> I had the mother and the daughter,
> Got them both 'twixt wind and water,
> And when they'd said they'd had enough,
> I shagged the father, bleeding pouff . . .

'That's rich,' said Roy, giggling, nudging Harry with his elbow. 'Who buys these?'

'Clubs,' said the printer negligently, 'some of the pubs, like the old free and easies—though you wouldn't remember them—and backstreet newspaper shops.'

The 'clubs' were wooden shacks, often set behind factories and roofed with corrugated iron, and fading signboards showed what they once were. There was the Digbeth Workmen's Educational Club, the Deritend Social Club, the Bradford Street Institute and, most exotic of them all, the League for the Rehabilitation of Working Men, housed in a former chapel. They were open only at night, and much of the boys' work was done between eight and ten. The clubs varied; sometimes there were just three or four men, clad in the usual mufflers and dirty jackets, with moleskin trousers tied with string below the knee, leaning against an improvised bar downing ale and adulterated continental gin; sometimes there were twenty or more crowded in a room ten feet square reeking of sweat. There was usually a piano in the corner and the singers, men and women, sang the obscene songs lustily, the women singers ogling the men as they mouthed the lines, the men eyeing the women in the audience.

14

Harry was shocked that so many women frequented these places.

The time came when he was too busy to fetch the children from school, and he told his parents that he had got a job, working for a Bradford Street printer. 'A pound a week, Dad,' he said, putting on a show of proudness, 'and I'll give mum ten shillings of that for my keep, if that's enough.'

'Not many lads get that much a week,' said George suspiciously. 'I was reading in the paper that the average working wage for a man is only twenty-five shillings a week.' He had been watching Harry with increasing trepidation. The flash of insight when he had sensed that, like recruits, Harry was trying to put something over on him, had never left him.

Harry and Roy found that if they concentrated on the clubs they could ignore the other outlets, and they could also forget the respectable pirated songs. They bought the dirty songs at three-halfpence and sold them to the clubs at sixpence a sheet, and they made arrangements with the clubs to provide them with half a dozen new songs a week. Digbeth in Birmingham had a long history of printing broadsides and scurrilous pamphlets, and men who called themselves Grub Street poets, equipped with thesauruses and rhyming dictionaries, plied their craft for half a crown a song.

The double life became difficult for Harry to keep up, and the hole behind the brick was used not only for cigarettes but sovereigns. His mother was a great one for hanging up his clothes on hangers, and if three or four sovereigns fell on the floor there would have to be some explanation. Harry was making considerably more than a pound a week and was actually earning more than his hard-working mother. He would occasionally stay home in an evening but would spend much of the time in the parlour picking out music-hall tunes on the piano. Life was treating him well.

3

It was possible that Harry was mixed up with bad influences, George considered. In his army career he had seen how a nice lad could be thoroughly perverted by the bad apple which every platoon gets sooner or later. Maybe it was this mysterious Roy. He was musing about this when Captain Griffen strolled into the recruiting office at the time of the morning when George was making himself a cup of tea.

'How is business, Oaky?' he asked breezily, laying his cane on the counter and pushing the flap up. He usually popped in at least once a week. It was one of his duties to supervise the running of the office, but Colonel Ludlow thought him rather too assiduous, suspecting that Griffen was taking the opportunity of getting out of the barracks.

'Two yesterday, sir,' said George.

'I got the 1903–4 army estimates in yesterday,' said Griffen, 'more than two hundred thousand men still in uniform. Including a trained reserve of seventy thousand. Trained reserve, my arse! Young men playing at soldiers, turning up at a drill hall when it suits them and occasionally at manoeuvres if it can be sneaked out of their working time. I think I've got you back to sergeant-major, Oaky. Back to five shillings a day instead of two and fourpence as a sergeant.'

George nodded his appreciation. Jane was getting far more than he was; even Harry was earning a pound a week. He mentioned Harry to Griffen.

'Not in the army yet?' asked Griffen, looking at his watch. It came to something, he thought bitterly, when his declining years were spent swapping chat with a sergeant.

'Harry's a strange one,' George admitted, 'not like I hoped he'd turn out. I've more faith in young Leonard. He's always reading about the army and asking me questions.'

Griffen hesitated. 'If you'd like me to have a word with Harry I'd be happy to. Just send him up to Thorpe Street.'

'He's sure to say that's he's too busy or something,' said George, 'but thanks for the offer, sir.'

'Nice cup of tea, Oaky,' said Griffen, getting to his feet, 'I'll be over next week as usual.'

'Always welcome, sir,' said George, saluting. Not like the old Oakwood salute, Griffen thought, it was more like a casual wave to an old chum.

George had spoken without real conviction, and if he sent Harry to someone it would be to an officer like Captain Griffen as he used to be. There must be some about. They cannot have all been chewed up by the reaction to the disastrous Boer War, cannot have all had their spirit drained away. He stood by the counter, suddenly aware that someone had entered the recruiting office while he and the captain were chatting. He could see the feet of a man reading posters hung up on a framework that ran the length of the office. He thanked God that they were the feet of a civilian. Someone who wanted a son to enlist— someone like himself, perhaps; or a prospect; or some tramp wanting to cadge a few coppers.

He waited for the man to show himself but he only saw the stranger's back as he walked out of the office into the busy street outside. He shrugged his shoulders. He often had them like that, men who could not make a decision. A row with a wife, an argument with a workmate, simple things such as these could urge a man to sign for the king's shilling. It was good of Captain Griffen to get him back on his old sergeant-major's pay, but unfortunately for Oakwood it was not so easy as that. The stranger's visit was to have unforeseen consequences.

'Sorry I had to ask you to go in mufti,' grunted Colonel Ludlow. With his waxed moustache, he was often mistaken, allegedly, for Kaiser Wilhelm, and was rather pleased by the resemblance.

'I didn't intend to spy on a fellow officer,' blurted out Lieutenant Culpeper.

'Good God, man, it was not your fault that he was there. It was a spot of luck, if anything,' said the colonel, 'and you say Griffen was sitting at the table *gossiping* with Sergeant Oakwood. And drinking *tea*?' He shook his head disbelievingly. He had asked Culpeper to look in on the recruiting office to see if he thought Oakwood should be made up to sergeant-major. Now there was no doubt in his mind.

'Oakwood was quite a man in his day,' he said absently,

17

'but he's too damned old. And he was in the South African War.'

'Put up a show there, sir,' said Culpeper eagerly, anxious to be fair to the aged warrior.

'My son was killed at Spion Kop,' said Ludlow curtly, 'don't remind me of the South African War. Too many old men there. Fifty-year-old NCOs such as Oakwood, sixty-year-old generals. And my son was twenty-four, just twenty-four.' He gripped the arms of his chair. No, Sergeant Oakwood would remain Sergeant Oakwood, an ex-Sergeant Oakwood if he had his way.

That evening George decided to take the bull by the horns and go and see this fellow Roy. Several weeks before, Harry had let slip the address, and George had carefully memorized it. He put on the neat dark suit that he had bought in town and left the house. He had told Jane where he was going, and she had nodded, for she, too, was worried by the secrecy and furtiveness shown by her son.

It was a fine night and he breathed in the air, smiling at the young children playing underneath the gas lamps, absorbed in a world of their own. A football came towards him, and he tapped it back to the young player. 'Are you a Birmingham supporter, sonny?' he asked.

'Nah,' said the urchin, grinning at him with gap teeth, 'Aston Villa. Birmingham, why they're a bunch of cripples.'

'You've got the Birmingham rosette on,' said George, pointing to the rosette pinned in the boy's grubby cardigan.

'Oh, that was free,' said the boy. 'Roy gave it to me. He's got lots of them. Doesn't do that any more though.'

'What does he do now?' George asked.

'Sells music,' replied the boy, moving to his right to intercept a hard shot from the wing.

Sells music? That did not fit in with his mental picture of Roy. From what Harry had said, Roy was one of those obnoxious young men who propped up four-ale bars and hung around outside the stage-doors of variety theatres. Perhaps he had wronged him. He had sometimes made mistakes about men in his platoon or company.

The house that Roy lived in was one of those big places with a high wall, lots of hedges, and big bay windows, but as he approached he realized what a shocking condition it was in.

The front door was boarded up, and at first he thought the house was derelict, but a plume of smoke from one of the chimneys at the back caught his eye. They must be living at the back. He had not thought what he was going to say when he finally cornered the elusive Roy but doubtlessly something would occur then.

Between the rubbish ran a narrow dirt path and George followed it until he came to a door, paint-blistered and resting on one hinge. 'Anybody at home?' he called out, when a knock on the door had failed to rouse anyone.

'Come in, can't yer?' called a quavering voice. 'Me leg's bad and I can't get up.'

Shrugging his shoulders, George pushed open the door, careful that he did not topple it from the one existing rusty hinge, and found himself in a damp-smelling corridor. There was the drip of water. Whoever it was, no wonder his or her legs were bad. Never had he seen a place more sacred to rheumatism.

At the end of the corridor was a chink of light from under a door, and George groped his way forward. The door was clammy to the touch, and as he opened it the fug from the room took him by the throat.

'Have to keep it warm', said an old man sitting in a chair in front of a blazing fire, 'for me legs. Dotty always sees I have a good blazing fire.'

'Dotty?'

'Me old woman,' said the man. 'Who are you? I don't know you, do I?' Suspicion flickered in his eyes. 'You aren't the bobbies, are yer?' he asked.

'No,' replied George, 'I've come to see Roy.'

'And you still ain't the bobbies?'

George's heart sank. 'Is he in trouble a lot?' he asked.

'Not to my knowledge,' said the other, 'have I seen yer before? I'm good at faces. Think I've seen yer before somewhere.'

'Don't suppose so,' said George, not very interested. 'I don't live round here. Who's the girl?' He nodded to the photograph on the mantelpiece. It was a pretty girl, heavily made-up, with bare shoulders. Someone had hand-coloured the photograph, so the make-up was probably added. He looked more closely.

'If you haven't seen me before, I daresay you've seen *her*

before,' said the old man, giggling, 'maybe in your young days, eh?'

'What are you getting at, old 'un?' asked George, puzzled. He looked back at the photograph. The face seemed vaguely familiar.

'That was Dotty in her prime,' said the old man with pride. 'I rescued her from a life of sin, you might say. She was a tabby in Cherry Street.'

'What, a prostitute?'

'Made no bones about it. Doesn't still, either.'

George closed his eyes, remembering back. This was the first woman he had ever had.

'Have her again for old time's sake,' said the man, egging him on, enjoying the situation. 'She ain't as pricey as she used to be.'

'Good God!' breathed George.

'You look like you've been a soldier,' said the man. 'She liked soldiers. She'd turn down her regular customers to do a turn with a soldier. She didn't fancy 'em so much when they went khaki. I was a soldier, too, that's how I met her.'

George was too shaken to pursue further enquiries into the life of Roy. Nor did he bother to find out more about this senile old man, sitting in front of the fire in a chair with all the flock hanging out, sticking to his baggy stained trousers. For this wreck, living vicariously through his wife's fornications, had been the recruiting sergeant in Dale End who had signed him on. The man whom, a seeming eternity later, he had replaced behind that counter, as a smart front to the army machine.

When he got back home, George merely said that Roy had not been in and Jane did not pursue the matter, though she thought that her husband looked as though he had had a shock. Probably the walk had taken it out of him; he was not so young as he used to be. Feeling sorry for him, she went into the kitchen and made him a cup of tea while George put a record on the gramophone. Harry had more records than Jane but he soon got tired of his. Jane liked the old ballads, and he enjoyed the old army songs. 'Comrades' was one of his favourites, and 'Dolly Gray'. He had heard that a lot in South Africa.

'It's nice to hear the old tunes,' said Jane coming in with the teapot, 'these musical comedies are all right if you like that kind of thing, but they're really for London people aren't they?'

'The toffs, you mean?'

'No,' said Jane with spirit, 'I do not. My customers, and they're ladies, they like the old songs best. And Mr and Mrs Motley. They've got a gramophone upstairs and I sometimes hear it. It's nice to listen to music when you're in the shop waiting for customers.'

'Do they ever ask about me?' asked George suddenly.

'They said that if you wanted to be in the men's department there would always be a job for you', she said, 'they're really patriotic people, the Motleys. They had a nephew who was killed in the South African War.'

'That war cost a hundred and fifty million pounds', commented George, 'and what did we get out of it? Only a casualty list as long as your arm. Sometimes I don't think wars do any good at all. Look at the Napoleonic wars and now, after we beat them, what did it do? The French are our allies. And when we fought the Ashanti War, who would know that in thirty years the blacks would have another go? You knock 'em down, and they come up again like a kid's toy.'

'Strange,' said Jane, 'I don't remember seeing your *Soldiers of the Queen* about lately.'

'It's about somewhere,' said George casually, 'tucked under something I daresay. But it's out of date now.'

'Leonard brought that book from the library, the one you asked him to get.'

George brightened up. 'That's good', he said, 'I'll read a few pages before I go to bed. Harry's late tonight.'

'He seems to be getting later and later,' said Jane with a note of despair in her voice. 'I know I stopped you being hard towards him but I think I was wrong. I know, dear, that the army can stop a young man going to the dogs. I've seen it myself a dozen times.'

'You're in favour of Harry joining the army?' asked George.

'Yes,' Jane said simply.

The book was Conan Doyle's *The Great Boer War*. George had read the Sherlock Holmes stories in South Africa, and when the author had decided to write about the war George wanted to know what he thought about it. Though it would need more

21

than Sherlock Holmes to make sense of some of the mysteries that he had heard about. He read on, and it came as a shock when he realized that it was one o'clock and Harry was not yet home.

As it happened, Harry and Roy were in trouble. They went on the usual Friday round, their carriers slung over their shoulders, the dirty songs fresh from the press with ink still damp, but at the Bradford Street Institute, their first call, the club manager had not been at all eager to buy. It was early in the evening and only three or four people were present. The piano still had its cloth on.

'They're bad times, boys,' said the manager.

'Your customers won't like it,' said Harry angrily. 'They like their dirty songs. I've heard them laughing their bloody heads off. And a tanner apiece won't break you.'

'Sorry, lads,' the manager had said with finality.

'Suit yourself,' said Roy, 'plenty more clubs who do want to buy.'

'Go and see then, me old cock-sparrow,' the manager had said with a thin smile.

Harry and Roy had the same reception at the Deritend Social Club. Almost the same words, thought Harry; there was something funny going on. At the next port of call the singing had started earlier. 'That's not one of our songs', said Roy suddenly, 'listen.'

> I poked her in the parlour,
> And I poked her on the stairs,
> I poked her till she cried, 'No more!
> You're clogging up my hairs.'

'That's not as good as ours,' said Harry, 'that's not witty, it's just dirty.'

'Come on,' said Roy, 'let's go on in and see what it's all about.' He swaggered in, but nobody took any notice of him. He looked at the sheet of music on the piano. It was printed on buff paper. It came from another printing firm.

Roy was fuming, but Harry put his hand on his arm and went to speak to a young man leaning up against a wall whom he knew casually. 'What's going on?' he asked.

22

'That's a saucy ditty ain't it?' countered the man, joining in the chorus, and Harry patiently waited for the song to finish before he repeated the question. 'Oh', said the other, 'some blokes came in a motor-car, quite toffs, really, and they had a natter with the manager, and before you could say Jack Robinson they'd unloaded this music.'

At that moment Harry spotted the manager, and their eyes met. The manager disappeared out of a side door, but Harry caught him by the arm. 'What's happened, Bill?' he asked. 'I know about the men in the car, but why?'

The manager shuffled his feet uncomfortably. 'It's not my wish, Harry,' he said, 'I've been happy with your songs, but they said that if I did not take theirs they would close us up.'

'What do they mean?'

Bill shrugged his shoulders. 'Put the coppers on us, I suppose, but they looked very hard customers, very hard customers indeed.'

'We're not going to stand for it,' said Roy shrilly, his thin shoulders quivering with fury.

'All right then, dear,' said a woman, 'sit down for it.'

'And that ain't easy,' said another woman lewdly.

'Nothing we can do here, Roy,' said Harry, 'let's try the Rehabilitation.' They stamped down the street, the stench of the leather market where Harry's grandfather used to get his hides in the 1860s in their nostrils. A high square motor-car was standing at the kerb outside the converted chapel, and from his open seat a man in goggles and a check cap buttoned under his chin looked down. 'Lost your way, sonny?' he asked.

'That must be them,' whispered Roy.

The man in goggles improvised a comic song:

> Selling dirty music
> Is not an easy job,
> If your face it doesn't fit,
> You'll get one on the nob.

'Get my meaning, sonny? Why don't you just go home and play with your toys?'

'Why should we?' asked Roy, 'we were here first.'

'What's that got to do with it?' asked the man in the car. 'It's

23

every man for himself in this sort of game. Though I suppose you're new to it.'

'Don't bother with 'em, Cotman,' said the driver, 'we've got three more lots to deliver round here then over to Aston.'

The man addressed as Cotman lifted up a leather-gloved hand. 'Patience, love, patience. The lads might need some advice.'

'Like keep out of our way,' grunted the driver.

'Something like that,' said the other.

'We have to make a living, mister,' said Roy in a whining tone, 'why don't you leave Digbeth to us? We won't go to Aston.'

'No, your little rocking-horses won't get you that far,' said Cotman. 'All right, let's be on our way.'

There was a third man in the car, who got out and put the starting handle into the socket. He turned it a dozen revolutions before the engine fired.

'These foreign cars,' said Cotman contemptuously, and settled himself deep in the seat.

'We'll tell the police of you!' yelled Roy above the noise of the engine.

'You'll what?' shouted Cotman. He opened the door, and jumped down off the high running-board, seizing Harry by the arm and twisting it. The man with the starting handle came round the side and struck Roy a crunching blow across the shoulders. The men bustled Harry and Roy through the arch that led to the chapel and beat them to the ground. Cotman took out a bottle of gin from his leather jacket pocket, unscrewed the top and poured the contents on to the young men, dropping the bottle between them. 'Go and tell the coppers in Digbeth Police Station that there are two fellows dead drunk in front of the old chapel', he ordered, 'and you, Rusty, scarper into the chapel and tell them to stop those disgusting songs until the coppers have carted them away.'

But the police had their hands full with a promised strike of factory workers at the sheet-metal factory down the road, and did not fancy dissipating their energy rounding up drunks. By the time a policeman on the beat did reluctantly pay the chapel a visit Harry and Roy had picked themselves up, shaken but unharmed, retrieved their bicycles and ridden off.

'It's back to rosettes then, is it?' asked a chastened Roy, his shoulder bruised and aching.

'For the time being, anyway,' agreed Harry.

4

The printer looked up from the machine with a start when he heard footsteps on the oily cobbles. He had heard disquieting stories of his runners being scared off, of their supplies being taken from them, of the clubs and public houses having to pay money to stop hooligans throwing stones through the windows. He relaxed when he saw who they were—the tall fair-haired lad and the thin weedy fellow with the ferret-like eyes.

'You don't have to tell me, boys,' he said, waving his hands solicitously, 'they've been at you as well, have they?'

'Three men in a motor-car,' said Harry. 'Have the others come up against them?'

'The little squint-eyed fellow is in hospital with a broken jaw', said the printer, 'and Alex, you know the one who's a bit funny in the top storey, he's got something the matter with his kidney where they kicked him in the guts.'

'We got off lightly then,' speculated Harry.

'What's to be done?' asked Roy, scowling. 'It was a good little business.'

'And you did well at it, Roy,' said the printer consolingly. 'I'll tell you what I've done with the boys who did round Bristol Street—I sent them down to Balsall Heath and Sparkbrook. I haven't heard from them yet, but no news is good news, ain't it?'

'So what about us?' pressed Roy.

'You can try Smethwick, or you can go back to the respectable music which you can sell in the daytime,' suggested the printer. 'Have you brought last night's music back?'

Harry and Roy unloaded their carriers and the printer held

the music in his arms, looking from one to the other, waiting for them to decide.

'Let's take some of both kinds', said Harry suddenly, 'and see how it goes. You'll have to tell us how to get there, and the good cribs.'

They followed the printer into his office, and Harry took down a list of names and a set of directions.

It was a longer ride than they thought it would be and going through town on the bicycles, the music strapped to the metal grille above the rear mudguard, was irksome. They had to dodge old ladies on shopping sprees, the iron-bound wheels of the horse waggons, and a large number of tricycles, used by messengers and shop-assistants to deliver food and other commodities. There were more and more motor-cars on the road, tall slow-moving vehicles that could not compete with the boys' bicycles for speed, and when they backfired Harry would deliberately wobble his cycle and pretend to be shot. When Roy disdainfully refused to respond he stopped it.

They made their way over the cobbles of Hockley Hill past the isolation hospital, gaunt and forbidding ('That's where my father used to be,' volunteered Harry, 'it used to be a barracks.'), past the factories puffing sulphurous fumes into the atmosphere, over the canal bridges and under the railway arches. There were still a few houses crouched at the edge of the road, but they would soon disappear as industry stretched further into the suburbs.

Not that there was anything like suburbs as Harry knew them—no leafy boulevards as in Acocks Green or Sparkhill, a mile or two from where they lived, very few stretches of park. Just an acre or two of scrubby grass with a tree trying desperately to gain sustenance from the thin soil. There was no let up in the ribbon-building, and the first sign that they were out of Birmingham and into Smethwick was the different colour of the omnibuses.

They would not know whether the man in the motor-car was selling his dirty music until the evening, and the two men became more and more depressed as tradesman after tradesman refused to have anything to do with their respectable pirated music.

' "Martha Thumps the Grand Pianner",' read a newsagent

sarcastically, his straw boater hat at a rakish angle, 'why, me old woman does that, and sometimes she thumps me too when I've had a pint too many. No, lads, there ain't no call for it.'

'You might be just the man for our other line,' said Roy slyly, delving into his carrier bag for the obscene music, but Harry sensed that he was not when he saw the lips tighten as the newsagent looked at the woodcut on the front and read the lyrics.

'Get out of my shop, you little bastards,' he said gritting his teeth.

For half an hour at lunchtime, when the shopgirls were having a break and factory workers were sitting on the pavement outside their firms eating sandwiches and drinking tea from their enamel flasks, Harry and Roy touted the musical comedy songs.

'The latest successes from the musical comedy *The Girl from Kay's* at the Apollo Theatre, London,' shouted Harry, 'normally costing four shillings, but for you at the special price of one shilling.'

The workers, their faces covered with grease, looked at them as though they had come from another planet. One of the men deliberately spat on Roy's foot as the two walked by, calling their wares, and the other workers roared with laughter.

'Why don't you idle sods get yourself a job?' shouted one of the factory men.

'And work with pigs like you?' retorted Roy from a safe distance.

Harry scowled. 'Not one bloody penny,' he said. 'Let's find a coffee-house and have a cup of tea. My legs are killing me.'

'You remind me of old Abbott when you say that,' said Roy. 'Someone came looking for me last night. He said it wasn't the coppers. It might be someone offering us something good, so we can forget these bleeding songs. I wouldn't mind making a lot of money so that I could buy myself a motor-bicycle. Have you seen the way they can rip along?'

Talking of old Mr Abbott made Harry think of Roy's sister, Judy. He had not seen her since that exciting evening at the music hall when she had lifted up her skirt and showed him her thigh. The thought of it still thrilled him. For some reason he did not ask Roy where she was. He knew—out skylarking with

27

one of those monocled knuts, having a good time like her mother.

He was still shy about women, though he was becoming increasingly suspicious of Roy's vaunted conquests. He was with him almost every night and day (except those nights when he reluctantly stayed at home) and so far he had seen none of Roy's lady-friends who wore silk knickers and corsets you could see through.

The day wore on. Although they had sold three songs and thus made themselves one and sixpence between them, they considered it was one of their worst day's trading. Their worst day ever was when both Aston Villa and Birmingham were playing away from home and they had to try and sell rosettes to the couple of hundred men and boys who went to watch a reserves football match.

By five o'clock they had had enough and went into a public house to recuperate. Roy did not believe into going into what he called a cacky pub and usually chose the most luxurious and flashiest in sight, with lots of coloured glass in the windows, polished leatherette seats and marble-topped tables. He swaggered to the bar and ordered two pints of bitter beer.

'How are you then?' he asked the barman breezily.

'Not so bad,' answered the barman automatically, eyeing the narrow-chested lad, 'how's yourself?'

'Can't grumble,' replied Roy, 'up and down, you know, like a bishop's what's-it.'

'Pardon?' asked the barman, putting the young shaver in his place. Some of his lady customers did not like smut. This cocky little bastard should have gone to the Station Inn where they appreciated that sort of thing.

Someone was watching the boys from the other side of the room, a shifty little man dressed in a neat suit with a loosely tied bow at his throat. He saw Harry open the canvas bag he was carrying and take out a couple of sheets of paper. It looked like music and when Roy hurriedly took the papers from Harry and stuffed them back in the bag he had a shrewd idea what sort of music it was. He went outside, found a post office, and sent a telegram. He resented paying ninepence for the eighteen words, but he knew that the recipient would be grateful and refund him the money.

It was dark when Harry and Roy left the public house, somewhat glutted with beer, and it was some time before they could remember where they left their bicycles. They had left them in an alley, securely chained to railings that edged a railway siding. The brisk evening air sobered them up, and they trotted through the gas-lit streets.

'Half a sec,' said Harry suddenly, stopping, 'I'm not going back until we've seen the lie of the land. We've still got a lot of dirties to get rid of.'

'Where do we start?' asked Roy amiably, and Harry got out his instructions.

'The West Smethwick Working Men's Club,' he said, 'it should be by the railway line somewhere like where we left the bikes.' They walked slowly, looking at street signs, stepping out of the way of homeward-going workers smelling of suds and oil, occasionally stepping into the road to avoid children jumping over skipping-ropes attached to garden fences. Gas lights went on in the houses as men and women returned from work. Occasionally they peered into parlour windows, seeing elderly couples sitting in front of the fire, staring at nothing.

'What a life!' said Harry with disgust.

'Quick!' whispered Roy, 'look in that last one. A couple having it off on the sofa!' Harry rushed back, but could see nothing. 'Ever been had?' asked Roy, giggling.

This road seemed familiar to Harry. They must have walked up it before, for he seemed to remember that neglected church with a spire too big for it. Churches always gave him the shivers. Thank God mum and dad did not bother with them. More than once at Aldershot he had heard his father snort contemptuously about knee-drill, compulsory church services when the men would have been better occupied in shining their brasses and going over their belts.

The bicycles were still chained to the railings as they had left them.

'Honest lot round here,' commented Harry, 'I suppose they're not Brummies, strictly speaking, but they sound like Brummies.'

'It's all the Black Country right up to Dudley and beyond,' said Roy knowledgeably. 'I went to Dudley once with Ma. She

29

had the bloke in one of them ruins. "Go along and play, little boy," he said to me, "here's twopence".'

'What did you do?' asked Harry.

'What did you expect me to do?' asked Roy belligerently, the drink still in him. 'I went and spent my twopence on sweets. He was a short time one, though. In and out in ten minutes.'

'You can do it quicker than that,' said Harry.

'Who can?' asked Roy loudly.

'Keep your voice down,' ordered Harry irritably, 'there's the club at the end of the alley.'

It was very much like the clubs around the Digbeth area of Birmingham. The lettering on the notice-board was faded and illegible and there was a smell of stale beer and sweat partly hidden under asphyxiating clouds of cheap face powder and eau-de-Cologne bought by the small chemists by the gallon and retailed in gaudy little bottles. Still too early for the club to be even half full, a pianist was in full flower, singing lustily the Vesta Tilley music-hall song 'Daddy Wouldn't Buy Me a Bow-wow'. He had a surprisingly rich baritone voice which made nonsense of the lyrics.

One of the local whores pirouetted around on high-heeled shoes, occasionally flicking up a leg waist-high and grinning with pointed teeth as she saw the two newcomers staring at her white knickers. 'Have another look, boys,' she said, bending over and flicking up the hem of her skirt. One of the men made a motion of taking out his penis and pressing it into her and everyone roared with laughter. Roy, too, joined in and swaggered to the dirty wooden-topped bar.

'Two pints of bitter, mine host,' he said loudly, 'and something for the lady.'

'D'you hear that?' cooed the whore, winking at the assembly, 'a lady. I don't mind if I do, young 'un. A gin if you'll be so good, Bert.'

As if to the manner born the barman whisked up a glass to the water-filled inverted gin bottle. 'A big 'un, gents?' he asked.

'Of course,' replied Roy in a lordly manner, 'for the lady nothing's too good.'

'I think I like you,' the girl said speculatively, going to Roy and stroking his arm. The heavily-rouged face, the belt of crimson about the mouth, the crackling powder round her eyes;

these, for Roy, merged into a blur. Harry, disgusted that Roy should want this hideous woman pawing him, collected his drink and went to the pianist.

'You're a real good singer,' he said. 'They don't get them like you in the Digbeth clubs.'

The pianist looked pleased, but his significant glance towards the piano top, where his tankard stood empty, went disregarded.

'Do you know any of those saucy songs', Harry went on, 'they used to sing them in Digbeth?'

'Yes,' said the man, 'I've got some here.' He stood up and turned up a pile of music on the piano top. Harry saw that they had buff covers. The men in the motor-car had been here, too.

'Oh, I know who brings them in,' said Harry, 'a bloke in a motor-car.'

'It's a sort of contract,' said the pianist, rubbing his forehead with a fingernail. Harry saw to his distaste that he was picking at black-heads. 'The guv'nor gets half a dozen new ones each week, then these are collected and another half a dozen come in. Between you and me, the tunes are nearly all the same, but nobody notices it except me.'

'And me as well,' bragged Harry, 'I play the piano as well.'

The pianist ignored the comment. 'The audience likes them, though, really gets them going, and I've seen 'em popping out the back, all red in the face, and doing the naughty. I bet there's more kids brewed up in this stinking bar than there is in all the beds in bloody Smethwick.'

Occasionally bits of chatter came through from Roy and the whore.

'Of course, I've been to see all the shows in town,' said Roy.

'What's your name, dearie?' asked the girl, more interested in essentials.

'I'd call him the man who broke the bank at Monte Carlo,' said a bystander, 'to judge by all the drinks he's been buying you.'

'Go on with you, Ginger,' said the whore, punching the other amiably on the shoulder, 'a few drinks from you might get you somewhere other than a bit of a grope at locking-up time. Like the young man, here. I don't think he's going to let me walk home by myself, along them dark and nasty streets.'

'I don't think I am either,' said Roy, heart thumping. He peered down between her breasts.

'Naughty,' the girl said coyly. 'Why, I don't think I'm going to be able to wait till locking-up time. I feel myself going all hot and bothered.'

'No time like the present,' put in Roy, joining his hands across his chest, and widening his shoulders.

'Reminds me of one of my pigeons,' commented a rough-looking man smoking a pipe. 'Got any good racers this year, Bert?'

'I've got one I fancy,' replied the barman, 'I think he's a good 'un. Bit too cold for them yet, though, I don't believe in forcing them . . .'

Soon the room began to thicken with smoke, and more and more people joined in with the singer, who went on to the buff-covered songs. Harry looked for Roy, but his friend had gone off with the girl. It would serve him right if he caught the pox, thought Harry bitterly. Not a word, just hopped it. Still, Roy had done it, not like him, just thinking about it like one of those daft blokes in Tennyson's poems that they pumped into you at school. It was about time he left, he thought. Dad would begin to get nasty if he was late every night—and he had not arrived home until two o'clock that morning. Fortunately the graze on his face where he had been knocked to the ground had disappeared by the morning.

He was walking across to the bar, pushing between the singing people, when the door opened and a big man of about thirty-five came in. He had hair neatly parted in the middle, wide-spaced eyes, and a dark moustache. What made Harry look at him were the leather jacket and the leather gloves. The man was not wearing the goggles but Harry knew him as the man they called Cotman. His blood froze as from Cotman's expression it was certain that the visit was no accident.

Mumbling something to the people he barged by, Harry returned to the side of the room, sinking down on a chair. While he was in there he was surely safe from a beating. Cotman looked around him casually, found another chair, and placed it facing Harry, ignoring the elbows and the hips of the mob, now happily dancing. He took the carrier from Harry's hands, and leafed through it. With a lift in his heart, Harry realized that

Roy had all the dirties while he had the musical comedy tunes.

'Is that all you've got?' asked Cotman.

Harry nodded.

'Where's your mate?'

'He got hurt last night,' improvised Harry, 'nasty crack on the shoulder.'

'You won't get anywhere with these,' said Cotman shaking his head, 'it's the wrong sort of party altogether.'

'I sold three today,' said Harry, nearly biting off his tongue as he was about to say 'We'.

'Not much profit in that is there?' asked Cotman, 'you can't take more than sevenpence or eightpence a copy.'

'I have to make a living somehow,' said Harry, putting on a show of pathos that could always soften his mother. 'I'm an orphan you see. Have to make a copper when I can. And it's not easy these days.'

'It's never been easier,' said Cotman, 'except amongst these poor working-class sods. You've had a decent education, I can hear that. Good speaking voice. Good speaking voice goes far these days, love. I don't hear any Brummy twang in your voice. Do you want a lift in the motor anywhere?'

'I've got my bicycle, thanks', replied Harry.

'Sorry about last night,' said Cotman, 'but we thought you were Leatherby's boys coming into our territory. We have to put on a show of strength sometimes *pour encourager les autres*. Do you know what that means?'

'To encourage the others,' Harry translated.

Cotman looked Harry over thoughtfully. 'Have you any decent togs?' he asked.

'These are my working clothes,' said Harry, falling into a trap.

'Orphans do all right then, eh?' suggested Cotman, 'No, love, you're right to cover up. One of these days come and see me.' He gave Harry a card from a silver card-case.

Harry read:

C. S. Cotman
Manufacturers' Agent

'What's that number down there?' Harry asked with curiosity, all trace of apprehension gone.

'That's a telephone number,' replied Cotman. 'I was one of the first business men in Brum to have one. The only snag is that my men can't use it. The fools send me telegrams and I have to fork out the money for them. I'm in my office every morning from ten to twelve. You can do better than selling "Come into the Garden, Maud" and the likes of that.'

He nodded and left. Harry looked at the card for a couple of minutes then tucked it into his upper breast pocket. He did not know what a manufacturer's agent was, but if it meant that Cotman could buy a motor-car then he certainly would not mind learning.

5

Harry did not see so much of Roy nowadays. A break had occurred between them one Saturday morning when Harry, looking at the rain falling, had decided that he was not going to the football ground to sell rosettes. 'And my advice to you', he had told Roy, 'is to stay behind too. You've got a rotten cough.'

'Some of us haven't got a ma who thinks the sun shines out of your arse,' Roy had said sardonically, and had stamped out of the house.

Harry was now working for Cotman and acting as a messenger. He gradually realized how many irons Cotman had in the fire. Parcels were sent from Holland and France, a couple of girls in the office untied them, took out books and packed them up individually, posting them to private addresses or to bookshops. For some reason, Harry was sent out with certain of the parcels and told to deliver them to specific persons, collecting money from them on the spot. Only when one of the parcels burst open in the driving rain did he realize what the books were; even he, accustomed to the obscenity of the sheet music that Cotman sold to the clubs and public houses, was shocked by the material contained in the books. There were photographs of men being flogged by women, of close-ups of women's bodies, of men and women coupling in a variety of bizarre ways.

It was then that he understood why customers were so intent on having their books delivered to them personally. He could imagine the effect on a wife who happened to unwrap one of the books. Funny, he thought, you would never think that the men to whom he took the books were that way inclined. They all lived in big houses, often had a motor-car and were mild, shy people, surreptitiously handing Harry the money in a sealed envelope. He had felt the coins in the envelopes and guessed that they were sovereigns. He never gave any indication to the customers—Cotman called them clients—that he knew what the parcels contained.

He saw little of Cotman, for the pornographic book business was only one of his many business interests. He saw more of a man named Bellamy, a middle-aged clerk with thin receding hair and a perpetual sniff, and the girl in the office, forever pounding a typewriter. The typewriter fascinated Harry and one morning, while he was waiting for the books to be packed for the day's round, she looked at him through the door and said, 'Don't stand there. Come in.'

It couldn't be said that Carol was a pretty girl, not like Judy, but she had a perkiness that made her attractive. She had a pointed chin and big brown eyes, though they could scarcely be seen behind the low fringe of hair.

'What are you doing?' he asked.

'Writing to Amsterdam,' she said, 'that's in Holland, you know.'

'I did geography at school,' retorted Harry.

'Fancy that,' said the girl amiably, 'here you are. Here's a fresh sheet of paper, you have a go.'

Harry sat down and painstakingly typed out his name and address. 'Why don't they have the letters in the right order?' he complained. 'A to Z. They're dotted about all over the place.'

'Fancy you spotting that,' said the girl sarcastically.

'What do you do in the evening?' Harry asked idly.

'Nothing much,' replied Carol, looking at him brightly and, stumbling over the words, Harry asked her if she would like to go to the Hippodrome. Eagerly she agreed, and Harry booked seats in the stalls for the next night, first house, as Carol had to get back home to look after her baby sister. Harry gathered that her mother went out charring and that her father worked on the railways.

It was clear that Carol did not go out very much, for she was awed and thrilled by the occasion, dressing neatly but simply in a close-fitting high-waisted dress that did the best for her slim figure, and obviously taking considerable trouble with her hair, even to the extent of cutting the fringe. In the interval Harry bought her a box of chocolates and she gorged herself on these, her eyes fixed to the stage. The most humdrum of comedians brought out extravagant laughter and the knock-about turn had her bending over in her seat, tears streaming from her eyes with hilarity. Feeling bold, Harry put his arm around her waist, and she put her hand on his.

'I've never had such fun,' she said as they walked out into the autumn dusk, her eyes sparkling. She looked at the clock over the jeweller's shop in Hurst Street.

'How about a quick drink?' suggested Harry and she nodded eagerly. Harry led her into one of the flashy places that Roy liked so much and went up to the bar. At one time he would have felt out of place, but no longer. He dressed well, with a gold pin set neatly through his wide-knotted tie and his check suit was dashing without being loud.

He ordered a whisky for himself and a gin for Carol and the way she screwed her eyes up made it clear that she was not used to the drink. After another whisky and gin he waved down a passing cab. It was not a night to stint things and on the journey to Carol's home he kissed her on the mouth, the sensation thrilling him, and cupped his hands over her breasts, soft and yielding. She clung to his mouth eagerly and the driver waited patiently outside the house until he considered that the youngsters had gone far enough in his cab.

It was a small two-up two-down terrace house, similar to the one his father had lived in before he joined the army. Carol, clutching his hand, led him into the house by the back-door which opened off a large yard, surrounded by other houses, some of which had no access to a street and consisted of one room up and one room down. The living room was clean and tidy, and on the snow-white tablecloth was pinned a note. Carol bent down and said, giggling, 'I can't read it. All the letters are swimming.'

'It's just to say that your mother has put baby to bed,' said Harry.

'That means there's just you and me downstairs,' said Carol saucily. 'What are you going to do about it?'

'What about your dad?' Harry asked.

'He's on the night-shift,' replied Carol, 'he won't be back before six tomorrow morning.'

The invitation was there and he made love to her with an energy that astonished her. Mr Cotman was never like this.

Harry considered that love was all that it was cracked up to be and on the walk home he sang lustily all the way. He was not to know that Carol was aggrieved by his lack of interest in her once he had had his way with her. He had only pecked her on the cheek as he left. Men, she reflected, they were all the same, but at least you did not expect more from Mr Cotman. Having him was part of the job. Typewriting girls who made mistakes in spelling did not usually get two pounds a week.

It was something of a surprise to Harry when he went to the office next morning and found that Carol was not there.

'Where's Carol?' he asked Mr Bellamy, the clerk.

'I sent her back home,' replied the other, 'she looked a bit peaky this morning.'

Satisfied with the explanation, Harry went on his rounds, returning at five o'clock with six envelopes which he handed to Mr Bellamy.

'Mr Cotman's in the office,' said Bellamy, looking up from his desk. 'He'd like to see you.'

Cotman was sitting in Carol's chair, reading the letters that she had typed the previous day. 'That girl will never learn to spell,' he said regretfully. 'Had a good day, Harry?'

'Six envelopes, Mr Cotman,' replied Harry, 'and I took those two big parcels to those bookshops as you asked.'

'Harry,' began his employer, 'let me tell you a little story. When I was a young fellow like yourself my father said to me: "Do what you like, my boy, but don't do it on your doorstep. You've had a good education but they won't have told you that." They don't, do they, Harry, schoolmasters?'

'No, Mr Cotman,' Harry answered.

'One day you might be the director of a company,' Cotman went on, taking out his cigar case and offering it to Harry. Harry took a cigar, and Cotman handed him his cigar-cutter. 'When you're boss you get the pick of everything. Even the girls. You weren't to know, of course, about Carol and me. She should have told you, by rights, but you know what girls are like when they've had a drink or two inside them, especially when they're not used to it. You see, Harry, Carol is more of a daughter to me. I don't let her drink.'

'You're not going to give her the sack, Mr Cotman, are you?' asked Harry, suddenly feeling apprehensive.

'I wouldn't dream of it,' said Cotman expansively. 'Boys will be boys, and girls, bless their little hearts, will be girls. Now the last few weeks I've been thinking about promoting you and so, as they say, it's an ill wind that blows no one any good, or blows no one no good, as the Brummies say. I've got better work for you than being a delivery boy. Come and see me at my office tomorrow morning. You can have the rest of the day off. By the way, do you know anybody who'd like to take over your job? A young fellow you could trust? That mate of yours, for instance?'

'You mean Roy,' said Harry, 'well, speaking bluntly, as soon as he knew what was in the parcels he would turn awkward, and Roy's one of those fellows who bears grudges.'

'That's what I like about you, Harry,' said Cotman, 'common sense and knowing where your bread's buttered. All right, love, come and see me tomorrow morning.' He felt in his pocket, and handed Harry two sovereigns. 'That's a bonus for seeing my point of view,' he said.

On the way back to Sparkbrook, Harry felt guilty about not putting Roy in the way of an easy job and decided that he ought to go over and see him, find out how he was getting on. It was some weeks since they had met and Harry wondered how Roy was making a living in the cricket season when there was no opportunity to sell rosettes. He resolved to call on him the next morning.

The house was as derelict-looking as usual and, surrounded by swirling mist, made Harry think of those mystery stories in the *Strand* magazine that dad bought for the sake of the war stories.

The basement door was open as usual and he went into the subterranean passage, calling Roy's name. There was no response, so he pushed his way into the living room. There was no one there except an elderly woman sitting in front of a glowing fire, her skirt above her knees, her legs bulging with surgical stockings. Her mouth was open and she was snoring, but when she sensed that someone else was in the room she came to life, coughing. She looked at Harry blearily, and reached for the packet of cigarettes at her elbow. Not until she had lit one did she say anything.

'You must be Harry,' she said, blowing smoke through carmine lips. 'Roy was wondering where you had been.'

'I've been so busy at work,' said Harry apologetically, 'lot of night-work, too.' This must be Mrs Abbott, decided Harry. She did not look much like the photograph of her on the mantelpiece. She reminded him very much of the whore Roy had picked up in the Smethwick club, but it was far too early in the morning for Dotty to come up with any artificial brightness.

'You might have come over and seen him before he went to the sanatorium,' said Dotty accusingly.

'What?' asked Harry.

'You didn't know?' went on Dotty in surprise.

'No. What's wrong with him?'

She shrugged her shoulders. 'Some say TB, some say rheumatic fever, but the docs all they talk about is X-rays and God only knows what that means. I can't get over there so often as I'd like, but Judy, she's a wonder that girl is, an absolute wonder. Only his half-sister, but she's like a mother to him, just like a mother.' Maudlin came easily to Dotty. Her eyes bulged with tears. 'More than me,' she said, her voice quavering. 'I ain't been a good mother to him, that I ain't, and this is the Lord's vengeance, that's for sure. I should 'ave brought 'im up in the paths of righteousness, that's what I should've done.' She took another drag of the cigarette, which seemed to settle her somewhat. 'Still,' she said philosophically, 'we can all be wise after the event, can't we? And anyway, Abbott won't go and see him. Says it's his legs.'

'Where is it?' asked Harry. 'I might pop over and see him.'

'Earlswood,' replied Dotty, 'it's easy by train.'

Roy was sitting in the garden looking disgruntled, a red

39

hospital blanket round his shoulders. He did not seem particularly pleased to see Harry.

'How are you feeling?' Harry asked sympathetically.

'All right, I suppose,' said Roy churlishly, 'my cough's gone, anyway, though I expect I'll get pneumonia being stuck out in the garden all the time.'

'Is it catching?' Harry asked.

Roy did not answer, but browsed through the magazines that Harry had brought him. 'You know I'm not one for reading,' he said. 'Have you got any fags?'

Before he could reach into his pocket, Roy seized Harry's arm. 'Careful', he whispered, 'I'm not allowed to smoke. Sort of smuggle them to me.'

'Anybody come to see you?' Harry asked.

'No,' replied Roy, 'I might be dead and buried for all the trouble they take.'

'How about Judy? She comes and sees you.'

'No, she don't,' said Roy. 'She comes and sees one of the male nurses. That's where she is now. Hullo and cheerio is all I see of her.'

On cue Judy's voice called out, 'I'm off now, Roy. See you next week.'

Harry turned. Behind a hedge he could see a man's face, with Judy's in proximity.

'Oh, it's you, Harry,' said Judy, coming from behind the hedge. 'I'll go back with you. You can't be certain who'll you meet on the train. Lot of dirty old men about.'

If there were, they would not have had much chance that day, for a school outing from the Birmingham slums made any kind of communication between the sexes impossible. The train puffed its way through the countryside, sidling through the outer suburbs with their lines of clean washing and pastel-dressed children playing with hoops, the occupants of Harry's carriage hurling obscenities from the window. Judy was sitting opposite to Harry, being remorselessly stared at by the more adventurous children, and when the train drew in to the Birmingham terminus Harry was glad to be out of it.

'Come back and have a cup of tea,' requested the girl and Harry nodded, his head aching from the noise of the children. He did not feel that Judy warranted a cab, so they returned to

40

the house by bus. They discussed Roy. Harry thought that he looked all right, Judy that Roy was poorly. 'I don't think he'll be out of there except in a wooden box,' she said forebodingly, and Harry felt guilty about giving Roy the half-packet of cigarettes.

'I'm back, grandad,' yelled Judy as they clambered down the basement steps. 'He's not really my grandad', she explained, 'but he likes to be called that. And he always likes to know when I get back.' She led the way into the living room. Dotty had gone, leaving the debris of half a dozen cigarettes scattered on the bare linoleum, and making a tch-tch of annoyance Judy kicked the stubs towards the fireplace. She went outside to the kitchen and Harry heard the flare of a gas jet. 'We was one of the first houses round here to have a gas oven,' Judy said proudly.

As his headache ebbed away, it suddenly dawned on Harry that for the first time he had Judy with him alone. Always before there had been Roy in the background. On an impulse he went into the kitchen and wished he had not. His mother's housekeeping had not accustomed him to the squalor that he encountered, the blobs of jam on the newspaper spread on the table in lieu of a cloth, the plate of mouldy cheese, the bucket in the corner full of cabbage and tea-leaves and the sink covered with slime.

As it seemed that Judy was content to empty the dregs of the cups into the sink and refill them without washing them, Harry thoroughly cleaned them under the running tap, though he was unable to remove the brown stain that clung around the rim and it seemed bad-manners to scrape away the patina of lipstick. 'Proper little housewife, aren't you?' asked Judy pertly, 'I bet you can do more than that, though, a great big man like you!' Harry nipped her bottom, and she giggled. 'I know your sort,' she said archly, 'can't wait for it.'

'How about you?' Harry asked.

'Oh, I got my pride,' she said, pouring out the tea.

'Got something else I'll be bound,' suggested Harry.

'I might have,' she said cheekily, eyeing him as she sipped her tea. She put the cup back on the saucer and wiped her mouth with the back of her hand. 'You haven't drunk your tea.'

41

'I've got other things on my mind,' Harry said. 'All right, in the other room.'

He followed her into the living-room and while she rolled her dress above her waist he stepped out of his trousers.

Pleased that the night with Carol had not curbed his ardour, Harry took Judy without ceremony.

'You've torn my dress,' Judy complained as she brushed the hem down.

'I'll pay for that,' Harry said, turning away from her feeling somehow ashamed, and as he picked up his trousers he saw something move on the wall and there was a click. He went over to the wall, holding his trousers, and found a square panel. As he opened it he heard shuffling feet.

'Somebody's been watching us,' he said, aghast.

'Of course,' said Judy complacently, 'it's old Abbott. Why did you think I gave him a call when we got in?' Furiously Harry pulled up his trousers and strapped on his belt. 'It's his only pleasure in life,' explained Judy. 'It doesn't do anybody any harm.'

Harry was never to find another woman in whom compassion and hard-heartedness were so evenly mixed.

6

Sergeant Oakwood stood behind the counter staring into space, focusing his eyes sufficiently to see that the plate-glass windows were rather grimy. He had lost his enthusiasm and the ponderous black apparatus at his elbow unnerved him. The War Office had decided to fit telephones into their recruiting offices. 'It will keep them on their toes,' said a red-tabbed major in Whitehall, 'there are too many sinecures today.'

A young man came through the door, and looked at Sergeant Oakwood nervously.

'Yes, lad?' asked Oakwood automatically, and waited while the man coughed. They were long racking coughs.

'It's not usually this bad, sir,' said the young man.

Oakwood bit his lower lip. 'It's no go, boy,' he said, 'I've heard that sort of cough before.' He did not say that it was, in common parlance, a churchyard cough. 'Here,' he said suddenly, reaching into his pocket and bringing out a half-crown.

'I don't want charity, sir,' said the other. There was blood on his handkerchief when he brought it out to choke off another bout of coughing. He did not say anything more, but silently took the coin and left.

Oakwood watched him go. He hoped that the telephone would not ring. He was not good with the telephone, he knew, and Colonel Ludlow's adjutant had been very acrid on the subject. He watched Captain Griffen cross the street outside. He was disappointed in Griffen; he had not been made up to sergeant-major, as arranged. He steeled himself for a welcoming grin, but Griffen was subdued.

'I can't stay,' he said, 'I've been posted to Warwick.'

'That's good, sir,' said Oakwood uncertainly.

'Good?' asked Griffen, puzzled, 'what's good about it?'

Oakwood shuffled uncomfortably. 'Promotion, sir?' he suggested.

'It's not good for you and it's not good for me,' said Griffen. 'I know you don't like the telephone, but for God's sake do your best with it.'

'I was trained for the telegraph not the telephone,' said Oakwood coldly.

'I've got a list of complaints,' said Griffen taking a paper from his pocket, 'made by Colonel Ludlow at six the other evening.'

'I went to a restaurant with my wife,' said Oakwood.

'I don't want your excuses, Oaky,' said Griffen sadly, 'you can go to the restaurant whenever you like. It's a pity you went that particular evening. Your hours are, specifically, half-past six.'

'Let's have the complaints, sir,' said Oakwood heavily.

'Dirty window, dog fouling the step, paper on floor of office, telephone incorrectly placed, tea cup on counter,' said Griffen.

'Five shillings a day goodbye then,' said Oakwood ironically.

'Oh yes,' said Griffen, 'oh yes, indeed!'

43

Since Africa, George Oakwood had encountered bored officers, negligent officers and officers who wanted nothing more than to get him out of their sight. It was a long time since he had been face to face with a hostile officer. Colonel Ludlow kept him waiting in the outer office for twenty minutes, and when Oakwood was marched in Ludlow did not look up from the papers he was reading for a full five minutes. Twenty years ago Oakwood would not have minded, but now, at fifty, his back ached and the sinews of his legs felt like overstretched elastic.

Slowly Ludlow raised his head and stared at Oakwood. Suddenly Oakwood realized that Ludlow was half-mad, and the hairs on the back of his neck stood up.

'What I know of you I don't like, Sergeant,' said Ludlow softly, 'you seem to have spent your entire army career detached to some regiment or other, the Telegraph Corps or the Manchesters or someone. Then in America you had the impudence to impersonate an officer. Unfortunately the Americans couldn't see through you. I can. I wanted to tear this obscene nonsense up, but my adjutant persuaded me not to. As he says, there is a copy elsewhere. There may be dozens of copies. Don't you like the Warwicks?'

'They have been my life, sir,' replied Oakwood.

'It doesn't look like it,' said Ludlow. He scribbled something on a piece of paper. 'As for your part in the South African War,' he said viciously, 'there is something nasty about it. Tracking mercenaries! That was an excuse, wasn't it, Sergeant, an excuse for rape and looting?'

Oakwood felt anger bubble up inside him. 'Is that an accusation, sir?' he asked.

'Don't be impudent!' snapped Ludlow, 'the facts are there in black and white.'

'I would like this interview to be witnessed by a senior officer, sir,' said Oakwood.

'Senior officer?' echoed Ludlow, standing up, his knuckles white against his desk, 'I am the senior officer. Where do you think you can find a senior officer in this god-forsaken hole?' He sat down, his hands shaking. 'I am in two minds whether to court martial you, Sergeant, for dereliction of duty. Or perhaps a court of inquiry. Then there is this business with Captain

44

Griffen, ingratiating yourself, hoping for promotion. Did you know my son, Sergeant?'

'No, sir,' replied Oakwood.

'He was butchered at Spion Kop. The shock killed my wife. It is my considered opinion that he was shot by one of his own men. In your experience in the war, did that happen?'

The change of tone and attitude startled Oakwood. 'Not in my experience, sir,' he replied.

Ludlow nodded. He seemed to forget Oakwood, and began to scrabble about in a drawer. A sergeant-clerk opened the door softly, and beckoned to Oakwood. With one eye on Ludlow, Oakwood backed through the door. 'A pretty kettle of fish!' said the sergeant heavily, 'you realize he's as mad as a hatter?'

'I guessed it,' said Oakwood.

'And what the bloody hell can be done?' asked the clerk, 'he accused me yesterday of urinating against his desk. The adjutant's no bloody help either.'

'Why don't you have a word with Captain Griffen?' Oakwood asked, 'he used to be my old commanding officer.'

'Oh, him!' spat out the clerk, 'he's no bloody use either. It's yes, sir, no, sir, I ain't got nowhere to go when the army's finished with me, sir. Still, he ain't as bad as Lieutenant Culpeper. The old man send Culpeper out spying. He sent him to your place in Dale End in civilian clobber. Of course, he went himself as well. Saw a dog shitting on your doorway and marked it down against you. As if you was responsible. That's what got Griffen posted. It was partly his fault, too. At one time he thought it was Griffen's dog that did it, just out of spite against him.'

Oakwood went back to the recruiting office, numbed. The man he had seen should have been in an asylum. The shrill clang of the telephone broke into his thoughts. It was the orderly room clerk to tell him that his replacement as recruiting sergeant was on his way. The new sergeant arrived reeking of drink, and did not seem to take in the instructions Oakwood gave him.

'I can do this job on my head,' the sergeant boasted, a tall gangling man with a red nose. With the inner assurance that his replacement would not last long, Oakwood went home. He sat down, and told Jane what had happened.

'But, George,' she said, her brow puckered, 'something ought to be done about it.'

'If he drinks it's his own look out,' said Oakwood.

'Not the sergeant,' said Jane impatiently, 'I mean this colonel. And all the things you have done for the army! It's not fair, really it isn't.'

'Life's not fair,' said Oakwood, 'you have to make the best of it. Still, better for Colonel Ludlow to be stuck on his backside in Brum than on active service. He wouldn't have lasted long with old Stryker, I can tell you. Stryker would have put a bullet through his nut before long. And so would Cartwright. Poor old Cartwright. I heard say he was dead. Most of 'em are dead. Captain Griffen, now that's a hard one to take.'

'Waiting for his pension, I dare say,' said Jane, 'do they give officers pensions?'

'Don't know,' said George, 'it just shows that you can never take officers on trust. Only one I knew who was gold all the way through, a captain named Barnett. But I never thought it of Griffen . . .' He paused. 'Well, my dear, I may be out of a job.'

'It doesn't matter,' said Jane, 'we can manage.'

Leonard had overheard the conversation. 'Don't worry, Dad,' he said eagerly, 'I'll get a paper round. I'll help.'

George Oakwood felt his eyes moisten. 'I know you will, lad,' he said gruffly, 'but it won't come to that.'

Nor did it. The following morning a messenger arrived with an urgent message. Sergeant Oakwood was promoted back to sergeant-major and reinstated as recruiting sergeant. He never found out why, and imagined that Captain Griffen had come up trumps after all. It was a visionary thought. All that had happened was that a court of inquiry into the curious behaviour of Colonel Ludlow had restored the status quo.

An impromptu visit by Colonel Ludlow to the recruiting office had also helped. The spectacle of George Oakwood's replacement asleep on the floor grasping an empty whisky bottle by the neck had impelled Ludlow to go berserk, and a policeman attracted by the smashing of the plate-glass window was in no mood to inquire about the status of the well-spoken hooligan.

The colonel who took over from Colonel Ludlow had decided against cancelling Captain Griffen's posting to Warwick.

46

There was no doubt, he thought, that Griffen had become slack. Officers could, it was agreed, drink tea when the occasion arose. But not in a recruiting office open to the public or with a serving NCO, old soldier or not.

7

During the years of Edward's reign there were enormous advances in motor-car technology and a car that was right up to the minute could be rendered obsolete by some new discovery. It was an age when the rich were enormously rich, unaffected by modest income-tax demands, and buying a motor-car was no more significant than buying a new toy for a child or a coat for a wife. No woman of standing reckoned that she could get by on a dress allowance of less than a thousand pounds a year, and the owner of a motor-car was not concerned that the trade-in value of his old car was fifteen per cent of the original amount.

Cotman seized upon this point and offered garages a small profit on the second-hand cars they took in. He purchased cars, renovated them and even carried out modifications at a workshop that he owned on the outskirts of the city. A moderately wealthy man, unwilling to spend four hundred pounds on a new car, was often more than willing to speculate half this sum on a slightly older car with no more than five hundred miles on the clock.

Along with the cars, Cotman had a subsidiary company dealing in motor tyres. Many motorists had regretted the passing of the solid tyre for comfortable rides using pneumatic tyres could be expensive—tyres cost twenty-five pounds a pair and even then were often bursting. Cotman and his mechanics conceived the idea of remoulding rejected tyres and selling them at a third of the price of new ones. Business was booming, and gradually Cotman began to drop the more or less illegal activities that had made money for him in the past, running down the business in pornographic sheet music though keeping the book trade, the profits of which were too large to be idly dismissed. He had a staff there he could trust. Bellamy was able to operate without supervision and the new girl who replaced Carol, whom he had set up in an apartment in fashionable Edgbaston after her fleeting night of pleasure with Harry, had proved to have a sound business sense, knew what to order and in what quantities, and what to avoid.

For his best customers, Cotman did a good job so far as cars were concerned. Mechanically minded himself, he did not disdain donning a pair of overalls and getting beneath a car to see what was wrong and whether his mechanics were doing what he asked them to. But for the fringe of the trade he set up cut-price garages, the mechanics of which were not over-scrupulous. Cars had few instruments, and the first sign of overheating was the smell of burning paint. It was expected that car owners should spend at least an hour a day cleaning, oiling and adjusting and, as this harsh regime taxed all but the most enthusiastic, a car engine that seized up was partly a result of the motorist's own neglect.

There was no way to get at an engine except underneath, and Cotman was one of the first men in Birmingham to build well-equipped and well-lighted pits so that engine inspection could be carried out conveniently. When Harry was introduced to the motor trade he spent a good deal of his time beneath cars and having blueprints explained to him, but he did not mind the dirt and the grime, and when he got back at night George was pleased to see that his son was clearly doing a hard day's work.

Secretly George envied the boy—he still thought of him as a boy though he was now twenty—the motor bicycle that he had bought, and he often went into the yard to watch Harry servicing it.

'What does that do, Harry?' he asked, pointing to various parts and Harry explained.

One day Harry drew up to the house in a 1903 ten horse-power Panhard, and George felt a glow of pride in his son. He looked so smart sitting high in the car, his cap strapped securely beneath his chin.

'It's all turned right after all,' he said to Jane as they watched him through the window.

'To think that Harry's driving a motor-car,' breathed Jane, sharing in her husband's pride.

There was more to Harry than driving a motor-car. Sometimes Harry chuckled as he imagined what his mother would think had she known about Judy. And his father would do more than strut around playing soldiers. He stroked the steering wheel tenderly; the motor-car was worth every Judy in the British Empire, even though it was Mr Cotman's and not his. One thing about dad, he thought suddenly—he was a cut above that other old soldier, Abbott.

He did not bother about Abbott any more. If the old fellow wanted to stare into the living-room at him and Judy having their fun, let him. Mind, he and Judy did have fun, though he was getting a bit tired of it now. Judy had no more tricks to show him, that was the truth of it, and he was bored. He remembered that night he had taken Mr Cotman's girl, Carol. Now that was an experience to cherish. Judy, he was afraid, was the short-timer par excellence—up skirt, in, out, finish. Like making love to march rhythm, fitted into the two minutes of a gramophone record. Still, he mused as he drew up outside the old house with its sightless windows and the garden growing deep in rubbish (now that Roy was no longer there to occasionally weed it out), it was nothing more than you could expect with a mother like Dotty. Dotty's face, the patched and garnished wreckage of beauty, remained in his memory, though he had seen it only once, when he had learned that Roy was in the sanatorium. Poor old Roy. It was not fair.

Feeling that he knew the exact tempo of every drip, the location of every broken brick on the path, he entered the basement. Sunday night was one of his usual times. Judy would be waiting for him, a bottle of gin on the sideboard, the curtains drawn over the windows to stop the local brats looking in and the gaslight flickering. And in the next room would be old Abbott, knees trembling, waiting for the great sensation of the week.

But there was no bottle of gin on the sideboard and Judy was staring in a lack-lustre manner at the few burning coals in the grate.

'Snap out of it, girl,' said Harry cheerily, 'and after you know what we'll go for a spin in the motor. I'm full up with petrol.'

There was no response from the moody girl.

'What's up?' asked Harry.

Probably old Abbott had snuffed it. Or Dotty.

'You've done it this time,' said Judy lugubriously.

'Done what?' asked Harry quickly. 'The coppers haven't been here, have they?' There was that car that he sold that he was certain was stolen; there were the new tyres that he had bought from the man in West Bromwich and sold to Mr Cotman at half-price; there was that man who had stopped him at the coffee-house on the way to Warwick to whom he had sold a quick-repair job, there was . . .

'It must have been that time I didn't take precautions,' said Judy, turning a tear-stained face towards him.

'Oh, is that all?' asked Harry, relieved. 'You've got a bun in the oven.'

'I've got witnesses it was you,' said Judy, 'old Abbott.'

'He wouldn't say anything, the dirty old bastard . . .' began Harry.

'I would,' shouted Abbott from behind the hatch.

'Give us a fag,' Judy said harshly, and Harry did so.

'Are you going to make an honest woman of me?' Judy asked pleadingly.

The situation was too much for Harry. He roared with laughter until tears were streaming from his eyes. 'I should phrase it differently to that,' he said when he had partly recovered.

'I know where you work,' Judy carried on savagely. 'You've never let on where you live, but I know where you work. I was going through that little cupboard in the motor one day and I found out where the car was repaired and that's where you work. I don't want to cause no trouble. And I want the baby. It's all I've got.'

Realizing that he was up against something other than a hysterical woman Harry asked, 'What makes you think it's mine?'

'The others take precautions,' Judy replied.

'Yes, yes,' said Harry casually.

'You're going to marry me then?' pursued Judy.

'It needs some thinking about,' parried Harry.

'If you don't,' warned Judy, 'there's going to be trouble. It will be all right anyway. It's not like as if you're one of my gentleman friends. I mean to say, I never ask any money from you, do I?'

'Where would we live?' asked Harry.

'Why,' answered Judy, puzzled that such a question could be put, 'here, of course.'

Harry pretended to give the matter some thought. 'There doesn't seem any choice,' he said. 'All right.'

Cheered up in a fraction of a second, Judy turned up the gaslight for the benefit of Abbott, and began to pull her knickers off. 'Not tonight', said Harry, 'it's been a bit of a shock to me, you must admit.'

'Yes,' agreed Judy, 'it's a special moment, ain't it, for the two of us.'

'Not to forget your mum,' Harry pointed out.

Judy's eyes softened. 'Yes, she'll be real pleased. She's always liked you, and she was saying that it was about time I left off my flighty ways and settled down and got married and had kids and all the rest of it . . .'

Resolving that this was the last time he would see Judy, Harry left the house and drove rapidly, as fast as the car would take him, to Cotman's big house in Shirley. He was told never to go there except in emergencies, but this seemed like one to him, and Cotman was not put out when Harry told him what had happened.

'What do you want me to do, Harry?' he asked.

'You're the only person who knows where I live,' Harry said. 'If you'd just forget it when Judy or her mum turns up. You don't know me, nor do the mechanics.'

'And how are you going to get out of it?' asked Cotman.

'There's one sure way, Mr Cotman, where there's no questions asked. The army. I'll enlist in the regulars for the short service.'

'I'll be sorry to see you go, Harry,' said Cotman, nodding, 'but I would do the same thing if I was in your shoes.'

'Who is it, darling?' asked a voice from the drawing room, and the most exquisitely beautiful woman Harry had ever seen in his life appeared framed in the doorway.

51

'My wife,' muttered Cotman. 'Mum's the word, love.' He turned to her. 'Just one of my men, dear,' he said, 'a small emergency. Nothing that can't be put right.'

8

The sergeant looked from under the peak of his cap, his eyes glittering. 'You 'orrible men', he shouted, 'of all the 'orrible men I've dealt with in my time you are the 'orriblest. Mr Lloyd George and his like are going to give the old 'uns pensions. Why are you lot 'ere then?' He turned dramatically to his corporal. 'Why are they 'ere, Corporal?'

'Don't know, Sergeant,' said the corporal, clicking his heels.

'They're 'ere to make my life a bane, that's why, Corporal. But they won't do it . . . wipe that grin of your face, Private Oakwood, I saw that.'

But it was all very routine; there was no acrimony in the voice.

'I want two men who are mechanically minded,' he shouted. 'Two paces forward all those who are mechanically minded.'

Harry Oakwood and another soldier stepped forward.

'All right, you two. Take the Maxim to the stores. At the double, you idle men.'

Harry and his companion lifted up the gun, one taking the body the other the tripod, and trotted to the stores. The sergeant-armourer came up to the drill sergeant, and watched them go.

'What are this lot like, Arthur?' he asked.

'Not bad at all,' the drill sergeant reluctantly conceded. 'You see the tall one with fair hair? Do you know who that is? Oakwood, son of Sergeant-Major Oakwood.'

'I never met him,' said the armourer.

52

'Me neither, but he's partly responsible for me being in the regiment.'

'How's that, mate?' asked the other as they slowly walked back to the sergeants' mess.

'Long story,' said the drill sergeant, 'my eldest brother was enlisted at about the same time as old Oakwood. Went over the wall when he was at Hockley Hill barracks'—the sergeant did not drop his aspirates in normal conversation—'and got took a few weeks later. The bastards broke his toe in the glasshouse. My mum and dad wanted nothing to do with him—dad was a clerk, very respectable, y'see. Sullied the family name. They had a provost sergeant almost camping on the doorstep looking for young Dicky. Then out of the blue we had a letter. I'll show it you if you like.'

He dug into his pocket and drew out his wallet. The letter he handed to the armourer was thin and beginning to get tattered at the edges, but the firm slightly schoolboyish writing was easy to read:

> *Dear Mr and Mrs Marchbanks,*
>
> *It is with regret that I have to tell you that your son, Richard, has been killed in battle. I knew your son when he enlisted twenty-five years ago and, to be honest, when he deserted I thought he would never make a real soldier. But he put his back into it, put his troubles behind him, and died a brave soldier. I felt honoured to be his NCO. I am enclosing his personal belongings.*
>
> *I have taken the liberty to have him buried amongst his own kind in the Church of England cemetery in Khartoum.*
>
> *Yours respectfully*
> *George Oakwood*
> *(Sergeant-Major, Royal Warwickshire Regt)*

'Mum was dying when the letter came,' said Sergeant Marchbanks, 'it helped her meet her maker in peace. Dicky wasn't a failure after all. So I joined up after the Battle of Omdurman where Dicky fell to scotch any idea that there's anything wrong with our family.'

Unaware that Sergeant Marchbanks had a friendly eye on him, Harry Oakwood walked back to the barrack room. Stern training, little drink and good food had tightened up his muscles. He had been in the army a year now, and had stuck it out well. He remembered the moist look in his father's eyes when he had enlisted.

'This is the happiest day of my life, Harry,' George Oakwood had said, choking.

'I won't let you down, Dad,' Harry had replied, uncomfortably. For him it was merely a way of shaking off Judy, of putting behind him part of his life that he wanted to forget, but he knew that for his father his enlistment was equivalent to going into the family business. All events had been leading up to it since he had been born.

His NCOs had found Private Oakwood a good-average soldier, diligent at drill but not over anxious to impress his personality, perhaps over eager to get into the town when passes were issued and known as a lad with the ladies, even on a shilling a day's pay. His kit layout was never less than acceptable and he had never been caught out on parade for sloppy dress or dirty equipment. But those with eyes to see saw that Oakwood was determined to get by with just the right amount of effort, and one or two of the elderly sergeants who had known his father shook their heads and declared that Private Oakwood would never be the man his father was.

The platoon corporal, acting as echo to the voice of the master, had been surprised that Oakwood had volunteered when the sergeant had asked for men with mechanical minds. He could not recall Oakwood volunteering for anything before. On the way to the corporal's canteen he looked in on the men's barrack room. Four men were playing cards on one of the bunks, including Oakwood. Oakwood had a pile of silver beside him, and seemed to be winning. You couldn't stop the men gambling if they had a mind to it, thought the corporal, though it was a damned silly way of getting rid of your money. He had heard that Oakwood made himself a bob or two playing billiards in the men's recreation room.

In the officers' mess there was boredom. One or two of the officers had been down to Olympia to the motor show, and they were the only ones showing any animation, raving about the new six-cylinder Ariel and the £700 Crossley.

A captain was browsing through one of the society weeklies.

'Look at this,' he said, 'the War Office has six hundred and forty rooms. Not all are sleeping compartments.'

'What's funny about that?' grunted his companion.

'It shows what they think of the War Office,' rejoined the other.

Another officer said, 'I read that they're trying to sell one of the Spithead forts and turn it into a hotel.'

'Sometimes I think this is a hotel,' said a fourth man, looking out of the window. 'The men are getting sloppy and all look like porters or window-cleaners. Oh for a war!'

Back in the barrack room Oakwood pocketed his winnings—five and threepence. Not bad, nearly a week's pay. He had won enough now to get down to London for his forthcoming leave, though he would have to find some excuse for not going home. He could say that he had volunteered for a course or something. That would please dad. The motor show at Olympia was more interesting than having to chat with his parents or listening to young Leonard playing the piano (though, he had to admit, he was getting on all right, if you liked those soppy pieces by Mozart and Beethoven).

A conversation in the company commander's office scotched Oakwood's leave. The adjutant was compiling a roll of other ranks to act as guard of honour for the state visit of King Haakon of Norway. The Home Army had recently been reorganized into seven commands, and the General Officer Commanding-in-Chief of West and Midland Command had decided that it would be a good idea if a company of the Royal Warwickshire Regiment showed its paces in London.

So Private Oakwood went to London not on leave but with a company of Warwickshires. Still, it was better than being stuck in Warwick with officers breathing down your neck all the time, and eternal drill, drill with and without rifles, machine-gun drill, map-reading and exercises in the field. He stared out of the train window at the countryside, brittle and frosty under the November sunshine.

'What are you going to do, Oaky?' asked Private Saunders, a dapper little man with a toothbrush moustache and a slight squint.

'The motor show at Olympia,' replied Oakwood.

'It's the Tivoli for me,' said Saunders, 'they've got Little

Tich there and Gus Elen, you know the one who sings about if it wasn't for the 'ouses in between.'

'I saw Gus Elen at the Brummagem Hip,' recalled Oakwood, 'wasn't bad, but not a patch on Albert Chevalier.'

'Be lucky if we get half a day off,' predicted Saunders gloomily. 'We're in with the Middlesex regiment, and they're keen as mustard on bull. It will be kit layouts morning, noon and night, and tramping round their bloody parade ground.'

The company climbed off the train at Euston, stretching their legs, and a fleet of motor-buses took them to the barracks in Mill Hill. 'Miles out of London,' complained Saunders. 'Look, we're almost out in the country.'

'Well,' said Oakwood stubbornly, 'nobody's going to stop me going to the motor show.'

'And nobody's going to stop me going to the Tivoli,' countered Saunders. How they would set about it, though, neither could say.

For a time it seemed that Saunders' gloomy predictions were right. For two days the Warwickshires were drilled off their feet, their company commander determined that the men would not let him down, and Oakwood watched longingly as the troops of the Middlesex regiment made their way to the recreation room. 'They've got a ping-pong table there,' he told Saunders. 'That's a game I'd like to play.'

'Stick to billiards, Oaky,' advised Saunders, 'you're good at that. You must have made a bob or two at billiards.'

'I've got no opposition,' said Oakwood. 'I hope we get sent to India one of these days. They're all playing sport there, and you get a native servant to do your chores. They even shave you in bed.'

'What?' said Saunders, 'you'd let one of them blacks shave you? He'd cut your throat as soon as look at you.'

'The Indians aren't like Dervishes, mate,' explained Oakwood, 'they're almost civilized.'

'That's enough of that chat,' barked out Sergeant Marchbanks, his cap pulled over his eyes as was his style. 'Outside you lot.'

For an hour it was left wheel, right wheel, mark time, but at last the sergeant released them and the corporal took over. 'Big day tomorrow,' he shouted, 'so get your kit looking real smart or it's a fizzer for the lot of you. Day after tomorrow you might get an afternoon off. That's what sarge tells me, if you act and look like guardsmen. Now it's like this. King 'aakon is going to get the freedom of the City of London at the Guildhall. That's where we're going to be. And the word is that there's going to be a cinematograph man there who's going to take moving pictures of it.'

The following day the buses drew up outside the depot gates, and the men clambered aboard, their uniforms neat, their brasses shining, the wood of their rifles oiled and the slings blancoed. They were deposited at the Guildhall many hours before the Norwegian king was due to arrive, and Sergeant Marchbanks had them at the stand easy. His men made the lot from the Worcestershire Regiment, also involved in the reception, look dullards and he was fuming when the colonel in charge ordered the company commander to march the Warwickshires off as there were too many sight-seers arriving and the streets were already becoming blocked. The sergeant deliberately held his platoon while the man with the cinematograph put up his tripod and whirled the handle.

'Thank God for that,' muttered Harry, 'we might have been stuck there for another six hours.'

The company commander had more desperate problems. He had a word with his sergeant-major. 'Damn me,' he said, 'do you know what's happened?'

'Yes, sir!' barked the sergeant-major, 'the companies have got mixed up. We've left some of our men behind and we've picked up some of the Worcesters.'

'Keep your voice down,' said the officer irritably. 'Don't let the men know for Christ's sake, otherwise it'll be chaos.'

'What's to be done then, sir?'

The captain looked around desperately, sweat oozing from his brow despite the nip in the air. 'The buses won't be here for five hours any way', he said, 'you know your London, don't you? Is there any open space near Euston Square where you could fall the men out?'

'There's a garden there, sir, big space. And we could send the men in groups to the refreshment room on Euston station. That would keep the men happy.'

'I'm not interested in keeping the men happy, Sergeant-

57

Major,' retorted his captain. 'Thank God the buses for the Worcesters are rendezvousing at the same place. We can sort 'em all out there.'

But the men had already realized what had happened and when Sergeant Marchbanks looked at them sharply he could see the vestiges of grins. A brisk march through the City, up through Islington and along to Euston would soon curb their spirits and there would be no way for the odd soldier to slide out of the march. When they got to Euston it might be another matter, especially as the sergeant-major had told him that the men would be sent in small groups to the refreshment room on the station for tea and sandwiches.

One of the first of these groups to go included Oakwood. He deposited his rifle in the left-luggage office, already noticing three rifles there. 'Tuck 'em under the counter, there's a good fellow,' he pleaded, and the railwayman grinned and did as he was asked. Oakwood sneaked out of a back entrance and took one of the new motor taxis to Olympia.

'Blimey,' said the driver, 'you got more money than I had when I was a soldier.'

'Do you know what a gentleman-ranker is, cabbie?' asked Harry in his haughtiest voice, slurring his words like a Hussars subaltern.

'Yes', said the driver, 'a nob who joins the ranks 'cause he don't want to be no bleeding officer.'

'That's just it. And I'm off to Olympia to take delivery of my new six-cylinder Napier. I haven't got much time, so keep your foot on the pedal.'

'Right-o, sir,' said the cabbie, momentarily awed.

Girls gave Oakwood the eye as he went round the show, but his eyes were on the motor cars not them. He visited each of the two hundred and sixty stands in turn, the names of the cars ringing in his ears—Fiat, Napier, Vinot, NEG, Arrol-Johnston, Lanchester, Armstrong-Whitworth, and Beeston-Humber. Limousines and tourers, landaulettes and racing-cars, their steel glittering in the artificial light, the carriage-work so polished that Oakwood could see his face reflected in it, tyres spotlessly clean, and engines fragrantly oiled. He acted as though he had been vouchsafed a glimpse of the Holy Grail.

Time went rapidly and it was with a shock that he discovered that he was one of the few people left in the vast exhibition hall. He rushed for one of the exits and mercifully a prowling motor-taxi saw his waving hand and drew into the kerb. He felt relief as he saw the soldiers still on the gardens in front of the great Euston arch, but he was only just in time, for they were getting to their feet as a queue of motor buses rounded the corner.

Suddenly he realized that his rifle was in the left-luggage office and he pushed half a sovereign into the driver's hand, not waiting for change. His heart sank. The left-luggage office had closed up for the night. He closed his eyes and saw visions of shot-drill, everlasting fatigues, and racing at the double round the parade ground with full equipment and his big pack full of sand.

Suddenly a small voice called out, 'Oi, soldier!'

He looked.

A boy in a porter's hat much too big for him peered up at him from below his shoulder.

'I've got your rifle,' he said, nipping behind the left-luggage office and bringing it out. Oakwood fumbled in his pocket for some money. 'Naw,' said the boy deprecatingly, 'I want to be a soldier when my old man lets me.'

'Thanks, mate,' said Oakwood, clapping the lad on the shoulder, 'you've saved my life.'

'You'll have to run,' the boy said anxiously, 'they're just getting on the buses.'

Oakwood took to his heels and came up against Sergeant Marchbanks.

'You're too late for the last Olympics and too early for the next', said the sergeant ironically. 'That was a bloody long cup of tea you've been having, Private Oakwood. I haven't seen you about all night. Get up with you.' He pushed Oakwood on to the steps of the bus, and waved his hand to the driver to give him the signal to start.

'That was a narrow squeak,' he said sitting down next to Saunders. Saunders did not answer but was humming softly to himself the old music-hall song 'Champagne Charlie'. So old Saunders had got to the Tivoli after all. But who on earth would want to see a lot of people prancing around on a stage when they could see hundreds of motor cars? You had to admit it, people were funny.

9

It was not often that Jane went out in the evening but when she and George heard that they were showing at the music-hall moving pictures of the Warwickshires in London they met each other after work, had a snack at one of the new cafeterias and caught the bus to the Aston Hippodrome. George was hoping that the programme was clean and inoffensive and was agreeably surprised. There was no vestige of smut about the comedians and the other people in the stalls were middle-class folk like themselves, respectable and well-dressed. He found himself enjoying the programme and even the knock-about comedian got him smiling, though he could not understand why the old fellow on his right was roaring his head off.

The flickering pictures of the arrival of King Haakon in themselves were not outstanding, but the cinematograph was still something of a novelty to the mass audience and there was interest in whatever was showing. George stared at the screen, peering for Harry. The scene moved to the City.

'There he is!' whispered Jane, gripping George's arm, 'he seems to be smiling at us.'

'Nice turn-out,' said George admiringly. 'Who would have thought that we'd see our Harry dressed up to the nines like that!'

There was not much of Harry, barely five seconds, but the Oakwoods stayed on until the end of the programme. George was glad, for the finale was a patriotic tableau with the full company singing the songs of the Boer War. 'Goodbye, Dolly Gray' always had a powerful effect on him.

Back in Warwick, Harry found that the routine continued as ever before. There were parades, field exercises in which nothing happened and which were mainly excuses for brew-ups behind hedges out of sight of officers, and drill. When Sergeant Marchbanks called out for someone to step forward, someone with mechanical knowledge, Harry, observing that there was no Maxim gun within eyeshot, obeyed. Anything to relieve the monotony.

'This isn't a joke, Private Oakwood,' said Marchbanks

severely, 'if you haven't got mechanical knowledge, two paces, back!' But Harry stood his ground, and after the sergeant had dismissed the rest of the platoon he approached Harry. 'One of the officers can't start his motor. Is that something you can fix?'

'I think so, Sarge,' said Harry confidently.

'We'll see,' grunted Marchbanks. 'You'll find it in front of the motor-house behind the officer's mess. Draw a pair of overalls from the quartermaster's stores, and get busy before it's too dark. I'll have a word with the sergeant-cook so that you get your grub.'

It was a fairly new 28–36 horse-power Armstrong-Whitworth, and Harry approached it with affection, rubbing his hand over the leather. He examined the engine, tried to start it, but nothing happened. A major, drawing on leather gloves, came round the corner, and watched him. 'What's wrong with it, soldier?' he asked.

Harry, unaware that he was being looked at, started to attention. 'Ignition, sir. Pretty sure of it. There are two systems, but neither's working. There's a low tension magneto with automatic advance, and a stand-by high tension. A feature of this model is that the whole make and break is contained in a circular plug . . .'

'There's no need to try and sell it to me, young fellow,' said the officer with a grin, 'I've bought it.'

'So you have, sir,' said Harry, 'might I ask if you have a spare plug?'

'There's all kinds of things in the box on the running board,' said the major.

Harry untied the straps and peered inside. He took out a plug, and replaced the old one. He invited the officer to get into the driving seat, adjusting the ignition lever fixed to the steering pillar beforehand.

The engine spluttered into life, and the officer climbed down. 'Good work,' he said. 'What are you, private, corporal, sergeant? I can't see under that overall.'

'Private Oakwood, sir,' replied Harry.

'Oakwood?' queried the officer, brows knitted. 'No relation to Sergeant-Major Oakwood, are you?'

'He's my father, sir.'

'He was in my company for a short time in South Africa,' said

61

the major meditatively. 'Where is he now? Out of it all, I'll wager.'

'He's recruiting sergeant in Birmingham,' explained Harry.

'I hope you do as well as he did, Oakwood,' said Major Barnett. Harry saluted, and went away, the major watching him. He did not have the march of old Oakwood, thought Barnett, but there was something of a soldier there, not like some of the recruits who were cluttering up the modern army. He spotted Sergeant Marchbanks, and called him over to him. 'I'd like young Oakwood to keep my motor groomed, Sergeant.'

'Yes, sir,' said Marchbanks. He knew what would happen. Oakwood would turn up on parade less and less and always the excuse would be the same—he had been washing Major Barnett's car, seeing to Lieutenant Wilcox's Bianchi or the colonel's Daimler. And he was proved right. 'He's either a soldier or a car engineer,' he complained to the sergeant-major.

'It keeps the officers happy,' said the sergeant-major sardonically, 'that's a mercy, ain't it, that's a mercy?'

'It'll be different when we have a war,' said Marchbanks.

'Oh, no, my lad, it won't,' said the sergeant-major, 'look at 'im, Lieutenant Wilcox, look at 'im. Keeping his motor-car nice and clean is more important to 'im than the future of the British Empire and the old nasty Kaiser.'

Lieutenant Wilcox, Eton, sent down from Oxford, father a High Court judge, mother a once-fashionable beauty who was said to have been one of the mistresses of the king when he was Prince of Wales, did not think of war and could not understand all the fuss about Haldane's reforms. If they cut down the army, as Haldane was pledged to do, there would still be plenty of room for people like him. A Wilcox always went into the army. It was a law of Nature. There had been a Wilcox, knee-breeched and ineffectual, at the Battle of Waterloo, one for the troubles in India, and one, no doubt giggling and trembling as was their wont (Wilcox had no illusions about his ancestors), in the Boer War.

He found the talk in the mess reverting to the Germans and, bored, he went out to find Oakwood. He ignored the soldiers' heel-clicking and stiff-armed salutes, acknowledging them all with a vague wave of his cane. He called Oakwood's name, and waited for him to come to him.

'Did you get to the motor show, Oakwood?' he asked.

'Just made it, sir,' replied Harry.

'On the qt, eh?'

'On the qt, sir.'

'And what did you see there that you fancied?'

Harry thought. 'I liked the Lanchester,' he said, 'it's got a lot of features that other cars haven't. But I didn't like the body-work. If I had to pick, sir, I would still go for a foreign car. There's too many English makes, you see, and most of them are bound to pack up in a year or two, and what'll you do then for spares?' He realized that he was speaking to an officer as though he himself was a car-dealer. 'Sir!' he added, clicking his heels.

'That's good,' said Lieutenant Wilcox, 'that's very good.' He looked at Harry speculatively. 'When I'm ready I'll rummage you out and we can find a motor that will suit me,' he said. He tapped his leg with his cane as Harry rejoined his mates.

'These bloody officers,' said a lance-corporal enviously, 'they buy a motor like you and me would buy a newspaper.'

'It's aeroplanes next,' ventured Private Saunders, 'I read in the *Daily Mail* that they're offering ten thousand quid to the first man to fly from London to Manchester.'

'That don't surprise me, Saunders,' said the lance-corporal. 'Shall I tell you what does surprise me?'

'Yes, Corp?' asked Saunders innocently.

'That you can bloody well read,' said the other; 'as for you, Oaky, sucking up to officers won't help you none. They're a different breed.'

Harry looked at him and grinned. He was on to a good thing, and he knew it.

As requested, Harry found a suitable car for Lieutenant Wilcox, a six-cylinder Darracq with bodywork by Sayers of Vauxhall. It cost Wilcox not far short of a thousand pounds. He wrote the cheque with a flourish, and motioned to Harry to get in. 'Give it an outing,' he said.

'Sir, I've got to get back . . .'

'Rubbish', said Wilcox resolutely, 'I'll square the sergeant or whomever. We'll take it on that straight stretch of road on the way to Warwick.'

Satisfied when the speedometer needle went off the dial and revolutions kept steady, Wilcox stopped and gave the wheel over to Harry. Harry's eyes glowed as he put the machine into gear.

'It doesn't take much to make you happy, does it?' Wilcox asked. 'Damn it, I wish I was like that. I'm always after some novelty, some girl who's not been had before, some car faster than anyone else's, I'm almost inclined to be a Tommy Dodd to see what that's like . . .'

'What's that?' asked Harry.

'Tommy Dodd? Tommy Dodd, sod, sodomite. You must see 'em at it in the barrack room. I'm told, though without actual knowledge I might point out, that the private soldier is a great one for pederasty. It must be like Eton, a private soldiers' barrack room, a pederast's paradise.'

'We don't get much of that in the Warwickshires,' said Harry stubbornly.

'Ah, the old pride of regiment,' said Wilcox softly. 'I heard your pater was a sergeant-major. I suppose you were always destined to be a soldier.'

It was odd, considered Harry, that he had never stuck up for the regiment before. Anyway, he did not like men having men. It offended his sense of propriety, though he remembered photographs of them doing the naughty in those pornographic books that Cotman sold. He sometimes wondered what Cotman was doing and sometimes thought of Cotman's beautiful wife. He had never known that Cotman was married. What did he want with the Carols of this world when he had such a beauty back home, free and for nothing? He supposed that Cotman was somehow like Lieutenant Wilcox. He had all the money he wanted and so got tired of everything he could buy. Would he ever get that way?

10

The years rolled on. Mary was becoming a pretty young woman, and Leonard had found employment with an import firm run by Germans. Jane and George heard little from Harry.

'I was no great writer,' said George, hiding his disappointment, 'but he seems to be enjoying himself.'

Harry was. When an officer wanted a car he was called on to advise and try out the car and this meant there were hand-outs from garages and agents. He also contrived to get himself attached as Lieutenant Wilcox's batman. Consequently Sergeant Marchbanks saw very little of him, and when he did he considered that Oakwood was distinctly cheeky. Harry had also acquired, without trying, a lance-corporal's stripe, and had no conception of the pleasure and excitement this gave to his father when he wrote home and told him.

If this was the British Army, thought Harry, he wished that he had had a go at it before. He was well-fed, parades were minimal, and he had not seen his rifle for several months. Lieutenant Wilcox had given his batman a chit to the quartermaster, and Harry had handed in his rifle. 'I wouldn't want you to get your finger caught in the bolt,' Wilcox had told him, 'you need that for the delicate adjustments on the motor.' He had traded in the Darracq and bought a 120-horsepower Mercedes which did 108 miles per hour over the measured mile. Wilcox boasted that he had the fastest car in Warwickshire and few would argue with him as they watched him, often accompanied by Harry, speeding along in the huge car.

For George and Jane life went on uneventfully. Their middle age was a placid period that most of their contemporaries envied. The Motleys sold them the house in Brunswick Road at a figure well below the market price and there was no need to stint themselves for little luxuries. Jane was one of the first women in the district to have a sealskin coat and would have bought one of the new-fangled vacuum cleaners had the salesman not reluctantly told her that it would not work until the road was fitted up with electricity as well as gas.

The Oakwoods saw few outsiders. Occasionally Jane would have tea with one or other of the shopkeepers but attempts to involve her in playing bridge were short-lived. Every Christmas she received a Christmas card from the corporal's wife who had helped her in the bungalow in Aldershot, and she dutifully responded with a New Year's card. Jane did not want very much to be reminded of those long drab years in married quarters, though she did think back with pleasure on the cycle trips with Alice Burgess. Aldershot too often meant the dreadful recollection of the meeting with Mrs Bland and her bombshell—the news that George had had an affair with her in Africa.

George, too, wanted to bury the Aldershot days, and in retrospect his life there had been pointless—drilling men day after day. But one day the epitome of Aldershot arrived on his doorstep—Miss Burgess herself. Her hair had greyed until it looked like brittle steel wire, and the gruff masculine voice had become a raucous croak.

'Too many meetings, my dear,' she said to Jane as they sat down to tea, 'you don't stock many *sensible* shoes in your shop, do you?'

Jane did not tell her that there was not much demand for stout walking brogues.

'Meetings?' asked George politely.

'The women's movement,' she said airily.

'You don't approve of this digging up lawns and chaining yourself to the railings of Parliament Square, do you?' asked George.

'Ah, you know about that, do you?' countered Miss Burgess.

'For my part, what would I want with the vote?' asked Jane.

Miss Burgess was aghast. Jane was not the shy uncertain woman she once knew, but was now rather formidable. Just the kind of woman who should be demanding equal rights. 'Where's Mary? She must be grown-up by now?'

'Twenty-two, nearly twenty-three,' said Jane, 'it seems extraordinary, Alice, that I've known you that long. It must be eleven years since we left Aldershot.'

'What does she do?' Miss Burgess asked.

'Do?' asked Jane. 'Why, she helps in the house. Plays the piano quite nicely.'

'Isn't she bored?' Miss Burgess asked.

'She doesn't seem to be,' replied Jane. 'Leonard works at an import firm in town.'

But Miss Burgess was more preoccupied with Mary's idleness. Young girls should have a mission. They should not wait around hoping for marriage. She only half-heard the news about the shop, that Mrs Motley had fallen over and broken her hip and would never walk again.

'She's something of a trial to poor Mr Motley,' said Jane intensely, as if the information was of great importance, 'and it means I'm left in charge. I do all the ordering, and all the accounts. And I've got two girls working for me. Would you ever have thought I would be managing a shop, Alice?'

'Some of the women in the movement *own* shops,' said Miss Burgess crushingly, 'one is a doctor.'

'I don't hold with lady doctors,' said Jane.

Miss Burgess bit her lip. Jane Oakwood was proving a disappointment. 'I'd like to see Mary,' Miss Burgess said.

'She walks the baby next door in the park nearly every afternoon,' said Jane, somewhat surprised by the interest. Alice had never taken more than casual notice of Mary as a child.

After she had gone, George said, 'Funny, her asking after Mary.'

'I didn't seem to want to talk to her much, dear,' said Jane, 'it's such a long time ago. She wears well, you've got to admit that. But we don't have much in common. I never realized before how mannish she was.'

'You've come on in the world, you see,' said George. 'When you met her she was something new. Wouldn't say boo to a goose. Now you can hold your own with anybody.'

'You too, George,' said Jane, but George shook his head.

'Not quite,' he said quietly. 'I've always got to have someone above me. Our kind of folk always have to call someone "sir." I daresay Leonard has to, and I'm sure Harry has to. You, too.'

'It's part of business,' said Jane briskly, knowing what her husband meant but disagreeing with it. She called her customers 'madam' but she would not have dreamed of calling them madam outside the shop. She and George almost forgot the visit of their old friend as they thought about the curious question of class. Had they been at home the following day they

67

would have been surprised to see Miss Burgess loitering at the end of the street. A tall girl pushed a pram by her, looking at Miss Burgess idly. Funny looking woman, Mary Oakwood thought. And she was staring at her as if she knew her.

'Mary?' asked Miss Burgess uncertainly.

'Do I know you?' Mary asked.

'That reminds me of your mother when she was younger,' said Miss Burgess.

'What?'

'Tossing your hair over your shoulder,' said the older woman sentimentally. 'I came to see them yesterday.'

'Oh, yes?' asked Mary politely. 'Do you want to see Horace?'

'Horace?' echoed Miss Burgess.

'The baby,' explained Mary, 'his name is Horace. Women do, you know. They chuck him under the chin and make funny noises at him. Horace doesn't seem to mind.'

'No, I wanted to see you,' said Miss Burgess, 'your mother was saying that you don't go out to work.'

'Dad doesn't think it would be right,' said Mary. 'I wouldn't mind. I would like to have some money in my purse for myself.'

'And so you should,' decided Miss Burgess.

'I don't suppose I could earn a lot,' speculated Mary, 'but even ten shillings a week would seem an awful lot to me.' She looked at the baby blankly.

This, thought Miss Burgess, was the kind of young woman who could be worked on. She had seen her kind at her meetings, bored, anxious to escape from any routine.

'I don't suppose you know anything about the women's rights movement,' she began.

'Oh, but I do,' said Mary, 'I read the papers you know. Dad always gets the evening paper. Are you in it?'

As they walked together to the park Miss Burgess explained what she and her colleagues were out to do, making it seem as fascinating as possible, and by the time they reached the park Mary was almost enthusiastic. At least, thought Miss Burgess, Mary had given some sort of commitment to attend a meeting in the town at which she herself would address the audience, though she did not fully expect her to turn up. But Mary did, for her boredom had been played on with extreme cleverness. The woman in the next seat was elderly with beady eyes whose

68

glasses kept slipping off her nose, and she clapped loudly when one of the speakers spoke of the coming phase of the battle, the fighting in the streets and the sabotage. At the end of the meeting Mary followed her out, and was thrilled but at the same time shocked when the woman picked up a stone from the kerb-side and hurled it through a shop window. Coming out of a side door of the hall, Miss Burgess heard the crash of plate-glass, blinked and went the other way. The new recruits were volatile and inclined to be rash.

A policeman ran up, shouting for the culprit. A crowd of women stood by the hall steps jeering at him. The woman who had thrown the stone stood forward in self-satisfied martyrdom and screamed, 'I did it. Arrest me!'

'All right,' said the policeman, and took her arm.

One of the spectators stepped from the crowd and knocked the policeman's helmet over his eyes with her umbrella. He staggered, arm flailing, and inadvertently brought down the woman who had thrown the stone, who yelled and scrabbled for her glasses. The policeman stepped on them as he pushed his helmet up.

'Come along with me!' he shouted.

'My glasses,' said the woman, 'my glasses. I can't see.'

'Serves you right!' rapped out the policeman, thoroughly out of temper.

'You brute!' shouted Mary, her colour rising.

'You keep out of it, missy!' warned the policeman, one hand grasping the stone-thrower's arm, the other wagging at Mary. Mary stooped, and picked up a stone. Her aim was erratic, and instead of flying towards the policeman the stone went off at a tangent and smashed the window of a respectable draper's shop. The policeman fumbled for his whistle, gave three piercing blasts and the crowd dispersed, some of them rushing back into the hall, others running down the street. Three policemen appeared, pushing into the hall, one losing his helmet from a stoutly wielded handbag.

Young and fit, Mary outdistanced most of the pack and, feeling safe at last, she leaned against a post, breathing heavily.

'That was wonderful!' said another woman catching up with her. She pushed a leaflet into Mary's damp hand, 'So young too!'

69

She began running again as a policeman appeared from a different direction, but Mary realized that there was nothing to connect her with the disturbance and stood still. She watched the policeman go after the other woman, and read the pamphlet. 'Women of Britain, unite!' she said aloud. The pamphlet gave the date of another meeting.

On the way home she felt little chills of excitement run up and down her spine. There was something satisfying about throwing a stone at a glass window. It must be like, she thought, dad shooting a black man in the jungles of Africa. The only difference was that that was approved, and what she had done was not. She wondered if she could be sent to prison, and exhilaration turned to apprehension. Her interest in the movement died overnight.

Her parents did not notice her agitation. They never noticed her at all, Mary thought with some bitterness but she sensed that they had something occupying their minds. They had. George had been placed on the reserve; his days at the recruiting office were over.

'One thing, George,' said Jane, 'you won't be a commissionaire or a night-watchman. I'll see to that!'

'What a change in you, my dear,' said George wonderingly, 'what a change!'

'We have money saved,' said Jane briskly, 'there are no problems. You're nearly sixty, George. You've done your share. Let's celebrate your retirement by going away to the seaside!'

They were surprised that Mary did not want to come, but Leonard jumped at the opportunity. His German employers took every opportunity to denigrate the British and a week away from them would be heaven.

11

As they were packing, Jane picked up a copy of the sensational-
ist weekly *John Bull* which George had bought to read on the
train journey. 'What's this mean, George?' she asked, ' "To
Hell with Servia!"?'

'They mean Serbia,' said George, 'you would think they
would be able to spell it right. An archduke's been assassi-
nated.'

'It's not that German menace again is it?' said Leonard. 'I
thought the papers had tired of it.'

They started their journey early in the morning, for the
weather was fine and the Oakwoods feared that everyone
would be piling into the trains. But the station was no busier
than usual and the refreshment room where they had a cup of
tea and a sandwich was almost empty. A platoon of soldiers
clattered across from one platform to the next, George watching them admiringly. A fine body of men, but did they have the
discipline that he and his comrades had had? Discipline was a
word that was lacking in Harry's vocabulary. Or so it seemed.

'Here comes the train, George!' called out Jane.

The locomotive puffed in, and the Oakwoods scrambled
aboard, Leonard hurling the cases on to the racks and seeing
that the carriage door was securely closed.

'We've got a carriage to ourselves,' Jane said, pleased, 'what
a nice day it's turned out to be. Where do we go through,
Leonard, you're the scholar amongst us?'

Leonard had it all pat. 'Worcester, Cheltenham, Bristol and
Weston,' he said rapidly.

'I went this way when I enlisted,' said George nostalgically.
'They were hard wooden benches then.'

Halfway to Bristol Jane opened the sandwiches and
uncorked the flask of tea, pleased that it was still hot. Leonard
had been to the seaside with school outings, but it was a long
time since she had seen the sea, and from Bristol onwards she
kept her eyes glued to the horizon, waiting for the telltale flash
of blue. When it came it took her by surprise. It was so blue and
inviting.

They took a motor-taxi from the station to their boarding house, where Mrs Jones was waiting with a pot of tea.

George had insisted on having full board. 'You are not doing any cooking this holiday,' he had said patting Jane's hand. Incredible what a transformation there had been in George. Solicitous, gentle, who would have thought that this was the brusque stubble-haired martinet of Aldershot?

The days passed far too swiftly for the Oakwoods. They went on motor charabanc trips to Minehead, to Cheddar Gorge, where they looked at the stalactites and stalagmites with an awe that the guide reckoned would net him an extra sixpence, and in the evening they watched the pierrots or went to hear the band. Occasionally they went on the pier and played the machines in the amusement palace, but George thought them a waste of money. The high spot of the entertainment for Jane was a visit to the picture house to see the Italian film *Quo Vadis?*

'We ought to go to the pictures more often, George,' she said. 'I didn't realize they were like that, and so life-like. You could almost imagine you were there. Only two more days. Oh, dear, I wish we could stay longer. I can't think when I have enjoyed myself more. And the weather has been so lovely.'

'Did you send those postcards to the Motleys?' asked George. 'You asked me to remind you.'

As he was feeling the pace too hectic, George suggested that the next morning they spend the day on the beach. He and Jane hired a couple of deckchairs and settled on the sands, while Leonard went for a walk.

He liked a part of the town called the Old Pier, though there was no pier in evidence. The waves, subdued and calm elsewhere, here dashed against the rocks with magnificent force. He was watching them as if hypnotized when he was aware of someone by his side. He turned round.

'Hullo', said a girl. She was as tall as he was, with long flaxen hair, and a pert little hat on the back of her head.

'Hullo,' answered Leonard, 'isn't it a lovely day?'

'Lovely,' she agreed, leaning over the iron railings, her head on her arm, 'and we've only two more days to go.'

'So have we,' said Leonard, 'then back to Brum.'

'Are you here with your ma and pa?' the girl asked.

Leonard nodded.

'I am, too,' said the girl, 'my father works on the railway and so we get free travel. We always come to the seaside twice a year.'

'Lucky you,' said Leonard smiling.

'We come from Coventry,' volunteered the girl.

And so they began to talk. Leonard had chatted with girls at the night school, but it was usually about the work. The plainest of girls, he considered, went to night school. This was different. He talked with her in a way that he had never talked before. His parents would have been astonished by his love of music and shattered by the knowledge that he did not play too much because he knew the music he liked irritated and mystified them. They also did not realize that Leonard had another passion—aeroplanes. George had often seen the books on aeroplanes about the house but assumed that his son was merely broadening his general knowledge.

'You sound as though you're frightened of your pa,' said the girl, puzzled.

'When I was young he was very strict,' explained Leonard, 'but now he's old he's sort of mellowed. He was a soldier, you see, a sergeant-major. And my brother's a soldier. We never got on together. He used to get up to the most awful tricks when he was my age. Mum and Dad never found out, but I knew. It's rotten to say, I know, but I was glad when he went away.'

'Yes', said the girl, 'families are funny things. I mean, I have aunts and uncles and they're just not like each other at all.'

'I wish I had some aunts and uncles,' said Leonard thoughtfully. 'Both Mum and Dad were only children.'

'You can have some of mine,' said the girl, and they both laughed.

'You don't know my name,' said Leonard, and told her.

The girl told him hers—Elizabeth—and somewhat awkwardly, as though this was a stage that they had passed through ages ago, they shook hands. Leonard held her softly gloved hand long after it was necessary.

He spotted the clock above the café. 'Goodness', he exclaimed, 'I'll have to go. It's lunchtime.'

The girl's face fell. 'Must you?' she asked.

'I can be back this afternoon,' Leonard said eagerly.

'Oh, yes,' Elizabeth said, 'half-past two?'

73

He nodded and sped away, catching his parents up as they walked up the steps to the boarding house.

As soon as he had eaten he had gone again. George looked at Jane. 'Where is he going do you think?'

Jane had a flash of intuition. 'I think he's found himself a girl', she said. 'I hope she's a nice girl. They get all sorts at the seaside in the summer.'

'I found a nice girl', said George gallantly, 'and so can Leonard.'

'I hope he won't make her wait six years,' Jane said wistfully.

Elizabeth was waiting for Leonard, even though it was only a few minutes after two. Without self-consciousness they held each other's hands, watching the waves dashing in, sprinkling them with spray that they hardly felt. The silence lasted a long time.

'Do you feel the same way as I do?' he asked quietly.

'Yes,' she replied in a small voice, 'I wish we could stay here for ever.'

'We have all day tomorrow,' he said happily.

A cloud drifted across the sun and Elizabeth shivered. Leonard put his arm round her shoulders and drew her to him. Somewhere overhead an aeroplane buzzed and Leonard peered up at it but could not see it. The noise from the children on the rocks seemed a hundred miles away. Time stood still. There was a sound of voices from the promenade and in the distance a newsboy approached them with the early evening editions. They watched him getting nearer, then turned back to the sea, happy in their own blossoming feelings.

Only when the boy was ten yards away did they hear what he was calling.

'War!' he shouted, 'war with Germany. Read all about it. War! War! War!'

'What do we do?' Leonard whispered.

'We must go back to our parents,' she said. Her eyes were suddenly damp. He held her head between his hands and kissed her on the lips.

Somewhat formally they exchanged addresses. The magic was being dissipated by the tension that they sensed around them. Parents were gathering their children from the beach and trundling off towards their boarding houses and hotels, and the

74

café proprietor was boarding up his windows. Leonard could hear him explaining to the fortune-teller in the kiosk next door that this was in case the Germans bombarded the resort.

'You didn't tell me about this in your blooming stars,' he said.

'They sometimes withhold their secrets', the clairvoyant said casually. 'I'll tell you something though.'

'And what's that?' asked the café owner.

'That young couple are in love, and I don't reckon much on their future if there's a war.'

The two young people parted in silence. There did not seem anything to say. On the way back to the boarding house a gang of hooligans were smashing the windows of a shop that bore a German-sounding name. Mr Blum, thought Leonard grimly, would have a job to get rid of the ten gross of toy German soldiers that he had just had sent over. And he hoped that someone would see the name of Blum in faded gilt paint on the fifth floor of that dirty terracotta building in central Birmingham and throw a stone at that.

12

There was a rumbling in the distance as of far-off thunder. The battalion of the Royal Warwickshire Regiment marched mostly in silence, though a few irrepressible soldiers, stimulated by the wine that the French peasants had handed them in long thin bottles, sang 'It's a Long Way to Tipperary' and 'La Marseillaise'. They passed a column of French infantrymen resting, whistling at them roguishly, for the French troops were dressed in dark blue coats, red breeches, and kepis, helmets that savoured more of the musical-comedy stage than war. In the background were French dragoons in cuirasses and plumed helmets who eyed the more soberly dressed British troops with disdain.

As the march went on the gunfire became louder and the countryside around began to be pockmarked. The trees were lopsided and many had lost huge limbs. The men began to ascend a steep hill and the road started to wind. The soldiers looked uneasily into the ditches at the side of the road. A French soldier was kneeling on the bank, with his head hanging down, as though sobbing, but the British troops knew that he was dead. A middle-aged grey-haired man was lying flat on the back, clutching his rifle, eyes staring. One man had put his elbows on the edge of the ditch to die and his eyes were fixed, seeming to watch the passing column.

'Eyes to the front,' shouted Sergeant Marchbanks, his stomach churning over. 'You, Lance-corporal Oakwood, get that file straightened up. You've got a stripe. Use it.'

Wounded men were coming back, one of them staggering from one side of the road to the other, coming up against the marching men as though engaged in some ghastly country dance. This was something the men had not come across in their drill, and as they stood still to let the wounded man through, their comrades barged into them from behind. The wounded came on handcarts, on improvised stretchers, on ladders. A Belgian private, supported by two of his mates, stumbled unseeingly forward; his open tunic and torn shirt let the British see a scarlet chest with a small black hole in the middle from which trickled thick blood. A battalion commander, crouched over a bicycle, was being led by a stretcher-bearer.

A cavalryman as white as a sheet galloped by, the horse steaming with sweat and the bit snowy with foam and the company commander of the Warwickshires drew rein to let him go by.

'Sergeant-Major Jenkins,' he ordered, 'call a halt.'

Jenkins, although only in his early thirties, was the type of sergeant-major George Oakwood would have understood—brusque, no-nonsense and devoid of fear. He drew the men to a halt, and while the captain and his subalterns went into conference he harangued the men. 'Now, you lot, you've seen a lot of dead men on this march. They're dead because they don't know the meaning of discipline. Remember that. You get a mob of Froggies running around and the Huns will whip the arses off them. And remember this. You are supposed to be the best-trained, best-disciplined army in the world, including the Huns. Let's see you live up to it. Any questions?'

A voice piped up from the ranks. 'Where are we, Sarge-Major?'

Jenkins grunted. 'Your guess is as good as mine. It's my opinion that we're nearly out of Belle France and into Belgium. But the word has it that we're somewhere near a place called Mons.'

He stopped talking to watch a bunch of soldiers going the other way, away from the fighting. Any order that they had started with had long since disappeared. There were infantry and cavalry mixed up together and among the mass of horsemen a short-snouted artillery piece was being hauled by four horses. Some of the horsemen were without saddles or bridles; a few had ropes through their horses' mouths, others were using sacks for saddles and string for stirrups.

The captain had a word with Sergeant-Major Jenkins, and the order to fall out at the side of the road was given. A field kitchen rumbled along and there was the clatter of mess-tins and metal mugs as the men waited for the cooks to get busy. A few of the retreating soldiers tried to join in with the British troops.

'Get moving, you buggers!' shouted Jenkins, 'this grub's for fighting men.' He turned to Sergeant Marchbanks and told him. 'Once you start they're all over you. We've got to keep our strength fighting the Huns not the Frogs. You look a bit green about the gills, Sergeant.'

'Them bodies, Sergeant-Major,' said Marchbanks.

'It gets easier,' said Jenkins breezily. 'After a time it affects you no more than a leg of pork hanging up in a butcher's shop. You may not believe it now, but that's the truth.'

Harry Oakwood lined up and drew his mug of tea and then went back to Saunders, who was rubbing the side of his leg reflectively. One or two of their companions had been about to take their boots off, but Jenkins had put a stop to that, telling them that once the boots were off the feet would swell so much that they could not get them back. No one knew how many miles they had marched. The troops had been cheerful as the train had chugged out of Le Havre, but since they had got off

77

their spirits had sunk. The word had been passed around that the Germans had already captured the so-called impregnable fort of Liège, and the Belgian front was open to all comers.

This was not much fun, thought Harry as he sipped his tea. He had been reading a postcard from his parents when Saunders had run up to him to say that war had been declared and new company orders had been put up. 'Jolly good,' he had said, but no one had told him that all war would mean was being packed on a train, pushed on to a crowded boat, and then being marched all over France. He had watched Lieutenant Wilcox's Mercedes being wheeled away into the garage with a lump in his throat.

'Come on, Corporal!' Sergeant Marchbanks had shouted, 'draw your bloody rifle from the stores and get the grease off before next parade. No batman's privileges, my lad!'

'You sound happy, Sarge,' Harry had said.

'I am happy, Corporal,' Marchbanks had said.

Well, Marchbanks did not look so happy now, Harry decided. He amiably cuffed a French private who had grabbed at a chunk of bread near his elbow. The Frenchman had bloodshot eyes, and his three-day growth of beard was clogged with filth. 'All right,' said Harry, 'here you are.' And he threw the Frenchman the bread.

'Very Christian, Corporal Oakwood,' said Sergeant-Major Jenkins, 'but don't make a habit of it. This grub's for fighting men. And that means you, Corporal Oakwood!'

He grinned menacingly, and looked at Lieutenant Wilcox over the heads of his men. Grim-faced and thin-lipped, Wilcox was determined not to let his company down.

'No motors for you here, Corporal,' Jenkins taunted.

A dispatch-rider, grey with dust, his brow wrinkled with fatigue, roared in on his motor-cycle, and handed a message to the captain before going on again, ignoring the retiring French troops who were forced to get out of the way, even jump into the ditch.

'I wonder what that means,' muttered Jenkins to Marchbanks, 'but I daresay we'll know soon enough.'

They did not have long to wait for the news that the concentraton of the British forces was sufficiently complete for them to go into action, and an advance would begin on the following day in the direction of Mons. It was now 21 August. The war had been going for just over a fortnight.

After the meal the march continued until late afternoon. A barn was requisitioned for the men. The officers and senior NCOs took over the farmhouse, now deserted. But the people who had been there had left plenty of food, and by seven o'clock the spirits of the troops had been restored as they had found a cache of wine and were singing and joking. Harry dug out his erstwhile mates and they played pontoon in the light of the guttering candle.

Throughout the night they heard the rumble of the artillery, and one or two of the soldiers went outside to see the show—the orange glow on the horizon, the star-shells in the sky. On the road a quarter of a mile away they could hear the steady tramp of more troops making their way to the front and could see the occasional hurricane lamp, swinging from a gun-carriage.

Reveille was early and never had the bugle call sounded more depressing. A light drizzle mingled with the pale sun and the dawn to cast an eerie light on the men as they rose to their feet, yawning and stretching their arms. Sergeant Marchbanks did a quick check of his squad. Even at this stage, before the men had seen action, nerves could occasionally crack.

As the war got nearer the roads became full of civilians. A grey mob, grey because most of the men and women wore black clothes which were covered with dust, blundered by, heedless of the sergeant's barks to get out of the bleeding way. Oakwood saw two young women, blood from torn feet oozing through their fragile low silk shoes. A very old couple, who for years had probably done no more than walk round their garden, staggered along arm-in-arm, utterly bewildered. They were bustled on by an officious gendarme who did not hesitate to prod them in the ribs with his truncheon if their pace was too slow. There were waggons piled high with children, silent and dejected, wondering where their meals had gone to or what had happened to their parents.

The artillery fire now crackled rather than rumbled, rending the air like a clap of thunder, and when this happened the long unending column seemed to buckle, then reform. Oakwood found that there was a piece of rag clinging round his ankle; irritably he kicked it off, and read 'Welcome to our saviours, the

79

Tommy.' 'Thanks very much', he said sardonically. Saunders, marching alongside, looked at him sharply. Was Oakwood cracking already?

The officers and NCOs urged on their men. Tall slag heaps rose up out of the ground like desolate hills, and these obscured the horizon, though smoke could clearly be seen as the grey ground met sky, and the crackle of the artillery was accompanied by the clatter of machine-guns and the uneven volleys of rifle fire. To Oakwood and the other soldiers new to battle it all seemed vaguely unreal, the backcloth to some patriotic tableau at a music hall but as the battalion topped the crest of a rise it was clear that this was no play.

A great arc of water curved through the panorama, the Mons canal, and on either side there were thousands of scurrying figures, moving without apparent rhyme or reason. In the foreground, tucked in a hollow, was a little village, from whose church tower a Red Cross flag hung drably. An arterial road sliced across the country. Parallel with this defending troops were hastily entrenching themselves and behind them the guns were being drawn up. As they were pulled into position they were fired, almost before they were still, and the recoil of the barrels often slewed them at right-angles, a source of danger to the artillerymen. Countless flashes of light scintillated against the green and gold of what was left of the countryside, and occasionally a chance shell hit the side of a slag heap, starting a miniature avalanche.

Almost as soon as the extent of the battle was revealed, the troops began descending. Far too close for comfort they could see the white and yellow smoke-clouds of the enemy shrapnel and high explosive, the nearer of which were tongued with flame. The thunder of the guns rolled and reverberated in deep waves of sound, spreading in growing circles.

Suddenly a staff officer appeared on a dappled horse. 'The right has gone', he said tensely, 'God knows what's going to happen now. The First Gordons are covering.'

'We have our orders,' said the Warwickshire captain crisply. 'There is nothing about retiring.'

'It's not an advance any more,' said the staff officer irritably. 'You passed the French troops on their way back, surely?'

80

He rode off and the men marched on. For some reason the battle seemed to be receding rather than getting nearer and over the brow of a hill they found themselves in country again. The road was petering out into a track, but other soldiers had been along here before, for it was churned up by the feet of men, the wheels of the gun carriages and the hooves of horses. The pace of the march slackened as the men found themselves gripped by the mud, sometimes up to the ankles and the sound of the oozing mud, sucking and squelching, seemed almost louder than the artillery.

Over to their right a company of other infantry were digging in, the soldiers looking up incuriously as the Warwickshires marched by. The trenches were shallow and the troops, not yet experienced in trench warfare, were picking at the surface. On the left was a company of heavy artillery, which had previously been silent but which, one after the other, boomed out. Involuntarily Sergeant Marchbanks's platoon put their hands to their ears, and their eyes stung with the cordite.

Harry Oakwood was not one given to self-analysis but he wondered how his father reacted in a situation like this. His stomach felt like lead, and his teeth were chattering. With an effort he turned to Saunders. 'How are you feeling, mate?' he asked.

'Terrible,' replied Saunders. 'It's not knowing what's going to happen that's the worst part of it.'

Oakwood averted his eyes from the dead horses and the wounded men. And these were Englishmen. A boy no older than seventeen, with a bloody sling round his shoulder, was being sick. A man was lying flat on his back, a blanket tossed over him. Oakwood turned away, bile in his throat, as he saw the mangled stump of a leg sticking out.

A captain who had lost his cap and whose hair was frizzed up on end put his hand up to stop the company. 'Two miles up the path', he said, 'you'll be among the odds and sods I'm afraid. The Royal Scots will be on your right wing, Fourth Dragoon Guards on your left. The Germans have crossed the canal and we know which way they're coming. They're a bit uncertain because they think they're up against the whole of the British Expeditionary Force.'

'And are they?' asked the Warwickshire captain.

'Don't think so,' replied the other, adding, 'you've got some Frogs with you, too. So watch out for them for they're as likely to run away as fight.' He was dabbing at the side of his face with a stained handkerchief. 'A bit of shrapnel', he said, 'only a scratch.'

Men were feverishly laying down rolls of barbed wire in front of their trenches and requisitioned French tractors were hauling carts piled high with the wire. A large canvas-topped lorry that had somehow managed to get that far up the lane and had then become bogged down was being manhandled to the side of the track, and twenty yards further on the troops had to skirt a large crater in the lane. It was still smoking and stones were clattering into it.

It took an hour to reach the company of the Royal Scots. Their barbed wire was laid and their trenches dug, and they were taking it easy. A lieutenant with binoculars was scanning the horizon. A large field of beetroot was ahead, sloping down towards them. It was a good defensive position and machine-guns were posted at intervals. There seemed plenty of men about and Oakwood was glad to see that the Royal Scots seemed relaxed and were even able to joke. His comrades exchanged pleasantries with the troops as they marched by.

Over on the left Oakwood could see the artillery, but as they made their way to their own trenches, already begun by a company of the French Fifth Army, the number of guns seemed to be getting less. He knew what this meant—a 'tactical withdrawal to prepared positions'. A French officer began to jabber away to the captain, so he summoned Lieutenant Wilcox, who understood French and translated to his company commander. 'Can we help laying barbed wire? His men have been marching for three days and are at the end of their tether.'

The Frenchman started off again.

'Not that it will do any good,' the lieutenant went on with a wry smile, 'he's laid barbed wire before and was then ordered to withdraw. Anyway, the wire doesn't stop the Germans.'

The men got busy, laying their rifles down. Boxes of rifle ammunition were being piled up behind the trench, which was merely the ditch at the side of the lane enlarged and deepened, with the earth removed piled up as a parapet. The four men detailed to manage the Maxim gun struggled to rig up their weapon and one of them poured water into the chamber surrounding the barrel.

'Don't throw the rest of the water away,' ordered Sergeant Marchbanks, 'you'll need it to refill the barrel when the water starts to boil.' There were always little things like that to point out, he thought, and what was Oakwood doing? He seemed to be supervising. 'Get stuck in, Corporal,' he shouted, 'the Huns are coming for you as well as them.'

The Warwickshires were joined by a company of the Hampshire Regiment, who helped with the wire laying and began work on enlarging the trench.

'What a bloody game,' said a Hampshire private to Oakwood. 'They never said that I'd be bundled into a railway truck which read eight horses or forty men. These rotten Frogs must live real rough. My dad was right. Who cares about bleeding Belgium? If this is Belgium we're in now they can sodding well keep it.'

The sergeants of the infantry companies were working out how far the telegraph post was, so that they could gauge distances. They reckoned it at twelve-hundred yards. 'Don't fire at anyone beyond the posts', ordered Marchbanks, 'it will be just like throwing stones at them.'

'What if they come across that field of stubble, Sarge?' asked Corporal Wilkinson, whose breast sported medal ribbons of the Boer War.

'The captain thinks that they're going to come across the beetroot field,' said Marchbanks.

'Officers!' exclaimed Wilkinson with disgust, 'my bet's on the stubble field for, look, there's a wood there to give them cover. I don't know why the guns haven't clobbered that already. As we can't see where the wood goes to my bet is that they're going to come out of that.'

'It's a bit too obvious, Wilkie,' observed Marchbanks, 'that's the most likely thing to do and if they've got any sense they'll know we expect it from them.'

But Wilkinson was right. The lieutenant of the Royal Scots up the line shouted that he had seen them just coming to the outer fringe of the wood and, as if to confirm this, a herd of cows, taking shelter among the trees from the occasional shell that came their way bolted across the stubble, upturning cornstooks. Almost immediately the German artillery, out of sight behind the brow of the hill, opened fire and the British guns retaliated, sighted on the wood. The trees were soon hidden by smoke, and the German troops dispersed, joining up and advancing in a line. Lieutenant Wilcox focused his binoculars. He saw that the line was extended to more than two paces between the men and the German infantry were keeping a bad line, evidently very weary and marching in the hot sun with manifest disgust.

The wire layers dropped their bundles and scooted for the trenches, uncertain whether to dive in or wait for the order. A high explosive shell nearby made up their minds for them. It burst harmlessly but clods of earth were flung over the troops. The sun was drying up the earth and the ammunition carriers were able to move more easily.

The command came, 'Five rounds rapid at the stubble field nine hundred yards', and as the Warwickshires and the Hampshires opened fire the Germans hopped into cover like rabbits. Some threw themselves behind the corn-stacks and when the firing stopped they got up and bolted back into the wood. Two or three who had thrown themselves down remained motionless. German guns appeared over the brow of the hill and opened fire with shrapnel at the British troops. Great numbers of troops appeared in the beetroot field, and the men in the wood crossed the stubble field in two quick rushes, losing only a couple of men.

Although the British infantry were good shots, they did not often hit their targets, even though the beetroot field had no cover. The German gunners kept up a steady stream of shrapnel that burst just in front of the trenches and broke over the top like a wave. Shooting at the advancing enemy had to be timed to the bursting shells and the soldiers adopted the plan of firing two rounds and then ducking down at intervals, determined by the arrival of the shell. The company commander, standing up and giving his orders regardless of danger, was bowled over by a chunk of shrapnel as big as a tea-cup, and the stretcher-bearers rushed up to him, though it was a waste of time as the officer was dead.

The leading German troops were soon out of sight. Lieutenant Wilcox feverishly drew the map from the pocket of his dead commander and perused it. He was joined by the commander of the second Warwickshire company.

'It's the Route Nationale', he told Wilcox, 'four hundred yards away. It runs along an embankment and one can't reach it except with artillery. Who have you lost?'

'Three men wounded, but NCOs all right. Why didn't we get more of them?'

The captain shrugged his shoulders. 'That's the way it goes, I expect. I've never been in a war like this before. I honestly expected their artillery to cause more casualties.'

They were still coming. The grey groups raced across the fields, losing one or two men, but there were still no more than twenty or thirty bodies lying in the corn. Wilcox looked at his watch. It was three in the afternoon. They had been firing for an hour. He ducked as a high-explosive shell burst uncomfortably close and saw the captain looking anxiously to the left, up the lane. The French were throwing in their hands. Ducking, weaving, they left the ditch and scampered along the lane. Before they had gone fifty yards they had lost three of their number from shrapnel, and panicked taking to the fields towards the artillery. Somewhere amongst the artillery a protecting machine-gun clattered out. The gunner had thought that the French soldiers were Germans.

'Serves them right,' muttered Corporal Wilkinson, peering again through his rifle sights and squeezing the trigger before the next shrapnel shell came.

You had to hand it to the youngsters, Wilkinson reflected glancing down the trench, they were not losing their heads. Even Oakwood, the playboy of the platoon who he thought would crack when the going got tough, was cool and collected. Harry's trepidation had disappeared as soon as he had fired his first shot. The comfortable surroundings of the trench gave him a sense of security. It did not seem that the enemy had any howitzers to lob shells into the trench and it was a long shot against a high-explosive shell hitting the ditch. The German artillery seemed to be concentrated on their British counterpart, which was ominously quiet.

A corporal on a motor-cycle roared up. 'The line's broken up

85

the lane,' he shouted, 'pass it on. The line's broken up the lane. Pass it on.' In half a minute he was out of sight, skidding on the track but keeping his balance.

'Fix bayonets,' ordered Lieutenant Wilcox.

Sergeant Marchbanks went amongst his platoon, head low. 'Remember your drill,' he warned, 'the Huns can't stand cold steel.' He saw Lieutenant Wilcox take his revolver from his holster and check it.

Suddenly a white flash burst right over the road behind which the Germans were massing. It was followed by another and yet another. The enemy fled back up the hill, towards the wood, mingling with those who were coming down. A detachment of the Royal Scots cheered and scrambled out of their trenches, but became entangled in their own barbed wire as they went forward to attack. Their screams as they were caught in the fire of a concealed enemy machine-gun rang through the August air.

'Hold your ground!' shouted Marchbanks, 'no bloody heroics here.'

In ones or twos, then in squads, the Dragoons on the left flank of the Warwickshires and Hampshires raced along the road. One or two of them were stumbling along haltingly, pitifully inadequate bandages on their legs, oozing blood. They crouched when the shrapnel shells burst, their injuries making it impossible for them to join the British infantry in the trenches as their mates were doing. A machine-gun was being hauled by two men, the tripod bouncing in the ruts. With a curse the men let it drop.

'What's it like up there?' asked Oakwood of the man who had leapt into the trench beside him.

The man's lips were trembling. 'Got a fag?' he pleaded but as his hands were shaking and he could not hold the cigarette Oakwood pushed it between his lips and lit it for him. 'They told me that the British soldier was the best in the world', said the man, inhaling deeply, 'but he ain't. I was in St Quentin only yesterday. There was every regiment under the sun, Dragoons, Hussars, Irish Horse, Lancers and the blokes were just hanging around in the town square waiting to give themselves up. They'd thrown away their rifles, their water-bottles, their belts and their packs. The mayor had surrendered the town and they

86

were just sitting there in the sun waiting to be collected. The officers had scarpered.

'I'm no bleeding hero, but I said to one bloke, "What are you doing, mate?" He said to me, "Our old man—meaning the colonel—has surrendered to the Germans and we'll stick to him. We don't want any bloody Dragoons interfering." And him in the Hussars! Some of us couldn't stomach it and a sergeant rounded us up and marched us out. And there's the sodding Fourth Division for you, the cream of the British Army. It makes you fair puke, don't it?'

Sergeant Marchbanks, who had listened to the narrative in silence, handed over his brandy flask and the Dragoon gulped down the spirit greedily. 'Any one of my platoon who gives himself up does it over my dead body, officer or no bloody officer,' Marchbanks grunted. 'A retreat's one thing, surrender's another.'

As he spoke, many of the men who had streamed past a quarter of an hour before reappeared.

'They've blocked the lane,' said one. It was as though the artillery men had heard him, for gradually the guns were disappearing from behind them. An officer rich in red braid rode up, for some reason waving a sword, though Marchbanks noticed that it had a splash of red near the tip.

'Orders to retire', he shouted, wheeling his horse, 'across the fields.'

As the men clambered from the trench, the shrapnel storm seemed to increase in savagery. Oakwood saw two of the men in the platoon go down, one of them clutching his face, the other grasping his thigh and toppling over in slow motion. Sweating, the machine-gunners tugged their gun backwards, but it fell over and threw them momentarily into the ditch. The troops grabbed all the ammunition they could carry and swarmed across the field. They were now exposed, in the same position as the German troops had been earlier, but the German fire was no more effective, and as they ran forward the range was extended. Harry felt something strike his buttocks as if someone had thrown a stone.

Although the only men left near the trench were the medical men, the shrapnel still came, and only when the Germans realized that the trench had been evacuated did the gunners

87

alter their range. But by that time the British had gained cover in a wood. Branches and leaves rained upon them as the Germans left their protected road and scrambled over the barbed wire. A few of the braver elements, including Corporal Wilkinson, hung back, and their accurate fire momentarily halted the German advance, but as the Germans took possession of the trench Wilkinson and his comrades retreated. Harry had certainly not remained behind, and he was one of the first men through the wood. He was caught up by Saunders.

'Where are the rest of them? Saunders asked.

'Search me,' said Harry, 'but I'm hopping it.'

Back in the wood, Sergeant Marchbanks was gathering up his men to stop retreat turning into a rout. 'One of you is worth three of them,' he shouted.

He was joined by a cavalry major, still with spurs but lacking a horse. 'What are you doing, Sergeant?' he screamed, 'you haven't had orders to retire.'

'We have, sir,' said Marchbanks.

'Well, I'm countermanding them,' the major said.

'It's no go, sir,' said a Hampshire corporal, bleeding profusely from the arm.

'We'll see about that,' said the major grimly, drawing his revolver, but before he could do or say anything more a bullet caught him in the back, whipping him round, and sending him, face distorted in a grimace, into a prickly bush. No one would know who shot him, thought Marchbanks.

One of his platoon rushed by, yelling. He had discarded his cap and his rifle, but caught his foot in a root and fell sideways. 'Help me up, Sarge,' he urged, but Marchbanks ignored him.

'We can't help the wounded,' he shouted to no one in particular.

'I've lost my pack', said one man, 'what will happen, Sarge?'

'It doesn't matter', replied Marchbanks, feeling suddenly tired. He was coming to the edge of the wood, and he waited at the fringe, waving on his men as they blundered by, the breath burning in their lungs. They did not need encouragement. They were moving as fast as their legs would take them. He wondered how far the Germans were behind and then ran with them, the ground soaking up his energy. A squadron of Lancers went by ahead of him, pennons flying. As he clambered over the brow of yet another hill he saw a village beneath him, from which were exuding thousands of ant-like creatures. He realized that they were French troops, and they were moving diagonally across his path. One or two of them fired speculative shots at him at a range of more than a mile, and he stopped, uncertain. A second-lieutenant in the Royal Fusiliers caught him up, his breeches torn, and his holster empty.

'No need for panic, Sergeant,' he said grimly, 'the Royal Scots have stopped them. The Warwickshires won't get many battle honours over this one. Your Lieutenant Wilcox had hopped it. Borrowed a horse and was away like the breeze. Can't blame you, I suppose, with officers like that.'

'What are you so bloody complacent about?' retorted Marchbanks, his tiredness disappearing as adrenalin flowed back with anger.

'I'll have you on a charge, Sergeant,' threatened the second-lieutenant.

'Balls!' spat out Marchbanks. 'Who do you flaming Territorials think you are? What are you in civvy life—a bank clerk or something?'

Beyond the village Marchbanks could see a company of artillery. Thank God they were not moving away, and as he got nearer to the village he could see British soldiers marching through the streets, watched by silent villagers whose enthusiasm had run dry. There was a line of waggons approaching the village and far-off he could hear the skirl of the Scots pipers. He was never so pleased to hear them in his life.

A number of Warwickshires and Hampshires had gathered in the town square, wandering about as though waiting for a proclamation. All, Marchbanks was pleased to see, had retained their rifles and equipment. Sitting in a corner with Saunders was Oakwood. They were drinking from bottles of wine. Trust Oakwood, he thought grimly, to seek out the pleasures of life in this humiliating shambles.

13

The war was not yet abated for Harry Oakwood. Gradually more of the retreating troops collected in the village and were formed into something like order by Sergeant-Major Jenkins and the other company sergeant-majors, livid that their men had been forced into something near a rout. Sergeant Marchbanks had kept to himself the information imparted by the second-lieutenant that Lieutenant Wilcox had made a run for it, and was relieved when he learned that Wilcox had been sent to headquarters to tell them that the entire front at Mons was folding.

The British Expeditionary Force marched two hundred miles in thirteen days, often with only four hours' sleep a night. It had been a surprise to the officers and men crammed into that narrow salient, who had fled leaving arms and ammunition and even one or two large field pieces, that they were regarded as heroes. Captured German prisoners had admitted that the rapid rifle-fire of the British infantry had convinced them that they were facing massed banks of machine-guns (instead of two per battalion, twenty-four to a division).

On one of the night stops the new commander of the company of Warwickshires held a conference in his billet, a farmhouse nearly on the Marne. Captain Whitehouse, red-faced, choleric, with years of fighting experience in India, was not one who liked turning his back on the enemy. His contempt for the Germans was only rivalled by his contempt for the French and his suspicion of the commander-in-chief, Sir John French. 'French or French', he commented enigmatically, 'there's not a pin to choose between them. He's joined hands like pattacake with the French Fifth Army and whether we like it or not we're stuck with them. It's because of the French Fifth Army ordering a general retreat that we've got our arses to the Hun. The only reason that they are not following it up is that the German Army is more intent on taking a line south-west, and we're going south. It's also taken us away from our lines of supply. Still, most of our fellows kept their weapons, and I want none of this business of quartermaster-sergeants putting men on charges for losing their packs. Tell your sergeant-majors to make that clear.'

The message had not yet got through to Captain Whitehouse that Joffre, the overall commander of the French and British forces, was preparing to strike back. As it happened, the order was delayed, through the Allied inability to evaluate the merits of the telephone and the British Expeditionary Force received it when they had got beyond the Marne.

With tears in his eyes, Sir John French told Joffre, through the interpreter, that 'We will do all that men can do.' He had visions of his men being cut to pieces by ruthless Germans, who had not yet met defeat and who had had no traumatic war in South Africa to void from their systems. But when the men, tramping listlessly, march-weary, turned and marched back there was no enemy to be found.

As the Warwickshires moved north, their spirits quickened by the news that they were not aimlessly wandering in an alien country, they were passed by squadrons of cavalry, pennons flying, anxious to get to grips with the Huns. Many of them were fresh from England, and these included Captain Bland, not so fresh-faced as when his father, George Oakwood, had encountered him after the Battle of Omdurman in 1898.

Since his cadet days Captain Bland had had a number of shocks. The first was the news that his father was held, throughout the British Army, in amused contempt. Secondly, somewhat cancelling out the first, was that his real father was a certain Sergeant Oakwood (his mother had confessed this to him on her death-bed a few hours after turning Roman Catholic, the religion of her parents). The third was that the British Army was not the hell or glory organization he had thought it would be. With memories of his 'father's' ineptitude still a legend there were attempts to keep Bland tucked away in a staff job where he could do no harm, but he had managed to impress on his grandfather, still at the War Office despite his immense age, that he was of the stuff that heroes are made and had managed to get himself transferred to a cavalry regiment.

As he rode past the lines of British troops, for the first time taking the offensive, Clive Bland felt a sense of exhilaration. He had heard, on landing, about the British retreat from Mons, but no one at headquarters was particularly concerned. It was all blamed on the French. And the British had suffered a mere sixteen-hundred casualties; there were battles in the Boer War that had cost more British lives.

This happy mood was shared by the staff officers at head-quarters near Paris. They had all received copies of Joffre's Order of the Day, dated 6 September 1914:

> *At the moment when the battle on which the fate of the country hangs, is about to open, it is necessary to remind all ranks that it is no longer the moment to look to the rear. Every effort must be made to attack and throw back the enemy. A unit which can no longer advance, must at all costs retain the ground it has gained, and rather than retire, be killed on the spot. In the present circumstances, no weakness can be tolerated.*

Full of enthusiasm the cavalry went forward, regardless of risk and ignorant of the great unwieldy armies engaged in the ceremony of trying to turn the enemy's flanks. On 7 September the Ninth Royal Lancers were well beyond the German line and learned from the villagers, silent and reproachful, that the Huns were not far away. Behind a stone wall Captain Bland and his squadron halted. Bland took out his binoculars. The stubble stretched away towards a line of woods and diagonally, across the broad road that led north from the village, came a line of horsemen. Magnificent in the morning sun the First Garde Dragoner Regiment of Berlin, of the Garde Kavallerie Division of the Garde Korps, rode, a dense line rising and falling as if mechanically operated—the proudest, finest cavalry of the German Army—more than a hundred. Envy seized Bland, but there was no time for contemplation for the German cavalry were on the attack, like machine-made waves on a machine-made ocean.

Pennons flying, the Lancers skirted round the field, and it seemed that the two groups of horsemen were not to meet. Then the British broke abruptly across the field, hurling themselves into their slower-moving foe. The Germans momentarily paused, and wheeled, their lances held horizontally, but the British force did not stop. Crunching against bone, one of the British lances went straight through the chest of one of the dragoons and came out the other side. Two of the British squadron went down, but by the time the Germans had reformed they had lost six of their men. The Lancers squadron disappeared out of sight round the village, exhilarated by its small victory. A couple of the dragoons dismounted, going through the pockets of one of the two dead Lancers. While the merits of the British officer's watch were being debated, a dismounted squadron of the Eighteenth Hussars approached stealthily with a machine-gun, and when this opened fire the Germans fled and swung full into the line of fire. The dragoons who had got off their horses did not have a chance, and one of them fell across the body of the man he was robbing.

The Hussars fired until the German dragoons were out of range, and when the Ninth Lancers returned, one of them, spying a wounded German trying to crawl away, casually pinned him to the ground with his lance and turned to his comrades, grinning. Bland felt physically sick, and was glad to move on, joining in the debate as to when the British Army would reach Berlin only after the incident had been suppressed in his mind.

To this small force of cavalry and to many of the infantry officers pressing forward without opposition, the whole business seemed cut and dried. But it was not to be. Although the Belgian Army was intact and tucked away in the German rear at Antwerp nothing was made of this. Although Kitchener had eleven Territorial divisions mobilized he did not send them. A division of the Regular Army, the only one available now that the other troops were committed in the fighting that had taken place already, was not flung into battle.

Few of the ordinary infantrymen knew what was happening. Harry Oakwood trudged on, hardly knowing whether he was asleep or awake. Bright spirits who began singing 'Tipperary' soon fell into silence as the chorus was not taken up. The officers on horseback were jogging along, their heads tucked on their chests, dozing. Occasionally a motor-cyclist would appear with a dispatch from headquarters couched in such grandiloquent terms that the company commanders were sceptical of its contents. The marchers were passed by a fleet of Paris taxi-cabs, packed with sleeping French soldiers on the way to the front. If there was a front.

It was the morning of 8 September when the Warwickshires came across a dozen heavy guns blocking the road. They took to the fields and as they did so, they were just in time to see a scurry of field-greys swarm up a ridge and disappear half-way up as if by magic into a sunken road. Captain Whitehouse rapped out his orders and the Warwickshires fell flat on their faces, jamming cartridges into their magazines and opening fire at fifteen-hundred yards' range. The German infantry responded, but neither side was able to make much impact. The bullets whistled harmlessly over heads and after half an hour Whitehouse ordered his men to cease fire to conserve ammunition. Thankfully the men rubbed their bruised shoulders.

For half an hour nothing happened.

'He's waiting for something,' said Saunders to Oakwood, looking over his shoulder at Captain Whitehouse, who was waiting nonchalantly, smoking a cheroot, while his minder held his horse. The reason was not far away. There was a crackle of artillery, and Oakwood could see the shrapnel bursting over the sunken road. The order came to resume fire, and presently a white flag was waved.

Whitehouse ignored it. 'Can't trust the bastards', he said to the sergeant-major.

More white flags came up.

'Looks like washing day in our road,' observed Saunders.

After a few minutes, Whitehouse ordered cease fire, whereupon the Germans opened fire again, the white flags being withdrawn.

'Damn silly,' muttered Oakwood.

'It's no good waiting here, Sergeant-Major,' said Whitehouse, 'the range is too far to bother them. We'll send two platoons and give them covering fire. The Huns haven't got any machine-guns.'

Sergeant-Major Jenkins looked around and motioned to Sergeant Marchbanks.

Marchbanks' knees were knocking together, and he was sweating heavily. 'All right, you lot,' he said to his men, gritting his teeth, 'it's us for the chop. Don't let me down.'

This is it, thought Harry. He looked up at the sky. To think, this might be the last time he would see it. He clenched his fists to make certain that they were his hands.

Then he was on the move, trying to move faster than he had ever moved before, yet wondering whether it was safer to fall behind the rest of the running men. Pray God that the bullets, humming amongst them, would hit them and not him! Mostly the soldiers could not hear the bullets, the sound of them being drowned in the jangle of equipment. Somewhere on the right a soldier went down.

'Get up,' roared Marchbanks, 'it missed you by a mile.'

And the soldier obediently got up.

The covering fire seemed almost as likely to hit them as that from the enemy. Suddenly Harry found that he was in dead ground, a part of the field not covered by the Germans on the sunken road or by the back-up British force. He loitered, looked around, saw a private being sick and deliberately took a tumble.

Saunders rushed up to him, his mouth open with apprehension. 'Are you hit, Oaky?'

'No,' hissed Harry, 'I'm shamming. I'm not going to get my head blown off. This ain't my idea of a good time. Bend over and let me hook my arm round your shoulder as though I've been hit. If old Marchbanks creates a stir I can pretend I've wrenched my ankle.'

'Marchbanks has got an attack of the collywobbles,' said Saunders, 'I had a good look at him. He's as white as chalk. I don't fancy Jenkins coming across us though. He won't be put off by a yarn like this. And, anyway, you're bloody heavy and they've stopped firing.'

The troops following them were not going forward, but moving sideways, along the dead ground and over the grass parapet.

'Come on, you idle buggers,' snapped Sergeant-Major Jenkins appearing from nowhere, 'we're taking them in the flank. What are you up to, Corporal, diddum's wrench your little ankle? Get along there or I want to know the reason why.'

There was a sporadic outburst of firing, and then silence. Oakwood and Saunders clambered up the grass and found themselves at the outskirts of a wood. They brushed their way through, came across a lieutenant looking intense and carrying his revolver as though it was going to bite him, and slackened

95

their pace as the wood thinned out. There did not seem to be any firing. Harry and Saunders discussed it. Would they hear the rifles in the wood?

'We heard them at that other place,' recalled Harry, and so they took a chance and emerged near the sunken road, their mouths dry.

About fifty British soldiers were engaged in plundering a large body of prisoners. The Germans were grinning, their hands held high and were assisting in the operations. Harry could see one of his comrades thrusting a pair of binoculars into his pack. Watches were being unstrapped from wrists, and pocket wallets were being remorselessly gone through. Only the arrival of Sergeant-Major Jenkins put an end to the looting.

A private nudged Harry. 'I've got a watch, Oaky. Seventeen-jewel Swiss. Yours for five bob.'

'Done,' said Harry immediately.

A German sergeant-major was found, and told to form the prisoners into fours. The order was slackly obeyed, and the sergeant-major screamed at them, one eye on Sergeant-Major Jenkins. Jenkins, all animosity forgotten, watched the display with admiration. The simultaneous click of heels, the instantaneous response to orders, these were real soldiers. He was sad that they had been taken prisoners. He turned to Sergeant Marchbanks.

'Sergeant!' he barked, 'search your men. And if they have any loot they're going to cop it real bad.'

Harry moved unobtrusively away from the man who was going to sell him the watch. Slowly the contents of British pockets were disgorged, and the personal effects handed back to the prisoners. The German sergeant-major's face broadened in a smile. He clicked his heels, and bowed towards Jenkins. He said something.

Puzzled, Jenkins looked round. 'Anyone know German?' he demanded.

One of the platoon translated. 'He says that you are a real soldier, Sarge-Major,' he said.

'Tell him that I'm sorry I'm fighting the likes of him,' growled Jenkins. 'I'd rather be fighting the Frenchies.'

The German sergeant-major thought this a great joke and when Oakwood and his comrades were being marched on he was still roaring with laughter, and slapping his thigh with the flat of his hand.

'What was that altercation about, Sergeant-Major?' asked Captain Whitehouse, riding up.

'Nothing, sir,' replied Jenkins.

It was a matter between senior NCOs, an understanding reached between two enemies who yet knew that they had more in common with each other than Jenkins and his commanding officer. It was none of the officer's business and consequently the sergeant-major never pressed any charges against the looters.

14

Speculation about whether the British troops would reach the Rhine in three weeks or six was shortlived. The Germans, as weary as the Allies and unable to march further, stopped on the River Aisne and dug in. Trench warfare had begun. On 16 September Sir John French issued his first instructions for the new kind of war.

The British Expeditionary Force was wedged between two French armies, and it was arranged that it would move north with the intention of outflanking the Germans. But by this time there was no room for manoeuvre. The head-on collision between 12 October and 11 November was known as the first battle of Ypres. The Germans had twenty divisions, the Allies fourteen.

The Warwickshires had been marching for fifteen miles, mainly over the French cobbles. It had been raining most of the day and Harry Oakwood was no longer aware of the water seeping through his cap and down his neck. He hardly noticed when his platoon was led into a school, and in a daze he helped collect some coal from an outhouse and build up a fire in the old iron stove. Spirits arose as the men removed their wet clothes and cloaked themselves in blankets that had been deposited in one of the classrooms. A corporal was detailed to issue a ration of rum and Harry downed his greedily.

There was no sound to overlay the crackle of the fire. Even before the food had been brought in, sizzling bacon and eggs, most of the men had fallen asleep swathed in their blankets. Sergeant Marchbanks came in, peering at his platoon through the clouds of steam that arose from the drying-out clothes. He spotted Corporal Wilkinson painstakingly pulling his rifle through and smoothing oil on to the working parts. He went over and sat down on a child's chair.

'This is a rum do, Wilkie,' he observed.

'Ain't it just, Sarge?' commented Wilkinson. 'Where are we?'

'A place called Hazebrouck,' replied the sergeant. 'How are the men taking it, do you think?'

'Not bad,' admitted Wilkinson, 'damned glad that they've been given a breather.'

'We'll be in the trenches tomorrow,' said Marchbanks. 'We'll be billeted in a village called Romorin. The front line is at a place called Ploegsteert. They call it "Plug Street".'

'I didn't hear any artillery,' said Wilkinson.

'The Germans are having the same trouble with the weather as us,' said Marchbanks. 'They're digging in trying to get dry. That's what the officers think, but they thought that we were going to walk right up to the Rhine so you can sort that out as you like. Who do you think'll crack out of this lot?'

'Morton's done it in his breeches,' said Wilkinson, 'if that's any clue.'

Reveille was early and the men, refreshed by a good night's sleep, stirred themselves. They brewed up some tea and went foraging for breakfast. A private from the cookhouse brought in more bacon and eggs, and the men supplemented their rations with more eggs that they had taken from a farm a couple of hundred yards away, frying them in their mess-tins on the stove, which the more wide-awake soldiers had kept alight all night.

Marchbanks checked the rifles in the morning. He was pleased to see that the men of his platoon had shaved. On the way forward to their billets they passed a column of Hampshires, returning from their tour of duty in the front line, led by a bearded officer on a horse.

'It's a full company,' observed Sergeant-Major Jenkins with satisfaction. 'It proves that casualties aren't heavy.'

Harry, Saunders and three more privates were billeted above a shop in the main street of the village. The owners, who were still in residence, intimated that they would supply the soldiers with extra food for a little cash.

'*C'est bien*', said Harry in schoolboy French, '*omelette à trois oeufs avec pommes frites pour cinq, s'il vous plaît.*' As the shopkeeper's wife busied herself, grinning, Harry lay back on one of the iron-frame beds and lit a cigarette. 'It ain't so bad after all, then, this war,' he said.

'I didn't like the sound of the artillery,' muttered young Morton.

After three days taking it easy, the company was attached to the eleventh brigade on the Fourth Division and moved to a large farm immediately behind 'Plug Street' wood. The farm buildings were completely intact and the farmer, his family, and the cattle, were still in occupation. The troops could now hear the ping of rifle bullets and the occasional rat-tat-tat of machine-guns but there was little shelling. At night Harry could see the German Very lights rising into the sky.

Each evening from twilight to midnight Harry and his mates were busy carrying stores to a line of barricades in the middle of the wood. Engineers had laid down duckboard tracks to the front line, and the barricades, made from logs, sandbags, and earth, were being constructed because the forward trenches had already become waterlogged.

One evening at dusk two platoons were told that they were to go into the front line for instruction with the Somerset Light Infantry, and they set off, each man wearing his overcoat and carrying full equipment together with a waterproof sheet. Rations for forty-eight hours were carried up behind them in sandbags by a fatigue party. They followed the duckboard trail through the woods for about an hour and came to a low line of trenches cut across the wood.

The trench here was nothing but a shallow ditch, and the occupying troops sat casually around, cleaning their rifles and equipment by the light of the moon. A Somerset Light Infantry officer carrying a stout stick and wearing a rabbit-skin hat on his head directed the NCOs to their section of the trench.

Sentries were posted at intervals, whilst about a hundred yards in front of the trenches there was a line of barbed wire festooned with empty jam tins which it was anticipated would give warning of the enemy's approach. The rain had cleared up and Harry felt it was almost like a picnic. On the evening of the second night he was nominated as one of the party to go out on patrol under Corporal Wilkinson.

There was nothing to see but the flashes of light in the skies and Harry, feeling protected by the wood, was quite happy to keep abreast of Wilkinson, though he felt that the corporal was moving forward at too rapid a pace. After a time he was relieved when Wilkinson found a tree stump to sit upon and lit his pipe.

'Miss your motor-car I'll be bound, Oaky', he observed.

'I don't suppose the war will last very long', said Harry, 'then back to Warwick, eh? Hope so, anyway.'

'The war will last for years and years,' said Wilkinson.

'We've got our medals for the Mons do,' put in Private Sampson eagerly. Sampson was an old soldier like Wilkinson, with a face bleached by the tropical sun. 'How long we going to wait here, Corp?' he went on. 'My mate's cooking me some bacon back at the trenches.'

'We'll give it another ten minutes', said Wilkinson, 'I've got to get my pipe puffing away first.'

The ten minutes expired, and the patrol went back to the trenches. The forty-eight-hour tour went without incident and the two platoons made their way back to the farmhouse, where Harry maliciously put the fear of God into Morton. 'Heads stuck on the barbed wire', he recounted, 'and rotting bodies. I've never seen so many. And stink, strewth, did they stink!'

'He's having you on, Morton,' cut in Saunders, but when Morton went out the next evening for his 48-hour shift he looked hard about him for dead bodies and dismembered limbs.

The rains had come again and Private Henry Morton waded through the sludge, the mud sucking at his boots. His platoon was ordered to a line of trenches to the north of those occupied by Oakwood's. A foot of water had collected in the trench and the men they were relieving thankfully relinquished their rum jars, improvised seats that brought them a kind of rest a few inches above water-level.

100

Morton, a pale thin youth who had joined the regular army to escape domineering parents, heard noises to the front, and looked over the parapet of the trench. There were lights showing. He was told that the Germans were only a hundred yards away. There was a strange sluicing noise; this, he learned, came from the German pumps. They were having difficulties in their trenches, but were systematically emptying them.

The fatigue men came with the rations but with the rain driving down there did not seem any way of warming them, though the Somerset Light Infantry had rigged up a corrugated iron shelter. The sergeant in command of the platoon had taken this over for himself and was reluctant to let Private Morton in. Smothered to the neck in his waterproof sheet, the sergeant sat broodingly on a folding chair he had brought.

'If you can't eat your rations warm eat them raw', he said bluntly, 'and send the corporal to me.'

The corporal came and joined the sergeant in a swig of brandy.

'Get a patrol out, will you,' ordered the sergeant, 'and take that poxy white-faced fellow with you, the one who wanted to brew up in my hut.'

So Morton went on patrol. Mercifully the corporal had no wish to go forward. They walked down the trench and did a brief spell in the woods where there would be little chance of coming across the enemy. The branches of the trees gave some protection from the rain and the group lit cigarettes, chatting amongst themselves in undertones. Swishing of branches was the first indication that something was happening. The patrol stood absolutely still in the hope that they would escape observation, not realizing for several seconds that their glowing cigarette ends would give them away.

'Cigarettes out!' hissed the corporal.

There was a crackle of branches.

'Who's there?' shouted one of the privates nervously.

'Bloody fool,' said the corporal. 'Come on, lads, back to the trench.'

Half a dozen speculative shots rang out, divided equally among the two patrols and Morton felt his legs taken from him as though he had slipped on ice. 'I've been hit!' he screamed.

101

'I've got a Blighty!' There was silence. A voice infiltrated through the swish of rain.

'Is that Englanders?'

'Yes,' replied the corporal hesitantly, bending low on the ground in case it was a trick.

'We shall not shoot if you do not shoot,' said the voice.

The corporal took out his handkerchief and waved it. 'I am holding flag of truce,' he said.

The two groups approached in the light of matches held up on both sides.

'We hit somebody,' said a German corporal, rain trickling down his spiked helmet and into his eyes, making him blink.

'Fellow named Morton,' said the corporal, speaking slowly as one does to an idiot.

'I was a waiter in the Savoy in London,' said the corporal. 'I speak English well.'

'You do, too,' said the British corporal. 'How many are there of you?'

'Five,' said the German.

'There are six of us,' said the Englishman. 'Do you smoke?'

'Thank you,' said the German, laying his rifle against the trunk of his tree and taking off his woollen mittens. He took the packet from the British corporal's hands and handed it around. Feeling self-conscious, the Warwickshire troops lit up more cigarettes.

'I'm wounded,' whimpered Morton.

'Oh, shut up, for Christ's sake!' said his corporal irritably.

The Germans went over to examine the wounded man as though he were a strange species of plant.

'It is a flesh wound,' volunteered a German private, 'it is nothing.'

'He's a lucky devil,' said the British corporal. 'It'll be back to billets for him. It means we've got to lug him all the way back to the trenches.'

The German corporal thought. 'Unless we could have him as prisoner,' he suggested, 'the Commandant, he is always asking for prisoners.'

'Good idea,' said one of the British privates, 'you have him.'

So Morton went out of the war, lamented by none.

Harry Oakwood was moderately surprised to learn that one

of his room-mates in the billet had been taken prisoner but, as Saunders pointed out, Morton was no great loss. The only person who seemed sorry to hear of his capture was the shop-keeper's wife.

'Damned nuisance,' grunted Captain Whitehouse. 'It means a lot of paperwork. As much for one man as for ten men, or a hundred men. I don't know what they were doing patrolling in that wood, anyway. A patrol's meant to go forward not rambling in the rear. Who do they think they are—sightseers?'

It seemed to Harry all very leisurely. They would do a week at the farm, then back to the billet in Romorin, then a spell behind the battle area where there would be girls and cafés.

'It's too good to last, Oaky,' confided Corporal Wilkinson, 'they're not going to leave us here when things are bad down in the south. I was speaking to a mate from the First Loyal Regiment.'

He was right, and the Warwickshires were relieved by a tired battalion who had been fighting near Gheluvelt. The situation at Ploegsteert was stabilized and could be left to battle-weary men to cope with.

As the Warwickshires marched south the noise of battle got louder and when they entered Gheluvelt it was a ghost town of shattered buildings, brick dust mingling with cordite fumes. They passed the doors of a chapel, turned into the field hospital. There were stretchers on the floor without space to walk between them. A motor lorry was burning in the street and another was upturned in a crater. Squads of pioneers were clearing the rubble from the streets. A car roared past the column with a staff officer sitting bolt upright in the back seat. The driver was sounding the horn, though it could not be heard above the constant roar of the guns and the explosions that wracked the town every few minutes. There was a roar and from behind a line of windowless houses a plume of smoke rose up into the dull grey sky. Boots crunched on broken glass as the Warwickshires were led into an empty house. The roof was missing, and the floor above sagged dangerously. Half a dozen fatigue men were bracing it with a beam.

As evening drew on, the bombardment slackened and Harry and his platoon settled down for the night. Casks of rum were brought in and the men had ample rations slopped into their enamel mugs. They are trying to get us drunk, thought Harry, so that we don't know what is happening, and he handed his mug over to a neighbour.

All night long he could hear the creak of waggons down the road, intermingled with the cries of the wounded, but somehow he slept a little, though at dawn he was awakened by a gargantuan roar as though the house was falling in on top of them. A lieutenant in the engineers came in. His uniform was dusty, and he had a bandage round his wrist.

'It's the morning bombardment,' he said. 'The Catholic priest is coming round to any of you who follow the true faith.'

A couple of the men rose from the floor and waited for the priest and Harry watched them cynically.

'It sounds as though it's going to be bad,' said Saunders uneasily. 'That hasn't happened before. What did they mean when they were talking about whizz-bangs and Jack Johnsons?'

'Whizz-bangs are shells,' explained Harry, 'that's all you hear of them. Whizz and then bang, and then it's too late. Jack Johnsons are the big shells.'

'Thanks for nothing,' muttered Saunders. 'The cookhouse man's just come in. Give us your mug and I'll get you some tea . . .' but before he could finish the sentence Sergeant-Major Jenkins entered and the men tottered to their feet, many of them still reeling from their massive intake of rum. Jenkins ignored their uncertain gait.

'The Huns are trying to recapture the town and we've got to stop them. Savvy? This place has been going backwards and forwards for a couple of weeks now, and it's vital that the Allies hold on to it. You may think that you're the only ones being clobbered by artillery, but don't forget that the Huns are being clobbered by ours. It's just as bad for them. Worse, for they're not the soldiers that you are. Get your ammo before you go. At least a hundred and fifty rounds. The pioneers will keep you well supplied. Fall in in fifteen minutes after you've had your char.'

The soldiers formed up outside, with detachments of other regiments, including spare transport men and engineers. They were addressed by a colonel, who winced at every explosion. The upshot of his speech was that matters could be worse.

As the force moved nearer the battle the houses became more

and more battered; some consisted merely of a chimney-breast, others a single wall. Amongst the rubble there were legs and arms poking out. Near a corner of a street that ran off the main road, a headless soldier was lying, his hands clutching his cap. The German artillery was firing smoke shells to confuse the defenders and there was no attempt to keep order. The men moved forward into the gloom, stepping around craters, avoiding bodies, the whistling of bullets and the ricochets off the walls of the ruins mingling with the bursting shells and the fevered neighing of horses.

Although Saunders was only five paces away, Harry could barely see him. Sergeant Marchbanks was standing at the side of the road, his face working, waving the men on. A shrapnel shell burst fifty yards away, and Harry could hear the metal shrieking across the ground, clinking at the walls. The black smoke lifted sufficiently for Harry to see a barricade being built up in the middle of the street. There was furniture from the houses, sandbags, and half a dozen men were laying barbed wire at an angle from the obstruction, rolls that curled back at the men already in position.

An officer motioned the men forward, brandishing his revolver. Harry could see it was Lieutenant Wilcox.

'Good luck, Harry,' the lieutenant called as Harry went by.

A shout came from behind. 'Make way for the guns', and the soldiers had to race for the side of the road as the four horses tugging the eighteen pounders reared up, nostrils dilated.

'What a bloody place to build a barricade,' shouted an artillery captain.

Four men ran forward, their breath wheezing, carrying a machine-gun. They clambered on to the top of the heap, and set it up.

Suddenly the enemy artillery ceased firing, and the deathly silence that followed was broken by the clatter of the machine-gun. Harry noticed a pile of what looked like jam tins. They were improvised bombs with pieces of metal, gunpowder, and a detonator crammed into an old tin. Hardly knowing what he was doing, Harry climbed up to the top of the barricade, which was eight or nine feet high, and joined the others who were lying at the top. Everyone was firing indiscriminately into the smoke and he joined them. He was surrounded by what sounded like buzzing insects. Occasionally there was a dull thud as an enemy bullet embedded itself into one of the articles of furniture that helped to make up the barricade.

The man next to him suddenly grasped his shoulder and turned to Harry with a surprised expression, while blood oozed from between his fingers. He was pulled from his position, and his place was taken by another soldier. The order came to cease fire and gradually the men laid down their rifles.

'That's taught them a lesson,' a corporal said with satisfaction.

The order came to advance, and the men feverishly clambered down from the barricade as engineers began dismantling it to let the artillery through. Harry joined in with the rush down the street. There was no opposition. A few German bodies littered the road and one or two of the wounded were kicked as the British troops ran by. They were nearing the outskirts of the village when a concealed enemy sniper opened fire from behind the shell of a house. He accounted for three men before he was dispatched.

'Fix bayonets!' screamed a major and clumsily the men stopped and obeyed, Harry with them. This was not him, he thought, this was someone else. It was just running at nothing, a nightmare journey through black smoke which ebbed and weaved. Abruptly the town ended, and Harry could see, between billows of mist, the countryside full of ant-like creatures rushing forward without apparent meaning. He became one of them. The bullets began again, zipping, sending running men headlong into the grass. There was a bunching as the men tried to avoid two large craters set together. One or two men were lying in one crater, pretending to be dead. Harry could see their eyes flicker at him as he looked down on them.

How do you get out of this? he thought. Where was the sense in it? The run had slowed down as the men mounted the hill. Unbelievably there were half a dozen cows munching grass in a corner of the field.

A voice came to his ears. 'Range nine hundred yards.'

He dropped to the ground, adjusting his sight, and feeling in his ammunition pouch for more ammunition which he laid down in front of him. Crawling on his belly he frantically sought for some kind of protective hollow.

On the brow of the hill a mass of grey uniforms clustered together, and then began to descend. Somewhere to the right of Harry a machine-gun opened fire on them. The grey uniformed men broke, and disappeared from sight. To the right of Harry men were moving back down the hill.

'Haven't you heard the order?' screamed a voice in his ear. 'Retire. Get back.'

Harry did not need any more encouragement. The town was quiet when he got back. The street was littered with dozens of bodies. He saw Corporal Wilkinson and asked what had happened.

'They came from the side,' said Wilkinson, 'where the hell were you?'

'I was up the hill,' said Harry indignantly.

'That was the Worcesters' business, not ours,' said Wilkinson sharply, 'your mate Saunders has bought it, and Marchbanks has got a Blighty. I never thought he had it in him. He went wild, went straight at them with his bayonet, carved half a dozen of them buggers up before one of them got a shot in at him.'

Shame about Saunders, Harry thought. He'd have to look the family up when he went home as he'd promised. But it could have been worse. It could have been him. He was rather glad that he had followed the mob and gone up the hill.

15

If George Oakwood had imagined that Harry going to war would bring them closer together he was disappointed. The field postcards bearing a sentimental picture of Tommy marching away to the front line watched by a weeping woman or a child asking where its daddy was were laconic and inexpressive. George explained it to Jane by saying that Harry was obviously forbidden to say more.

Although their way of life had not been altered an iota by the war, things perceptibly changed. Leonard, though introverted, had never been moody before, and Mary was beginning to cause problems. She had taken up a secretarial training course at a technical college, but had suddenly dropped it without a word of explanation. She mooned around the place, occasionally going to the picture house in Ladypool Road, but it seemed that matters would improve when she agreed to go and work behind the counter at the shoe-shop to replace one of the shop assistants who was marrying a soldier.

It was a great time for marrying soldiers, thought George. On any weekend the cars were queueing up outside the local church bedecked with white ribbon, and a large proportion of the bridegrooms wore brand new uniform, having succumbed to the huge posters depicting Lord Kitchener with finger pointing, and the caption:

Your King and Country Need You

A CALL TO ARMS

An addition of 100,000 men to His
Majesty's Regular Army is immediately
necessary in the present grave National
Emergency.

It did not seem like a grave National Emergency. There were as many shoppers in town as ever before and Mr Motley, totting up his accounts, found that he had never done better. Like many of his age group, Motley found the whole business of war exhilarating, and he wholeheartedly approved of the torrent of hate directed towards the Germans. He had not taken any part in the window-smashing of likely traitors' property, but he had viewed the results with satisfaction.

There did not seem any chance of the Zeppelins coming over and bombing them to kingdom come. As he said to Mrs Motley, it was all wind.

'Jane's girl is coming in this morning,' she said to him, nodding her head. 'I'd like to meet her. She's got such a lovely mother and I'd like to make sure she feels at home.'

'I've given her half-a-crown a week less than Sally', said Motley, 'but I'll make that up at Christmas. After all, Sally was with us three years.'

Without knowing why, he was slightly disappointed when he met Mary. True, she was a pretty girl but there was an air of aloofness about her. Still, there was a bit of that in Jane. And she had a sullen turn of her mouth. There was no doubt that she was an intelligent girl and he watched her surreptitiously in the shop, pretending to busy himself with reordering. When she put herself out Mary had a nice smile that completely changed her.

In the evening when she went home Mary would go into the parlour and play the gramophone. She would occasionally put on the latest ragtime records but preferred the sentimental ballads. Her favourite hobby remained the moving pictures; sometimes she would go with a girl friend, sometimes alone, but it did not matter much, for Mary became so immersed in the film that she completely forgot her surroundings. The maudlin romances enacted for the benefit of the threepenny stalls had her moist-eyed, the patriotic dramas had her full of ideals, and when she was introduced to Alfred, her best friend's brother, who was just about to enlist, she credited him with qualities that simply did not exist. He was the romantic lover of the screen come to life.

Alfred was an amiable good-looking young man without any great individuality, but when his sister left him and Mary alone they held hands and kissed each other enthusiastically as they did in the films. A few days later Mary took her first boy friend home.

George liked Alfred, more so when he heard that the boy was volunteering next week for the army.

'We have to beat the Germans,' he said earnestly to George. 'They're the scourge of mankind.'

It was a phrase George was familiar with, as he had read it too in the *Daily Express*, but he was not disposed to argue, though he had reservations about the ability of the British to deal with this scourge. Well-read in military history, he was contemptuous of the airy claims of the generals and did not boil over with indignation, as Jane did, when he read of German atrocities in Belgium. Why should professional soldiers want to toss babies in the air and spear them on their bayonets? Technically it was not an easy thing to do, anyway.

It came as a surprise to Alfred when, on the eve of departure, he proposed marriage and was enthusiastically accepted. The young couple had never done more than kiss, and it had not occurred to Alfred to try anything more.

'I'm not a fellow to be fresh', he said loftily to his colleagues at the office when they ribbed him. 'We go to our marriage unsullied in word or deed.'

'I heard that in that picture *The Sorrows of Satan*', commented a chum wickedly, 'but it ain't like that in real life, Alf, really it isn't. Women, they *like* a hand up their leg or round their bubbies.'

Alfred ignored him but secretly wondered if it were true.

There was no time to find out. He went down to the recruiting office, joined in the queue and signed on the dotted line. Before he knew what was happening he was standing on the railway platform, Mary sobbing with her arms draped round his neck, with miscellaneous parents doing likewise. It was a festival of the lachrymose and after the train had steamed off the bystanders and relatives congregated in the refreshment room, hardly a dry eye among them.

'My poor lamb,' whispered one woman, 'it's the first time he's been away from home!'

George had gone along, too, to speed the hero, but he was untouched by the sentiment. Never in his life had he seen such a rabbity lot of young men with their jug ears, big caps, best suits with cuffs two inches too short, and highly polished patent leather shoes. The Prussian cavalry would go through them like a dose of salts. But he kept his thoughts to himself and was irritated by Mary's show of grief. Damn it all, she had only known him a couple of weeks.

As he and Jane went back home on the electric tram, the cold autumn wind whistling through the open upper deck, he wondered about Leonard. Leonard was out of work, for the Blums had unceremoniously shut up their firm when the mob broke the windows of their office, and a vast quantity of mechanical German soldiers remained in their cardboard boxes for the duration. The Blums had been a little slow off the mark and when Leonard heard about their internment as enemy aliens a

110

thrill of pleasure went through him. He had not realized before that he had hated them.

He had spent half a day walking round the local park, watching the children playing with hoops on the grass or splashing around in their tiny Wellington boots in the muddy pool. Tomorrow he was going to Coventry to see Elizabeth, the girl he had met at Weston-super-Mare. They had written to each other, but somehow the magic that had been conjured up in August was missing. The ache in his heart had been replaced by puzzlement and indignation.

When he got back home he encountered a scene of misery. His mother and Mary were crying, joined in desperation.

'Who's dead?' asked Leonard sardonically.

Mary wiped her eyes and looked at him. 'I've got a hero as a fiancé', she said coldly, 'and an out-of-work coward as a brother.'

His mother looked at him and to his horror Leonard saw distaste in her face.

'You've never wanted me to join the army', he blurted out. 'It's no good going hoity-toity on me. You've always said that you never wanted me to join the army. It's those bloody newspapers, they've got at you, have they? Run by fat old men sitting on their backsides. Look at the casualty reports. A quarter of the British Expeditionary Force lost at Ypres.'

'And your brother may be amongst them,' said Jane.

Leonard flapped his hands at his side. 'All right,' he said, 'tell me I ought to go. Change your mind. Tell me I ought to go.'

At this point his father came in. 'What's all this?' he asked, bewildered.

'They're on about me joining up, Dad,' said Leonard rapidly. 'Mum's changed her tune. She wants me to go.'

'She's always wanted you to go, Leonard,' said George, 'but we're not parents who would push you. Harry went, and it was the happiest day of my life. You're a thinking lad, Leonard. You could do far better than Harry could ever do. You could be an officer. I could never be because I didn't have the schooling, and Harry couldn't because he's not one to really work at anything.'

'It's important to you, is it?' asked Leonard.

George looked at him as though he was crazy.

111

Jane had calmed down. 'It's not the army, Leonard,' she said, 'it's your country. Your country needs you. To protect us, the womenfolk. There's young Alfred, he's gone to fight for king and country.'

'It's no good talking to him,' said Mary. 'He's a coward.'

'You wouldn't know what a coward was unless it was written in the titles on the pictures,' said Leonard violently.

Mary relapsed into tears again, comforted by her mother who eyed Leonard as, Mary reflected through her anguish, the mother had eyed her son in *His Mother's Secret*.

George found it difficult to understand what the trouble was about and why Mary was going on like this. A son of his would certainly never be a coward. And in the back of his mind was the certainty that the sacrifices on the battlefield were insane. It was not the British Army that was fighting, but a ramshackle lot led by mad generals. His Army was gone for good.

What depressed him most was that it appeared that only he seemed to think this. Jane had always seemed to him to be the epitome of robust common sense, but even she was infected by this war virus.

'Your country needs you,' she had told Leonard.

Stuff and nonsense, thought George. The generals wanted him to make mincemeat of him. And, to his embarrassment, he had backed her up. He had been delighted when Harry had volunteered, but how far was this an expression of his wish to get him off their hands? Harry far away, he had to admit, was preferable to Harry up to his antics.

Then there was Mary. The Mary of old had seemed too cool for her own good, but just as her elders had been sent off their head by war propaganda she had been twisted by rubbishy films. Leonard was right. Mary would not know what a coward was unless it was on the flickering sub-titles of the motion picture.

The Oakwoods did not receive many letters. Occasionally Jane got a postcard from one of the girls who was on holiday from the shop or who had just left to get married. Sometimes a letter came for George from the War Office, duplicated and smudgy, ordering him to hold himself in readiness for a recall to the army but he knew in his heart, though initially cheered, that this self-same letter had been sent to hundreds of thousands of other ex-soldiers, most of whom were no doubt dead.

On the morning after the row Leonard received a letter. His heart sank when he saw it on the table. It was from Elizabeth saying that she did not want to see him. So he thought. But when he saw the postmark was Birmingham he opened it, and a white feather drifted to the carpet. It was just the sort of melodramatic gesture Mary would make, he thought. It savoured of a scene from *A Blot on the Escutcheon*, recently playing at the Olympia picture house.

There was no need for him to explain the letter to anyone, for everyone else had gone to work and, after toast and marmalade and a cup of tea, he went on the tram to town. He looked down on the scurrying people. Who would have thought that there was a war on? Christmas would soon be with them, and the men and women were laughing, joking, examining turkeys hung up in their hundreds and peering into the lighted shop windows at trashy toys.

It was a brisk walk from Coventry railway station to the home of Elizabeth's parents. It was a neat little house built just before the war, with round windows and stained glass in the front door. A typical jerry-built job, the white stucco was already peeling off the wall and the woodwork was splitting. The door was opened by a heavy middle-aged man in a drab three-piece suit, the effect of which was spoiled by scarlet carpet slippers.

'Come in,' said Mr Elkin, 'you must be Leonard. Elizabeth has just gone to get some milk from the corner shop. The milkman's gone to the war, and we never know when we are going to get our milk delivered.'

It was not like his parents' house, considered Leonard looking around. The Elkins were obviously 'artistic' and had gone in for plain wood furniture, self-coloured mats and curtains and odd-shaped vases. There was no welcome in the gas fire in the grate. Mr Elkin motioned Leonard to a so-called easy chair, no different from a dining-room chair except that it was bigger. He realized how comfortable his home always was—a bit dowdy at times but always cosy and comfortable.

'I've got a rotten cold,' explained Mr Elkin, 'so that's why I'm not at work.'

'It's very bad weather for colds,' said Leonard uncomfortably.

'Our boys at the front must be feeling it,' said Mr Elkin.

Leonard agreed, wondering whether this meant that Elizabeth had brothers or whether Elkin was encompassing the whole of the British Army. Fortunately Elizabeth came in, breathless. She looked at her father and then at Leonard and decided that it was all right to go up and shake hands.

It was not the Elizabeth of his dreams. The best summer dress of August had given way to a blue-check linen skirt and a high-necked white blouse, partly hidden under a woolly jersey that was much too big for her and obviously put on to go to the corner shop in.

As if aware that the jersey and the blouse were not compatible, Elizabeth struggled out of the former, making her hair untidy. Flustered, she patted her hair into place. Leonard noticed that her tip-tilted nose was red, and that there was a cold sore on her upper lip. The virus seemed to have struck all the family.

'I'll make some tea,' said Elizabeth, anxious to get away, and once more Leonard was left with her father, who spent some of the time sneezing into his handkerchief.

'My wife would have liked to have met you,' said Mr Elkin unconvincingly. 'She is working mornings at the bicycle factory. She's on war work.'

'That's nice,' said Leonard.

'My daughter tells me that you are studying to be an accountant,' said Mr Elkin, 'that's the kind of work I'm in. Bookkeeper, you know. Have you learned about double-entry book-keeping?'

'Oh, yes,' replied Leonard, 'I can do work up to a trial balance.'

'And profit and loss account?' went on Mr Elkin, eyeing the young man.

'I can manage,' said Leonard defensively. It was very much like the interview he had had with the Blum brothers when he went to get the job.

There was an embarrassed silence and Elizabeth came in with a tea tray. Mr Elkin looked at the contents and then at his daughter. Leonard knew that look. It meant that she should have used the best tea service. He sipped his tea, telling them what a quick journey it had been from Birmingham and what a wonderful thing railways were. Elizabeth hardly looked at him, staring into her cup as if reading tea leaves.

'I see you haven't joined up yet,' said Mr Elkin.

'I have to finish the term at night school,' lied Leonard.

'I should have thought a war to save mankind from barbarism was more important than finishing a term at night school,' suggested Mr Elkin.

'My father was in the army,' said Leonard. 'He always thought that we should have to fight the Germans.'

'We shall have to fight the Russians, too,' said Mr Elkin. 'I read rather a lot, and this Bolshevism is dreadful. The curse of mankind.' He went on a good deal about the Russians, and Leonard tried to show an interest that he did not feel.

'I suppose you'll be catching the twelve-thirty back,' said Mr Elkin, and Leonard agreed, and supposed that he would.

'I'll walk with you to the station,' said Elizabeth but her father put up his hand deprecatingly.

'Not with your cold, my dear,' he said. 'I think it much better for you to stay indoors.'

'But . . .' protested the girl, and Mr Elkin repeated that it would be much better to stay indoors.

Surprised by the frosty reception that he had received, Leonard got to his feet, and shook hands with the man. Elizabeth saw him to the door, her father in close pursuit. A gargantuan sneeze on the part of Mr Elkin enabled her to whisper, 'Sorry about this, it won't be always like this. I didn't know father would be at home today.'

She held out her hand and Leonard took it. She squeezed his rapidly, and then withdrew it. Mr Elkin was already shutting the door.

Leonard did not go back home. He made a small detour, and enlisted not in the Royal Warwickshire Regiment but in the Royal Flying Corps, subject to a medical examination.

'He seems an intelligent enough lad,' said the captain who had interviewed him, watching Leonard leave the room. He read through the enlistment form. 'Father a sergeant-major, that's good. His brother a serving soldier. He knows his aeroplanes, too. He couldn't have crammed that up in a couple of

115

weeks. A well-spoken lad, considering his class, but you can always tell a Brummy a mile away, no matter how they try to disguise it and go all lah-di-dah.'

'Might make a fitter', said his colleague, 'though you never know. The chaps are going down like ninepins behind the Jerry lines.'

'Well,' said the other philosophically, 'they're captured not dead. Still, that's not much good to us unless we can do a swap with some of theirs.'

The war in the air was still an affair of gentlemen and if there was any quality that would stop Leonard being a flyer it was the certainty that, well-mannered and presentable as he was, he was not a gentleman.

16

Alfred came home in his smart new uniform and he and Mary were married in the church of St Paul. George, uncomfortable in his new suit, did not know who half the people were, even those on his own side. His cousins were dredged up, old men in baggy trousers who sniffed; he had not seen them since the funeral of his mother forty years ago. It all seemed very remote to him, as though the womenfolk were trying to make a life that was drifting into the unutterably humdrum significant.

Thank goodness, he thought as he watched Jane, neat and trim in a new tailored suit, that his wife was still going strong. Quick and brisk in her movements, it seemed amazing that she would be sixty in a year or two. Of course, they were both too old to go cycling and it seemed ages since they had left Birmingham. Though, of course, there had been that seaside holiday last year. He went up and spoke to Mr and Mrs Motley. Mrs Motley walked with a stick and was obviously a sick woman, not really knowing what was going on. They clearly thought the world of Jane. He was still thinking of the years that had gone when he realized that Mr Motley was making a startling proposition: now that the children had gone why not take the option of buying the flat above the shop?

'We are going to live in a bungalow that we have bought outside Birmingham,' said Mr Motley. 'Mrs Motley is not at all well, and the country air may help her get better.'

George looked hesitant and Mr Motley said with a smile that he had spoken to Jane and she had asked him to talk it over with George.

It had been assumed that Mary would continue to live at home and it had been a shock to Jane to find that her daughter much preferred to live with Alfred's parents. 'It's no life for me here,' Mary had complained. 'Mum's at work at the shop and is tired when she gets in, and you're always reading. We never go out anywhere. Alfred's mum and dad, they're always going to the pictures.'

'Does that mean that you want to give up your job in the shop?' Jane had asked slowly, her lip trembling.

'I shall be a married woman,' Mary had said breezily, 'and it's not proper for a married woman, especially one married to a soldier, to work behind a shop counter.'

So although the wedding was going according to plan, George knew that there was a good deal of anguish behind Jane's bright and breezy exterior.

The clergyman had gabbled through the service and had hardly looked at the father of the bride. These working people always looked the same at weddings, he thought. He found it difficult to relate George to his wife. She, he considered, as he droned out the final words of the wedding service, had decidedly married beneath her. She had that no nonsense air about her that he often found with the middle classes. He felt sorry for the bridegroom, another poor lad destined for the slaughter of the Western Front.

Mary thought that she would feel more emotion than she did. It was like taking part in a film. None of this was real. She said goodbye to her parents, sorry to see that her mother was crying, and went outside to the taxi that was to take them to the reception and then the railway station. They were going to Llandudno for their honeymoon, at the expense of Alfred's parents. Mary liked them, she admitted to herself, more than her own mother and father. They were easier to get on with,

and much more fun—much more fun, to be honest, than
Alfred. You had to admit that he was a hero and looked so
spanking but he did not have much to say for himself.

They arrived at Llandudno tired and had difficulty in finding
their boarding house.

'You've got our best room,' said the landlady smirking,
'you'll have some supper, won't you, love, and then you won't
be disturbed.' She winked at Alfred, which Mary thought was
rather low.

'Nice fish,' said Alfred appreciatively.

'Do you always pour sauce on your fish like that?' asked
Mary curiously.

Alfred looked up, bright-eyed, full of anticipation, and
nodded.

Supper over, they went upstairs to their room. Mary had a
bath, and then went to bed, wearing her new nightdress. It was
like the one that the heroine wore in *Her First Love*. As she lay
back in bed, her hands locked behind her head, she reflected
that the films never told you what marriage was really like. She
knew what was expected of her, though it had been hopeless
trying to extricate information from her mother. Who would
have thought that she would be married? Alfred came in. For a
moment she wondered what he was doing there.

Clumsily Alfred switched off the gas-light and she heard him
stumble about the room. She stretched out her hands and
touched Alfred's naked body. It was the first body she had
touched. She felt a spasm of terror and her limbs go rigid
as Alfred pushed up her nightdress and pressed down upon
her.

'That was *lovely*,' he breathed after it was over.

'Yes, it was, wasn't it?' Mary lied. It had been painful and
unexpected. And there was more to come. Falling into an
uneasy doze, she felt Alfred's hands about her and once more
gave herself to him.

In the morning the landlady eyed her roguishly. 'I've
changed your sheets', she said conspiratorially.

Mary blushed self-consciously. 'Thank you,' she said, picking at her breakfast while Alfred, revelling in his newly-found
manhood, ate heartily.

They went for a walk on the promenade, and Alfred gave

118

sixpence to a man who saluted him with the words, 'Tanner for an old soldier, Captain?'

'But he's nothing but a beggar, Alfred,' said Mary disapprovingly.

The second night followed the same pattern as the first, though when Alfred wanted the light on during their lovemaking Mary refused.

'It's not proper,' she said, pulling up her nightdress. Alfred did not demur. Perhaps she was right. He wished, even as he made love to her, that there would be some kind of response from Mary, even a word of admiration for his ability in accomplishing what he termed 'the act' four times in one night. Mary found it all less painful, though she was disappointed.

They walked up the Great Orme, and peered into shops closed for the winter months. Mary sent postcards to everyone she could think of, and regretted that she had not kept the addresses of the girls she had met at the secretarial college so that she could send postcards to them, too. They had tea in quaint olde-Englishe tea rooms, with Alfred holding her hand beneath the table, and Mary deliberately led Alfred off on long walks so that he would not trouble her so much on the third and last night. In this she succeeded, and Alfred only managed it once before falling into a long dreamless sleep—broken into by the hooting of a motor-car that he imagined as reveille, so that he jumped out of bed, waking Mary. Mary looked at her husband. It was nothing at all like the films.

Tears came easily to Mary, nurtured on a hundred trivial film romances, and she put up a truly magnificent show as Alfred joined his train at Birmingham that evening to take him back to camp to continue his training before being shipped overseas. Alfred's mother joined in, sobbing plaintively.

'There, there!' she soothed, 'Alfred will come back to you soon, and we will all be together again.'

The two newly-married people kissed, then Alfred climbed on to the train. They watched him waving until he was an indistinguishable blob sticking out of a window.

'We'll have a nice cup of tea in the refreshment room', said Alfred's mother, 'and then we'll go back home. And tonight, if you're a good girl and stop crying, we'll go to the pictures and see that new film on at the Regent Palace.'

Nothing was more calculated to cut short grief than a film and, by the time Mary had settled in with Alfred's mother and father flanking her, it was as though nothing had happened, that the honeymoon in Llandudno had been a strange episode that had no sense in it.

Jane and George were disappointed that Mary had not come to see them after her return from the honeymoon, but were too busy arranging the move to the flat above the shop to worry about it for long. There were a lot of things to dispose of—first of all Leonard's piano, for which they got a surprisingly good price.

'Patriotic as I am,' the piano dealer they had bought it from told them, 'there's nothing that beats a good German upright.'

They lost only five pounds on the purchase price. All the bicycles were disposed of, and so were most of the pieces of furniture. George and Jane were taking over much of the Motleys' fixtures, fittings and furniture.

It was amazing how much the couple had accumulated during their time in the house. George was surprised how many books he had got and decided not to take the old volumes of the *Strand* which he had bought for the war stories. War was not like that at all. Jane helped him, wiping her eyes for she had just uncovered a cache of Mary's dolls and toys, and picked up George's old tattered *Soldiers of the Queen*. George looked at it sentimentally.

'That was the first book I ever had,' he said, 'and old Stryker gave it to me.'

'Stryker,' said Jane, smiling, 'I don't think that man has ever been out of your thoughts over all these years. I feel I know him better than almost anybody.'

'In a way I'm glad Stryker's not alive to see the mess they're making of the war,' George said. 'This book's a sort of link with sanity. Who would have thought that it would turn out like this?'

Jane took his hand. He seemed these days to be a pathetic old man, a shadow of his former self. 'We've kept together', she said softly, 'sometimes at Aldershot I wondered if it was worth it. But I'm glad we did. Mary was complaining that we don't go anywhere. But why should we? You've got your books, I've got my knitting, and then we can play the gramophone and listen to

120

the old songs. What do we want to go to the silly pictures for and see a lot of foolish actors and actresses playacting? And I've got the shop. I don't know what I would do without the shop and all the nice people I meet there. There's just two of us now, George, like it was when we started. No more worrying about where Harry is at night, or taking the children to school, or what to do about Mary and whether Leonard ought to give up his piano lessons.'

'I wonder how Harry's doing,' asked George. 'It's a long time since we heard from him.'

'No news is good news,' said Jane with the air of making a discovery, 'and things are quiet on the Western Front. Or so the papers say, though I know you don't believe all you read in them.'

'I think I do this time,' said George. 'It's when they talk about huge successes and marching on to Berlin by Christmas that I get sort of sceptical. Yes, I believe it this time.'

George was right, for the Western Front had settled down into a state of impervious defence. The trench systems stretched all the way from the North Sea down to the Swiss border, like the nerve system of a living creature. There were often as many as half a dozen series of trenches, intricately connected at places known as Piccadilly Circus and Hyde Park Corner, while the Germans, feeling that it was going to be a long war, were burrowing deep into the earth. There were often three levels to their trenches, with modern sanitary equipment built in and electrically-operated pumps to keep them dry. The British and the French, ablaze with the offensive spirit, considered their trenches to be temporary expedients, soon to be left far behind in the march on the Rhine and Berlin.

In Flanders the trenches were often waterlogged for months at a time. In one sector the trenches became full to the brim with foul green-grey water, so that the men lived in island breastworks standing at intervals across a nightmare wilderness. If a duckboard tilted, or an enemy machine-gun opened up, a man could slide into the water, two feet of mud clawing at him, and never come up again. Rats as large as rabbits lived in the festering conditions, sport for boyish subalterns who hunted them with revolvers.

Between the trenches was no man's land, varying in width

between a hundred yards and a mile or two. Mined, criss-crossed with barbed wire, humped into mindless ugliness by thousands of craters, it was ventured into by black-faced night patrols, crossed by thousands during offensives, and recrossed by thousands more on a counter-offensive. The rotting bodies of unidentifiable soldiers lay beside the skeletons of those who had gone before. A charnel-house under the sky, witness of the success of defensive warfare and the triumph of the machine-gun.

Harry Oakwood, after his indecisive role in the first battle of Ypres, was sent back to depot and resolved that never again would he let those idiots of generals put him at risk. One night he sat in his billet and thought it through. What could he do that few others could? The answer came to him right away. He knew about cars. So while his comrades were whoring and drinking he systematically went about on a borrowed motor-cycle trying to find some officer whom he had helped when he had been stationed in Warwick, preferably one who did not know why water should be put into a radiator and why a motor-car did not run on paraffin (easily available from the quartermaster on an indent).

Eventually he found one. He would have preferred to have got himself re-employed by Lieutenant Wilcox, but that officer had apparently been posted to a front-line division and was out of reach. What Harry wanted was a red-braided staff officer, not especially endowed with courage, and he found one in Major Cross, a Territorial Army officer who, although Harry's age—and Harry was now thirty—tried to behave like a twenty-one year old subaltern, and who, although middle class, tried to give the impression of belonging to the top ten thousand. Harry had met him briefly when driving Lieutenant Wilcox's Darracq.

Harry had preened himself to the eyes and, compared with the mass of soldiers, he looked like a recruiting advertisement. Searching for likely officers he went to the best *estaminet* in the town.

'Only officers in here,' said the proprietor coldly but Harry ignored him, looking round and spotting Major Cross, with a good meal under his belt and bleary with gin.

'Excuse me, sir,' he said deferentially, 'do you remember

me? I advised on the motor-car you bought in Leamington. I was Lieutenant Wilcox's driver.'

'It was a bloody good car,' said Cross benevolently.

'You have it with you, sir?' asked Harry politely.

'They wouldn't let me bring it,' growled Cross. He brooded on this for a while.

'They're useful to have', observed Harry, 'and I know where there is an old Darracq. A bit old but it only needs a little work on it.'

Cross put his finger on the problem. 'There are no bloody French mechanics,' he said. 'They've all bolted like the bloody rabbits they are.'

He eyed Harry speculatively, found out who his company commander was, and when he went to the headquarters the next morning, pulled a few strings. Harry found himself on attachment to divisional headquarters. The Darracq was no figment of the imagination. He had spotted it in a garage, apparently owned by the local mayor who had fled when the shelling became too close. It was a similar model to that owned by Wilcox and he knew it inside out. He told Major Cross that it would cost thirty pounds to put it in working order and when he had received this in francs, he searched out a needy sergeant-armourer who made one or two parts for a mess of tattered French money.

It was like old times, thought Harry as he took off his jacket and prepared to give the car a good clean. A few of the villagers looked up when he drove it out, but no one attempted to argue with him.

Major Cross was in raptures when Harry brought it to him. 'It's none of my business where you got it from, Oakwood,' he said. 'Have a word with my transport sergeant about petrol, and we'll go for a spin tomorrow. I've got to visit a mortar-training regiment.'

Major Cross, formerly looked upon as a desk-bound fellow who drank too much gin, became more highly regarded as he eagerly sought out jobs. Visits to retraining depots, machine-gun schools, and experimental stations built to deal with the poison gas threat, all were carried out by Major Cross— provided that the trips did not go too close to the front line.

The weeks passed into months. Harry was happy. He had his

123

own billet, and did a deal with the farmer who owned it, selling him army petrol at a cheap rate for the farmer's tractor. While the men in the trenches were surviving on hard biscuits and bully beef Harry ate steak, fresh vegetables, with ample bacon and egg. Always well groomed, subservient and willing to turn out any time day or night to drive Cross where he wanted, whether it was to a regiment fifty miles away or a château where Cross had ingratiated himself with the local aristocracy, Harry had no fear that he would be rudely despatched to the front, though he kept in touch with events. In the summer of 1915, with the Western Front stagnant, Joffre insisted that the British should attack at Loos in a district of mining villages. The German line was shaken, and the British command was urged to throw all the reserves into the attack including cooks, clerks, storemen and, by implication, Harry.

As it happened the reserves were kept by Sir John French too far in the rear to keep the attack going and the British suffered 50,000 casualties (against 20,000 German). Harry breathed again. He listened as Major Cross explained the political inferences to him.

'French has done it this time,' Major Cross said, grinning. 'He's blamed Haig in his official report. I was shown a copy this morning. Kitchener doesn't like French, Haig doesn't like French and, come to think of it, I don't like French. And Haig's got backstairs influence, Harry. He's in with royalty and he and the King write to each other like old pals. Haig's the coming man, and anyway I like a man who reminds me of one of my favourite beverages. I even had a soft spot for General Booth, though I was never of his persuasion. Is he anything to do with Booth's gin, do you think?'

'I don't think so, sir,' said Harry, keeping a straight face.

'You can never tell with these religious jossers,' said the major, brooding. 'Never mind, I've more important things to think about. Tomorrow we've to go to the trials of the new Lewis gun, and the day after that we're back at that bloody gas experimental station. I got a whiff of that chlorine gas which the Huns used at Ypres last April. They thought they were doing me a favour.'

Thinking no more about the major's engagements, Harry went off that evening to his mademoiselle in the town brothel—a clean, pretty girl, promising to put on a bit of weight with the chocolates that Harry took her. Major Cross, toddling over to the mess for a few gins to prepare himself for the trials of the Lewis gun, which he knew were noisy and gave him a headache, gave Harry permission to use the car.

Whilst Harry was engaged in love-making, a provost-sergeant and a French gendarme were doing the rounds of the red light district, and saw the big car parked discreetly off the road.

'That is something that our officers would not do so blatantly,' said the gendarme stiffly.

'It could be one of your officers,' said the sergeant, sniffing. He privately considered the French a dirty lot of swine having been given a pack of obscene postcards the previous night.

'All right then', said the gendarme, 'let us wait. They are what we call dix minutes girls there—what do you call them?'

'Short timers,' said the sergeant.

They lit cigarettes, and stood in a doorway. Harry came out buttoning his tunic. The gendarme scratched his head, puzzled.

'But he's not an officer,' he protested. 'What does it mean? A motor-car? Is he one of your, what do you say, gentleman rankers?'

The sergeant did not know. There were all kinds of odds and sods about these days; you could never tell whether a Terrier was a gent who had joined to fight the Huns or just a common soldier. He resolved to look further into it and jotted down the number of the car in his notebook.

Harry rated the visits of Major Cross on interest. The Lewis gun demonstration ranked low on the list, as Harry made a vow to keep as far away from this dangerous-looking weapon as he could. The trip the following day to the gas experimental station seemed to be equally boring. The very thought of poison gas gave Harry the shivers. He had seen, behind the lines, the effects of it, the yellow-faced men coughing up blood, and the mild attacks, croaking and unable to speak, eyes staring wildly. He had also examined with detached curiosity the early respirators made from impregnated army shirts and consisting of a bag, enclosing the head and neck, eyepieces, and a rubber breathing valve held between the teeth. After a few minutes a

125

man was bathed in sweat, half-suffocated and unable to see because the eyepieces misted over.

The experimental station consisted of a group of widely-spaced huts around a large field, the centre of which was dug into trenches to simulate front line conditions. An ash-covered patch served as a parking area for the motor-cycles and cars and Harry drew up alongside a long lean foreign car that he did not recognize. Major Cross climbed out, dusted down his uniform, and made his way to one of the huts. Harry lit a cigarette, and got out to examine the car, peering inside, and aimlessly tapping the tyres with his boots.

'Hi, soldier!' shouted someone.

Harry looked up. He was being addressed from a distance by an officer whose badges of rank were almost obliterated by yellow powder, and whose trousers were scorch-marked and frayed, bulging out of high boots. His hair was long and lank and as Harry, realizing that he was the only soldier within yelling distance, walked over, he could see that the officer wore thick pebbled glasses.

'What are you?' asked the officer. 'Oh, a lance-corporal. Never mind, that doesn't matter. What are you here for?'

'I'm Major Cross's driver, sir,' said Harry.

'Major Cross? Who's he?' asked the man. 'Yes, yes, I know. He won't be out for half an hour or more, so you can help us.'

'My instructions, sir, are to stay with the motor-car,' said Harry, and the officer hesitated, rubbing the back of his hair with his fingers and scattering a film of yellow dust over his shoulders.

Unobserved a sergeant-major had crept up and was listening to the exchange. 'I'm certain that Major Cross would not mind the corporal helping you, sir,' he said benignly, and turned his attention to Harry. 'My, my,' he said *sotto voce*, 'a real chocolate soldier. All right, boyo, have you anything else to say?'

Heart sinking, Harry replied, 'No, Sergeant-Major.' He followed the officer into one of the huts and looked dismayed at a collection of respirators and masks on a long trestle table.

The officer picked up a contraption of rubber and celluloid. A tube connected with a meat tin crammed with layers of gauze. A sergeant looked at Harry and then at the officer, and

126

sprinkled in some liquid from a bottle on to the gauze. He then put the lid on the tin, taping it airtight.

'If it just dangles down it will fall off the tube, Sergeant,' said the officer.

'Suppose he stuffs it in his tunic, and then buttons over it, sir,' suggested the sergeant. He, too, wore glasses, and had an educated voice.

'Good idea,' said the officer approvingly, and undid Harry's tunic, pushed in the tin, did up the buttons, while the sergeant got the respirator and thrust it unceremoniously over Harry's head, tying straps behind.

'Breathe through your mouth,' said the officer. 'Can you understand me?'

Harry nodded, his nose jammed against the rubber, and the eyepiece already misting up and sliding sideways. The sergeant took Harry's arm and led him to one of the trenches, helping him down wooden steps, while the officer followed, carrying a canister.

Another trench, covered with corrugated iron, led off the main trench, and Harry was thrust into this. The officer looked at his watch.

'We'll give you five minutes, Corporal.'

He tossed in the canister. Harry retreated from the swirling yellow smoke, only to find that the trench was a dead-end. By now, the eyepieces were completely opaque, and Harry stumbled clumsily towards the hissing canister, panic beginning to seize him as he found more and more difficulty in breathing. He tried to wrench the respirator off and struggled wildly, but all that happened was that the tube connecting the mask with the tin came away.

He rolled the bottom of the mask up, and caught the acrid stench of smoke, but found it impossible to get the contraption off any further. He held his breath, and made a dash for it over the canister and into fresh air, but he came up against iron railings that jarred the breath out of his body. The bastards, he thought, he was going to die of gas. He staggered again to the back of the trench. He remembered that gas and smoke rose, and he lay on the ground, trying to gauge whether there was air down there.

The air seemed to sob in his lungs. What a way to go, he

127

thought bitterly, and resigned himself to his fate. The iron railings clanked as the sergeant pulled them across the entrance and from a distance Harry heard the two experimenters walk towards him, hoisting him to his feet and dragging him into the main trench.

'That hasn't told us much,' complained the officer, looking at Harry speculatively.

'We should have clipped the tube in,' said the sergeant, looking angrily at the victim. 'These soldiers don't realize that we are trying to help them.'

'You bastards!' Harry wheezed out, 'you tried to gas me!'

'Nonsense', retorted the officer sturdily, 'it was only smoke. It was, wasn't it, sergeant?'

'Just a touch of chlorine to make the experiment more realistic,' admitted the sergeant, 'but it shouldn't have been dangerous.'

He untied the strap around Harry's head and drew off the respirator.

'He shouldn't have gone that colour,' he said disapprovingly. 'They must have put more gas in that smoke bomb than they said.'

'Major Cross can take a memo back to headquarters,' said the officer. 'If you can't trust your suppliers, whom can you trust?'

'Indeed, sir,' agreed the sergeant. 'Major Cross will have to drive himself back. I think we ought to send this chap to hospital. Otherwise divisional headquarters will scream to have us closed down again. Like they did after the last man we had here.'

So Harry found himself in hospital with a mild attack of gas poisoning. While he was there the provost-marshal made discreet enquiries about a car seen outside a well-frequented brothel. Although he was satisfied that Lance-Corporal Oakwood was in the clear and was about to drop the matter a transport corporal, whom he had interviewed, remarked about the vast quantities of petrol the Darracq consumed. Although it was never established that Harry was selling petrol on the black market, the suspicion was sufficient to encourage Major Cross to drop his driver like a hot brick. Anyway, the fellow had behaved like a silly fool by taking off the respirator and it was his own fault that he was in hospital. He felt no animus against Harry, and was sorting out some safe behind-the-lines unit to have him sent to. Only when the gendarmerie began making enquiries about the disappearance of the mayor's motor-car did Major Cross have second thoughts about his one-time driver, and the day it was retrieved by two French gendarmes was the day that he arranged a front-line posting for Lance-Corporal Harry Oakwood.

That was the trouble when you gave ordinary soldiers a helping hand, reflected Major Cross. They took advantage of you. To the chagrin of his colleagues, Major Cross lost interest in visiting out-of-the-way places, doing the necessary chores of a staff officer at divisional headquarters, and once more became a mundane desk-bound Territorial nobody, given to bouts of hard drinking.

17

The company of the Lancashire Fusiliers came to their positions in the front line amidst a constant crackle of machine-gun and rifle fire. There was a buzzing round the heads of the troops. Private Alfred Bates, recently married to Mary, only daughter of ex-Sergeant-Major George Oakwood, asked his guide what the noise was.

'Bloody rooky!' muttered the man to himself, and then told Alfred that they were German bullets flying by and intended for any fool who cared to stand upright.

The men arrived at the front-line breastworks. One of them stood up and looked over the top.

'Get down, you bloody fool!' screamed the guide.

'Is that where the Germans are?' asked a soldier politely. There was no time to answer him, for almost at once he fell in a heap. 'Somebody knocked me over. I've been hit on the jaw.' As he spoke he spat out a bullet. It had gone through his cheek, knocked out a couple of teeth and lodged inside his mouth. 'Is that a Blighty?' he asked innocently.

'No,' growled the guide. God, he thought, these newcomers. The twenty-year-old subalterns were bad enough, going over the top without encouragement and usually dragging a dozen seasoned veterans with them. But these boobies . . .

He bumped into the men in front of him and cursed. A shell had landed an hour or two before in the trench and the dead were still lying there half-hidden in puddles of muddy water.

'Use 'em as stepping stones,' shouted the guide. 'They can't feel nothing. They're all dead, you see, all dead.'

Shuddering the men did as they were told, averting their eyes from the upturned faces, looking like hollowed-out hallowe'en turnips.

Other soldiers watched the newcomers from caverns cut in the side of the trenches, lit by hurricane lamps and candles. Some of them called out 'Good luck!' but most of them were silent. Alfred was surprised that they looked so dirty and grubby.

'Keep yourself clean and tidy,' his sergeant had yelled at him and his companions, 'then the bugs won't get yer.'

Eventually they reached their own stretch of line and the guide left them. Alfred and a dozen others were led into one of the dugouts, treading gingerly on the duckboards, eyeing the bunks set above the mud level. A fatigue man brought in two sandbags and plonked them on the table, kept in place by sandbags piled around the legs.

'Your rations,' he said, and went.

The men sorted out the spirit stove and began to cook themselves bacon and eggs. With food inside them, stomach-churning fear gave way to apprehension.

The tea was stewed and bitter but eagerly drunk. Alfred, a great one for tea as Mary had found out at Llandudno, drank three cups, and then went out of the dug-out to find the latrine. There did not seem any about, so he looked about him and not seeing anybody, went to the side of the trench, unbuttoning his flies. For the moment he forgot where he was and stood upright. A bullet caught him between the eyes. Mary was a widow.

130

She received the news philosophically. Alfred had already joined the pantheon of film star heroes, too good to live. His death made little difference to the Oakwoods' life. Mary wanted to stay with her in-laws. Jane was resentful, but George shrugged his shoulders and accepted it.

Occasionally he would get a postcard from Harry. It had been a shock to get one from a military hospital. Poor lad, he had thought as he read that Harry had got a small dose of poison gas. Harry had turned out to be a fighting soldier in the tradition of the Oakwoods after all. And he had made lance-corporal, that was something. Harry was writing about possible convalescent leave. Maybe they would see him.

Although never really ill, Harry had stretched out his mild attack of poison gas. When he was sent home to England in hospital blue he was inclined to play up the role, though a nurse in the convalescent home at Tunbridge Wells had realized the truth about Harry when he had put his hands up her skirt when she was bringing him his late-night cocoa.

'If that's what gas does to you', she had said primly, 'I don't want to know.'

And she had meant it.

One morning the surgeon examined Harry and patted him on the shoulder. 'Nothing much the matter now with you, young man, it's back to your unit. I'll telephone your commanding officer at Warwick and see about a spot of leave.'

The officer at the other end agreed. 'He's due to go into the front line so I think we can stretch a point, though they are screaming for infantry for a new offensive.'

One of the privates in the orderly room in France had told Harry that he was being posted to the front, so he knew that the days with Major Cross were over. Not that he was worried. He had scrambled out of the fighting area before and he would do it again. He was more interested in the leave and what he could accomplish during that time. And because Harry had no wish to go up to Birmingham to see his parents, he settled down to ten days of pleasure.

However, as the days sped by, Harry thought more and more of his return to the Western Front. He tried to increase his heartbeat for the benefit of the local military hospital surgeon by smoking a cigarette with aspirin on the glowing end but the

131

doctor had come across this one before and denied him extra leave. There did not seem any way out of it, except deserting, but this he knew would do nothing except land him for a long spell in the glasshouse. Or they might shoot him.

He was rekitted at an infantry depot in London and found himself on a troop train bound for Southampton. The animation and high spirits of the early days were dissipated. Many of the men travelling with him had heard that conscription was about to be introduced and had joined non-fighting arms like the Pioneer Corps. Harry found that his war stories were greeted with derision.

'I got gassed,' he began.

'More fool you,' interrupted a man reading a newspaper.

It was odd, decided Harry, trying to boast about his bravery when he felt exactly the same as these men, only interested in survival. He leaned back in his corner seat, deliberately knocking the ankles of the man opposite him with his boots, then leering at him and pointing to his stripe in case the man got obstreperous.

He thought about life, about his first girl, the typist who worked for Cotman. He could not remember her name, but he could recall the smell of that house in Montgomery Street and, by God, he could remember the smell in that foul house of Judy's, with the old man peeping through the wall at them doing the naughty. If you wanted to blame somebody for getting him into this mess there was a prime one for you—Judy.

He wondered where she was now. Probably riddled with syphilis in some isolation hospital but not before giving it to half the Warwickshires who haunted the stage doors of the Birmingham Hippodrome. They would probably give it to the French whores, and when he took another one he would probably catch it. And all from Judy.

Harry had found a scapegoat and he brooded on this all the way to the docks. Another lance-corporal took his arm as he edged his way down the platform towards the quayside.

'Do you want to be i/c draft with me?'

'No thank you,' growled Harry. 'I'll pig in with the rabble.'

18

'He knows his aeroplanes all right', said the drill sergeant, 'but he's got two left feet and always will have.' He was speaking of Private Leonard Oakwood, RFC.

'A quiet one, that Oakwood,' said the corporal, 'always got his head stuck in a book.'

The war-time lot, he thought, were different from the pre-war recruits. A lad like Oakwood would have had a sorry time of it, badgered and bullied by the barrack-room tough nuts. But where were they now, the loud-mouths who made life hell for the quiet and the inconspicuous? They were dying in France by the bucket-load.

Of course, the corporal considered as he made his way to the cook-house, you still had your braggarts in the RFC just as you had them in the infantry. But they were more unsure of themselves. They had to do more than polish their boots and click their heels on the square. They had to learn things and if they did not learn them they would be sent to some undemanding service which only needed a steady finger on the trigger. So blokes who knew their aeroplanes were one step up, even if they did keep their heads in a book. This wouldn't help Oakwood to become an officer; it wouldn't help him become a pilot, but it would make him a damned good mechanic.

When Sergeant Erskine came across Leonard Oakwood he was at one with the corporal.

'Civilian mechanics are all very well, Sergeant,' his officer had told him, 'but you can't deal with them as you can with your own. They want sheets on their beds, and that sort of pampering.'

Captain Lucas, RFC, was disillusioned with the air force. He remembered with what enthusiasm he had joined in 1913 when the total number of aircraft in the corps was one hundred and one, none of which was suitable for warfare. He remembered reading what the MP Joynson-Hicks had said in Parliament: 'The right honourable gentleman might have 101 aeroplanes which can fly: so he might have 101 tomtits that can fly.' He recalled Joynson-Hicks turning up at the aerodrome where he was stationed counting every aeroplane he could, while cynics said that the RFC had but one aircraft and had been instructed to fly it round ahead of Joynson-Hicks's visiting commission so that the MPs had counted the same machine each time at a different airfield.

And the absurdities of it all! Lucas had been trained in artillery spotting, and one of the methods he had been encouraged to try was using Klaxon horns fitted beneath the fuselage. 'It will chill the hearts of the enemy', said his commanding officer ironically, 'but it won't help our gunners one little bit. You'd better try coloured flags, old chap, and if that doesn't work, coloured lights. Then you can go on a bombing course at Montrose.'

'But that's in Scotland, sir,' Lucas had pointed out.

'You may be able to get in a little salmon-fishing,' said his CO.

The bombing had been no more impressive, because no one had invented an aerial bomb and two-pound bags of flour had been substituted. The course had been terminated when a laird with friends in high office had had one of his sheep killed by a bag of flour that had been inadequately stored and had acquired the qualities of concrete.

With his CO, Major Brooke-Popham, Lucas had taken up a Henri Farman biplane to shoot at kites with rifles. This was more dangerous to the ground observers, and the kite was usually drawn back to the ground without as much as a single bullet-hole in it. As for night flying, Captain Lucas shuddered when he recalled his experiences with petrol flares that went out when he was coming in to land, or blazed up under his wing-tips, or simply blew away and tempted him to land on a ploughed field.

Sergeant Erskine had had his moments, too, as he had speculated on the sheer incompetence of the French aero-engine manufacturers. With brows knitted he had looked at fractured petrol pipes, broken rocker bars, push-rods flying loose, cracked engine bearers, and petrol leaking from the tank, all due to the lack of balance of the 50 h.p. Gnome rotary engine. Given a hundred pounds, Erskine considered, he could produce an engine that would knock spots off this bloody Frog thing, which he deliberately pronounced with a hard G.

'Do you know my worst experience in the corps, Sergeant?' Captain Lucas had once asked Erskine.

'Watching a G'nome fall apart, sir?' asked Erskine brightly.

'The G is silent as in gnu,' said Lucas automatically. 'No, Sergeant, it was when I was flying a Maurice Farman Longhorn, went into a cloud, and came out of it to see a huge hill directly ahead of me. I knew every inch of Salisbury Plain, and this hill wasn't on it. After a few seconds I realized that I was pointing vertically downwards and this was not a hill but the ground below. I pulled back on the stick, but nothing happened, not a bloody thing. I thought it was all up with me. So I pushed the stick foward, and came out of the dive, upside-down.'

'If the Maurice Farman had had a G'nome instead of a Renault engine your wings would have fallen off, sir,' Erskine had said.

'You may be right, Sergeant, you may be right,' Lucas had speculated.

Sergeant Erskine was never slow in pointing out the defects of French aero-engines to his mechanics. 'Now, Oakwood,' he said, 'always remember this. Anything can go wrong with a Frog engine. You may think you have got it mastered, but you will be wrong. When you go to France you may have the luck never to see a G'nome rotary but I doubt it. So watch out for the warning signs—paint coming off the petrol tank showing some defect in the metal, petrol pipes that look a bit crinkled, and nuts and bolts dropping on to your bloody feet.'

'I'll remember it, Sergeant,' said Oakwood.

'Good lad. Any questions?'

'Any chance of me being a flyer?' asked Oakwood.

'We'll wait and see,' said Erskine evasively.

Oakwood would be too useful on the ground, and so it seemed as Leonard spent his time swinging propellers for the flyers, scraping carbon off the valves of engines and occasionally acting as cook's mate.

His enthusiasm for such mundane duties caught the eye of Lieutenant Webb, a dapper, monocled figure who, owing to the absence of any medical examination for likely RFC officers, managed to conceal the fact that he only had one eye.

135

'You can be my mechanic,' he told Leonard. 'Care for a spin?'

Leonard could hardly speak with delight, and he looked down at the countryside around Farnborough from the observer's seat in Webb's Blériot.

In early 1915 he was promoted to first-class air mechanic, and flew with Lieutenant Webb to France as a minor member of Number Three Squadron, equipped with the new Morane.

'It's still got a Frog engine', Sergeant Erskine had told him, 'but it's a Le Rhône. Better than the G'nome or the Renault. The guv'nor has asked me to fix someone up with a course in wireless sets. You'll take that in France. It might get you into the air, my lad, now that they're putting wireless sets in aeroplanes.'

He gave Leonard a friendly pat on the shoulder. After the cretins who could not tell a crankshaft from a tail-plane Leonard was a welcome change.

'Wireless?' Major Strangeways had asked him, bemused. 'Nothing about wireless here. No, what we want is a good hand with the new Lewis gun.'

'I'm going to fly then, Sir?' asked Leonard breathlessly.

'Course you are,' said Strangeways. 'Get a few hours in on the rifle-range and I'll send you and Lieutenant Webb out on a reconnoitre.'

'Well, Oakwood,' said Webb one morning, 'we're going after the Germans today. Get yourself wrapped up and make certain you get a scarf round your face. It helps to keep the oil off it.'

They took off at 10 am, made 6,000 feet in twelve minutes over Béthune, and crossed the lines, moving north-east. Over La Bassée Leonard saw three tiny yellow specks. It was his first view of the enemy.

Going north at 8,000 feet over Violanes, Leonard heard a noise rather like china being flung to the ground and saw several balls of white smoke floating away. He watched, fascinated. The anti-aircraft shrapnel fragments each left a thin line of smoke, so that as each shell burst the shrapnel seemed to come from each explosion in the shape of a fan. The three German craft were climbing at a faster speed than the Morane could make and, turning to throw off the anti-aircraft gunners, Webb flew east.

There was little to be seen and although Leonard peered anxiously through his binoculars at the pattern of fields and woodland below, too far behind the front line to be pitted by craters, there did not seem any targets for the six melinite bombs that he had by his feet. Webb looked at him, shrugged his shoulders, and turned for home, dipping over the front line to see if there were any German transport waggons or lorries about. But all was quiet and the aircraft returned without incident.

Leonard was disappointed, but this was overlaid by the depression that hung over the whole squadron, for three pilots had been lost that day. One had been burned alive when his plane had force-landed nearby, another was posted missing after his plane had been hit by British anti-aircraft fire and had glided over the German lines and a third had been killed outright when his aircraft blew up in mid-air. Two of the squadron's mechanics, doubling as bombers and gunners, had also been lost. Leonard found himself promoted to sergeant, in charge of all the engines in his particular flight.

A batch of civilian mechanics arrived from England, several of them having been motor mechanics.

'I wouldn't trust half of them with my daughter's bicycle', said a grizzled veteran to Leonard, 'but I'll keep an eye on them, Sergeant. Those lads up there depend on us, and I'll make that bloody plain to them. I ain't above giving them a clip around the ear.'

Leonard was approached by Major Strangeways regarding the abilities of the civilian mechanics. 'Pretty good, Sir,' he said. 'Mr Cliff knows about aero engines.'

'He should do,' said the major, 'he did some work for Blériot.' He eyed Leonard speculatively. 'We were expecting replacements but the War Office have held them up to repel supposed air raids on London. They've even got the cheek to ask us if we can release any flyers. So you may be called upon to act as artillery spotter.' He nodded and moved away.

Three Vickers Gun Buses were flown in from England. Sergeant Oakwood and his team checked them over. They were small pusher aircraft with a reputation for unreliability, and as Leonard signed receipts for them Lieutenant Webb came up, putting on his gloves.

'Come on, Oakwood,' he said and ten minutes later they were in the air.

Ten minutes later, they were landing, petrol spluttering from a fractured pipe.

'As bad as the others,' said Lieutenant Webb in disgust.

The mechanics blamed the Morane aeroplane for the spate of losses the squadron had been suffering. Leonard found that some of the engine-trouble that the plane was subject to was due to the type of sparking-plug, which became incandescent after the engine had been running for a while.

'Good work, Sergeant', said the commanding officer, clapping him on the shoulder, and Leonard flushed with pride. He was sent to Paris to the Le Rhône works to collect replacement plugs, and when he returned he found that Lieutenant Webb had failed to return from a patrol flying a single-seater Bristol Scout. Two days later a German plane flew overhead and dropped a note to say that Lieutenant Webb's machine had been shot down by anti-aircraft fire over Fournes and that the occupant had been captured near the village.

In late spring the squadron was moved to Auchel, and Leonard was approached by Captain Lewis. Lewis always had a cigarette in his mouth and a way of lifting up his head and squinting to escape the smoke as he spoke. 'Plenty of old men to do the mechanic's job, Sergeant,' he said. 'Fancy a bit of flying?'

'More than anything, sir,' said Leonard enthusiastically.

'There's an old Blériot we can take out without anybody knowing,' said Lewis. 'Give us a whirl, and jump in. It's a damned slow thing and it's got a big cockpit so we can swap over when you feel you have the hang of it.'

Before Leonard could swing the propeller, the squadron commander came over and spoke to Lewis.

'There's a German peppering the trenches north of the Bois de Beiz. You'd better take a Morane. There's a Lewis gun aboard and a couple of drums of ammunition. Just show the flag, there's a good fellow. The divisional commander has been on the telephone and he wants to show the boys in the trenches that we are doing something.' He looked reflectively at Leonard, but did not say anything.

'Come on, Sergeant,' said Lewis urgently, 'he means you as well.'

Happily Leonard settled himself in the observer's cockpit and sighted up the gun, and they were soon on their way. As they neared the line they saw a speck in the sky about the same height as the Morane, going swiftly backwards and forwards but as they got within half a mile the German plane turned east. As it banked Leonard could clearly see the black crosses on the upper surfaces of the wings. Lewis pursued him for a while but the German plane clearly had a speed advantage over the Morane, and eventually Lewis broke off contact.

Something caught Leonard's attention, and he leaned over, bracing himself against the swirling slip-stream, pointing down. Lewis nodded. It was a small German machine just above the lines, ripe for attack. Lewis slid the machine sideways and Leonard saw the rudder flap on the tail click over. He was to fire his first shots in anger but, excited, he pressed the trigger too soon. It was just like throwing pebbles, he reflected, and held himself back until the enemy machine was closer. As it drew within range a light signal came from the German side of the line, and three other German machines appeared from nowhere.

Lewis climbed desperately, but the enemy aircraft were quicker, and gained on the Morane. Thank God they were not fitted to fire through the propeller, as the new Fokker was, thought Leonard. He knew what their procedure would be. They would fly alongside, and then turn off to allow their gunner to fire over their tail as they turned. That was the way they were trained. He knew that his pilot was aware of this and Lewis flashed him a quick nod. The aircraft reached their level and prepared to take their turn in flying alongside. The four men in the two aircraft stared at each other across thirty yards of airspace. Suddenly Lewis dropped like a stone, and Leonard, expecting such a manoeuvre, opened fire with the machine-gun at the exposed belly of the German plane. He could see clearly a pattern of holes appearing in the underwing of the enemy and almost heard the twanging of broken wires and struts. A shot struck the left wheel, which spun eccentrically and flicked off like an athlete throwing a discus, and the axle crumpled in.

Pieces were dropping from the fuselage, and the enemy plane

slipped away. The second plane in the line was now above them, the pilot not reacting to the British manoeuvre, and Lewis held the machine steady to let Leonard have a few shots at that one, too. But the third plane had changed direction and was at them sideways, the gunner hanging on and pumping bullets along the whole length of the Morane. Fragments of paint and wood flew into Leonard's face as Lewis broke off contact and dipped his nose.

Ground batteries were firing at them, but it was impossible to say whether they were friendly or enemy. The crackling shrapnel forced the enemy off, and they flew off towards the east, one of them limping nearer and nearer the ground. Fortunately it seemed that the Morane was not badly damaged, for Lewis gained height without anything amiss happening. At 4,000 feet Leonard looked about him, to see what damage there was. He took off his goggles to facilitate inspection, and although the wind made his eyes run he could see more clearly. The tail-plane had a few ominous holes in it, and the wing wires had suffered considerably. He then looked at the pilot. To his horror, the flying jacket of Captain Lewis was stained red all over the shoulder.

Lewis turned his head with difficulty, giving his sergeant an appealing look. Leonard swallowed, and while Lewis kept the plane at a level keel at a speed that was steady yet above stalling Leonard, clinging by his fingernails (he had discarded his gloves) to the framework of the machine, sidled above him, head low to avoid being blown off, and pulled himself into the pilot's cockpit. The pilot gave a cry of pain, but tried to suppress it, giving instructions through clenched teeth.

Ice cold but sweating at the forehead, Leonard tried to follow them, his fingers clumsy and raw with the wind. 'Try climbing,' Lewis urged, 'now rudder left, good, good, now level up, careful, throttle, man, throttle, otherwise we'll stall . . . that's it . . . try nose down, not too steep, now look for a level field.' Leonard peered out of the cockpit. He could see figures below, apparently waving. However as rifle bullets bit into the wings he realized that they were not waving but shooting. They were still over German territory.

Although Lewis was not in a state to note the compass and seemed only concerned in giving Leonard rudimentary instruction, Leonard cursed himself for not taking any notice of the direction. He carefully banked the plane until it was going due west, but as the air speed dropped he realized that they were flying directly into a stiff wind. The primitive fuel gauge was flickering near the empty mark. Coming up Leonard saw the black line of trenches, a scar across the countryside. Beyond that must be safety. He counted three trenches close together, then a wide open space.

The engine stuttered and the two-bladed propeller stopped, and seemed to turn backwards. The silence was unearthly. Only the wind through the struts, the click of the rudder flap and ailerons, the sighing of the wings. Leonard gripped the controls, remembering that to move in too slow was as bad as going in too fast. A stall at this height could send the machine toppling back on its tail, shaking him and Lewis out like dice from a games box.

Occupied with keeping the speed regular, Leonard only realized slowly that this was no ordinary open field. Near at hand there were savage ruts, crater holes, mangled tree trunks, all hazards to a learner flyer or, indeed, the most experienced aviator in the Royal Flying Corps. Had there been fuel in the tank he could have climbed up for a more cautious landing, but he felt helpless. He sensed rather than felt the wheels skimming the surface, then lowered all flaps. The plane bucked, put its nose up, and crunched back on its tail, before sliding in an arc. Giddy, terrified, Leonard crouched as low as he could, arms over his head, his eyes closed. Somehow the plane stopped. 'You still need some instruction, Sergeant,' said Lewis drowsily, 'but not bad for a first attempt.'

Smoke was pouring back at them, and there was the crackle of fire. As if from far off Leonard heard a voice.

'There's nobody in the back seat. Try the front.'

A strange face peered through the mist. 'Two of them in here, Corp,' said another voice.

'For Christ's sake pull 'em out before the bloody thing goes up in flames,' said an authoritative NCO.

Leonard felt strong arms beneath him, and then passed out.

He awoke in a dug-out. There was the smell of frying bacon and egg, and a mug of hot sweet tea was thrust into his hands. His first words were about Captain Lewis.

'He's wounded, but not too badly. Caught one in the shoulder. Struck the shoulder blade and bounced off, that's what the sawbones said. Lost a lot of blood but he should be all right. We thought you were wounded at first, but it was his blood on your tunic. Who was flying that bloody thing, you or him?'

'He was, until he was wounded,' replied Leonard. He sat up, but his head ached so much that he lay down again.

'We watched you coming in,' said the man disapprovingly. 'You were wobbling all over the place and, by God, you had to drop into no man's land. Lucky the trenches are a long way apart and the Huns are a bit lax these days. You've got one of my corporals to thank for getting you in.'

Leonard felt that he had to say something in his own defence. 'No fuel', he said indignantly 'and besides I'm a sergeant-mechanic. Never flown before.'

'I'm not making criticisms', said the other gruffly, 'just my chat. We're bally glad to have you with us.'

Leonard's eyes were becoming accustomed to the gloom. He saw that the man talking to him was an officer, probably in his late thirties. His cap was pulled over his eyes, and his uniform was dusty.

'Who are you, Sergeant?' he asked. 'What squadron?'

'Third, sir,' replied Leonard.

'Hmm,' said the officer, 'we've had your lot around here before. They've had a bit of a pasting from those new Fokkers.'

Leonard realized that he had not answered the first part of the question.

'My name's Oakwood, sir.'

The officer looked at him sharply. 'Not a common name', he said, 'I once knew a sergeant of that name. In the Royal Warwickshire Regiment.'

'He was a sergeant-major, sir,' corrected Leonard. 'He's my father.'

'It's a small world,' said Captain Bland softly, 'damn me, it's a small world. He must be getting old now.'

'Just over sixty, sir,' said Leonard.

'I never knew him well', said Leonard's half-brother, 'but my mother knew him in Africa. Tell me about him. I'd like to know more.'

Leonard was surprised, but perhaps the officer was merely

142

passing the time. It must be boring at one of these outposts, never knowing when the enemy was going to sweep along in force. Leonard talked on and on, the candle guttering in its improvised holder. The corporal who had saved Leonard came in with fresh tea and went away again, silently, not wishing to interrupt the monologue. Fancy Captain Bland listening to all that stuff from a bloody sergeant! Who's interested in his dad?

'You must be very proud of him,' said Bland at the end of the recital.

'I've never really thought about it,' said Leonard in surprise.

'I thought his sort had gone for good', said Bland quietly, 'but you still see them. They're the ones who lead their men over the top, the ones who crawl back into no man's land and pull the wounded to safety. And when they finish with the army what happens to them? They have to be commissionaires outside theatres and music halls, or night watchmen! I'm glad he's happy.'

He got up and stretched his legs.

'Eight o'clock', he said, 'we'll be relieved in a quarter of an hour. The Jerries don't shoot on us from eight to nine, and we don't shoot on them. You can go back with us and I'll arrange for a car to return you to your squadron.' He paused at the entrance to the dug-out. 'When you get back home,' he said, 'tell him I asked after him. Captain Bland, the young Captain Bland. And tell him that I don't drink or smoke either. He'll know what I mean.'

19

They waited in the trenches for zero hour, 7.30 am, 1 July 1916. It was the first day of the Battle of the Somme, which witnessed the worst catastrophe to befall British soldiery since the Battle of Hastings. Deafened by the artillery barrage, the bark of the eighteen pounders, the cough of the howitzers, and the surging boom of the heavy guns, Harry Oakwood, lance-corporal the

Warwickshire Regiment, wondered what the hell he was doing there.

As the minutes ticked by, he thought longingly of the days before he had joined that damned army to escape from that cow Judy and her talk of being pregnant, of his easy sovereigns working for Cotman, delivering his pornographic books and then selling his hashed-up cars, with their pistons painted with aluminium paint to disguise their burnt scuffed reality and their tyres wafer-thin, remodelled by a secret process invented by Cotman.

Men like Cotman were profiteering from the war. There was plenty of food for them on the black market. Not that he was jealous of Cotman. He would do the same if he was in his shoes and he admitted that he started the war well, just like a Cotman, worming his way into cushy jobs, batman to Lieutenant Wilcox, driver to Major Cross, picking up a quid here and a quid there from a grateful officer whose car he had put right, fifty francs from a French farmer for whom he had got army petrol . . .

A voice broke into his thoughts.

'All right, Corporal?' it said.

It was Sergeant-Major Jenkins, his face like some kind of mask, his lips compressed.

'Yes, sir,' Harry Oakwood replied.

Jenkins was like his father, he thought savagely, never happier than when leading men to their death. Corporal Oakwood thought about his family. Dad was beneath contempt. If it had not been for him Harry would have kept out of the army, waited for Kitchener to issue his summons and then dropped under cover. Cotman would have found a place for him out of sight.

Sergeant-Major Jenkins did the tour of his company. He looked at Sergeant Marchbanks, who had just returned to the front after a Blighty wound.

'Your promotion is due any day now,' he said.

'If I live to see it,' said Marchbanks with a wry smile. 'What do you think will happen, Sergeant-Major?'

'It's the biggest artillery barrage I've heard', admitted Jenkins, 'and the lads know it. Even Oakwood's lost the gift of the gab. There's smoke and gas out there, but it's not hanging.'

144

He looked at his watch. Not long now.

The shrill blast of the whistle cut into Oakwood's bones like a rapier and, his stomach as heavy as lead, he pulled himself out of the trench and ran. The others were warm and stupid with rum, but Harry had given his mug to a comrade. If he was going to die he would die sober. As he stumbled across the uneven ground, it seemed that he was alone in a pelting storm of machine-gun bullets, shell fragments and clods of earth. Alone, because the other soldiers were like figures on a cinematograph screen, remote, and detached. He could recognize some of the figures but in an uninterested way. Some of them stopped and fell down slowly, as if half-supported by the swirling smoke that clung in water-filled craters. He saw with indifference the man who had been standing beside him in the trench disappear in a fountain of earth. He made a point of not collecting any mates these days. He had been sorry to lose his mate Saunders.

Oakwood mumbled as he went forward, cursing as he ran into the German barbed wire that had not been destroyed by the bombardment. He cut his hand on the wire and the metal of his gun burned his flesh. He ran backwards and forwards trying to find a gap in the wire, broke through a partial gap, and tripped into a flattened trench. He bent his head; if he was to be shot it was not to be in the face. How would he face his mother with his face half blown away?

A hurrying foot cracked into his ribs, and he winced.

An officer ran by, shouting 'Get forward! Don't bunch!'

Wearily Oakwood got to his feet and ran on into the smoke and the spurting soil. A hand clutched him from the choking blackness and he brushed it off. The deep German trench took him unawares and he rolled into it, amongst the men, alive and dead, crawling along in the earth. Corruption and blood stung at his cut hand.

Men were climbing over the other side of the trench, blindly going onwards, but Oakwood carried on down the trench, treading on dead and wounded, their eyes staring up at him beseechingly as fingers crunched beneath his boots. In a hollow off the main trench a German soldier stared at him. Oakwood screamed, took out a grenade and hurled it at the man, forgetting to take the pin out. The grenade hit the man on the bridge

145

of the nose, which burst open, but the eyes continued to stare. The soldier was already dead.

He could hide in there, bury himself in the loose earth at the back in the dark. He seized a German entrenching tool. He dug at the back of the hollow frantically, expecting every minute a bullet in the back from friend or foe. Friend or foe—what was the difference in this madness? He pulled himself into the hollow, retching as a human bone poked through the earth. He heard things that sobbed and moaned and sang and whistled, not knowing whether they were in his head or not. This was the kind of war his dad should have been in! he thought bitterly and anger spurred him on to grope further into the protection of vile-smelling, gas-saturated mould.

His hand throbbed unmercifully and he began to talk to himself, going through the names of all the motor-cars he could remember, wincing as the earth trembled with more shelling. This meant that the battle had either gone forward or backward, he decided, and the crump of a heavy shell nearby threw soil over him as if deposited from the back of a lorry. Fear of suffocation was stronger than fear of being shot, and he felt his arms pinned to his side by the weight of the earth. He tried to scream, but his mouth was full of earth, and his eyes were pressed close shut.

Something in his mind said careful, Harry, take it easy, you're a survivor when these other fools aren't. You're still alive when the others went on and got mown down by Jerry. He tried to move his feet and gradually got movement up to his knees. He managed to twist his waist slowly, freeing one hand, and slowly he clawed his way free from the weight that was squeezing the last ounce of breath from him.

He heard voices.

One said, 'Don't know. Nobody's gone on. There's nobody left. We're wiped out.'

'We'll be all right when the reinforcements arrive,' said another voice.

A third said, 'There aren't any bleeding reinforcements. Look, there's somebody there!'

'There ain't', said the first man, 'and if there is we've got our own troubles.'

'If he's a Queen's Westminster Rifles we ought to see to him.'

'I ain't,' said the first man.

Startlingly near, a machine-gun opened fire, stopped like a man who had forgotten something learned by rote then continued again with greater rapidity. There was a silence. The men had gone or had been killed. It seemed to Oakwood that the thumps had a pattern to them, and he worked out when the next shell would drop, pleased when his prediction was true, disappointed when it was not. Another voice came to him.

'The Jocks are bombing them out of Mametz,' it said.

If that was a line from a music-hall song it wasn't much good, Oakwood considered.

The next thing he knew was that he was loaded on a stretcher.

'Miracle,' said the stretcher-bearer, 'the Jack Johnson must have missed him by a whisker. Good job it didn't go off.'

'My missis probably made that one,' said his mate, 'she works in a munitions factory. Just the damn silly thing she'd do. What's the matter with his hand?'

'Dunno,' said the first man. 'Let's get out of here bloody smart. Whoever you are, hang on, we ain't St John's Ambulance and we're moving sharpish.'

Oakwood did not care which way they were taking him.

'Infection,' said the harassed medical officer at the medical tent, 'tetanus I daresay.'

Did they mean him? thought Oakwood, in a daze. 'Water,' he croaked, 'water.'

A mess-tin of lukewarm water was thrust into his good hand. A white football-like object sufficed for his other.

'Come on, you two,' said the medical officer impatiently, 'we can't spend any more time on that one. There's one here without an arm. For God's sake give him some more morphine.'

The orderly did as he was told, and the screams subsided.

The other orderly looked at Oakwood. 'This one looks like he's had a whiff of gas as well,' he said.

'It's the infection,' the medical officer said tetchily, 'but put him down on the sheet as a possible gas victim.'

The ambulances were running in relays between the field unit and the base hospital. As the drugs wore off Oakwood looked around him, at his fellow sufferers and the stretcher-bearer who was taking the opportunity to get a few hours off, away from the constant rumble of gunfire.

'Want a fag, mate?' he asked, seeing Oakwood's eyes flicker open, and when Oakwood nodded he thrust a cigarette between his lips and lighted it.

'Is it a Blighty?' asked Oakwood.

'Depends,' said the other cautiously. He did not add it depended on whether the bloke had tetanus or not.

20

The major in charge of the flight read Captain Lewis's report, and looked at the man facing him.

'You can fly after a fashion,' he told Leonard. 'We're short of mechanics, but we're short of everything. We're getting some good civvy mechanics coming over.' He looked at Leonard again, sharply and intently. 'So you're to be a pilot. You'll start your instruction on a Henri Farman under Sergeant-Major Holland, and then go on to Gnome Avro. That's all, Sergeant. Good luck.'

Within two months Leonard did his first solo flight. He got off the ground safely enough, but only had a vague recollection of what happened while he was in the air. He went up to 500 feet and came down all the way with the engine roaring away. Only when ten feet from the ground did he switch off, and came in, tail high, at nearly seventy miles per hour. He had seen so many stupid accidents through want of speed that he was determined not to stall on his first solo, even if it meant driving through the aerodrome buildings.

'You've got the idea, lad,' said Sergeant-Major Holland. He liked to see confidence in a pilot. He had seen all sorts of men come in from the first solo; some as white as a sheet, some red-faced and sweating, some of them falling over. Leonard peeled off his gloves and blew on his hands, pleased by Holland's taciturn praise.

'I thought you was going to knock my bleeding head off,' Sarge,' whispered a mechanic as Leonard walked back to his quarters.

He was posted to 20 Squadron at Clairmarais, where FE 2ds were used. Leonard knew about them—powerful two-seaters with a 250 horse-power Rolls-Royce engine at the back, giving the pilot an unrestricted view. Four days later Flight-Sergeant Leonard Oakwood made his first war flight as a pilot, patrolling to stop enemy aircraft from crossing the lines. Down there was one of the heaviest battles of the war. He peered down amongst the smoke. Maybe Harry was amongst that lot.

He had not heard from Harry except through his parents, who had told him that his brother had had a mild attack of gas. But that was some time ago. In the distance he could see a solitary Fokker chaser, but as the FE2 had a range of only three hours he decided not to tackle it, especially as the Fokker had a mile or two of extra speed.

It was odd, he thought, that he should be a sergeant, while his observer, a quiet amiable man in his early thirties, was a lieutenant. It was all this funny thing, class, he considered. Lieutenant Bell was a gentleman, and he was not. There were certain things that the elementary school had never taught him and as he grew older he realized that his mother, whom everyone in the neighbourhood had considered a real lady, was also at a loss when dealing with social niceties.

For four successive days he and the lieutenant went out on patrol, seeing no enemy aircraft and he asked the CO why this was. Leonard learned then that the main force of the enemy was further up the line where the Battle of the Somme was progressing.

'They say it's going well', the CO said idly, 'but that's only relative, isn't it, Sergeant? Talking of relatives, have you got anyone in the war?'

'My brother, sir,' replied Leonard, 'he's in the Warwickshires.'

'Poor bloody infantry, eh, the old PBI. He's probably in the Somme, then. Wish we could do more for the poor beggars. But for the most part we're irrelevant.'

Leonard found the FE2d a delight to fly, and it was so stable that when flying near its ceiling of 16,000 feet he sometimes stood on the seat and looked back, over the engine and tail. His observer was worried by this unconcern, and when Leonard's flying glove came off and glanced off the propeller Leonard himself realized that he was being cocky and did not do it again. Lieutenant Bell was replaced by Lieutenant Scott as his observer. He was a bouncy young man who insisted on calling his pilot Lenny and took him to the *estaminet* in the village for lavish meals.

'War does funny things to one, Lenny,' he said, picking at the creamy cheese, 'it's a true social leveller. What were you before the war? A bank clerk, or something?'

'Something like that,' admitted Leonard.

'I was an upper-class idler,' said Scott, 'sent down from Cambridge, did a bit of hunting and shooting, hung around the Gaiety and Daly's and occasionally did a bit of four-legged frolicking. Liked dancing a lot. Ever been to Murray's?'

'Never heard of it,' said Leonard.

'Never heard of Murray's?' echoed Scott, aghast. 'My dear chap, you don't know what you've missed. They had all the best bands there. You should have seen me dancing the Boston. When I think of before the war I always think of Murray's.'

'It's not my kind of thing,' said Leonard, smiling. 'I was always a quiet one, night school and reading and playing the piano. I left dances and women to Harry, my brother. He was up to all kinds of tricks, was Harry.'

'You sound as though you envied him,' said Scott shrewdly.

'He was just different,' said Leonard uncomfortably, 'a bit of a disappointment to my parents. They always wanted him to go into the army. He did, but there was some girl after him for putting her in the family way. So I heard anyway, though mum and dad never found out.'

'What do they do?' asked Scott.

'My father's retired,' Leonard said, 'he was a sergeant-major, one of the old professional soldiers. My mother's manageress of a shoe shop in Birmingham, and they live over it. I haven't heard from them lately.'

When he had heard, the news was vague. His father did not appear to be doing anything but running errands for his mother. If he knew little about them, he knew less about Harry. He

150

wondered what had happened to the girl Harry had made pregnant. Was he, by any chance, an uncle? He smiled.

Judy was in London, booking into a hotel.

She seemed a nice girl, the manager thought as he returned to his sanctum behind the reception desk; it made a change from the prostitutes who used his hotel as a convenient base for short-time stuff behind the station. And most of them seemed to come from Brum. He had one in now, would bet a pound to a penny that she was on the game. But he supposed her money was as good as anyone else's, and the soldiers en route for France deserved a bit of fun between Euston and Charing Cross.

No one in their right mind would have laid a bet on Judy Abbott. Harry Oakwood would scarcely have recognized her. The initial cause of all his woe, with her story of being pregnant, Judy had left behind her flounces, her frothy petticoats, her hats of chiffon and lace, and her little-girl look in favour of the mature approach. Her hour-glass figure was encased in a close-cut suit of dark material, with a discreet piece of lace at the throat. Her veil was never far away to add an air of mystery. Judy had caught on to the vulnerability of war widows and she had found that by pretending to be bereaved she could go anywhere. The most unlikely people took pity on her and she had been through the entire station staff like, as she put it, a dose of salts—all except the stationmaster. He was her insurance, the final deterrent to any saucy porter who told her to get the hell out of the first-class waiting room.

The years had added something to Judy and although a careful scrutiny of her impeccably made-up face would reveal tiny crevices, tell-tale crows' feet and a slight flabbiness about the neck, she was not the happy-go-lucky slut that Harry Oakwood had known. The old Judy had not smirked like this, though she only betrayed her contempt for men and triumph over them when she was alone.

But she was not quite alone. A young girl with a frowning expression was peering out of a bedroom door.

'Excuse me,' asked the girl anxiously, 'have you got sixpence for the gas meter?'

'I expect so, dear,' said Judy, poking in her handbag, 'hasn't your hubby got one?'

'I'm here by myself.'

'Oh?' queried Judy. She looked Mary up and down, assessing her as competition. No, she was not on the game.

'What are you doing here, then?' Judy asked, exchanging a sixpence for coins.

'I'm a war widow', said the girl proudly, 'but I have to work to scrape a living for me and my darling baby.'

'Don't you get a pension?' asked Judy with curiosity. Real live war widows were not usually amongst her acquaintances.

'I don't think so but I expect my mother-in-law would see to that.'

'You have to see to things yourself these days, dear,' said Judy, 'I lost my man in the war, too. Joined up with Kitchener's army to fight the Boche. Your country needs you, the poster said, and he went.' She was about to launch into her recruiting speech, but decided not to. This girl who was looking for a sixpence for her gas would not earn her anything.

Certainly Judy was not in Harry's thoughts as he was returned to England on the hospital ship. He had not got tetanus and his hand had almost healed. That in itself was hardly enough to take him out of the front line, but a casual comment by the front-line medical officer that it looked as though Lance-Corporal Oakwood had had a second dose of gas had initiated an enquiry at a higher level than mere divisional. When it was discovered that Oakwood had been gassed by his own countrymen at an experimental establishment in the first instance, there was a good deal of ill-natured acrimony flying about. Although the Battle of the Somme was going into its second phase and Harry Oakwood was only one of the 34,156 other ranks wounded on that fateful day, 1 July 1916, an inquiry was launched into the reason why a gas-affected soldier was thrust back into the fighting so soon.

It was irrelevant that Oakwood had not been gassed badly the first time and had not been gassed at all the second time. Major Summers, appointed to look into the matter, was an old time Fabian who considered that Oakwood had had a raw deal. He sought out Major Cross, who was employing Oakwood as a driver when he was gassed the first time, and who had now subsided into a gin-soaked lethargy.

152

'I keep an eye on my driver, Major Cross,' Summers rapped out. 'Would you let any Tom, Dick or Harry cart him off to experiment on? The way I see it is that this damned experimental station ordered Oakwood from the car, put him in a trench, and threw a gas bomb in after him.' He looked at his papers. 'I saw Oakwood in hospital a few days ago, and he claims that these men locked a gate on him, and refused to let him out. And that the respirator they gave him was deliberately faulty. Furthermore he attests on oath that he was terrified of making a complaint there and then because of the threats made by the commanding officer of the establishment. And I see it was part of your duty to visit this establishment and report any irregularities. It is not satisfactory, sir, not satisfactory.' And he rapped the table with his cane so hard that Cross winced.

'It was not quite like that, sir,' Cross protested. 'Oakwood stole a car from a French mayor and was also selling petrol to farmers . . .'

'That is no concern of mine', said Summers, 'and it is not the way of a gentleman to cast aspersions on a brave soldier. You are in serious trouble, Major, and to avoid a court martial I suggest you apply for a posting to the front.'

'What charge?' asked Cross, angrily.

'Any number,' replied Summers casually, 'dereliction of duty for one. I have already had a word with the CO. He is waiting for your application for a posting.'

'Oakwood did some favours for him,' said Cross venomously, 'repaired his car for him. I knew that man was trouble. And they did not throw a gas bomb in after him. It was a smoke bomb with just a little gas to give flavour. And he tore off the respirator deliberately.'

'It seems that you have discussed the matter already with the officers of the experimental station,' said Summers icily. 'I suggest you keep these comments to yourself, and I also suggest that you think carefully what you say to your defending counsel at your court martial. If you can find a brother officer to defend you.' Summers stalked out, smug with honest indignation.

After a short communication with Mr Booth's gin, Major Cross pulled himself together and went to see the CO.

Within three weeks he was in battle, and within four he was just another statistic, a huddle of bunched-up clothes in a half-filled crater in no man's land. His name in the casualty list published in the papers created little stir. Certainly Harry Oakwood, comfortable in the British hospital, had better things to do than read casualty reports.

He was managing to stretch out this gas attack longer than the other one, and although one or two of the doctors had some trouble finding out if he had been gassed they kept quiet about it, recognizing that Oakwood was a special case. The officer who came to see him thought that he had been used as a scapegoat, the nurses thought that he was not so bad as he pretended to be, and the senior staff thought that he was fit as anyone. He had played it cunningly, considered Oakwood. He had stirred up a hornet's nest by telling the major how he had been deliberately gassed by British experimenters and had built old Major Cross into a monster of infamy. Serve him right for having him posted to the front line. It was good getting even with the officers.

He remembered how his father used to go on about officers and how wars ought to be left to the senior NCOs. That, considered Harry, was just as bad. Fancy having a mob of Sergeant-Major Jenkinses under your feet all the time. At least with officers you could pull the wool over their eyes. Of course, there were some officers who were all right—Lieutenant Wilcox, for example, who had treated him well, man to man. He hoped Wilcox was still alive.

21

Flight-Sergeant Leonard Oakwood, RFC, had made his first kill. His FE2 had been grounded because of a broken axle, and he had been invited to take out the DH 2, a single-seater scout that was being introduced to the corps. Like his previous aeroplane, it was a pusher aircraft, with the French engine and the propeller at the back of the pilot. Oakwood soon got used to the fact that the engine was less than half the power of that of the FE2, though he found himself turning round to shout at an observer who was no longer there.

He was in a patrol between Armentières and Ypres and half way through the patrol he saw a two-seater approaching the British lines over Messines. He looked at the commander of the six-plane force on the starboard side, who waved him down to try to deal with the intruder. The enemy immediately turned eastward but Oakwood's initial height of 14,000 feet helped him to get to within four hundred yards. On the level, Oakwood could just hold him for speed and, tensing his muscles, he gripped the handle of the moveable Lewis gun mounted on the frame in front of him and let the enemy have a full drum, expecting any minute to see the brilliant sparkling of the enemy gunner's tracer bullets coming his way.

Nothing happened and Oakwood feverishly threw the empty drum over the side of the plane, grabbing another one near his feet and fixing it, all the time keeping the enemy at the same range. High above he could see the five aeroplanes of his patrol continuing on their way. A half-hearted burst of anti-aircraft fire distracted him for a second then he squeezed the trigger.

The other plane dived sharply through a thick bank of cloud at 2,000 feet, with Oakwood in pursuit but as the woolly masses rolled around him he put the nose up and emerged in the sunshine, rejoining his patrol. On his return to the aerodrome he made his report, slightly disappointed that events had not turned out so dramatically as he had hoped when he had dived after the enemy, the thrill of pursuit in his veins. Three days later a report came that a German machine had crashed on the Menin road at Gheluve, and as the time and the place fitted in with Oakwood's combat report he was credited with the kill. He had mentioned that he had found it difficult to see the enemy against the billowing white cloud and this predisposed the CO to think that the victim had been, indeed, Oakwood's for the crashed machine had been painted all white. The reason why there had been no return fire was also explained; there had been no gun.

'Probably a new crew learning the ropes', said the CO, 'but an easy one for your first Hun.'

Lieutenant Scott clapped him on the back, congratulating

him. 'I'll be glad when they fix the FE2, Lenny,' he said, 'you're having all the fun while I'm kicking my heels down here. This is worth a dinner in town. I've borrowed a motor for the night.' He was as good as his word.

He watched Leonard surreptitiously. It was evident that the lad had never been in a good-class restaurant before.

They seemed to be taking a good deal of time fixing the axle of the FE2 and Oakwood felt it was about time to chase up the mechanic. He went into the improvised hangar and looked at the aeroplane. The axle was as good as new, and as the CO was passing by he asked him when he could take the FE2 up again as Lieutenant Scott was anxious to be up and about. The officer hesitated, and took Oakwood by the arm, walking over the oil-browned grass to the mess.

'I have to be diplomatic, Sergeant,' he confessed. 'I take it you don't know anything about Lieutenant Scott's family?'

'Well, sir, I gather that they're pretty well off,' answered Oakwood.

'More than that I'm afraid,' said the other ruefully, 'very influential, and I've been told to keep the lieutenant out of the firing line. He should never have been posted here in the first place and some poor corporal in an office in Farnborough has no doubt had a twigging. All this is confidential, of course. The FE2 has been re-allotted any way. It will be better if you stay on the DH2 until we get the Sopwiths that we've been promised. You lads are always complaining that the Fokker's too fast for you to catch. The Sopwith's got the legs on that.' He patted Oakwood on his arm, smiled, and went inside the mess.

He liked young Oakwood, always so calm and collected. If he'd got a bit more social savoir-faire he could make something of himself. But he had heard Scott having the junior officers in howls about Oakwood's lack of finesse in the restaurant.

'Not exactly peas on a knife', Scott had said, 'but not far from it. And you should see him with cheese. As though he was trying to kill it, not eat it.'

The CO thought it was in bad taste, but said nothing.

A few days later Oakwood was sitting in his hut reading an old newspaper, when one of the other pilots poked his head round the door and said, 'Come on, Oaky, we're after a Zep.'

'The two-seaters are better for that,' commented Oakwood, laying down his paper.

'That's right,' the other agreed, 'the mechanics have just wheeled out your FE2 and Scotty is jumping with joy.'

Oakwood checked with the CO that all was in order.

'It's only a Zeppelin,' said the CO. 'I think Scott's safe enough for that. He's been such a pest that I'll be glad to get rid of him for a couple of hours.'

'Come on, Lenny, quick!' shouted Scott, seating himself in the observer's place and pulling down his goggles as the mechanic swung the propeller. Oakwood would like to have checked the plane first, but he trusted in the good sense of the mechanics, and the man swinging the propeller seemed to recognize this and put his thumb up in the air, pointing at the plane, as Oakwood taxied away.

Once in the air he looked at the map. It had been reported between Calais and Bruges, and Oakwood guessed that they would intercept it near Dunkirk. The three planes flew north, climbing and by the time they reached the coast they were at about 11,000 feet. There was no trace of the Zeppelin, and the leader of the patrol turned round, threw up his hands in incomprehension, and flew out to sea, then turning east, with the enemy anti-aircraft batteries opening an ineffective fire, the blossom-like puffs of smoke careering quite harmlessly past the wing-tips of the aircraft.

Down below was the smudgy and incredibly complicated pattern of Ostend, then Zeebrugge with its curious curved mole, like an earthworm probing into the grey-green of the sea, and as the trio reached the mouth of the Scheldt Oakwood looked at his petrol gauge somewhat apprehensively. It was as though he sparked off a telepathic message, for the leader immediately swung in a gentle arc until the compass read due west. The coastal anti-aircraft guns were exceptionally active and the three British planes flew further out to sea to avoid any trifling accident.

Oakwood commented on this to Scott. 'Archie's busy today,' he shouted.

Scott winced. 'Not so loud, old lad,' he shouted back, 'I went on a bit of a bender last night and my head's not all it should be.'

There was a crackle in Oakwood's ear and automatically he took evasive action, a couple of seconds after the other two aircraft had turned away. An aeroplane of a peculiar shape with enemy markings was zooming up under his nose, gusts of smoke from the exhaust.

'You should have seen that,' snapped Oakwood.

'What?' shouted Scott, cupping his hand to his ear, but Oakwood had more to do than exchange chat with his observer. A second plane similar to the first came out of a cloud, its machine-gun rattling, and Oakwood saw fragments of canvas flick off his upper wing. As it banked, Oakwood went with it, realizing that this unknown aeroplane was slightly faster. Scott sprayed the underside of the enemy with bullets as it moved away. 'I got it,' he shouted, 'I got it.'

Oakwood did not say anything. He knew that the range was too far for his observer to have much chance of downing the enemy, except by a fluke. Deceptively the enemy dived and Oakwood went down with it, instinctively, not knowing why.

'Get above it!' screamed Scott, 'you've got the height.'

Oakwood ignored him, for as the enemy plane banked he knew why he had not gone above it; the enemy was a two-seater, and the gunner would have loved the chance to get at the unprotected underbelly. As he looked down he could see the enemy circling enticingly, as though encouraging the FE2 to go down after it.

'After it, Lenny,' said Scott pointing down excitedly.

'Oh, shut up!' shouted Oakwood good-naturedly. There was a silence while Oakwood banked the plane, turning towards home.

'That's an order,' shouted Scott. Oakwood thought that his observer must be joking, but when he saw Scott's set face he knew that he was not.

'You get after it,' he said angrily, 'if you jumped now you might just about land on the observer.'

The petrol was running short, and the evening sun was low, dazzling him. The engine spluttered and looking down Oakwood could see a ruined town, with a shattered church the chief landmark. It must be Menin. With a bit of luck he could make the Ypres Salient, and as the engine coughed and stopped he peered down for a suitable landing place. The plane swept in, the propeller revolving noiselessly, wheels crackling against cut corn. A black circle appeared near the wheels, and Oakwood shook his head despairingly. A shell-hole would wreck him and his plane and the now mercifully silent Lieutenant Scott.

With a jerk the aeroplane drew up and Oakwood looked at the outlines of big guns silhouetted against the red sunset, shrouded in what looked like cobwebs. Without saying anything to Scott, Oakwood alighted, his thighs tense and his ankles aching. During the rough run across the cornfield a spare machine-gun drum in the floor of the cockpit had been rattling against his legs and he found he could hardly walk to the corrugated iron and wood huts that served as battery headquarters.

An infantry sergeant was shaving himself in the light of a hurricane lamp just outside one of the huts, and he looked round, startled, as Oakwood approached.

'I've just come down in the cornfield,' Oakwood explained. 'Can I telephone the squadron for petrol and oil?'

'Of course, my boy,' said the sergeant heartily, 'it's in the hut. It's temperamental, and if you wait until I've cleared this soap off my face I'll get through for you.'

The field telephone was battered, with bits tied up with adhesive tape, but the sergeant got through and handed over to the flyer. Sergeant Marchbanks' brows crinkled as he heard the sergeant give the name as Oakwood. Could he be any relation to that fellow Oakwood who had worked his passage back to Blighty after pretending to be gassed? He shook his head reflectively, but as he recognized the Birmingham twang he hovered in the background and when Oakwood had finished he asked him.

'He's my brother,' replied Leonard. 'I've not heard from him for a long time.'

Sergeant Marchbanks did not go into the matter further but went on to George Oakwood. 'I never met the sergeant-major but he knew my oldest brother. They joined up together. How is your father?'

'Not too happy,' Leonard admitted, 'he had to retire.'

'I'd like to write to him,' said Marchbanks. The old man had done his parents a favour by writing to them about his brother, Richard, and he would do the same.

159

By the time he had found Leonard a comfortable berth for the night, the tender and mechanics had arrived. There was a little damage to repair on one of the wings, so they left it to the morning. Oakwood looked round for his suddenly bad-tempered observer and found that Scott had borrowed a motor-bike and had gone back to the squadron without saying a word to him. If that was the way Scott wanted it that was good enough for him, and he crawled into the bunk, pulled the rough grey blanket over him, and was asleep almost before his head touched the pillow. Sergeant Marchbanks sat in front of a blank sheet of paper, sucking a pencil. After an hour he had finished:

> *Dear Mr Oakwood,*
> *We never met, but you knew my brother, and very kindly wrote to my parents when he was killed in Africa. I have just had the pleasure of meeting with your son Leonard, and I am happy to see that he has carried on the fighting traditions of the family. He downed his first Hun the other day, and I am certain that this is only the first of many.*
> *Yours sincerely,*
> *W. E. Marchbanks (Sgt, R. Warwicks. Regt)*

In the morning Leonard asked him why he, an infantry sergeant, was with an artillery battery.

'I got wounded in the ankle on the Somme,' replied Marchbanks, 'not enough for a Blighty but enough to keep me out of the front line.'

'Not the first time they got you,' observed Leonard, looking at the other's wound stripes. He noticed the medal ribbon of the Military Medal, but did not comment on it. Marchbanks was one of the old school, like his father. Medals came incidentally when doing one's duty.

It was mid-morning by the time the mechanics had finished patching up the wing fabric and Oakwood took off, watched by Sergeant Marchbanks and men of the battery, who suddenly appeared from nowhere. They were probably, Oakwood thought, taking it easy during a lull in the action; he knew how men slept the clock round after three or four days without sleep.

Back at the aerodrome he completed his report, and handed it in to the office corporal. He had made no mention of the

160

behaviour of Scott and when he saw the officer at the other end of the runway he deliberately walked the other way. Only when the CO called him in did Oakwood realize that he should have thought more carefully about writing his report.

The CO was somewhat stiff and starchy and kept his sergeant standing at attention longer than was his wont. 'Your report does not tally with Mr Scott's,' he said.

Oakwood briefly told him what had happened.

'I appreciate that the need to break off contact with the enemy was due to lack of petrol', said the CO, 'but according to Mr Scott you were a good deal ruder to him than you make out. I appreciate that an observer cannot interfere with a pilot's duties, but I must remind you, Sergeant, that he is an officer and you are an NCO.'

'In that case, sir,' said Oakwood icily, 'I consider it unfair for a sergeant to have to contend not only with the Hun, the Hun's better aeroplanes which have got ten miles an hour on us and two thousand feet, but with stroppy officers in the observer's seat.'

Not caring to comment on this, the CO asked him if it was true that Scott had bagged a Hun.

'Not a chance,' asserted Oakwood, 'he was going away and the range was too far anyway.'

'I have reprimanded the patrol leader for going too far on his limited petrol', said the CO, 'and I can't say more about you putting Mr Scott in danger.'

He dismissed the sergeant, calling him back at the door, and saying in a friendlier tone, 'It was a Halberstadt you saw, Oaky. It was very astute of you to see that it was a rather dangerous two-seater.' Recognizing that the CO was making amends for his ticking off, Oakwood smiled. The matter was closed to him.

But not for the CO. An ordinary decent officer would let the matter drop but not Mr Scott. The CO had accidentally learned that Scott was the nephew of a very important general and could do no wrong. With a shrug, he let Scott's claim for shooting down one of the Halberstadts through. The barney in the cockpit would do Oakwood's chances of promotion no good at all, however he himself hushed the matter up.

In the following days Oakwood saw nothing of Lieutenant Scott, but their brief friendship had encouraged him to go into the village *estaminet* and experiment with the local food. He took with him his corporal mechanic, who did not have the social inhibitions of Oakwood and was contemptuous of what he called Froggie food, launching into bacon and eggs with gusto. '*Le pot de thé*,' he said to the buxom girl who waited on table, 'OK with you, Sarge?'

An ironical voice echoed from another table. '*A pot de thé*,' it said, '*pour les coches Anglais.*'

The corporal reddened. 'It's that bloody Mr Scott,' he said. 'He's been after me the last three days. Corporal, do this, Corporal, do that, Corporal, wipe my backside. It's not fair, Sarge. And I heard the rumpus he kicked up about you. I would have chucked him out of his bloody cockpit. The corporal in the office told me that the CO had to send in Scotty's claim for one Hun. He's got some kind of pull over the CO.'

Surreptitiously looking at Scott over the rim of his cup, Oakwood saw that he was a good deal worse for drink, stretching his legs across the space between the tables and forcing the waitress to go round them.

'Excuse me, Sarge,' said the corporal, getting up, 'I've got to see a man about a dog. Where is it? Round the back?'

During his absence, Scott and the sergeant glared at each other.

'Still eating peas off your knife, Sergeant?' Scott called out. 'Murdered any good cheeses lately?' He went through the motions of chasing a piece of cheese around a plate.

Another officer tried to hush Scott up but without success, and when the corporal came back Oakwood paid the bill. As he went towards the door, he saw a hand-written notice at the back of the café: GENTELMEN.

'It's not spelt right,' noticed the corporal.

'But you went outside,' said Oakwood.

'So I did, Sarge,' said the corporal breezily, 'so I did.'

Thinking no more about it, Oakwood returned with the corporal to the station, and only when he heard the next morning that Lieutenant Scott had broken his collar bone, having run into a ditch on his motor-bike, did he wonder what his mechanic had been doing outside the *estaminet*. Only when

162

he found out that the corporal had been a motor-bike mechanic before the war did suspicions turn to certainty.

'I deny it all, Sarge,' said the corporal, grinning.

Little did Leonard know that the accident was another black mark against him, for it was felt that he could have been responsible for fixing the lieutenant's bike, as Scott claimed. Neither he nor the mechanic knew that the bike had been hauled from the ditch, and a sergeant-armourer from the Engineers had been asked to go over it carefully. Fortunately the mechanic had done the job with cunning, nothing so crude as cutting the brake-cable through.

Nevertheless, the mindless revenge of an aircraft mechanic who felt himself being victimized by a disliked officer had its effect. Sergeant Oakwood found himself posted. A blameless record sheet was becoming a little blotted.

22

On his first leave since arriving in France, Leonard Oakwood, neat in his newly cleaned uniform with the wings above the breast, sent a telegram to Elizabeth to say that he would be arriving at the house in Coventry at three in the afternoon. He remembered that house, austere and cold with 'artistic' uncomfortable furniture, and Elizabeth and her ghastly father. Neither had been well, and their off-hand reception of him may have been due to this. Not that Elizabeth's letters had been very encouraging but at least she had taken the trouble to write.

To think of the last time, he mused as he approached the house—so sadly fashionable a few years before and now seen to be jerry-built and pretentious, with its useless circular windows and the mixture of pebble-dash and stucco on the walls. Wondering what the family was like, and the sinking of the spirits as he met the father, red-nosed and snuffling, proud of being a book-keeper with the railways. And the way the father quizzed him. Could Leonard do a balance sheet, could he do a profit and loss account!

Leonard expected nothing but could not eradicate the glow of hope. Almost as soon as he had pressed the bell push, Elizabeth was at the door, eager and tremulous.

'Oh, Leonard,' she breathed, taking his hands and looking into his eyes.

Clumsily Leonard kissed her and his heart jumped as she pulled him to her. A neighbour in a house opposite poked her head through the lace curtains, eyes goggling, then scurried out of the back door to tell the news that Elizabeth had a young man, and an airforce man at that.

'Come inside,' invited Elizabeth, and Leonard followed her in.

How different an atmosphere could be. The same furniture but now seeming tidy and rational, the same look of stained unpainted wood but sensible and now not high-faluting. Elizabeth busied herself in the kitchen, making tea, and Leonard followed her in, slipping his arm round her waist. She did not say anything but smiled and put her hand in his. All her doubts were removed. No longer could her father say that Leonard was nothing but a common clerk, unworthy of her attention. Neat and handsome in his uniform, with his hair so trim and glossy, Leonard was the kind of man who broke the hearts of Coventry suburban girls. How her friends would envy her!

Within half an hour an understanding had been reached and it was decided that Elizabeth would go to Birmingham with Leonard to meet his parents. Leonard did not ask why her letters to him had been so cool and off-hand. He was happy with the situation as it now was and it was with pride that he tucked Elizabeth's arm beneath his as they walked to the railway station.

Leonard's mother was adding up the cash takings for the day as the young couple entered the shop. Jane's eyes clouded over with tears as her son came up to her and hugged her. Leonard was not a great one to show affection.

'This is Elizabeth,' said Leonard. 'We're going to be married.'

The initial shock made Jane blink but she knew that these things happened in wartime. The young people made up their own minds. And Leonard was no longer a boy; his self-assurance reminded her of George in his younger days, but there was a sensibility about Leonard, a delicacy of feeling that was foreign to her husband.

'I would like to have told you before', apologized Leonard, 'but we only found out what our feelings were today.'

'I shall make him happy, Mrs Oakwood,' said Elizabeth eagerly.

Jane warmed to her. She squeezed Elizabeth to her and kissed her cheek. How different Leonard was from her other son! Harry keeping his girl friends carefully excluded as though he was ashamed of them, Harry jaunty and selfish.

On her part, Elizabeth was amazed by Leonard's mother. When she had learned that she was manageress of a shoe-shop she had built up a picture of a harassed, worried little woman, like the owner of the corner shop, always complaining about the price of things and how difficult it was to get stock. Mrs Oakwood was quite a lady. And how nicely she talked, just like the ladies of the Women's Institute who came round for jumble and who put her mother into such a fluster!

Hearing the voices downstairs in the shop, George came down the stairs, slowly, for the doctor had told him not to exert himself.

'A little tremor,' the doctor had said reassuringly, 'not uncommon for a man in his sixties.'

George was annoyed with himself for being a greater burden on Jane, now not even able to stand in ration queues. His heart gave a flutter as he saw Leonard, and his eyes misted. He gripped Leonard's hand with both his.

'My boy,' he said, his voice choking, 'you have no idea how pleased I am.'

But who was the pretty girl with Leonard? Was it a customer who happened to be in the shop?

'This is Elizabeth,' said Leonard proudly. 'We're going to be married.'

His father took Elizabeth's hand. 'I'm so glad,' he said.

Leonard was beaming.

'This is the happiest day of my life,' he said, 'all together.'

But it was not quite all together, thought Jane.

A late customer temporarily stopped the family discussion

165

but then Jane closed the shop and they all went upstairs, George eager to find out about Leonard's adventures. Who would have thought that the quiet book-reading boy who never indulged in street games would turn into a sergeant? George had received the letter from Sergeant Marchbanks telling him that Leonard had downed his first victim but as Leonard did not mention it he did not either.

'All the years it took me to get to a sergeant', George Oakwood said wistfully, 'and look at you, up there already.'

'Things are different now,' said Leonard, smiling, 'after all, you can't have a private flying an aeroplane worth more than a thousand pounds.'

George shook his head, grinning, overflowing with pride in his son's success, though deep down he knew that war was responsible. 'If I had been educated like you,' said George, 'I might have got on faster.'

Leonard did not say that his father had been opposed to him staying on at school, that at fourteen he had had to make his own way in the world, stuffed into that terrible Birmingham office smelling of dust and blotting-paper.

With an effort George turned his attention to Leonard's fiancée. 'And how about you, my dear?' he asked, 'what does your father do?'

Elizabeth smiled. 'He's led a very quiet life compared to you, Mr Oakwood,' she said, 'he's a book-keeper for the Midland Railway. He has quite a good job.'

'And they live in a very nice house,' added Leonard, seeking to compensate for Elizabeth's father's mediocre qualities.

Elizabeth did not add that her mother worked in a bicycle factory, believing that this would make her appear common. Mr Oakwood seemed a nice, friendly old man, and so proud of Leonard, but Mrs Oakwood was rather daunting and made her feel inadequate.

There was an embarrassed silence when Leonard asked about Mary and he did not pursue the matter, though his father told him a little while Jane and Elizabeth prepared supper.

'It hasn't turned out very well, Leonard,' said George, 'we've heard that she's in London. But least said, soonest mended. When do you think you're getting married?'

'As soon as possible,' replied Leonard.

'We'd like to have your young lady living here,' said George awkwardly, 'your mother has really taken to her, and we've got plenty of room.'

This seemed an admirable idea but Leonard did not take it up there and then. He expected a somewhat abrasive time with Elizabeth's father when he took her back later that night. In the event he was pleasantly surprised, for it was clear as soon as he entered the house that Mr Elkin did not count for anything in the family. The dominating person was Mrs Elkin, whom he had not met before, a cheerful buxom woman who accepted him immediately. She agreed that the couple should get married as soon as possible, and when she learned that Mr Oakwood was not well she was more than willing for the marriage to take place in Birmingham.

'I'll go over and see your mother tomorrow, Leonard,' she said briskly, 'and now I'll get your room ready . . .'

'If it's no trouble,' protested Leonard.

'No trouble at all. Come on, Father, rouse yourself, get me the eiderdown out of the airing cupboard.' She gave Leonard a half-wink, as she piloted her ineffectual husband from the room, leaving it to Leonard and Elizabeth. What a nice young man he was, and how smart he looked in his uniform! An airforce sergeant! What would the women at the factory say when they heard! She would have a few words to say to father when the young people were out of the way, trying to turn her and Elizabeth off the boy because he was just a clerk.

She wondered what the family was like. Leonard's sister sounded a strange, wayward girl. As for Harry, he seemed to be the sort of young man a mother would despair of, though Leonard tried to be fair.

'I'm certain he's still alive,' he said. 'Harry's one of that sort. He'll come through smiling.'

He hoped he was right; sometimes his heart ached for his brother somewhere in that shambles in France.

At the time, Harry was having the time of his life, well-fed at the convalescent home, able to take afternoons off when he liked, with plenty of opportunities for adventure.

One afternoon he met a buxom land girl with as little time for the preliminaries as Harry himself, and after an exhausting romp in a farm shed he fervently hoped that he could stretch out his opportune gas attack until the end of the war. He looked at the girl's fat thighs abstractedly as she pulled on what looked like hessian knickers.

'You make a girl feel good,' said the land girl.

He went back to the convalescent home in high spirits, and he was still whistling under his breath when he was intercepted by the consultant doctor in the corridor.

'Corporal Oakwood,' he said coldly, 'we have been looking for you for two hours. You should have been back long ago. An afternoon pass-out means just that.'

'Sorry, sir,' said Harry abjectly, 'but my fiancée and I had a lot to discuss.'

'That's none of my concern', said the doctor, 'but your absence has made it easier to make a decision.'

Harry went cold. 'What decision, sir?'

'We had a colonel from the War Office', said the doctor, 'wondering why you were still here when there doesn't seem anything particularly wrong with you. And why you were not in the home. You are still, I might remind you, under military discipline although this is a civilian establishment. You might have persuaded him that you were still unfit for active service, but I could not. An officer of the Royal Army Medical Corps will be examining you tomorrow. Please hold yourself in readiness for his visit.'

It was a formal request; the doctor had already issued instructions to the porters at the gate not to allow Lance-Corporal Oakwood out.

There was no way out for Harry Oakwood. He waited for the RAMC officer, puffing desperately at a chain of cigarettes to try to raise the vestige of a cough. Aware that the case of Corporal Oakwood had been aired in the press, the captain of the Medical Corps went over his patient methodically from top to toe.

'Sound as a bell,' he said, 'I wish all my gas patients turned out like you.'

He sent in his report immediately, advising that Oakwood was fit for active service and, confined to the home, Harry knew that his happy days were over, though he sensed that there would be reluctance to send him back to the front line. A third attack of gas would start the newspapers campaigning. Without compunction a colonel of the RAMC downgraded Oakwood from A1 to C2, ignoring the recommendations of the captain who had examined Oakwood at the convalescent home. Harry found himself on a troopship for France, destined for a behind-the-lines job.

'I see you were a motor mechanic,' said an elderly major, gnawing his pencil. 'Done any clerking or anything like that?'

'No, sir,' said Oakwood, 'but driving, yes.'

'Can't have that,' said the major shaking his head. 'You might get sent into the fighting areas and what would the newspapers say then?'

Oakwood said nothing. His reputation as a trouble-maker had followed him across the English Channel.

'I don't know whether you follow the course of the war or have been too busy elsewhere,' said the major, looking down at some papers, 'but on 15 September the British Army used tanks for the first time. If we had had five hundred they would have won the war, but we only had fifty. A lot were damaged. If you know about motor-cars you might be useful in helping to put them right. Would you like to mess about with tanks?'

There did not seem any choice.

'I would like that very much,' said Harry heartily.

'Good,' said the major, 'you will be attached as a full corporal to the heavy section of the Machine Gun Corps which is at present operating them. You seem to have been a lance-corporal for a very long time.' He looked directly into Oakwood's eyes. 'Discrimination, Corporal Oakwood?' he asked sarcastically.

The colonel Oakwood met later was a good deal more friendly. 'You really seem to know your stuff, Corporal,' he said after giving the new full corporal an interrogation, 'when we asked for men with mechanical knowledge we got mostly agricultural labourers. I see that you have some knowledge of Daimlers. Well, tank engines are 105 horsepower Daimler units, though you will find the transmission somewhat different to that of the motor. If you have all-round mechanical knowledge you might help us to deal with some of the faults we have discovered. The tail-wheels have been breaking off. And our crews have been worried by the Hun *flammenwerfer*—flame-thrower.'

A captain walking with a limp entered the office carrying a sheaf of papers.

'Clive,' said the colonel, 'will you fix Corporal Oakwood up with documentation, and get the sergeant to take him to his billet?'

As Oakwood followed the captain down the corridor he wondered what the perks were. Tanks must use petroleum and petroleum was always a marketable commodity, suitable for sale to Frog farmers.

'Any relation to Sergeant-Major Oakwood?' asked Captain Bland.

'No, sir,' replied Harry smartly. They might think he was one of the bright keen soldiers and have him out on the barrack square. And he knew that his father was a legend, and did not want any part of it. If it had not been for the old sod he would be a war profiteer.

Reading between the lines of Harry's service record, Bland recognized that he was no glorious acquisition to the Machine Gun Corps (heavy section). He had apparently got himself conveniently lost during the Battle of Ypres; there was a story of his stealing a Frenchman's car and selling it to a Major Cross; there were rumours of his dabbling in stolen petrol and, although a few lines of the later record were heavily obliterated, it seemed that there had been a question-mark against Oakwood's participation in the Battle of the Somme.

After he had sent the corporal on his way, he took the record back to the colonel.

'What's this crossed out for, sir?' he asked.

The colonel looked at the deleted passage. 'Ours not to ask, Clive,' he said, 'there was a bit in the newspapers about young Oakwood. Sent into battle twice when suffering from gas. No evidence that he was really gassed at all. He's been spending months taking it easy in a convalescent home on the strength of his story, with everybody in kid gloves. If it had been one of us he would have been shoved upstairs.' He yawned, stretching his arms. 'That's nothing to us though, he seems to be a bloody good mechanic and if he can really read a blueprint, as he claims, he could have raped his sister for all I care.' The colonel was not one to be put off by inessentials.

170

23

Everyone was getting married, thought the vicar of St Paul's. The bridegroom's parents seemed familiar, and he remembered that another of their children, a girl, had been married at his church. He rattled through the ceremony, and asked Jane about her daughter.

'She's a widow,' said Jane, 'the husband was killed in France.'

'Your son's an airman, isn't he?' the vicar, embarrassed, went on.

'Leonard? Oh, yes, he's an airman,' replied Jane absently.

Elizabeth was a dear, sweet girl, but her parents were decidedly common; Elizabeth's father had called her 'Madam', exactly as if he was one of her employees. And she did not like to see the way he patronized George, as though he were some poor relation.

Elizabeth was deliriously happy. Even with wartime shortages her mother had managed to provide her with a marvellous wedding dress, and who could say how many hours of overtime had helped pay for this yardage of silk and satin? As for her new in-laws, Mr Oakwood was so amiable and kind, and Mrs Oakwood could not do enough for her.

'I'd love to live with you over the shop', Elizabeth said, 'but I don't want to offend Mother.'

'Leave it to me, Elizabeth,' Jane had assured her. Elizabeth would be a comfort, not a constant source of worry. Only a day or two before the wedding they had received a laconic postcard from Harry, so laconic it told them nothing.

Leonard and Elizabeth had their brief honeymoon in a hotel in the town.

'I'm so nervous, dear,' she said as she sat on the bed in her nightdress.

'I'll be gentle,' said Leonard uncomfortably but when he put the light out and crept into bed she was crying. He put his hand out to comfort her and encountered something hard and shiny.

'What's this?' he asked suddenly.

'It's one of my dolls,' she said, 'you don't mind, do you?'

'Not if she doesn't,' said Leonard.

This relieved the tension. She moved towards him and he held her in his arms, feeling her soft flesh against him.

In the morning he found that there were three dolls in bed with them. He considered this rather strange, and when the maid came in the morning with their tea he hurriedly thrust the three intruders out of sight.

'Did you sleep well?' he asked Elizabeth as she awoke.

'After all *that*?' she asked coyly.

'It's only half-past eight,' he said.

'What?' she asked, in mock horror, 'again?'

'Why not?' he said, untying the cord of her nightdress and gently stroking her stomach.

The day passed too quickly, and the couple's rare appearances outside the bedroom were the source of much sniggering among the staff. 'Let him have his oats,' said the head waiter preparing for a massive luncheon for trade unionists, 'he's in the flying corps and they don't last long.'

'Ah, the poor lamb,' said an aged waitress, 'she don't look as though she's had it before. You can always tell. When they're new to it they get that dopey far away look.'

Carefully Elizabeth packed her dolls away. It did not seem at all odd to her. They had always been with her. Leonard took his suitcase from the top of the wardrobe. He looked at Elizabeth and at the bed; he would never forget that bed. But his train went at six, and he had to take his wife to the shop.

'You don't mind working in the shop?' he asked.

'I'd love to,' Elizabeth said. It gave her an excuse to stay with the Oakwoods.

She saw him off at New Street station, one face among many and hers not the only one tear-stained. Jane was there too, watching from the footbridge that straddled the platforms. If she had been more religious, she thought, she would have prayed harder for him but she recited the Lord's Prayer, the words familiar but yet strange in her mouth. If Leonard came back safe and sound she vowed that she would go to church, go regularly, whatever George said about knee-drill and army chaplains. But now she would put a brave face on it and get the poor girl busy in the shop.

A few days after Leonard had returned to France, Elizabeth

was serving in the shop when an over-dressed girl entered. She seemed a girl to Elizabeth, but when she looked closer she saw that the customer was well into her thirties.

'I'm looking for Harry Oakwood,' she said aggressively.

Judy Abbott had followed a trail, and was determined on being a nuisance. The widow's garb had let her down badly in the end, and an unsympathetic magistrate with a son on the Western Front had sent her to prison for three months, reduced to a month on appeal. It had not been an experience to relish. Judy had come up against the old lags, the women who had been on the game for thirty or forty years and were diseased and shrivelled up, and their experiences amongst the down-and-outs in Wapping and Silvertown made her blood run cold. Too hard-bitten to reform, Judy had vowed there and then to return to Birmingham, where at least she could always count on a handful of old-time supporters.

She watched the girl behind the counter closely. Was this one of Harry's bloody sisters? She hated this pink-and-white type, with the butter wouldn't melt in the mouth expression. Could this even be Harry Oakwood's *wife*? The girl's reaction did not convince Judy that this was not the case. Hesitation and uncertainty made Elizabeth nervous. She knew what kind of woman this was, without being told. The long lashes, the carmine lips, the unconvincing beauty spots on the cheek, she had seen them all on picture postcards. Clearly the visitor was an actress, probably part of Harry Oakwood's exciting past.

'Harry isn't here', said Elizabeth, 'and his mother has just gone out. His father's in.'

Judy shrugged her padded shoulders. 'All right,' she said negligently, 'I'll see him.'

She bent down and ran a finger up her leg. The itching made her think that the cheap hotel room she had occupied last night had been full of fleas. Christ almighty! What did her ma think she was doing, just flitting home without leaving an address?

The old man who descended the stairs made her think of her stepfather, old Abbott, deceased (and no one had been sad to see him gone). He had the look of someone who had once been a soldier or something, trying to keep his back rigid and preserve a battered dignity. There was a barking sound in George's voice when he asked what she wanted. He knew to a copper or

173

two how much Judy would charge and was not fooled by the bravura.

'Your son Harry,' Judy began without preliminaries, 'I want to see him. I've got a little matter to discuss with him.'

'He's in the army, fighting for the likes of you,' said George coldly.

'And what about his nipper? Him too?' jeered Judy.

George put his hand on the banister knob. 'What?' he asked.

'Yes,' said Judy pertly, 'he had his fun, then scarpered.'

The mists before George's eyes gathered and cleared, and he could feel his heart pounding. He did not argue that Judy's claim was impossible; he knew only too well it was likely. Fortunately in the matter of paternity Judy was her own worst enemy. Old as he was, George had the answer to quell her. 'It could be anybody's,' he retorted, 'now get out of the shop before I call the police.'

'Now listen here,' said Judy angrily, 'I'm not going to have any old bugger like you threatening me with the police——'

George interrupted her. 'Elizabeth,' he said slowly, 'go up to the Arcade and fetch the policeman on duty outside Lewis's. I'll mind the shop while you're gone.'

It needed nothing more. Judy was about to say something, but checked herself and flounced out of the shop and out of the Oakwoods' lives. But she had done the damage she had wanted to do. The shock on George's constitution, the anger that had welled up in him when he saw the little whore standing in front of the shop as bold as brass, were too much for him.

'I'm going to have a lie down for an hour or so,' he said to Elizabeth, and climbed slowly up the stairs, gripping every inch of the banister as if his life depended on it, the knuckles white.

When Jane returned, Elizabeth told her all that had occurred. Jane did not say anything, but the same agitation that had sent her husband to his bed made her cheeks white and her nostrils distend. Damn that Harry, she thought, and damn the whole army that had made their home life in Aldershot and elsewhere a mockery. How old was the baby that this slut claimed was Harry's? A few months, a few years? Did it mean that Harry, not seen for more than two years, crept up to Birmingham to copulate with a common whore without bothering to look in on his parents? That was what it must have seemed to George and she hurried upstairs to him.

'Are you all right, George?' she asked anxiously.

'I'm all right, love,' he replied, his face set. He was sitting up in bed with his pyjama top loose about his shoulders. He seemed to be staring at a spot on the wall. 'It was just the shock', he added, 'but I'll be all right.'

'I'll make you a cup of tea,' Jane said, desperate to busy herself with something and to find an excuse to leave that room with her husband in that pitiful state.

'Is everything all right?' asked Elizabeth, poking her head round the kitchen door.

'He's just had a nasty shock', said Jane, 'but he'll be all right. All that that girl said was lies. Harry was hot-headed and impulsive, but he was never like *that*.'

Elizabeth nodded, ready to be convinced. She remembered once when she was a little girl seeing her father talking to a smartly dressed lady not unlike the woman who had been into the shop. She would never forget the look of alarm on her father's face when he saw her watching them. He had told her she was an actress and Elizabeth had believed him. It was all flooding back to her now.

Not all was flooding back. There were memories she did not want, memories that she refused to believe belonged to her. They concerned her father and a woman somewhat like that dreadful girl who had so upset her father-in-law. She was still thinking about this the next day when the postman arrived with a letter from Coventry. Elizabeth's father had fallen ill and her mother implored her to go back home to share the trouble. She did not put it so brutally but Elizabeth sensed that her father was more than usually tiresome. Both George and Jane were reluctant to let her go, for not only was Elizabeth a valuable asset to the shop but she seemed to take pleasure in sitting with George, talking and reading to him. In turn, George regaled her with his army experiences. It was strange, he thought, how deeply etched were his memories of the Ashanti War and the Boer War. That, he reckoned, was the happiest time of his life. He told Elizabeth about the long rides over the veldt and the amazing sunsets, glossing over the romance and omitting the distressing incidents, the looting and the brutality.

175

'If only Mary had been like Elizabeth!' he said to Jane after his daughter-in-law had left for Coventry, 'perhaps she should have gone to work after all. I think I made a mistake there. I've made a lot of mistakes about the children.'

It was too late to worry about them, thought Jane. They were by themselves again, as they were at the start of their marriage in that bleak bungalow in Aldershot, with nothing to break the monotony but the shrill bugle bleats and the hoarse shouting of NCOs on the parade ground. Who would have thought that after that depressing beginning they would be so comfortable in old age?

She wound up the gramophone, and sat on the edge of George's bed listening to the old tunes.

'Do you remember that one?' she asked. But George was asleep.

'It's been so quiet since you went,' said Elizabeth's mother.

Elizabeth looked through the pages of a magazine on her lap, frowning as her father knocked on the bedroom floor with a stick. 'My turn,' she said. It was not as though her father was really ill. It was merely influenza. He had had it before, and no doubt he would have it again.

'He's run down,' the doctor had said, 'we're all run down. The war's been going on too long.'

She entered the bedroom. Her father was saying something about wishing that she had not run off to get married to the first man she had taken a fancy to and how inconsiderate she was. She did not say anything but returned downstairs.

'I'm going back to Birmingham,' she said.

Her mother nodded. 'I wish I was going with you,' she admitted, 'and leave him here to look after himself. But it's not possible, more's the pity. But you're right. It's not fair to you. You have your own problems.'

Almost immediately Elizabeth felt guilt. 'No, I'll stay on a little while longer,' she said reluctantly, 'somebody has to be in when you're at work.'

Eventually the war would be over and Leonard would be back with her. And when she was sad she always cheered herself with the awareness that at least Leonard was safe.

Sometimes she felt guilty about her attitude towards Leonard. She had heard customers in the shop talking about

176

their anxieties over husbands and sons on the Western Front. They relived the terrors of the trenches, scanning the casualty reports every day, waiting for the dreaded telegram, while to Elizabeth it was all very remote.

As the weeks went by and 1917 rolled on, with food shortages and a quiet desperation all round at the prospect of the war going on and on, Jane began to be more worried about Mary in London. On 13 June fourteen Gotha bombers made a daylight raid on the capital, causing 588 casualties. Jane, having no conception of the size of London, felt sure that Mary must be among the injured, whereas her daughter had watched the raid with perfect calmness from the windows of the YWCA.

She was eking out her savings by doing part-time work delivering letters, but she was still dissatisfied. What the secretary of the YWCA had called 'like-minded girls' bored her and she had reverted to pattern, spending most of her leisure time in the crowded picture houses, laughing with the Keystone Cops and saddened by the innumerable heroines fighting off odious men.

Sometimes she thought about her parents. Should she return home? But that would mean serving in that shoe shop. A war widow selling shoes! It was indecent. She compromised by sending a postcard home. It reached the Oakwoods along with letters from Leonard and Harry, and Jane was reading it when there was an unexpected visit from the owner of the shop, Mr Motley.

'She went this morning,' he began gloomily, and Jane, puzzled, saw the black armband on his coat.

'Oh, I'm so sorry,' she said.

'It had to be,' said Mr Motley, 'surprising she's lasted as long as she has. Still, I don't want to burden you with my worries. You must have problems of your own with poor George.'

Mr Motley looked around the shop, noticing that it was still as spick and span as ever, with not a trace of dust on the box tops and the glass-topped counter gleaming.

'Whatever happens, people have got to buy shoes,' he commented. 'Is your assistant a good worker?'

'Very good,' Jane assured him, 'only fifteen but as bright as a button. It was a pity about the last girl, but when I heard her making sarcastic remarks about George she had to go.'

177

She led the way upstairs to make her employer a cup of tea, and when they had both sat down Mr Motley came to the reason for his visit. 'It must be over fourteen years since you came to us, Jane,' he began. 'I remember you sitting in that very same chair telling us about George and the first time you came to the shop. That must have been when my father owned it. My wife thought the world of you and I don't know how I would have managed to run the shop with an invalid to look after. Well, to cut matters short, the shop's yours.'

'What?' exclaimed Jane, her heart pounding.

Mr Motley smiled, patting her hand. 'Yes,' he said, 'I mean it. I've got enough for my needs. No family to leave the shop to. And I'm going to sell the bungalow and live at the seaside. I've arranged to see a solicitor this morning, so if you get your coat on we can trot along there now.'

He was as good as his word and after he had gone, promising to see Jane before he left Birmingham, Jane raced up the stairs to tell George.

'That's wonderful news, my dear,' said George, putting down his book.

'What's that you're reading?' Jane asked brightly.

'Oh, it's my *Soldiers of the Queen*,' he replied.

Jane shook her head, smiling. No book could be more battered; tied together with string and the pages kept intact with brown paper it was more than a book to her husband. It was a memento of his early days, given to him by the man on whom he had modelled himself, Sergeant-Major Stryker, a token of the past. When they had been living in Sparkbrook George, disillusioned by the Boer War and the role of the army in it, had scorned it, burying it beneath a pile of other books. But eventually it had been resurrected.

'You must know every page of it by heart,' she said.

'I think I do,' he said.

Although the news from Mr Motley was good, although her future was now secured, her heart was heavy as she went down to the shop. Poor George, reduced to lying in bed and reliving the past. She blamed it entirely on the visit of that odious little streetwalker who claimed that she had borne Harry's child. Mary's departure from Birmingham had been a shock but both of them realized that women were different nowadays, what with the Suffragettes and everything. Jane accused herself of not being a good mother, so why should Mary be any different? But that little whore, marching into the shop and upsetting George just for the sake of it, she could never forgive her. That was the day George went to bed and, except for stumbling to the lavatory, there he had remained ever since.

It was all brought back to her one afternoon a fortnight after the visit of Mr Motley when she was shopping in the Bull Ring. A woman in a dark suit with a veil over her face was walking through the market, threading between the stalls, pulling behind her a boy of about six. The boy shot out a hand and grabbed an apple off a fruit stall. Jane blinked. It was done so quickly that probably she was the only one who had seen what had happened.

As if aware that he had been spotted, the boy turned his head sharply towards Jane and looked at her insolently, as if daring her to do something about it.

'Are you all right, ma'am?' asked a stall holder as Jane gripped one of the wooden posts that held the tarpaulin up.

Jane nodded, but was not sure. For the boy was the reincarnation of Harry when he was a child, that same blond hair, that same cheekiness. This must be the woman who had been to the shop, but Elizabeth and George had said that she was gaudily dressed. Jane was not to know that Judy was reverting to her war widow role.

She felt that she ought to approach the woman, to find out all about her, but common sense won. She had the shop and security and had successfully avoided being landed with Mary's child. If that boy were Harry's—and there seemed no doubt about it, for the soberly dressed woman was ogling one of the porters in a manner that allowed for only one interpretation—she would be morally obliged to do something for the girl, if only to apologize for George's threats to get the police.

Had she realized it, Jane Oakwood had many of the qualities she deplored in Harry—selfishness and the awareness of on which side her bread was buttered.

24

On the Western Front, the spring of 1917 was uneventful. The struggle on the Somme had long died out and during the early months of the new year both sides were busy with their preparations. The Germans upset many calculations by an unexpected retirement to the much vaunted Hindenburg Line and General Haig, who had envisaged a drive north and south of Arras—and on, predictably, to Berlin—now found himself obliged to concentrate on an attack in the direction of the Vimy Ridge.

The troops in the line, knowing that the Somme offensive had petered out without gaining anything despite the immense losses, prepared for the worst. They knew that there was a good deal of bad feeling between the French and British generals owing to the establishment of General Nivelle as overall commander in the field, for no one had told the British generals Haig and Robertson.

The failure of the tanks on the Somme to accomplish miracles had temporarily downgraded them, and Corporal Oakwood found himself involved in more mundane preparations for the British onslaught. A thousand miles of cable had to be dug in, six feet deep. Pumping-stations had to be erected, pipe-lines laid and reservoirs constructed. Supply, deployment, and reinforcement were rendered difficult by the fact that all roads converged on Arras, and the difficulty was only overcome by extensive mining and tunnelling operations. A system of underground sewers was turned into subterranean barracks accommodating the back-up divisions.

Urgency suddenly became the catchword, and all the odds and sods were recruited for the work: drivers, pioneers, engineers, and clerks. Oakwood was thankful that his two stripes enabled him to avoid the really hard work, the backbreaking labour shifting tons of earth, the eternal fetching and carrying under the watchful eyes of irate sergeant-majors. He was underground in Arras when the preliminary bombardment began and when he went to the surface he could see lorries going forward, their loads consisting of shells and canisters of poison gas.

Hardly had the work ended on the construction of the underground barracks than British troops began to filter into them, dropping their groundsheets into convenient corners and falling asleep on them almost immediately. Oakwood listened to the conversation. All the troops predicted another bloody massacre, especially of the Canadians who were rearing to go and Oakwood was glad when he was recalled to the Machine Gun Corps section well behind the front.

The word soon got back that the bombardment had not done its job—to smash the defences and in particular the massive barriers of barbed wire, that the Germans had full control of the air because of their superior aircraft (not to be wondered at if young Leonard was up there, thought Oakwood) and that the driving snow and hail were holding up those units that had, in fact, advanced.

The colonel called his officers in. 'We're to contribute twelve tanks towards an attack by the Fourth Australian Division between Bullecourt and Quéant,' he said. 'Anzac Corps headquarters don't want to attack for they think the wire is insufficiently cut and they doubt the value of the tanks.'

'Twelve's not enough, sir,' said a major, 'It won't mean anything either way.'

'And it's got to be a surprise attack,' added the colonel ruefully.

Sergeant Wills, in charge of the workshops, called his men together. 'The officers have got a problem', he said, 'and they've passed it on to us. Twelve of our Mark I tanks are going in with the Anzacs and the CO wants it to be a secret.'

'What's the weather conditions like, Sarge?' asked a weedy private, surreptitiously puffing at a hand-made cigarette.

'What's that got to do with it?' asked the sergeant suspiciously. 'All right, light up if you have to.' There was a click of tobacco tins. The workshop crew were great ones for rolling their own.

'There's snow and blizzards, I've heard,' replied the private, 'if we paint the tanks white the Hun won't be able to see them.'

'Good,' said the sergeant approvingly, 'how about you, Corporal Oakwood, you're the brains of this lot, aren't you?'

'I suppose there'll be a bombardment,' speculated Oakwood, 'and if the artillery are laying down cover will the enemy hear the tanks? I can't see any way of stopping the noise of the tracks. We can cut down the engine noise.'

'How's that, Corporal?'

'By fitting a silencer to the exhaust. If we fit a chamber halfway along the exhaust it will reduce the noise.'

'Good, good,' said the sergeant rapidly. 'I'll put it to the officers.'

All day the workshop men were busy refashioning the tank exhausts, while another group began painting the tanks white. The sergeant kept his thoughts to himself. He had been with the tanks when they were first deployed on the Somme and until the generals began to think in terms of hundreds of tanks in massed formation the new weapon was no more than an eccentric toy. And they were so cumbersome and slow and, although he heard that the new Mark IV tank had improved armour-plating, the ones they had were vulnerable to medium artillery. Stalking away he felt that he could have designed something better, with a revolving turret turning through 360 degrees. It would have to be power-assisted. As he was working on this he almost collided with Captain Bland.

'A penny for them, Sergeant,' said Bland, smiling.

The sergeant explained what he was thinking.

'We've always got the weapons of the last war but one,' said Bland, 'I hear they've had the cavalry out on this one. Too late, as usual. The Huns had dug in again by the time it arrived.'

'Will you be with the tanks, sir?' the sergeant asked.

'If I can swing it, Sergeant,' said Bland. Whatever the colonel said, he would try and be in the tank attack. The days of cavalry were numbered, and the future of cavalry officers was with the new weapon, ridiculous as it looked, a stranded whale when motionless, but a tremendous menace when on the move. On the Somme one tank had captured a German company, paralysed with fear as the British secret weapon rolled towards them crushing everything in its path.

Realizing that Bland was determined to go, the colonel gave his sanction and in response to the telephone call the tanks crawled out of the sheds and moved towards the front line at a sedate five miles per hour. Captain Bland was in the leading tank. He had had a word with Corporal Oakwood. 'You're infantry, Corporal,' he had said, 'you're a fighting man. You can squeeze in somewhere.'

'I'd like to, sir,' said Oakwood earnestly 'but I'm C2. Got gassed on the Somme.'

'Oh, yes,' muttered the captain. 'I forgot.'

Catch him going in with the tanks! thought Oakwood contemptuously as they moved towards the horizon, masked by snow. God, it was perishing cold and, rubbing his hands, he scuttled back to the billet not expecting to see Captain Bland again. In many ways Captain Bland reminded him of his father. The army was everything to him and he would have been aghast to discover that the view was not universally shared. He was the sort of officer who kept the war going; Oakwood knew full well what the private soldier thought about the Western Front, that grey-brown phenomenon that dulled the mind, turned men into burrowing scurrying animals, and that seemed to have always been there.

Ejecting Oakwood from his thoughts, Captain Bland carried on, the tank crackling over the frozen ground, occasionally tilting dramatically as it went over a crater with the engine whirring, the track momentarily idling as it tried to obtain purchase. He was pleased to see that the white paint did effectively camouflage the vehicles. They were now passing groups of men on their way to the front, and the juncture between sky and land was lit by the flashes of guns.

An occasional shell exploded near at hand and Bland's heart sank. They were only medium shells, and this meant that the big push had not succeeded as well as had been hoped. The Germans were still in action with their artillery. A snarl up of lorries and waggons stopped the tank force, and Bland struggled out. 'Who's in charge here?' he snapped.

A sergeant saluted. 'Not our fault, sir. A lorry's frozen up with the cold. The driver forgot to put glycerine in the radiator. He's on a charge, sir.'

That seemed to the sergeant to solve the problem and Captain Bland choked back his anger. This war had seen the emergence of a new kind of soldier who took refuge from the horrors of trench warfare in pettiness and an adherence to the small print of King's Regulations. Although Bland had seen little actual cowardice, more and more men were trying to avoid their duties, failing to back up their comrades. Oakwood, for instance, cringing in the support lines because he was ostensibly C2. He realized that the sergeant was still standing to attention. He saw the tired desperate look on the man's face and the wound stripes. It was not his fault. 'Carry on, Sergeant,' he said, 'do your best to get them moving.'

Eventually the muddle was sorted out and the offending lorry was manhandled off the road. The driver was being tongue-lashed by a foppish young lieutenant who looked as though he had just come off the parade ground at Sandhurst. Bland felt a spasm of distaste as he looked at the pop-eyed officer; he had been like him once. He recalled how he had pranced about at the Battle of Omdurman on his white horse, paying more attention to his impeccable uniform than the men suffering from heat exhaustion.

The troops marched on, a few of them cheering the tanks as they got out of the way to let them through. The earth was churned up by the British preliminary bombardment. Twenty-four hours before this had been enemy territory and a few bodies lay around to confirm this. The slaughter became more evident as the tanks pushed on and Bland shut his eyes, grimacing, as the tracks smashed over the legs of a dead man.

The white-painted tanks became liberally splashed with mud, and Bland knew that the camouflage idea had not worked. He sat above the hatch, despite the requests of the driver to keep his head down. The smoke mingled with mist and drizzle until it was difficult to see more than fifty yards. Great rolls of barbed wire lay at all angles, usually surrounded by bodies, some of them with wire cutters still gripped in their hands. Stretcher bearers loomed out of the murk.

'What has happened?' shouted Bland.

'The Australians have been rolled back,' the stretcher bearer replied, bent double by his load. 'They've lost three thousand men. The artillery haven't cut the wire, the miserable bastards.'

As he finished speaking a shell burst nearby. There was a crunching of metal, and Bland turned his head to see one of his tanks blazing. Damn it all, he thought gritting his teeth, they were sitting targets. On a horse one could at least go faster than five miles per hour.

On the tanks went, the artillery fire becoming heavier and heavier until Bland climbed back into the foul-smelling interior. Men were moving both ways. No one could see whether this meant success or failure. A flash of wing-tip caught his eye through the visor, heralding an explosion; they were German aeroplanes, dropping bombs. They must be confident coming down this low. Where was the Royal Flying Corps?

Many of the British craft were earthbound, owing to the bad flying conditions. One of those who were keen to get aloft and help in the Vimy battle was Flight-Sergeant Leonard Oakwood, newly married and anxious to get the war over as soon as possible. Being in the air gave flyers delusions of grandeur; the scurrying men on the ground, looking like ants, seemed vulnerable and the artillery, represented by matchsticks, ludicrous. Only when these matchsticks pointed heavenwards and the dull crumps of exploding anti-aircraft shells sounded nearby did pilots realize that they too were expendable.

Oakwood's new CO came out and looked at the low-lying clouds and the banks of mist that swept across the snow. 'We'll have to go and help the Australians,' he said suddenly.

A few minutes later a flight of scouts took off, with Oakwood taking his post on the starboard wing in his Sopwith Pup. He liked the Pup. More difficult to control than the DHs and FEs he was accustomed to but the engine being in front of the pilot gave him a sense of control, of knowing what was going on, though he no longer enjoyed the extensive field of view.

The weather seemed to be getting worse rather than better but broke sufficiently over the front line for Oakwood to see that numbing picture that was to haunt him for the rest of his life, the scars of the trenches and the slow-moving creatures who moved from one set to another, as if drawn on wires like performing fleas. Victories measured in a hundred yards, thought Leonard Oakwood, this was something that his father could never have visualized. To think that more soldiers were killed in a day down there in the mud than were lost in an entire colonial war!

A group of slow-moving German two-seaters moved between the British flight and the ground, screening the front line. The leader of the British flight began his dive, with Oakwood breaking off at an angle in case the two-seaters were protected by fast moving Fokkers flying above.

The group of Albatrosses split up as the Sopwiths dived and Oakwood could see the tracer bullets from the rear-gunner heading towards the British aeroplanes. The Sopwiths zoomed up, ready for the second assault, and the German aircraft reformed. They were taken unawares by Oakwood, who approached them from the flank, coming on them out of a bank of grey snow-laden cloud. The extent of the cloud confused him and he emerged at point-blank range, close enough to see the startled expression on the face of the rear gunner, who began to swing his gun to deal with the danger from this unexpected quarter. Deliberately Oakwood pressed the trigger of the Vickers gun, firing through the propeller, but two seconds was all that he could manage before diving beneath the enemy, his upper wings almost scraping the wheels.

One of the Albatrosses, seeing what was happening, banked away from the smaller British machine to present a more difficult target and enable the gunner to have a go, but with the speed of his dive and his extra twenty miles per hour Oakwood went parallel with it, turning in sharply to rake the enemy from propeller to tail fin. Holes appeared in the fuselage as if burned in with a red-hot poker. Oakwood grinned as he saw the orange glow behind the engine and the tongues of flame beginning to sweep out, crackling the paint of the body. Abruptly the German plane broke off contact, giving the gunner time to get in a short burst at the underside of the Sopwith before Oakwood completed an arc and came in again, spraying the enemy from above. The flame could hardly be seen now in dense black smoke billowing from the engine. Suddenly the enemy dropped like a stone. The other craft were winging their way back to the German support lines, pursued by the rest of Oakwood's flight, but as the anti-aircraft fire became fiercer they broke off and climbed for height, disappearing into cloud.

A pattern of shots appeared on the lower wing of Oakwood's plane, and he realized that he was near enough to the ground to permit the German machine-gunners to fire. He climbed, looking down at the confused landscape and seeing a small section of tanks battling towards the enemy lines. Three of them were laid out already, two of them wrapped in flames that sent smoke hundreds of feet into the air. A slow enemy two-seater appeared near by and Oakwood, glancing at his petrol gauge, went in pursuit, though the German plane was soon lost in the clouds. It was time to return to base.

Suddenly Oakwood's altimeter disappeared with a smashing of glass. He put his foot sharply on the rudder bar, cursing himself for having been lured after the two-seater, but as he looked round he saw no enemy. It must have been an expended bullet fired from the two-seater as a parting gesture, a fluke hit. As he turned his nose towards home, he saw in the parting of the clouds a swarm of enemy scouts attacking a British two-seater. The observer's gun, pointing downwards, told its own story; he was dead.

The two-seater banked, white vapour pouring from the engine—steam from a punctured radiator or petrol from a severed lead pouring over the hot engine. If it was the first Oakwood knew the pilot had a chance; if it was the second, a spark from the exhaust, one tracer bullet, would fire the vapour. The German Pfalz scouts were too engrossed in finishing off their wounded prey to see Oakwood bearing down on them. Oakwood, determined to try and save the other British aircraft, pressed the trigger of his gun, but after a second it stopped. Two of the German pilots, seeing Oakwood wheel away, realized that his gun had jammed, and went in pursuit. Oakwood saw that they were closing on him, and desperately tried to ease the blockage—no luck. Seeing a large cloud formation swirling towards him he plunged into it, climbing.

The clouds seemed never ending, and he began to find it more difficult to breathe. He must be near his ceiling. His goggles began to ice up, and frantically he rubbed his arm across them. Engine stuttering, propeller vainly trying to cope with the thin air, Oakwood began to lose height. His arms were difficult to move and his legs were like lead, but as he went lower the engine picked up and some life returned to his numbed limbs.

With the altimeter not working and the clouds low he had to keep his wits about him to make certain that he did not emerge from the clouds at ground level and crash. He took some chocolate from the compartment in front of him but his fingers would not bend to remove the wrapping. The cotton-wool he

187

was flying in was replaced by drifting strands, and soon he could see the ground, a thousand feet below. He followed the trenches until he came to a configuration he recognized, and a quarter of an hour later he landed.

For a few minutes he sat still, his head thumping, then slowly climbed out, hanging on to the wing to stop himself falling over.

'Where have you been, Oakwood?' asked a fellow pilot. 'The North Pole? You're all iced up.'

Oakwood stumbled, and the other man caught him by the elbow. He told a mechanic to give him a hand to take Oakwood to the sick bay.

'What's the matter?' Oakwood muttered.

'Frost-bite, old lad,' said the other genially, 'pretty bad, too. You've lost all the skin off your lips. And you just married!'

The flight leader paid a visit to Oakwood, and later discussed him with the CO in the officers' mess. 'Too fond of going off on his own', he said, 'but he got a Hun. Went down like a Roman candle.'

'That's four,' said the CO with satisfaction. 'I had heard that he ran into a bit of trouble with Scott in his previous squadron, but he seems all right to me.'

'So long as he doesn't get made up to captain,' said the flight leader pointedly. 'We don't want his sort in the mess. Lower the tone, Sir. If he wants to be a one man band he should have joined a Jerry *jagdstaffeln.*'

'I'll get him on a bombing escort,' said the CO soothingly.

'It's not that I've got anything against him,' said the flight leader, struggling to be fair, 'but he's not one of us. And he's a Brummie.'

There was nothing more to be said.

25

British flyers had so long been equipped with inferior planes that when they were at last provided with aircraft that were the equal of, indeed superior to, those of the enemy, they failed to take advantage of them, and even the exploits of the young brash aces were put down to luck. Consequently many flyers suffered under a sense of inferiority and many were killed by their own lack of confidence. As more pilots arrived from England the front-line RFC men were given a break by being posted to a home station.

They also acted as ferry pilots and Leonard was allocated an ageing Vickers Gun Bus to fly to Northolt. It was a strange sensation to head north-west, away from the fighting lines, and it was not until he was over the Channel that Leonard stopped glancing over his shoulder or into the sun for the tell-tale glint of a German machine out for trouble.

England looked placid and peaceful from four thousand feet, as if the people down there had never heard of war or rumour of war. And as he flew in to land the aerodrome was empty of aircraft and the large hangars gave the impression of being evacuated for the duration.

'Where's everyone gone?' he asked a mechanic who trotted up to help him down and place chocks beneath the wheels.

'They've gone to London,' said the mechanic.

'What? All of them?' Leonard asked, astonished. He knew that leave was easier in the home stations but this was ridiculous. Only when he entered the sergeants' mess did he understand the situation.

'They're after Gothas,' explained Sergeant Foley. 'I would have gone only I've busted an ankle. There's Ben looking for you. See you later.'

'We've got your particulars in,' said Ben, flicking over a sheaf of papers, 'you'll be a big help. Have something to eat and I'll show you our prize exhibit.'

The atmosphere in the mess was formal and almost chilly and Leonard was uncomfortably aware that his casual wear was not the ticket. This was the peacetime RFC, he thought, with photographs of the aviation pioneers on the walls and a large four-bladed propeller mounted over one of the doors, the relic of some long-forgotten aeroplane. He was not impressed by the meal, which was cold and dull, and was glad to escape into the fresh air.

The prize exhibit proved to be a Gotha bomber forced down near Northolt. Leonard gasped. It was the largest aeroplane he

189

had ever seen, sixty-six feet from wing-tip to wing-tip, and he wished that some of the aircraft he had flown had been fitted with engines like these, which he learned were 220 horsepower Benz units.

'It carries a bomb load of a thousand pounds,' said Ben, 'and it's no slouch either. Ninety miles an hour and it can outpace us in the climb.'

It had three machine-guns, one of which was able to fire through a channel cut in the underside of the rear fuselage. An unsuspecting British scout coming up on what was usually an unprotected area would have a surprise.

'What's that?' asked Leonard pointing.

'Clever, these Huns,' said Ben. 'Sometimes the oil of guns congeals at high altitudes. The casings of these are heated by a dynamo driven off the starboard engine.' He looked at the big aeroplane with something like affection, pointing out the sophisticated bomb-aiming device. He also told Leonard of its defects—the main spars were glued not screwed, the ailerons were too small and the machine was sluggish in the air and, in general, it was flimsy. It had to be to get its heavy load into the air.

'I'll enjoy having a crack at it,' said Leonard.

'You will do, boy, you will do,' promised Ben, nodding, 'but rather you than me.' He looked up into the air as half a dozen aeroplanes came in to land.

'Not a chance,' said one of the pilots as he passed them, 'they dropped their bombs, but we lost them in the cloud.'

He did not seem very concerned. He was off to see *Chu Chin Chow*, and was relieved that he was back to get up to London in plenty of time for a decent meal and the show.

During the evening Leonard sat in the mess looking through the latest magazines while somewhere near he could hear a gramophone playing ragtime. It seemed a waste of time. Birmingham and Elizabeth were only four hours away. If he were a daredevil like Harry he would have borrowed a car and taken French leave—if only he could drive. In the morning he went to see the sergeant in the office, whom he knew only as Ben, to see what prospects for leave were.

'Thin,' said Ben without ceremony, 'the flyers here take things easy when blokes like you come in from France. You

190

won't be here long. Every two days there's a cry from your people over there to have experienced pilots back. You might have a chance of getting off for a couple of days if I push you in this afternoon's flight. Have you flown a Pup?'

The flight commander took Leonard on one side. 'When we approach London we go our various ways,' he said. 'We only know they're on their way at usually twelve thousand feet. So dress up warm. Good luck, anyway. You've seen our specimen, so you know what to look out for. Just one tip. The thing's so big you may feel inclined to bang off your gun before it's in range.'

'Wouldn't it be best to intercept them near the coast?' asked Leonard, perplexed.

'The Royal Naval Air Service does that,' explained the officer, 'not with any marked effect. But ours not to wonder why.' He waved nonchalantly, and strode away to his plane.

A mechanic came up to Leonard's Sopwith Pup and waited patiently to swing the propeller. 'Good luck, Sarge!' he shouted as the engine roared into life. Leonard nodded, pulled his fur-lined helmet closer around his face, tucked his chin well into his flying suit and, keeping his station, accelerated down the runway and into the crisp afternoon air.

It was fine flying weather with good visibility. Down below he could see the barrage balloons swaying to and fro like some creatures from a grotesque ballet. The serpent-like form of the Thames became thinner as he climbed. One by one the other aircraft in the flight of six split off to continue their sortie alone and Leonard let off a short burst to make certain his guns were all right.

Cloud was coming in fast, and for the first time Leonard appreciated the full difficulties of the pilots. It was like looking for a needle in a haystack.

He reflected on the stupidities and short-sightedness of the War Office, and, by implication, the brigadiers and assorted red-tabbed generals who administered the affairs of the flying corps. By ignoring the possibilities of aerial warfare they had let the French and the Germans take the lead in aero-engine production; by being slow off the mark when wireless came along they had relinquished the chance of providing an effective ground to air communication network. Some aeroplanes, he knew, carried wireless sets. But far too few. If he had a wireless set now he could get in touch with his fellows in the air to find out if they had spotted the Gothas. Or, if relationships between the RFC and the Royal Naval Air Service had been less tense, the pilots near the coast could have told him if anything was happening up high.

He could understand the off-hand attitude of the Northolt pilots to their patrols. The odds were against them from the start. He floated in and out of cloud formations and it came as a shock when he saw, not two hundred yards away, one of his own flight. The pilot was waving at him. Leonard, feeling foolish, waved back. The generally cool reception he had received had not prepared him for such familiarity. Then he realized that it was not a wave, but a gesticulation. To confirm it the pilot in the other machine pulled out his Very pistol and an emerald-green flare blossomed in the east.

The other man had sharper eyes than Leonard had; high above them flying north-north-west were fourteen aircraft. The two single-seaters began to climb, but it took several minutes before they were appreciably nearer. Another British plane of a type not recognized by Leonard joined in; it was not one of his flight. All three closed in on the Gothas; the German planes seemed immensely slow, though Leonard recognized that this was deceptive. From a distance he had seen a Zeppelin seem almost motionless, yet knew that it was going forward at quite a respectable speed. He heard the crackle of machine-gun fire. It was a long burst and he knew that at least one of the gunners in a Gotha was inexperienced, firing well out of range.

At last the Gothas seemed near enough to let them have a burst and simultaneously, as if they were telepathic, the German machine-gunners replied, their pilots keeping perfect formation so that their gunners would be able to cover all the vulnerable points. Out of the corner of his eye Leonard saw one of his fellows heading straight for the leading Gotha, without the constant alteration of course that would present a more difficult target. At the most conservative estimate therefore there were at least fourteen machine-guns trained on him. The German gunners made the most of their opportunity, reckoning this reckless English tyro worth a full drum each. The British plane did a half-turn, fabric flapping loose from the

192

upper wing, and sped away, a plume of steam from the radiator.

Vizfeldwebel Kluck, commanding Gotha number 660, saw his one adversary retiring ignominiously from battle and grinned, putting his thumb in the air at his pilot. The pilot was less sanguine. He was watching the tiny Sopwith Pup, veering and swinging so that his gunners found it difficult to sight it up. The third aeroplane could not be seen and he scanned the heavens anxiously. He had recognized it as a Bristol Fighter and he heard that they were formidable. Something intangible whizzed down fifty yards away. With a jolt he realized that the mad Englishman was trying to bomb them.

The neat Teutonic formation was for a few minutes in doubt, and Leonard, also seeing the Bristol Fighter high above, took the opportunity to rake the Gothas with a long burst. The Gotha bringing up the rear dropped down, the pilot a new-comer to the bomber and automatically covering up as if he were flying a scout. Leonard turned and raced down after the Gotha that had become detached. He fired a full drum at fifty yards, without apparent effect and, changing drums, went in again at right angles. He saw the tracer entering the wings of the aircraft. The Gotha jettisoned his bombs to give added lift, and a herd of cows in a field ten thousand feet below had a few awkward moments. Leonard could see tracer coming his way, heard the nick as his starboard wing was clipped, but as the Gotha slowly climbed, like a mastodon rejoining its fellows, he let it have the remainder of his second drum. He could see the machine-gun position beneath the fuselage, even the gunner struggling with his weapon. Feverishly Leonard reached down into his cockpit and picked up a fresh drum of ammunition, using all his skill to keep to his post beneath the fuselage of his prey, knowing that he was masked from the others and aware that for some reason the gunner was not firing on him.

The gunner was mortally wounded. Through a red haze he saw the British plane and then he collapsed. As Leonard jammed on his third drum of ammunition and emptied it through the rear-gun position the German gunner was hurled, a bloody mangled mess, back into the cockpit. Slowly the tail section of the Gotha toppled over with a rending of wood and the plane cartwheeled down. Leonard peeled away, out of ammunition and almost out of fuel. As he headed for Northolt he saw the Bristol Fighter dive down at the Gothas, apparently inconclusively.

'Your Gotha's confirmed,' said Ben a few hours later, 'it dropped like a stone near Wimbledon.'

'Good work, lad,' said Sergeant Foley gruffly. The pilot who had been driven away after his vainglorious attack stared through Leonard icily. It was not fair for a second lieutenant to be made to feel a fool in front of a common sergeant. He was therefore taken aback when a strange captain approached him and reviled him for his stupid behaviour in the air.

'I was in a Brisfit watching your bloody antics,' he growled, 'who was in the Pup?'

'I have no idea,' said the lieutenant, and his attitude got him posted back to the cavalry from which he had so briefly emerged.

Captain Thomas, who had left Farnborough to help start an interceptor station near Southend, soon found out who had been flying the Sopwith Pup.

'Sterling stuff, Sergeant,' he said, clapping Leonard on the back. Leonard stared at him blankly.

'I was in the Bristol Fighter above you,' Thomas explained. 'I tried to bomb the buggers. But that was a waste of time. I thought you might be from Northolt. It's the first time anyone's downed a Gotha from here. Though they won't thank you for it. They're gentlemen here, you see, Sergeant, damned bad form to bag a Hun. That's why I'm taking you back to Southend with me. You're only a slim 'un. I think we can cram you in.'

There did not seem to be any opportunity to say no. The commanding officer at Northolt, who had been playing golf and was resentful of the high-handedness of Captain Thomas, flatly refused to let Leonard go on leave.

'We bring you all the way from France to help deal with the Gotha menace, and then you are whisked away,' he said.

'That's not my fault, sir,' said Oakwood reproachfully.

'I know it's not, Sergeant,' said the CO, 'but that's how I see it.'

When the Bristol Fighter landed at Southend, Thomas explained why he wanted Leonard. 'As you know, we forced down one Gotha which Northolt has on show. We questioned

194

the crew. They're not happy with Gothas. We haven't done very well with them, but the Huns lose more when they are taking off and when they are landing, and to Archie. Especially Archie. The anti-aircraft people have a fine time with them.'

'We'd do better if we had better communications, sir,' said Leonard.

The captain misunderstood the statement. 'Between the corps and the Royal Naval Air Service,' he agreed.

'No, I mean wireless,' said Leonard.

Thomas winced. 'You know that, do you?' he said. 'I know it, but does anyone else outside these four walls? Well, three and a bit walls . . .'

He looked sardonically around him. The corrugated iron hut with a half-built brick wall at one end seemed to prove that Whitehall had a long-seated grudge against him and his ideas.

Captain Thomas went on to say that because of their high losses, mainly due to the inherent faults in the plane, and anti-aircraft guns, the Germans were going to try night-bombing. The interrogation of the captured Gotha crew had told the British that.

The atmosphere at Southend was more congenial than at Northolt. There was an easy relationship between the officers and the other ranks, and all made the best of the primitive arrangements: the urinals in the open behind green canvas sheeting, the cookhouse converted from an old stable and the quarters. Captain Thomas lived in a decrepit gypsy caravan and Leonard found he had been allocated a small section of a charabanc that had long lost its wheels and every vestige of paint.

In the morning he was shown his new mount, the Bristol Fighter, or to give it its correct designation, the Bristol F2A. Thomas explained that its prototype had flown in September 1916, but it had then needed modifications. The engine radiators had obscured the pilot's vision.

'The Brisfit didn't start off too well,' said Thomas, patting the fuselage, 'it first saw action in April just gone, six went out, and two came back. They'd run into five Albatross D.IIIs led by Richthofen. The Huns thought we were easy meat. But you know what the trouble was?'

Leonard looked over the aeroplane thoughtfully. It had a

forward firing Vickers machine-gun as well as a twin Lewis on a Scarff ring in the rear cockpit—well-armed enough.

'It flies like a single seater,' Thomas explained, 'and we were using it like an old two-seater. You saw the way I went at the Gothas? Banging them with the Vickers. That's the way to do it, use the forward-firing gun and the Lewis only as an alternative. You'll like it. It hasn't got the nasty tricks of the Pup. I don't suppose you've come up against the Camel yet? You'll be flying one of those before the year's out, or, better still, the SE5a. There are some SE5s at the front, but the SE5a is a winner.'

That evening Leonard had his first taste of night flying, acting as observer to Captain Thomas. The petrol flares in huge metal tanks gave off a lurid glow as Thomas taxied to turn the aeroplane's nose into the wind. Then they were off, the lights of Southend dimmed by blackout regulations but still in evidence to give the pilot valuable information about whether or not he was flying on an even keel. At five thousand feet Thomas turned to Leonard and in the dim light of the instrument panel Leonard exchanged places with the pilot. He looked sardonically at the instruments. Thomas had invented an instrument for finding an artificial horizon, but the indicator was revolving like a heavily magnetized compass needle. Thomas had admitted that it needed a few modifications.

Captain Thomas sat in the observer's seat, rubbing his hands, staring into the blackness below. There had been no reports of any Gothas coming over, and he was content to use the evening as a test run for young Oakwood. The lad had confidence and was already a first-rate pilot; with night flying experience he could be a superlative one.

Knowing that one's senses can let one down, Leonard kept a watchful eye on the subdued luminescence of London so that he would not panic and get vertigo. Thomas had told him stories of pilots who had suddenly discovered that they did not know which way was up and had spun to their deaths. He kept his engine revolutions steady, and with attention divided between the lights of London and his instruments he was startled when Thomas bent over him and shouted, 'Up! Up! Climb!'

Thinking that the officer had some new novelty in store for him Leonard climbed until he felt his ears pricking as if some-

196

one was putting sharp needles into the lobes. The air was thinner, and he gulped in the cold air. He straightened out. Ahead of him was a faint grey shape. Suddenly searchlights probed the dark, settling on the shape. Kapitänleutnant Eichler, commanding the Zeppelin, released ballast and began to climb, cutting off his engines as the searchlights began to concentrate on a different area of the sky. He had heard that the English were using sound detectors.

He relaxed and opened his packet of sandwiches. His second-in-command tapped him on the shoulder. In the silence he could hear aero-engines. He cursed as far below he saw anti-aircraft shells bursting but Eichler nodded comfortingly, pointing to the altimeter. They were at fifteen thousand feet, too far for all but the most lucky of shells. He was debating whether to carry on and bomb the Midlands when he, too, heard an aero-engine.

His hand ice-cold at that altitude even inside the gloves, Leonard pressed the trigger of the forward-firing Vickers gun. It was such a huge target that it was impossible to miss. He poured one drum into it, and then another. Nothing happened. Angrily he reached for the Very pistol at the side of the cockpit but it was not there. Apparently undamaged the Zeppelin floated yet higher and as Leonard banked and turned for home Eichler ordered the engines to be switched on. He saw the exhaust sparks from the Bristol Fighter dwindle and disappear. Providence was on his side again and, as a token of his deliverance, he decided to drop his bombs into the sea.

Perplexed Leonard took his bearings on that sleeping metropolis on the port wing and flew towards Southend, following the snake of the Thames, glimmering with the light of anonymous vessels, large and small. He was still pondering about the events of the evening as he came in to land. Any tension that might have arisen, any doubts that he might have had about his ability to land an aircraft at night, were forgotten. He noted the disposition of the petrol flares and the direction of the oily smoke, and that seemed to him sufficient. His wheels touched down, and he slowly braked, the propeller turning over and then twitching to a halt. He removed his flying helmet and wiped the oil from his face.

Captain Thomas looked tired as he sat back in his canvas chair in his caravan. He poured himself a brandy.

'What happened?' asked Leonard. 'What in God's name happened?'

Thomas looked at him dully. 'You're either a stickler for the small print or you're not,' he said. 'I'm not. I trust the men I command.'

'I'm talking about that Zep, sir,' said Leonard.

'So am I,' said Thomas. 'I assume every man under me is doing his duty. Then I'm proved wrong. It happened at Farnborough, it's happening here. Of course you hit the Zep, young Oakwood. But you know why it didn't go up in smoke? Because the buggers didn't put any tracer in the ammunition drums, or any exploding bullets, such as I ordered. The bullets just went through the sausage, right through it and came out the other side. They'll notice it in about three days when the Zep begins to look soggy. As for the Very pistol, one of the mechanics borrowed that this morning to experiment with a flare path. I thought a line of petrol could be fired to give direction at take-off. It didn't seem necessary after all, but he forgot to put the pistol back in its place. I should have checked on that. I'm getting sloppy, too. The war's beginning to go on too long, that's the truth of it.'

He poured himself a second brandy, motioning to Leonard to do the same if he felt inclined, but Leonard shook his head.

'I'm disillusioned, Oakwood,' he said, 'bloody fed-up. Tommy Atkins on the ground is being slaughtered by stupid generals who never get their fat arses near the fighting line. Tommy Atkins in the air is buggered and bewildered by incompetence at all levels: colonels and brigadiers who don't know an aileron from a spanner; mechanics who're only glad that they're not fighting and it's sod the men in the air; stupid bloody women in the factories who make bullets that won't fire and gun mechanisms that jam because they're too bloody idle to do a good job, and civil servants who won't follow up good ideas because they finish work at four and have to get back into the suburbs before the common men leave their jobs and pack the trains.'

He looked at Leonard quizzically. 'I'll be all right in the morning, Oakwood, but I've known aeroplanes since before the

Wright Brothers and aeroplanes could have won the war. I know designers who could build aeroplanes that would dwarf the Gotha and could drop a ton of bombs on Berlin every minute of every day. I know a designer of motor-car engines who swears he could produce an aero-engine of five hundred horse-power. But what stops it, eh, what stops it?'

'Money, sir,' said Leonard.

'That's it, Oakwood,' said Thomas slapping his thigh, 'they spend millions on a hundred thousand shells which they shoot into no man's land, millions on a navy that only goes out when the Admiralty is feeling perky, millions on dull dogs like Haig and French and the rest of that motley crew.' He brooded silently. 'Run along, Oakwood,' he said quietly, 'things will look different in the morning.'

26

Lieutenant-Colonel Blenkinsop and Major Hoare-Bentley sat at twin desks in their Whitehall office determining priorities, and wondering whether they could allocate the new batch of SE5s to the Royal Flying Corps without alienating the Royal Naval Air Service.

'They will want to stick floats on them and use them as seaplanes,' said Blenkinsop.

'I think we can forget them,' said Hoare-Bentley, his uniform tightly buttoned and his buttons shining.

It was said that when he first came to Whitehall he wore spurs. He did not speak with any enthusiasm. He was more concerned with the coming formation of the Royal Air Force, and was wondering how he stood. He knew that ranks would be renamed, and whether he would be a squadron leader or a flight commander was at present under discussion. He did not like the change. Whatever he was called he could only regard it as a poor substitute for major, if not actually a climb-down.

All the memoranda piling on his desk spoke of menaces.

There was the Zeppelin menace, mercifully on the decline; the Gotha menace, which seemed to be subsiding, and there were still plaintive epistles about the Fokker menace, though they were in a minority compared with the triplane menace. He had heard that the triplane was being scrapped, but from what he read it was still a subject of concern in France. He mentioned the Fokker menace to his superior. Blenkinsop waved his hand irritably.

'They're old applications coming back,' he said, 'those fellows in France don't realize how busy we are. Or rather they do, and they think they will get their aeroplanes if they trot out the same old excuses.'

The destinations and fate of thousands, tens of thousands, of airmen were in the hands of such as Blenkinsop and Hoare-Bentley. They were men who tried to be fair but were occasionally exposed to political blasts. The politicians who made noises and who were the biggest nuisances tended to get heard more often. It was they who, frightened to death by Gothas and Zeppelins in the clouds over their domiciles, urged the recall of squadrons from France. It was they who, when the Zeppelins appeared to concentrate their activities on such insalubrious localities as Wapping, had their priorities rejigged by powerful pressures from the French.

Blenkinsop and Hoare-Bentley detested, above all, unconventional pressures and when it transpired that they had their place of origin in an obscure establishment near Southend run by a mere captain, their chagrin knew no bounds. The winding-up of Captain Thomas's interceptor station was always on the cards. Thomas had made the cardinal mistake of not going through the proper channels, and when it transpired that his unit had only accounted for one Gotha, believed destroyed, it was left for the Royal Naval Air Service to take over the Thames estuary.

Sergeant Oakwood had been sent up on three successive nights after his disappointing encounter with the Zeppelin but, although he had found the night-flying experience stimulating, he had made no further contact with Gothas or airships.

Night flying at a height made his nose tender, and when a corporal mechanic saw him dabbing at his nose as he climbed down from his plane he said, 'Sarge, why don't you go sick?'

200

'Why should I do that?' asked Leonard.

'It's the only way you can get leave in this bloody place,' said the corporal, 'it's a bit of a wangle, you see. We've got no MO here, only a sergeant and he's all right. No MI room, so he shunts you off to London for an examination. If you want to go further afield, he covers up for you. In bed overnight for further observation. It don't say whose bed and what for, but a nod's as good as a wink.'

Leonard grinned, and nodded. He had agreed with all that Captain Thomas had said four nights before, but to some degree Thomas only had himself to blame. He expected his men to work like dogs but on the other hand he did not offer them any concessions. If they asked for leave he told them that they could not be spared and that the war was more important than their contentment.

'Nosebleed, eh?' said the medical sergeant slyly. 'Daresay someone will have to put some drops up your hooter. Not the kind of things we do here, no facilities. Is it Birmingham you want to get to? You'll have to pay your own way from London, but I'll arrange for you to get a warrant to Fenchurch Street.'

And it was as simple as that. He sent a telegram to the shop but when he stepped off the train it was not Elizabeth who greeted him, but his mother. Jane hugged her son to her.

'Where's Elizabeth?' he asked.

'She's at home in Coventry looking after her father. He's got influenza. Had it for weeks now.'

Leonard felt a wave of disappointment sweep over him.

'You look well,' said Jane lamely. To her surprise she did not feel deliriously happy. Leonard had always been quiet and remote; now he seemed a stranger.

'How's Dad?' he asked.

'He'll be so happy to see you,' Jane said, 'he's not well. He had a shock. A woman came in and said that she'd had a son by Harry. She was a tart, Leonard, nothing but a tart.'

'War does strange things,' said Leonard. 'Harry was always headstrong.'

'About going with a tart?' Jane asked.

Leonard was secretly shocked. His mother had never mentioned such a word before; it was as though she had lived without needing to know about prostitutes.

201

He was also ashamed that he was not more concerned about his mother, Harry or even his father. He wanted to get to Elizabeth, to climb into bed with her and enjoy her soft yielding body and as he walked out of the station he bitterly regretted sending the telegram. Though he could not have known that Elizabeth was no longer there. Why hadn't she written to him? Then he realized that she probably had and the letters were wending their way to and from France, read and re-read by busy censors, sent to Northolt, and perhaps, in the fullness of time, finding their way to Southend.

He had not written to her since France. He was always assuming that in the next day or two he would be granted leave. He looked sidelong at Jane. She was beginning to look her age and, throwing off his petulance and repressing his longing for Elizabeth, he put his arm round her as they walked to the shop.

As the door jangled Jane called, 'It's only me, George!'

George appeared at the top of the stairs. He had dressed himself for the occasion and solemnly he descended the stairs.

He moved very slowly. 'I get tired very easily,' he said as he reached the foot of the staircase, panting.

'We have only to go back up again, George,' said Jane briskly.

'I had to make the effort,' George said, moving to Leonard and gripping both his hands in his. 'Welcome back, son,' he said.

'It's not that long,' said Leonard, shocked by his father's rapid deterioration.

'When you've rested, George, come on back upstairs,' said Jane, 'I'll make some tea and something for you to eat. We don't do too badly for rations. One of my lady customers sends in eggs every week and somebody else sends us bacon. I think we can run to two eggs for Leonard, don't you, George?'

George sat down.

Jane waited for an instant at the foot of the stairs. 'Let him come up himself,' she whispered to Leonard. 'It helps him, gives him confidence.'

'You go up, Leonard,' said George. 'I'll take my time.'

Leonard nodded.

'It's partly in his mind,' said Jane to him as she busied herself in the kitchen. 'He's mentally weary, sees troubles where none exists. We're very comfortably off, Leonard. The shop is doing remarkably well. But every two or three weeks he goes on about the workhouse. I tell him that there is no workhouse these days. Try and get his mind off it.'

Leonard sat with his father and told him about his experiences in France, about Gotha-hunting, and his brief encounter with the Zeppelin. George sat silently, smiling absently. Leonard a sergeant, but never taken a squad of men on a parade ground. Officers did what Leonard was doing, in his experience, not sergeants.

'It's a strange old war,' he said, 'when I was your age a war was what happened somewhere else. The government sent soldiers out and that was that. Everyone forgot the war until they came back. Except the Boer War. I suppose that was a bit like this one, though I was out there all the time.' Memories of the veldt came back to him, the silent adventures into the hinterland. And the fighting, the Boers on their horses, their bandoliers across their shoulders, their beards bristling.

'They're on our side now,' he said suddenly.

'Who is, Dad?' Leonard asked.

'I was thinking aloud,' George apologized, 'the Boers. They were fighters.'

'So are the Germans,' said Leonard. 'Don't believe what you read about them being cowards. They go on, like us.'

'Half of them here wouldn't go on,' said George, musing, 'the other half are doing well by the war and would go on, no matter what—provided that they did not have to do the fighting. I've seen them come into the shop, working girls in the factories, spending a pound or more on a pair of silly slippers that will last them a week.'

He sounded, thought Leonard, like Captain Thomas. One of them long past it, sitting on the sidelines, the other still involved, but both of them depressed by what they saw. He wondered how he himself stood it, and was surprised to find that the stupidities and opportunities that irked both his father and his commanding officer meant little to him. He was doing a job he liked doing; the fighting was incidental, the flying was all. Even the pinpricks were of no consequence—Lieutenant Scott's arrogance, the disinterest of the Northolt flyers, the stubborn refusal of Captain Thomas to give his men leave.

'You've heard about Harry?' George asked.

'A little,' admitted Leonard, 'but it'll all come right in the end. When the war's over. Harry's been through the thick of it.'

'All the time,' said George half to himself, 'I thought that Harry would be a credit to the regiment, even when he was spending his time gambling and wenching. He was a disappointment. But you made up for it.'

Leonard was embarrassed. 'Wait until you hear his side of it,' he said. He looked at the clock on the mantelpiece. It was time to be going to Coventry.

His mother put her hand to her mouth. 'Oh, dear!' she said, 'we've kept you talking so long.'

'I'll have to go now,' said Leonard.

'She won't know you're here,' said Jane.

'I must go,' said Leonard, getting up. 'Perhaps I'll get a longer leave soon. I've snatched this one.'

'It's too late,' said Jane placatingly, 'the last train's gone.'

'I could cycle,' said Leonard, annoyed.

'We sold the bicycles,' said Jane, 'we don't cycle now. We're over sixty.'

So Leonard stayed the night, alone, staring at the ceiling, hearing the early morning scuffle of feet down the arcade and the bell on the door heralding the first customers of the day. George was still asleep, his mother told him. Leonard kissed her on the cheek, then made his way to the station. He passed the journey to Coventry in a fever of anticipation, and marvelled how events could alter the look of a place. The house which had seemed so uninviting when he had first visited it now looked almost beautiful. But why were the curtains drawn? Could it be that Elizabeth's father had died?

His first thought, which he realized was uncharitable, was whether this would throw a damper on the reunion. He had not liked the father. He knocked at the door but there was no reply, and as he stood pondering he saw a face at the next door neighbour's window, a thin pinched face. The neighbour's door clicked open.

'Good morning, young man,' said the woman, 'can I help you?'

'My name's Oakwood,' said Leonard, 'I was wondering where Elizabeth was. She's my wife, you know.'

'Oh, yes, we know,' said the woman coyly. 'My name's Mrs Busst—two s's, one of which is silent—not like me, my husband used to say. Didn't you know?'

'Didn't I know what?' Leonard asked anxiously.

'He's gone convalescent,' Mrs Busst said, 'to Weston-super-Mare where they always go for their holidays. The railway's paying for it. Not fair, if you ask me. Come in and have a cup of tea.'

As she poured the tea, Mrs Busst chattered with the persistence of a cage-bird. 'I'm so glad she married a nice young man like you, someone who would appreciate her *difficulties*, someone who would *understand* her . . .'

'Difficulties?' asked Leonard.

'We never thought she would marry after what happened,' Mrs Busst went on.

'I'm sorry,' said Leonard. 'What happened?'

'I don't suppose she would tell you,' said Mrs Busst, 'she was a loyal girl. But you must have seen the dolls? She never goes anywhere without them. We thought she would never grow out of them. My husband, before he passed over, thought she was childish. She never had a boyfriend, you know.'

'What happened?' Leonard repeated.

'Elizabeth found her father in bed with another woman,' said Mrs Busst with a rush, 'she was thirteen. Very impressionable. Her mother told me. She knew.'

She talked in so spasmodic a style that Leonard had difficulty in getting the gist of the message. What did Mrs Busst mean—that Elizabeth's mother knew that her daughter was impressionable or knew about her husband's amours? It did not matter very much. Elizabeth was not there, and that was the end of it. He thanked Mrs Busst for the tea, and left. At the station he conceived the idea of catching the train to Weston-super-Mare and bluffing it through when he got back to Southend. But the inspiration was short-lived; he was on active service, and could be shot.

It was not a pleasant journey to London. When he alighted from the train and heard his name being called on the railway loudspeaker he assumed that Captain Thomas had discovered his absence and was lining up a court martial for him. Apathetically he went to the stationmaster's office, half-expecting to see

205

a pair of grim-faced military policemen. But the stationmaster was smiling. Mrs Busst had been more effectual than Leonard had imagined, and was not just a twittering nuisance. She had telegraphed to Elizabeth in Weston-super-Mare telling her that Leonard was on the 3.40 to London.

The stationmaster looked at his watch.

'She'll be here at 7.20,' he said. 'Would you care to wait here?'

There were forty minutes to go. Leonard waited on the platform, his heart thumping.

She jumped from the train before it had stopped, raced to him and flung her arms around him, crying. She had no luggage with her, only a small handbag. As she nestled against him Leonard wondered if she had, even in the hurry, brought a doll with her.

'I don't care what they say about me having no luggage,' she said.

'What?' asked Leonard as they left the station.

'I want you, Leonard,' Elizabeth said fiercely, 'I've never wanted anything else so much as you. And I want you now.' She looked at the line of hotels outside the station. 'That one,' she said, pointing. 'I like the name.'

Leonard never found what the name of the hotel was. He allowed himself to drift behind this strangely changed and exciting Elizabeth. She ordered a hotel room, stared at the receptionist aggressively, and led the way upstairs.

Once inside the bedroom she tore off her clothes, letting them fall anywhere and fell upon him, wrenching off his shoes and socks as he pulled his shirt over his shoulders. They said nothing as they climbed on to the bed. Elizabeth took the lead, straddling him, her breasts and buttocks heaving, gasping as she reached her climax and digging her nails into his thighs. Even in her rapture she felt that this might be the last time she would see her husband and make love to him.

He rolled away from her exhausted but she coaxed him to new endeavours. When it was finally over it seemed to him that they had been making love for hours. But it was only nine o'clock. She dressed herself silently, suddenly ashamed of her exuberance and forwardness. They had scarcely said a word to each other since their arrival at the hotel; there had been nothing to say. Now Leonard was formal and guarded. They discussed Mrs Busst at length, and what a good sort she was for telegraphing; Leonard expressed mild distress at Elizabeth's father's illness; she asked him about the war, and he answered in the stock clichés of the popular press. Eventually she asked him the most important question, the one she had feared to ask. When was he going back?

Leonard was sexually satisfied. His limbs ached and he wanted to do nothing more than sleep. He knew that he could telephone the medical sergeant and see if he could cadge another night away from the station but the edge was off his appetite. This was deeply disappointing, because during that first frenzy he felt he could have gone on all night. Did Harry, with his train of conquests, have this problem?

'I'll have to go back tonight,' he said, 'this isn't a leave, you know.' He wrote his new address, and she tucked it in her handbag. As they left the bedroom he looked back. There was nothing in the room but a bed, a wardrobe, and a chest of drawers with the veneer peeling from it. There were hundreds of rooms like it, he thought, in London, rooms where men and women went for a half-hour of passion. It was the kind of room one did not pass a night in.

He paid the bill at the desk, and they walked out of the hotel, hailed a motor-cab to Fenchurch Street, where he caught the next train to Southend. She had clasped him to her and he had kissed her lovingly but without passion. 'Come back, my darling,' she had whispered. 'I will,' he promised. But as he sat back in the carriage he realized that he had said it automatically. Of course he would come back. What else would he do? Did Elizabeth think that he was going to be killed? He felt a chill. Did she have some premonition?

But Elizabeth had only read the casualty reports in the papers, seen the pages of photographs of men who had died for king and country, and knew that the average life of a new subaltern in the trenches was a matter of weeks. She had read that airmen were no sooner trained and sent into the skies than they were killed. The average flyer was one who lived a few bright weeks and fell from the clouds. As she went back to her parents she prayed that Leonard would remain safe and sound

207

in this place at Southend. That did not sound too dangerous at all.

Absently she looked at the route map on the side of the carriage, showing where all the lines of the network intersected. She was on the Great Western, she knew, but there were others that went north to Crewe, Manchester, to Scotland. She read the posters, volunteer for this, volunteer for that, work on the land, join the Red Cross, drive an ambulance, make shells for the guns on the Western Front. She had never wanted to volunteer for anything.

The train was approaching Oxford, and she peered through the darkness at the anonymous suburbs. Suburbs were the same everywhere. The guard came down the train, carrying his lamp. He intoned a series of place names. One of them broke into her reverie.

'What?' she asked.

'Birmingham, Miss,' said the guard, smiling.

The poor girl had been crying. Some lovers' tiff, no doubt.

'Change at Oxford for Birmingham,' he said, moving on.

Elizabeth looked at her ticket to Weston-super-Mare but it was not important. She changed trains. She was going back to the Oakwoods.

27

'You've missed the fun,' said the sergeant mechanic, grinning, 'we had a couple of brass-hats down here. The old man went on a bender the night before and he didn't take too kindly to them.'

Such was his summary of the visit of Major Hoare-Bentley and a lieutenant with a wispy moustache whose only qualifications were that he could drive and was friendly with the owner of Southend's leading hotel. So they had a good meal after their inspection of the Thomas establishment, which reminded Hoare-Bentley of nothing so much as a native village in the West Indies—where he had served in his younger days.

They discussed their findings over vintage port, the lieutenant deferential to a fault. If the meal had been less good, Hoare-Bentley would have been more caustic on the subject of Captain Thomas, whom he had last seen tottering to the communal urinal. As it was he was inclined to benevolence.

'I think he should be shifted back to Farnborough where they can keep an eye on him,' he said, 'while we are in the area we'll call on the Royal Naval Air Service station to see if they can cope.'

'We should have approached the Admiralty, sir,' said the lieutenant cautiously.

'I know them down here,' said Hoare-Bentley, lighting a cigar and deciding as he did so that his companion did not warrant such a munificent smoke.

In the aftermath of the inspection of the interceptor station many changes were made. As a final gesture Captain Thomas grounded all his Bristol Fighters and a low-flying Gotha returning from a daylight sortie, damaged by anti-aircraft fire, was allowed to escape without a token resistance. Thomas flatly refused to let Leonard take off to tackle the bomber; he thought it an odd coincidence that his best pilot should be away from the base at the very time that the brass-hats had made their appearance.

Knowing that Captain Thomas, despite his modest rank, had friends in high places, Hoare-Bentley put down his reasons for advising the closure of the station as duplication of Royal Naval Air Service duties, together with the high proportion of airmen seeking medical attention in London. No doubt the station was insanitary due to the lack of toilet facilities and its proximity to the Thames estuary and any effluvia associated with it. Fortunately for sergeants, corporals and privates no one checked with the Royal Army Medical Corps in London.

The members of the unit were dispersed. To his intense disappointment the MI room sergeant was sent to France to help cope with a new offensive, Captain Thomas went back to Farnborough, and the corporal mechanic who had told Leonard of the wangle was intercepted on his way back from Hull, having mysteriously caught some rare tropical disease that needed immediate treatment in London and being unfortunate enough to be sandwiched between the old order and the new. Sergeant Leonard Oakwood was sent back to France for retraining on the new SE5a.

His new CO was flabbergasted that a sergeant was expected to keep his end up among the officers, and wondered why it was. Obviously none of the sergeant's previous officers had considered Oakwood suitable material for upgrading. He would have none of it; he would have none of these damned toffee-nosed public schoolboys scorning a chap who had downed six Huns, with two probables.

It was not so easy as that.

'It's all very well, my boy,' said a general from divisional headquarters, 'but there are some bright lads coming along, with good backgrounds. You look like a shooting man. Now look at it this way—where would you be with all shooters and no beaters?'

The company officer had never fired a shotgun in his life, but got the message.

'Another thing,' the general went on, 'perhaps the lad deserves promotion. But can he afford it? Would he fit in?'

Even Leonard's keenest supporters could not answer that with any certainty, for the contretemps with Lieutenant Scott was still on his service record and a fellow who would mess up a comrade's motorbike could not be regarded as 100 per cent reliable. After the general had gone, roaring away to a cosy evening in his requisitioned château, the CO of Leonard's new unit had a word with Captain Lewis.

'You once flew with young Oakwood, didn't you?' he asked.

'Damned good pilot,' said Lewis, 'I was sorry he had to go with Scott.'

'I had thoughts of suggesting promotion for him,' said the CO casually.

'Sergeant-majors are a bit of an anomaly in the flying corps, sir,' Lewis said.

'I suppose they are,' said the CO, and shelved the idea of pushing Oakwood's name forward as a possible officer.

'There's something remote about young Oakwood,' said Captain Lewis, 'I liked the fellow, but he lacked gusto.'

'That might have been before he was married,' the CO said, looking at the papers in front of him, 'perhaps that's why he

210

stayed alive. You wouldn't say he was an ace, but six Huns and two probables is not to be sniffed at.'

'I'd rather have him than one of the aces,' said Lewis fervently, 'they're too damned cocky.'

As soon as he had the chance he sought out Sergeant Oakwood. Yes, Oakwood was quiet and self-contained still, wouldn't get into a panic.

'How are you finding the SE5a, Sergeant?' he asked.

Leonard snapped to attention. The trouble with officers was that you were never certain how far you could go with them, whether their interest was passing and that they felt that they had to chat with other ranks as part of their duty.

'Well, sir,' said Leonard, 'I like it. It's easier to break off battle and streak back home if the plane gets damaged or the guns jam. I've had trouble with guns jamming. I fixed up a Lewis on the upper wing, but that one jammed as well. My old CO thought it was the munition workers back in Blighty, didn't care as long as they got their week's wages.'

Certainly the SE5a was a great improvement on the Sopwith, with its inclination to go into a dangerous spin. With its engine of more than two hundred horse-power the SE5a could overhaul almost any German plane. Leonard was confident; soon he would be in action with it.

On 6 January 1918 Oakwood was up alone, patrolling at 17,500 feet, when he saw a formation of six German triplanes west of Cambrai. He was very surprised for he had not seen a triplane before, though one of his comrades had had a doughty fight with one piloted by the German ace Werner Voss. He had heard that the Germans had scrapped the triplane after Voss's death, but apparently the British were misinformed. Still, there must be something wrong with them, they looked so cumbersome, he thought, like flying sandwiches.

Oakwood was near his ceiling but climbed to get above the six planes, speculating how he could detach one. Since his experience with frostbite he took care not to go too high, and when the triplanes began to climb as well he decided not to venture any further as it was common sense that the greater wing area of the German planes would be a great advantage in the thinner atmosphere.

As he began his turn, one of the triplanes detached itself and

211

dived towards Oakwood. Oakwood saw that it was painted purple and black. He began to climb to get the height on the enemy. He had it for a brief instant in his sights but before he could press the trigger it disappeared. He caught a glimpse of it through the struts of the wings, losing it again as the triplane went into a tight circle. Damn it, thought Oakwood, it could manoeuvre better than he could. He turned in the cockpit and could distinctly see the pilot. It sometimes shocked him that he was actually fighting people. There was a temptation to believe that they were just automata, tin toys of the kind the Blums had been agents for.

He kept his head, put the SE5a into a vertical bank, held the stick tight into his stomach and kept the throttle wide open. The German pilot was evidently an old hand, letting his foe have short bursts. Newcomers, as Leonard had learned, sprayed bullets all the time and were soon out of ammunition. After all, the airman had only a thousand bullets.

'When you're in a spot,' the CO had said to him, 'put on full bottom rudder.'

This seemed to Leonard to be a spot, so he took the advice. But he did not shake off the triplane.

Cockiness, as the CO had warned, was the finish of a pilot. Oakwood took the ability of the triplane to turn in a tighter circle than him as a personal affront, and although reason told him to break off and use his extra speed to get away his pride kept him turning, jigging the rudder bar. Remorselessly the black and purple plane closed the circle and, before Oakwood could make the decision to break off and get away, he heard the crackle of a machine-gun, the tearing of canvas, and saw the tracer across his nose. Steam suddenly hissed from the cowling of the engine, his screen blurred over, and a spot of boiling water seared his cheek beneath the goggles. He brushed his hand across his face, hearing the sullen plop of bullets behind him and, revving the engine despite the damage it might have suffered, he dived, the airspeed indicator needle going off the dial, the wings flapping menacingly.

The other plane followed him, urging him downwards with short bursts. The triplanes had not been scrapped, Oakwood thought, gritting his teeth and trying to see where he was. It would be something to tell them when he got back. To him it seemed more than likely that he would get back. The engine, despite the punctured radiator, was going well, but as he was congratulating himself on getting out of the scrap in one piece and surviving a dog fight with an obviously experienced German pilot a flicker of flame emerged from the top of the engine. Looking over the side of the cockpit at the bullet-holed exhaust Oakwood saw that there were flames roaring along it.

He switched off the engine, trusting that no spark would get at the petrol tank, and peered through the smoke that belched from the engine. He saw trenches beneath him, unoccupied. If they were Allied trenches all might be well. The dull crump-crump of anti-aircraft shells forced him to rethink. Any field was better than no field at all, and as yet the plane showed no signs of going into that awful spin.

For a moment he wished that he had got one of the old planes that were almost impossible to stall. As the ground loomed nearer he pushed the joy-stick, and felt the wheels pumping over an uneven field. He was reminded irresistibly of the last time he forced landed. But this time there was no friendly British artillery battery on the skyline.

The wheels sent up the snow in great clouds and he could sense the tyres skidding. A patch of ice thinly covered with snow passed beneath him. Then there was a crunching sound as the undercarriage ploughed through it, chunks of ice folding up vertically and sawing through his wings like a carving knife. Braced for the final jolt, Oakwood was surprised by the jack-knife effect but managed to protect his face with his arms. The dampness he put down to the water which swept into his cockpit, but only when he removed his broken goggles did he find that there was blood oozing from his sleeves.

He was half-conscious of being hauled from the cockpit, and his last recollection was the sudden fire that seared his face, then subsided in hissing. He came to on the bank. Three men were shaking mud and water from their boots, a Red Cross ambulance was bumping over the snow, and in the middle of the lake was the wreckage of his plane. The uniforms of the men were unfamiliar. One of them looked at him. He was not a rescuer, but a captor.

'You are hurt,' the man said in slow English. 'My brother, he is a flyer. He is in the Richthofen circus. He says your SE5 is good, but not so good as the German aeroplanes. What have you to say to that?'

'He may be right,' said Oakwood, wincing as he clutched his arm.

Without a word medical orderlies got down from the ambulance and helped him into it. One of them cut away his flying jacket, looked at the arm and asked Oakwood something in German which was not understood. The orderlies looked at each other, and one of them took a hypodermic syringe from a wooden case. He smiled at Oakwood, made the motion of giving himself an injection, and when Oakwood nodded, showing that he understood, the orderly rolled up Oakwood's sleeve, sought for the vein, and pressed the plunger. The pain disappeared into the distance and the faces of the orderlies became indistinct. Oakwood passed out again, coming to his senses in a hospital bed.

After a while a doctor came to him. 'You are wounded', he said in good English, 'but not badly. You will be transferred to the hospital at Stuttgart, and then to a Stalag. The war is over for you.'

'Thank you for your medical attention,' said Oakwood weakly.

The doctor shrugged his shoulders. 'It is our duty. We know that captured German flyers are well-treated. Why should we be different? And you are not insolent, as some of your comrades are. You have been talking in your coma about your father. He was a soldier?'

'He was a sergeant-major in the Boer War,' said Oakwood.

'Yes, the South African War. The Kaiser did not like that war. He wished for Mr Kruger to win. We have examined your papers and will tell your squadron that you are captured.'

He nodded, and walked away. Another enemy accounted for.

So he was a prisoner of war, thought Oakwood. He knew that many of the soldiers in the trenches would give their right arms to be one. It was odd that he should have been talking in his sleep about his father, and not his wife. He hoped that the Germans got the message through quickly so that she would not worry too much. He wondered if he would ever see his father again; if the war lasted much longer there would be little chance of it.

28

January 1918 was bleak and bitter. Jane found it difficult to keep the shop warm as there was a shortage of fuel, and the rumours had it that the miners were going on strike until the war ended. She seemed to have an immense amount of stock of last year's summer shoes. How foolish they looked, these confections of patent leather and cotton, when all customers wanted were rubber boots and stout leather walking shoes of the kind favoured by her old friend Alice Burgess.

There was good news and bad news from her children. Leonard had been shot down, but was alive and well. Mary was foresting somewhere, incredible.

'She wouldn't know one end of a tree from the other,' George had said.

And occasionally there was a cryptic postcard from Harry. 'Still with the Tanks,' Harry had written succinctly. Jane wrote back, but there were never any signs that Harry had received these letters.

There were no indications on Harry's postcards about whether he was or was not having a good war. A good war, Jane knew, was the kind enjoyed by some of her customers who had never been so well off before. The kind, she confessed to herself, she enjoyed herself.

The tank had been upgraded, and the heavy section of the Machine Gun Corps had been renamed the Tank Corps. But Harry had not enjoyed the increased kudos. In November 1917, when the tanks had been thrown into battle in great quantities at Cambrai and had scored signal successes, he was under open arrest, suspected of selling fuel to French farmers.

He had eased out of that one, and the promised court martial had not materialized. However, the sergeant mechanic was keeping an eye on him, on the orders of Captain Bland. Harry found himself doing the dirty jobs, oil changes, mending the tracks of damaged vehicles, and going out with the recovery vehicles.

'Your couple of stripes mean nothing to me, Oakwood,' the sergeant had said. 'To me you're just a common soldier, out to skive as much as possible and dying to dip your fingers in the till. If another Frog farmer kicks up hell it's nick for you for a very long time. Captain Bland has given me the wink to fix you up with a big one.'

Perhaps this was an exaggeration, but certainly Captain Bland detested Corporal Oakwood, that malingering trouble-maker. Only two tanks had returned from that futile attack with the Australians. It had earned Bland the Military Cross, but had exacerbated his earlier wound. Before he had limped, but now he hobbled. He was happy that he had kept Oakwood working his guts out during the preparations for the tank attack at Cambrai. 165,000 gallons of petrol, 55,000 pounds of grease, 54,000 rounds of gun ammunition, and five million rounds of machine-gun ammunition had been stock-piled, and if Captain Bland had had his way Harry Oakwood would have carried the lot on his back.

There was plenty for Oakwood and his comrades to do even in a time of comparative inactivity. At last the Allied generals recognized that their offensive policy was misdirected and all troops were being reconditioned for defensive warfare. In accordance with instructions issued by GHQ the defensive line was to be organized in three zones to a total depth of eight miles. The British had learned from the Germans at Passchen-daele, who had avoided serious defeat by maintaining a thin forward line with more thickly-held lines in the rear.

Morale among the ground troops had never been lower. The Russians had sued for peace and hundreds of thousands of German troops were being released from the Eastern Front to fight the French and English. There was going to be a big German offensive soon and everyone knew it. The unfortunate soldiers posted in the thinly-held forward lines knew that they would either be killed or taken prisoner. Worst of all, there was no leave. The generals could not risk sending men back home. The most irksome thing was that the British Tommy knew that the French frequently had more than a quarter of a million soldiers on leave at any one time.

The commanding officer of the Tank Corps unit of which Captain Bland and Corporal Oakwood were members called his officers together and briefed them.

'The Huns are waiting for the word Go', he said, 'and we in

the Fifth Army will probably get the worst of it. We have a proportionately longer line to defend than the others, with less guns. We've got nine thousand labourers now to do the heavy work and fourteen entrenching battalions. The British Intelligence Service tells us that we'll be up against crack troops— what the Germans call storm troops—and I want to make it clear that I expect none of my company commanders to send their men to a certain death. Uncle in the War Office, gentlemen, has decided that our defences will be elastic. As for the tank, I don't honestly know what role it will play in the coming German offensive. The crews may have to fight as foot soldiers, I don't know. A little weapon training would not do them any harm, and would keep them on their toes. I've noticed one or two infantry NCOs amongst the men. Get them busy on the drill square.'

A dozen of the labourers were ordered to put down an improvised drill square and Corporal Oakwood was sent out to do his best as a drill corporal, Captain Bland watching him sardonically from a distance.

'Come on, Corp, give us a rest,' urged a private from the ranks as Oakwood marched them up and down on the ice-bound square.

'I can't,' shouted Oakwood, 'the buggers are watching me.'

'Get us behind that hut,' said another man. 'They can't see us there. We won't drop you in it, mate.'

So Oakwood drew them up behind the hut, posted one of the men as a look-out, while the rest smoked and shivered, rubbing their hands together. To think, this was what his dad *liked* doing!

When he decided that he and the men had had enough, he marched them back on to the square and dismissed them. So suppose they court martialled him and dropped him in rank! Even a spell inside the glasshouse might be better than facing the German offensive. Tomorrow they would be drawing their rifles from the stores. Even getting sodden with oil and grease was better than firing a rifle. A voice echoed across the square, and Oakwood immediately came to attention. An infantry sergeant-major beckoned him over.

'How did you ever become corporal?' he demanded. 'I've

217

never seen such a shambles in all my born days. What's your name?'

'Oakwood, sir,' said the corporal.

'Hmm,' said the sergeant-major, 'you had a namesake once. By God, if he could see the standard of drill I've just seen he'd roll over in his grave.'

'I'm C2, sir,' said Oakwood, defending himself.

'Speak when you're spoken to,' spat out the sergeant-major, tucking his cane beneath his arm and walking round Oakwood as if surveying a monstrous abortion of nature. 'You don't look C2 to me. I'm going to have the MO give you a look over. There are too many odds and sods amongst you tank people. Clever Alecs you looked at Cambrai but you didn't help us, the poor bloody infantry, didn't help us one little bit.'

He looked at Oakwood from under his peaked cap. Oakwood could just see the shadowed eyes glaring at him. Then the sergeant-major turned on his heel and went, leaving Oakwood trembling. He did not know that the sergeant-major had no intention of contacting the medical officer, and that it was not the infantry's business to meddle with the Royal Tank Corps. The sergeant-major had tried to buck him up and had succeeded. Somewhat chastened, Oakwood went back to his quarters. The encounter was a reminder of the peace-time army. At least Captain Bland did not have him doubling up and down the communication trenches.

29

On 21 March 1918 thirty-seven divisions of German infantry, supported by nearly six thousand guns, fell upon the British line of battle on the front of the Fifth Army. Later Winston Churchill was to describe it as, without exception, 'the greatest onslaught in the history of the world'.

The five-hour bombardment was directed mainly against headquarters, signals centres and battery positions. The network of cable communications and wireless stations on which the direction of battle depended were wrecked early in the day. Gas mingled with thick fog to demoralize the defenders. 3,500 trench-mortars battered the thinly held forward posts out of existence and the redoubts, the strong points that remained, were dealt with by detachments of the German Army while their comrades swarmed on, occupying the forward trenches without much opposition and moving on to the battle zone, the garrisons of which were hurried into position by the code word 'Bustle'.

At one stroke the Fifth Army lost more than a quarter of its infantry. The commander of the tanks prepared to move to the front.

'It's that damned fog,' he said to Captain Bland, 'the defences depended on the blob system, crossfire between dispersed posts. How can that work when you can't see more than ten yards? The code word should have been "Muddle" not "Bustle".'

Bland did not say anything; defeatism never got anyone anywhere, and there was enough of that about with the French. Even on the first day he had heard that the French were considering withdrawing the government to Bordeaux.

The battle was still far off but the rumble of the guns could just be heard, muffled by the pervasive fog. The tanks were herded together and given last minute checks by the mechanics. A dispatch rider rode up, his wheels spattering the mud in all directions. More bad news, thought Bland, going into the mess. The mess was getting more like a private soldier's canteen, he considered, looking round. Standards were falling all the time, while the crest of the Royal Tank Corps, newly made and shining, was propped up on the sideboard. No one had made the effort to put it on the wall. A couple of his fellow officers were writing letters. As the war moved into its fourth year the officers were getting older and quieter, with the percentage of wartime soldiers getting larger. No one in the company had been in the Boer War. As he surveyed these balding, dome-headed officers, many with spectacles, it came as a shock to realize that he was probably older than any of them. Did he

219

look like that, lined, haggard, with sombre desperation taking the place of the high spirits of the junior officers of the 1914 period?

The commanding officer's depression was shared by the NCOs. The mechanics' movements as they made the tanks ready were slow and disinterested, and the sergeants gathered in knots, discussing the future. One of them had been on a recovery vehicle to an infantry regiment.

'They're getting a lot of desertions,' he said, 'the men are just skedaddling. And when they get them back they're shooting the buggers. They had to shoot a lieutenant the other day. It made my blood run cold. We know the Frogs have firing squads but nobody told me that we had too. I'd like to see the general who didn't run away when things got too hot for him.'

'No chance of getting a thick 'un in their bloody châteaux,' said another sergeant.

The order came to move forwards, and the tanks drew out, their engines roaring, followed by the CO in his staff car and preceded by the wireless van. The wireless operator, not happy about being the front runner, intercepted a message from an infantry company:

> *Third Division. GB fifty begins. Germans have broken into right Corps sector. We still hold front line of third (purple) system roughly from right Corps boundary to St Leger wood, thence along Factory Avenue to Swift Support.*
> *Third Division will readjust its line along Croiselles Switch to Sensée River, thence to Brown Line. Aeroplane has dropped message to say infantry visible on wide front long way through British positions from Croiselles southwards.*

Corporal Oakwood was sitting in the wireless van, brooding on fate.

'Take this back to the CO, Corp,' said the wireless operator.

Oakwood jumped off the duckboard and trotted back, intercepting the CO's car. He gave the officer the written message. The CO did not say anything, but the news was disastrous. It meant that the Fifth Army had given way. He looked at the fair-haired man who had brought him the message; yes, this

220

was Oakwood, the malingerer. His much vaunted mechanical knowledge had not been much help after all.

'Well, Corporal,' he said genially, 'you may see some fighting yet. That'll warm the cockles of your heart, won't it?'

'Sir,' said Oakwood expressionlessly.

He ran back to the wireless van. The operator was listening intently to another intercepted message.

'It's from the First Royal Scots, they're burning their papers and dumping their Mills grenades down a disused shaft.'

'Fancy,' said Oakwood sarcastically.

'I don't like being in the front,' complained the operator. 'It's not fair.'

He winced as a shell landed a hundred yards away, the glow filtering through the fog, the smoke drifting across. The van braked abruptly and the operator held on to his equipment to stop it being dashed to the floor. Oakwood poked his head around the canvas flaps of the van. A number of lorries were mixed up with a mule train at a crossroads and a military policeman was trying to restore order.

The driver of the van got out and looked inside the back. 'Got a fag, Corp,' he said, shivering. 'Gawd, this fog gets into your very bones.'

He was a thin-faced Cockney with his tunic open at the throat. Oakwood gave him a cigarette and tucked another one in the man's breast pocket. The two men looked at each other and then at the operator.

'What's our chances of getting out of this one?' the driver asked.

'It's up to you, mate,' said Oakwood, 'you're the driver. But I wouldn't have any objection to losing this lot when we get the chance.'

'The fog's getting thicker,' added the operator eagerly, 'they wouldn't see us. Come on, the copper's getting restless.'

The van rattled over a hastily filled crater and, as the fog closed in, the driver imperceptibly increased his speed until the following tank was a blur in the gloom. He held this station, carefully watching through the driving mirror, oblivious to the increased shelling. His eyes were suddenly dazzled by a shell exploding to the right of the road. The van wobbled and the receiving apparatus crashed to the floor.

221

As the smoke and fumes wafted across the road, the driver put his foot on the accelerator and, ignoring the increasing ferocity of the shelling, he drove hard towards the front line, braking only when figures loomed up out of the mist, the walking wounded. An officer imperiously held up his hand to stop the van but the driver ignored him. Oakwood kicked the equipment out of his way and stumbled to the front of the van, pulling aside the canvas flap.

'If you see an odd wounded, stop and pull him in,' he said, 'if we're stopped we can say we're taking him to a field hospital.'

'Good idea,' muttered the driver, 'how about that one?'

'He'll do,' said Oakwood.

The man was tottering along, his left arm a bloody pulp and his tunic charred and torn to ribbons. He was too far gone to cry out as Oakwood jumped off the van and bundled him on board. The wireless operator had a flask of brandy and forced it between the man's teeth. The gurgle turned to a choking.

'He's a dead 'un', said Oakwood distastefully, 'but we'll keep him as insurance.'

The operator looked at Oakwood with horror and turned aside to vomit.

A narrow rutted lane appeared on the left and the driver swung the van up it. A headquarters post was blazing and as they passed, a small wooden hut blew up, sending flaming fragments over the road and van. The canvas top caught fire, and Oakwood feverishly dashed it out with the operator's message pad. They passed the protruding barrels of big guns, silent, their operators killed or gone and the pervasive odour of gas stung Oakwood's nostrils. He searched for respirators in the bottom of the van, without success.

A lorry blocked the road, the driver staring sightlessly through the shattered windscreen. Oakwood jumped out and climbed into the passenger's seat, pushing the man out into the mud. The engine was still turning over, and there was plenty of petrol in the tank.

'We'll take that,' Harry told the driver.

'I've never driven one of them,' protested the driver.

'I'll drive,' said Harry. 'Come with me if you want to. If we're stopped, we're delivering. There's bread in the back.'

'What about the other fellow?' the driver asked.

'Leave him,' said Harry, 'he's no use to anyone, and anyway he was sick on my boots. And the other bloke's dead. And for God's sake throw away your rifle. We're not going to do any fighting.'

The driver licked his lips and nodded, jumping into the lorry and hanging on grimly as Harry probed for first gear. For the first time for many months he felt alive and in control of his own destiny, no longer a reluctant cog in a machine for which he felt hatred. Leave the heroics to Captain Bland and the other fools.

All along the skyline the fog was lightened with splashes of red, orange and yellow, as if a child had flicked paint on wet paper. The occasional tat-tat-tat of machine-guns amidst the ground bass of the heavy guns told Oakwood and the cockney that they were not far away from the front. They passed a bunch of tired infantrymen wearing unfamiliar uniforms.

'Americans,' said the cockney.

Another traffic jam loomed up in front and the two men could see half a dozen military policemen checking the vehicles. Oakwood slowed down but an impatient hooting of a horn behind him told him that it would be foolish to get out and make a run for it.

'What'll we do?' asked his companion.

'Keep your hair on,' said Oakwood. 'I'll get through.'

A military police sergeant held up his hand.

'What have you got, Corporal?' he asked.

'Bread for the Warwickshires, Sergeant,' answered Oakwood succinctly.

The sergeant glanced at Oakwood's regimental flashes and at his cowering companion. 'What's up with him?' he asked suspiciously.

'He got shot up, Sergeant,' replied Oakwood. 'As you see we got a bullet through the windscreen.'

'All right,' said the sergeant, 'I'll just check your load.'

He was away five minutes, Oakwood drumming with his fingers on the wheel, his companion watching the expression on the face of a military police corporal.

'There's something up,' he said suddenly.

The sergeant reappeared. 'Something to show you, Corporal,' he said casually, 'get out.'

'Can't we get on, Sarge?' pleaded Oakwood. 'The boys are

223

starving, and once I stop the engine it's the devil to get it started again . . .'

'Out I said, Corporal, and out I mean,' said the sergeant menacingly.

Out of the corner of his eye Oakwood saw that the road had cleared itself and a hundred yards would land them back in obscurity. He elbowed the sergeant off the running board and the lorry jerked forward, the engine racing in bottom gear till the cabin throbbed and the man beside him had to grab his seat to stop being flung out. Not until they were lost in the fog did Harry dare change gear, with the danger of stalling.

There was a cart track on the left and he turned up this, the wheels sliding in the mud. A large band of soldiers blocked the way. Oakwood jumped out.

'There's some grub in there, mates,' he said, 'help yourself.'

'Here!' expostulated a lance-corporal but did not follow it through, and joined in the rush to the back of the lorry.

Oakwood could now understand why the military policeman had acted as he had done, for the troops were bringing out bottles of cobweb-encrusted wine, boxes of cigars, and all kinds of odds and ends, including, he noticed, a couple of clocks. One of the soldiers had found a silk negligée and was crowing with delight, holding it against himself as he splashed in the mud. The men smashed the necks of the bottles off against the mudguards of the lorry, downing the wine. They were hurling the clocks and ornaments into the fog as if they were hand-grenades. The layers of loaves were left untouched.

The previous driver had been shot whilst out on a looting expedition. 'Serves him right,' muttered Oakwood, 'let's get out of here.'

As they ran away from the group they tore off their identification badges. A military sergeant and an infantry lance-corporal would soon give the word that a corporal of the Royal Warwickshire Regiment was wanted for questioning. They both realized that their actions could be rewarded by a session in front of the firing squad.

'Gawd,' said the private, 'you've landed us right in it.'

'I didn't hear you saying no,' said Oakwood. 'If it wasn't for me you'd be very likely be a bunch of guts on the barbed wire in the battle zone.'

'What are we going to do?'

'I don't know,' said Oakwood. 'Just keep our fingers crossed that the Tank Corps is being cut up and that that bastard Bland is meeting his maker. If he hears about the lorry he'll figure that it's me. These old soldiers have a nose for it. My dad was like that but I got the better of him. Old Bland is a good deal brighter by half, though. Don't worry, mate, there'll be some platoon we can fix on to. Let's get some of this mud on us.'

Amply plastered with mud, the two men began walking, talking as they went. Oakwood found out that his companion's name was Hood, one of the reluctant conscripts.

'I was doing all right,' he said, 'helping me father with his barrow in Berwick Street market, fruit and veg, you know, then one morning I was in the army.'

He assumed that Oakwood was also a conscript, and he was not disillusioned.

'The sergeant told me to steer clear of you', he went on, 'as you were a bad influence.'

'He would, the old sod,' said Harry. 'We're coming to a town. Remember, we've got separated from our units.'

A few dozen troops were milling around in the village square, looking into shop windows. A large car was drawn up outside the town hall, and in the back slept an officer with his mouth open, his left arm hidden by a startlingly white bandage. Casually Oakwood and Hood mingled amongst the troops.

'What happened to you?' Oakwood asked one man, who had lost his equipment and his helmet.

'Bloody Heinies drove us back, didn't they?' the man said. ' "Stick it to the last man," said the major, and then he hopped it. I suppose some of them did. I dunno.'

In the windows Oakwood saw displays of food temptingly arranged—tins of lobsters, glass jars of caviare, foil-capped magnums of champagne. A sign read 'Smoke De Reszke cigarettes.' As they looked, a man kicked a cobblestone loose from its bed, picked it up and hurled it through one of the grocery windows. The crash and the splintering glass stilled the hum of conversation. The soldier stepped through the window and came out with an armful of cigarettes, tossing them to his mates. A second man followed him back into the shop then a third. Oakwood and Hood joined in and soon the shop was

225

filled with milling hungry soldiers, eating as they plundered, discarding their equipment and filling sacks with food and cigarettes. In the street officers were calling for order and there was a silence as a single shot rang out.

'Let 'em stop me,' said one private, pulling out a captured Luger revolver from his belt, 'are you going to stop me, Corporal?'

'Not me,' said Oakwood, as busy as the next man.

He and Hood made their escape through the back door and seeing an open window they climbed through it and prowled through the house. Obviously the inhabitants had left in a hurry, for in the dining room the table was set for the next meal. There was no sign of disorder. They piled their sacks on the table and within five minutes they were plundering into lobster salad, peas, bread and butter, and washing it down with champagne. Sated, they poked around in the sacks and found tins of Turkish cigarettes. They lit up, placing their mud-caked boots on the table, pivoting on the back legs of their chairs.

'This is what war should be like,' said Oakwood. 'In 1914 it was like this, cushy billets and plenty of good grub. I lost a mate then.'

As the evening wore on they bathed and shaved with the late owner's razor, and threw themselves on the massive bed in the main bedroom. Sleep overtook them immediately but they were awakened by the sound of crashing noises downstairs. A party was taking place in the drawing room. Drunks were sprawling on the gilt Empire furniture, kicking at the elaborate finials. Someone had found a gramophone and men were dancing together.

All the time more men were arriving. One of the new arrivals took out a revolver and took pot-shots at a row of china plates that lined the mantelpiece. Oakwood and Hood, rubbing their eyes sleepily, heard fragments of conversation. '. . . broke into the church and took all the gold and silver ornaments. There was some kind of a padre there but one of the lads knocked him down . . . there's wine-cellars in the town as big as a house . . . one of the officers said he'd send for the MPs, someone shot him, wasn't me, though . . . nor me, that's a topping offence.'

A group of Scotsmen arrived, one of them blind drunk and waving a Lewis gun in his hand. One of them broke up a chair and threw it into the fireplace, setting fire to it and throwing a bottle of brandy into the flames. His mate drew cartridges from his pouch and flicked them into the fire, giggling.

'Let's get out of here,' muttered Hood, 'they're stark raving mad . . .'

'I spy a little corporal,' said one of the Scotsmen. 'I can't abear bleeding NCOs . . .'

Oakwood ran for it, leaving his loot upstairs.

They walked down the main street. Men were lying in gutters, others were running down the street, howling. They went into a wineshop that had already been looted and found some cognac and cigarettes. Oakwood drank deeply and, sitting on the counter, watched the far end of the town bursting into flames.

'Why did they all leave?' asked Hood.

'I suppose because the Huns are near,' said Oakwood. Never before under the influence, he felt his senses reeling and was nodding off when shells began to rain into the town, and the crumbling of masonry vied with the roaring of the flames. A drunken officer peered at them through the shattered window and keeled over as Hood hurled his empty brandy bottle at him, striking him on the shoulder.

'Let's find a cellar,' said Hood, pulling Oakwood off the counter. 'Cor, you can't hold your liquor, can you?'

He looked into the street. Men were lying in the middle of the road, lit as clear as day by the bursting shells and a drunk was tottering forward, singing. Hood watched, making a private bet with himself that the man would get hit within ten seconds. A sudden crump above his head diverted him from his innocent hobby and he helped Oakwood down a flight of stone steps, closing the door with an iron bar in case other soldiers tried to come. He could do without them, especially the Scotsmen with the machine-gun.

The rafters overhead shuddered with the force of the bombardment, but despite the noise Hood soon dropped off to sleep on a pile of sacks. He awoke to the sound of brick fragments dropping through the small grating near the street side of the cellar. There was just enough light to see that Oakwood was still sleeping.

What a mess they were in, thought Hood gloomily, and the

sooner he dropped Oakwood the better. He was the one the military policeman would remember. He climbed the steps, sliding the bar across and ventured into the daylight. The bombardment had stopped and men were staggering around the streets, some wounded, some merely with hangovers. A number of soldiers had found a French quartermaster storehouse where some French officer uniforms were stored and cut ludicrous figures in the ill-fitting blue tunics.

The clatter of the metal bar made Harry stir and, head splitting, he looked about him. Hood must have gone to investigate. He got to his feet, and slowly climbed the steps but shrank from the street. Mercifully the bombardment had stopped but he could hear the sound of machine-guns not too distant. A short staircase led to some living quarters and he found some bread and butter in a cupboard. The butter was just beginning to turn rancid but Harry Oakwood was not one to cavil and tucked in. He wiped his mouth with the cuff of his tunic and went to the window, squinting through the broken panes at the scenes below.

Bodies were strewn across the street, some of them in pools of blood, others twitching, showing that the men were drunk not dead. A couple of French officers ran down the street. Why should they be wearing British Army puttees? They were followed by two helmetless soldiers and a Scotsman, waving a bottle above his head. Oakwood soon saw what they were running from—a group of military policemen mounted on horses. They cantered down the street and Oakwood stepped back. One of them was brandishing a revolver.

'Stop, or I shoot!' he shouted.

Oakwood stood stock still, in case they had spotted him but their orders were to a man who had just emerged from a dairy clutching a long loaf beneath his arm. The man panicked and ran and without compunction the military policeman shot him down. The dead soldier rolled over on his back. It was Hood.

It was the horsemen's turn to take cover as a two-seater German aeroplane zoomed low, machine-gunning the street. Oakwood could hear the crackle of slates on the roof and took refuge on the stairs, burying his head in his arms to still the throbbing. Nothing would be served by going outside and he was as safe here as anywhere. Huddled uncomfortably against

228

an angle of the staircase, he fell into an uneasy slumber, broken into by footsteps in the shop. He remained perfectly still. The door was thrown open and a startled German infantryman stared at him, his hand round the neck of a bottle of wine and a bread roll stuffed in his mouth. To make certain that there was no mistake Oakwood lifted his hands high above his head, though it did not seem that the German was armed.

'Kamerad,' said Oakwood. 'I wish to be prisoner of war.'

Before speaking the German swallowed his roll. 'Orders are we take no prisoners.' He grinned. 'You like my English? I was a waiter in your Soho.'

He pulled the door behind him and handed Oakwood the bottle. Oakwood took a swig of the wine, fumbled in his pocket and handed the German a packet of cigarettes. 'Nein,' said the German, 'I have the Russian cigarettes.'

'What is happening?' Oakwood asked.

The German shrugged his shoulders. 'Who knows?' he countered. 'We are breaking through your lines and we are back on the old battlefields of 1914 but I suppose we will be driven back. It is nothing to me. When the war is over I hope to return to London and have my old job back. Have you had a good war?'

'No, mate,' said Oakwood with feeling, 'a bloody bad one. I got gassed, and then they stuck me with the tanks.'

'Ah, the tanks,' said the other, his face lighting up. 'We have the tanks as well now.'

There was a short silence as they puffed their cigarettes in harmony.

'I must go now,' said the German, pressing his cigarette out against the floor. 'The best of luck, as you Britishers say.'

It was a funny old war, thought Harry, settling back on the stairs, who would have thought that he would be hobnobbing with the enemy? The enemy seemed to be not that friendly German soldier but the military police, sergeants and the people like Captain Bland. It would be irksome but he would remain until darkness fell. If the Hun were moving so fast he might be able to slip through their lines.

Eventually he climbed the stairs and looked out into the street. The French civilians were coming back in twos and threes, throwing up their hands when they saw the destruction and the chaos. One old woman was standing in front of a heap of rubble, crying, with a child trying to pacify her. Oakwood sidled into the street, but no one looked at him. Outside the house he and Hood had broken into there was a large car, piled high with cases. A man and a woman were arguing on the pavement; he hit her then unlocked the front door.

As he trudged on there did not seem any trace of friend or enemy. The fog had turned into a numbing mist. The sound of marching feet forced him into a field and he watched a squad of British prisoners of war being marched away, a guard jabbing at them occasionally with his bayonet. One of the prisoners collapsed and one of the German soldiers kicked him out of the way of the column.

Oakwood waited until their steps disappeared into the night, then went on. Sporadic gunfire indicated that there was resistance somewhere. A farm loomed up and through a window he could see a couple eating their evening meal by the light of a hurricane lamp. A bicycle was leaning against the building and he took it, heading towards the flash of the guns. If he managed to regain the British lines there might be a chance that the questions asked him would not be too searching. It all depended on how the tank group had done, whether the wireless operator in the van had survived, and if Captain Bland was still after his blood. There were a lot of imponderables, and the more he thought about them the less sanguine he was. He resolved that the next bag of prisoners of war that passed would include Corporal Harry Oakwood, Royal Warwickshire Regiment, deserter.

30

Gradually Leonard Oakwood realized the inestimable advantages of being a prisoner-of-war. His shyness in unexpected situations was construed as British phlegm and his willingness to co-operate was seen as acceptance of the realities of life. To his surprise he found himself enjoying captivity and when a

German airman was placed in the adjoining bed in the hospital the Englishman had an ample opportunity to talk aeroplanes with his neighbour and the German's comrades.

He was soon fit enough to get out of bed and the damaged arm was responding to treatment.

'The bone is cracked and you will never be a weight-lifter,' the doctor had told him, 'but it should not inconvenience you too much.'

He looked at Oakwood. The Englishman was so useful in the hospital that he was deliberately deferring sending him to a Stalag. Eventually the German airman was well enough to return to his unit but he occasionally came back to see Oakwood, as did several of his one-time visitors. Oakwood had picked up a working knowledge of German during his time with the import firm in Birmingham and, as he had plenty of time on his hands, he improved it and within a few months became extremely fluent. With the flood of English wounded from the Second Battle of the Somme, Oakwood was called in as an interpreter. In his neutral hospital blue he was taken by British soldiers for a German and, realizing the delicacy of the situation and wondering if he was contravening the rules of war, he did not contradict them.

'You sound like a Brummy', said one soldier, 'but as you're a Heinie, you can't be, can you?'

Occasionally a stern-faced German interpreter was brought in to see British soldiers taken to a private ward. Unhappily Oakwood realized that they were being interrogated and he was pondering on this when he was stopped by a familiar figure.

'Lennie,' said Lieutenant Scott, 'I see you've made yourself at home.'

'Anything I can do for you?' Leonard asked coldly.

'Sir,' added Scott mildly.

'I don't feel like it,' said Leonard.

'You don't feel like it, eh,' muttered Scott, his colour rising, 'yes, you can do something for me. You can explain your bloody position. I don't have to remind you, do I, of King's Regulations and your duty to behave in a proper manner? When I get back it will be my duty to report you to the authorities. They won't be so well disposed to you as a bunch of Hun quacks.'

'I have been thinking about this business of fighting,' said Leonard. 'I don't see why I should be fighting for your sort of people. My father spent his life doing it, and he ended up as nothing.'

Scott was silent. He was not interested in Oakwood's juvenile musings.

One of the doctors overheard the conversation and later took Leonard on one side. 'I see your difficulty, Sergeant,' he said, 'we are enemies, but my duty is to preserve life and heal sick bodies. The war to me is a sad business. But it will not last much longer. The Battle of the Somme was not the success we hoped for. I do not know your King's Regulations but if they prevent you acting as interpreter then so it must be.'

An army padre came up to Leonard one afternoon. 'Lieutenant Scott has spoken to me of you', he said, smiling uncertainly, 'but the men haven't heard your side of the story.'

'I was helping,' said Oakwood quietly. 'There were fellows in there in pain, trying to tell the Germans what was wrong, telling them their next of kin, all kinds of things like that.'

'There were Germans in there, too,' said the padre, 'you talked and joked with them.'

'You're not injured yourself?' asked Leonard.

'No, no,' said the padre, 'Red Cross, you know.'

'No, I don't know,' said Leonard. 'What I do know is that it's a different kind of war for the officers. They send out for meals, and pay by cheque. And the cheques are honoured.'

'You feel hard done by, do you, Oakwood?' asked the padre aggressively.

'I've heard they go into the village on parole,' continued Leonard.

'They give their word not to escape,' said the padre lamely.

'Escaping is their duty,' said Leonard scathingly. 'Go back to your billet and tell Lieutenant bloody Scott that I'm going to continue acting as interpreter, King's Regulations or not. And after the war we can sort it all out. Now, if you excuse me, I've got one of my German friends coming to see me.'

The visitor was a huge corporal with his arm in a sling. With the free hand he held a large paper bag. 'For you, Sergeant,' he said, clicking his heels and grinning.

'Cream cakes,' said Leonard opening the paper bag.

'It is not much,' said the German awkwardly. 'Now I must go. I am being returned to my unit.'

'Not to fight?' asked Leonard.

The corporal shook his head. 'I will be in the stores,' he said.

'I'm glad about that,' said Leonard sincerely. This was one of the anonymous dots on the battlefield.

About five o'clock he did the rounds of the wards, lamenting the waste and the futility of it all. A man with a bandage round his head looked up.

'Sarge?' he said, uncertainly.

Leonard looked hard. It was the corporal mechanic who had fixed up Lieutenant Scott's motor-bicycle.

'What happened to you?' Leonard asked.

'They were all over us,' said the corporal. 'I was in the rearguard helping to burn papers. Glad you got captured and not killed.'

'Is that how they got Lieutenant Scott?' Leonard asked.

'Oh, him!' said the mechanic scornfully. 'Muvver's boy. No, he went out to help shoot down an observation balloon. I'd hoped he'd gone west. I saw his ugly phiz about half hour ago. Broke his ankle or something by the way he was hopping about.'

'What about you? What's wrong with your head?' asked Leonard.

'Just a scratch,' said the corporal, 'I expect they'll be sending me off to the pen in a couple of days.'

'An old friend, Sergeant?' asked a doctor doing his tour of inspection.

'My old corporal mechanic,' said Leonard. The doctor nodded, and passed on but later he intercepted Leonard.

'There's a superficial head graze,' he said, 'nothing at all. But he won't thank me for sending him to a Stalag, will he?'

'He'd be happier here,' said Leonard.

'We'll see what we can do,' said the doctor.

Leonard told the corporal the news.

'Not many guards round here,' said the corporal.

'It's a hospital, that's why. You're not going to try to escape, are you?'

'Get to Switzerland,' said the corporal.

'What, and fight again?' asked Leonard.

233

'Come off it, Sarge,' said the other amiably. 'I'm a mechanic, and they're short of mechanics. When there's an SE5 to tinker with there'll be no fighting for yours truly. And if I get back I get leave and see the old woman.'

It all seemed so simple, thought Leonard but he did not know that escape was in the air. In the wards where the officers were kept there was a good deal of discussion, for the rumour had it that they were to be used as hostages in the event of a German retreat to the Rhine.

The most likely hostage was Captain Berry-Faulkner, related in a dimly understood way to royalty, though the only thing Berry-Faulkner knew on this score was that his father had shot stags with King Edward VII. Lieutenant Scott resented being upstaged by his companion in misfortune especially as Berry-Faulkner was a quiet modest man and had no time for heroics.

'My dear Scott,' he said. 'I was in the quartermaster's branch and if a company commander indented for too many small packs and coats GD I was the very devil. But escaping? And having these fellows chase me and perhaps shoot at me?'

Captain Culpeper was a different sort of man, thought Scott with approval. George Oakwood would not have recognized him; the tame sycophant of the mad Colonel Ludlow had turned, in the safety of the hospital, into a firebrand, though there was no record that he had ever fired a shot in anger and he had only been captured through the negligence of his driver who had taken the wrong road. On being chased he had taken his revolver from his belt and had inadvertently fired it at his foot. He was known to the more irreverent patients as Limpy. Lieutenant Scott was known as Limpy Mark Two. Culpeper had outstayed his welcome at the military hospital and was due for an oflag.

'Of course I want to fight again,' Culpeper asserted, 'they can't keep me holed up here.' In private he wanted to get back home as a censor had wielded an obtuse blue pencil and his wife in Birmingham had had the idea that Culpeper's life was wine, women and song, with the accent on women. Consequently she had threatened to go off with a local councillor named Bumpus.

'I want to get that fellow Oakwood court-martialled the

instant he sets foot on Allied soil,' said Scott. The padre had reported back to tell him that Oakwood was unrepentant.

'There's a corporal in the other ranks' wing who knows about cars,' said Culpeper. 'He was an aircraft mechanic before he was captured. I've watched him looking around and timing the guards. Chat to him, Scotty, find out if he's game.'

Scott did not recognize the corporal, though Corporal Bullfinch, RFC, was more observant. He was also sceptical of Scott's escape plan.

'You'd never get far with your ankle,' he said. 'I've seen you hopping around.'

'That's what I want the Huns to think, Corporal,' said Scott, 'my ankle's as good as anyone's.'

'I could get hold of a car,' said the corporal, 'there's always four in the field. Guards look at them once every two hours. I'd pick the big Mercedes and drive straight through the barbed wire. It ain't barbed wire as I understand it. It's just playing at being barbed wire, if you get my meaning, sir.'

'What's stopping you then?' Scott asked.

'Don't speak the lingo,' said Bullfinch.

'I do,' said Scott stoutly.

Bullfinch nodded. They wanted a moonless night, and one was coming up in forty-eight hours. In the privacy of the lavatory he unwound the bandage around his head, wincing as the clotted blood tugged at his hair but satisfied that he no longer needed it, a judgement confirmed by the nurse who replaced the dressings.

'I should keep it on for a time,' he said in excellent English, 'it's nicer here than in a Stalag, where they have turnips for breakfast, lunch, and supper.'

The next day Bullfinch did a final tour of the hospital, making certain that he had made no mistake. The guards, elderly men frostbitten from years at the Russian Front, did a four hour duty. They did not march but ambled, chatting and gossiping. Most of the time they spent playing cards in a small hut behind the hospital.

The hospital was built in the shape of a letter L, with surrounding lawn, kept neat by recuperating patients. The main gateway was built of brick and once it was planned to have a brick wall leading from it to block in the hospital. But either the supply of bricks or enthusiasm had run out, for after twenty feet the wall ended and the barbed wire began. It was in single strands, taut enough, but Bullfinch saw that the posts that held the wire were insubstantial and what paint they had was flaking, indicating that weather had been at work. The guards paid him little attention. If a patient made a break for it he would have to race over acres of flat grassland and for this contingency one of the cars had a rifle in the boot.

Well behind the lines, too far for strafing by British aircraft, occupied by the wounded, the hospital was not worth more than a cursory examination by the Wehrmacht. The commandant rarely wore his uniform but more often promenaded the wards in a white coat indistinguishable from the wear of the doctors.

'Are you all right, Corporal?' he asked. 'Head not aching?'

The clear precise English and the abrupt tone, friendly as it was, told Bullfinch that this was one of the top men in the hospital. He felt a momentary spasm of alarm, not relieved when the commandant said, 'I saw you out walking on the lawns today. It was a fine day. It is agreeable to see soldiers sunning themselves after the horrors of the trenches.'

He did not wait for an answer but went on to the officers. 'Gentlemen,' he said, entering their ward, 'have you everything you want?'

'Yes, Commandant,' replied Berry-Faulkner.

He sat on his bed. Scott was hobbling across the room, exaggerating his injury as usual. Culpeper was as red as a beetroot. Guilt, thought Berry-Faulkner, was written across him like a slogan from *John Bull*. Thank God he himself was not going into this ridiculous escaping business.

'Do you think he knows?' asked Culpeper anxiously afterwards.

'I once saw a fellow turn red like you at Murray's,' said Scott tersely, 'he had trodden on his partner's dress and it tore. She wore the most tasteless knickers I have ever seen.'

'Your mama let you go to Murray's, did she?' asked Berry-Faulkner casually. 'We thought it was rather low.'

'Of course we were not connected with royalty,' said Scott. 'Remember us when they march you away to Berlin.'

'As long as you don't want me to be a witness at the court

236

martial of young Oakwood I don't mind where I go,' said Berry-Faulkner, 'if you'll forgive my saying so, no one will thank you for it. He's remained a human being, after all.'

'I'll get the bugger,' said Scott fiercely.

'Is your corporal to be trusted?' Berry-Faulkner asked, picking up his book.

'He'll obey orders,' said Culpeper.

Ever optimistic, Corporal Bullfinch borrowed an atlas from the hospital library and planned a route to the Swiss border. As it was a school atlas, the scale was not large enough to be of any real use and it made the projected journey seem a formality. Although Bullfinch did not have his uniform his greatcoat was hanging up in the communal wardrobe at the end of the ward, and this would hide his hospital blue.

He had arranged to meet Scott on the lawn after lunch the next day. The commandant saw this through his window and pondered on the disgraceful democracy, not to say socialism, the rendezvous implied.

'Are we all set, Corporal?' Scott asked.

'I've planned the route,' said Bullfinch, 'no problems, sir.' He would have preferred to go with someone else.

'We're ready,' said Scott, 'I've got some German marks. Lost on the exchange, of course, but the Heinies get greedy.'

'We?' asked Bullfinch, puzzled.

'Captain Culpeper and myself,' said Scott.

'You didn't say anything about him,' protested Bullfinch indignantly.

'Well, it's settled, Corporal,' said Scott. 'Do we know the Mercedes is all right?' he asked as an afterthought.

'I had a look at it last night,' replied Bullfinch, 'one of the doctors took it out a couple of days ago. It'll go through the wire like a dose of salts. There's fifty horses under the bonnet if I'm any judge.'

Some of his optimism had evaporated. Culpeper had the mark of doom on him but perhaps he could jettison Limpy somewhere on the way to Switzerland. And the same went for Scott. A pity that Sergeant Oakwood was not keen on escaping but he saw that the sergeant had it pretty easy, with his own room, and he did not mention the escape plan to him.

It was the perfect night for going over the wall, dark and dry

237

with just enough wind to hide unusual noises. At five to ten he left his bed, put on his greatcoat in the lavatory and removed his head bandage, which he stuffed into one of the pockets. Carefully he opened the door and crept towards the cars, keeping close to the wall until he could make a quick dash. Scott was crouched between two of the cars and he slid into the driving seat.

'Here!' hissed Bullfinch, 'I'm driving!'

'Swing the handle, Corporal!' ordered Scott.

'I'm driving,' Bullfinch repeated. 'Where's the captain?'

'He's not coming,' said Scott, 'he's got the shits.'

'I tell you, I'm driving, or it's no go,' said Bullfinch.

'By Christ, I'll have you on a charge when we get back,' said Scott, fuming.

'Thanks,' said Bullfinch, edging away.

Lieutenant Scott irritably tapped his fingers on the wheel. That was two of them to deal with in due course. And he would have a word in the right quarter about Captain Culpeper. Unfortunately he was dependent on someone turning the starting handle of the damned Hun machine and, feeling foolish, he trotted back to the officers' ward. There was a new man there, from a Scots regiment, who had lost an arm and whose wounds brought a new dimension into the world of twisted ankles and injured feet. He lifted an eyebrow at Scott and Berry-Faulkner put the query into words.

'Back already, Scotty?' he asked. 'Wouldn't Fritz let you have his motor-car?'

'I want someone to swing the handle,' growled Scott. 'Where's Culpeper?'

Berry-Faulkner jerked his finger at the door leading to the lavatory. 'He's staying quiet until you go,' he said, 'that's my reading of the tactical situation . . .'

As he spoke there was the roar of a car, followed by the grinding sound and the splintering of wood. Then silence. The crack of a rifle shot acted as a warning to any daring patients who wanted to take a look. The commandant padded out in his slippers, his greatcoat slung over his shoulders. The stumps of the poles holding up the barbed wire were white and jagged in the light of his lantern and he trod carefully. Tetanus from rusty wire was more important than the loss of a patient. He watched with surprise the guard turning out. He never saw more than two at any one time but there were a dozen chattering among themselves.

One of the junior doctors climbed into one of the other cars, and one of the guards swung the starting handle until he tired, whereupon one of his comrades took over. Eventually the engine broke into life and the car shot off, coming to an uneasy halt as the strands of barbed wire burst one of the tyres.

The commandant made a tour of the wards. 'My apologies for troubling you, gentlemen,' he told the officers, 'but one of the patients has escaped. His name is Corporal Bullfinch, and I recollect you talking to him earlier today, Lieutenant Scott. Perhaps you will see me in my office in the morning to explain the nature of your conversation.'

Some time the next day he would have to make a report and the military would come and take over. There would be a few changes. The mildly injured would go to prisoner-of-war camps and, although he had some doubt about it, the man who helped Bullfinch to escape might be apprehended. He did not think it was Scott; the man was clearly too selfish. If he were a betting man, he would lay his money on the useful Sergeant Oakwood, who sat up in bed as the commandant and his entourage swept by taking their count.

'You're a good sort, Sarge,' Bullfinch had said to Leonard as he had released the brake. Leonard had thrown the starting handle into the thick grass at the edge of the lawn. 'Good luck,' he had said, wondering why he was not going with him, back to England, back to Elizabeth. Was he, deep down, a coward? Or was he, like so many men he had met, thoroughly battle-weary, caring for nothing but inactivity? Whatever happened, he could not see himself staying much longer at the hospital. A few weeks in a Stalag would probably tempt him to try and escape.

His thoughts turned to Harry. Perhaps his brother had been killed on the battlefield, though he really did not believe it. Far more likely that Harry would have found himself a snug behind-the-lines job. He had no conception of the trials and tribulations that Harry had gone through, Harry who would have given anything to be a hospital assistant, Harry who could not even get himself captured.

After he had left the town he had struck out westwards, his

239

head still aching from the large intake of drink. He had seen evidence of the path of the Germans but no more convenient columns of prisoners of war to latch on to. He had come across a badly damaged German tank and had taken a look inside, comparing it with the British. You had to say one thing for the Huns, he thought, they had learned fast. Their tanks were nearly as good as the Mark IV and he would have laid a bet on their having superior engines. The tank driver had been lying inside, eyes staring at the top of the tank and Oakwood had been through his pockets. There were some German marks, which he left, and there was also a bundle of French francs, of large denomination. The Heinie had been looting, no doubt about it, and Harry took the French money.

His heels were blistered and he rested in a derelict pigsty. Before he knew what had happened, a hard horny hand was jabbing him in the ribs. He opened his eyes and looked at his watch (it had seemed too good to leave on that dead German's wrist). He had been asleep nearly six hours. The French farmer did not seem particularly friendly and he babbled in a dialect that Oakwood could not understand, pointing towards the setting sun. Oakwood fumbled through his French vocabulary, telling the farmer he was hungry.

Carefully he drew out one of the notes. 'Pour vous,' he said, 'si je mange.'

The Frenchman analysed the quaint noises, and got the message, hauling Oakwood to his feet and dusting him down.

The war had not struck these blighters, thought Oakwood wolfing through a plate laden with fresh cheese and crusty new bread, followed by ham and eggs and steaming coffee. The farmer's wife grinned at him and fired brisk questions. The Frenchman fluttered the note in front of Oakwood's eyes.

A ferret-eyed youth sidled in. 'Mama asks if you 'ave ze more,' he interpreted.

'If you hide me,' Oakwood said, 'I will pay you more.'

He wished that he had come armed.

The farmer nodded abruptly and led the way to a straw-filled barn, motioning Oakwood to stay there.

The boy followed him. 'Until this evening,' he said. 'We will make plans.'

Oakwood's feet were too sore for him to tell the boy to forget the plans and he dozed, awakened by the reappearance of the farmer and two armed men. The two men looked at him sharply.

'We will get you through,' one of them said in English.

'Perhaps it would be best to stay here,' said Oakwood.

'Nonsense,' said the speaker roughly, 'the Boche will be back and we do not want an Englishman hiding here. They are going backwards and forwards like rabbits, or, as you English would say, like a hound trying to find the line. I know you English hunt.'

The farmer winked at Oakwood conspiratorially and as he followed the two men out into the darkness Oakwood pressed another note into the farmer's hand. War or no war, money still talked. He should have looked for some more in that damned town instead of getting stewed on filthy cognac.

As they walked to the lorry in the farmyard the man who spoke English explained what was happening. The fighting was extremely fluid and no side had yet dug in. He pointed to a grass-covered depression dramatically and said that it was a crater from the 1914 battles. Oakwood clambered into the back of the lorry and covered himself with straw. A feeble baa told him that he was not the only occupant.

The lorry jolted off, bumping Oakwood up and down, but soon they were on level ground and the lorry hurtled along, its headlights cutting swathes of light. Occasionally Oakwood peeped out, seeing gun flashes around and hearing the boom of artillery. He did not think that they were going west, for otherwise the lorry would have been into the fighting area long before.

He dropped off to sleep, waking to find a sheep lying on his legs. There were noises outside and he looked through a gap in the canvas top. He was in a convoy of refugees. Behind him was an old man pushing a hand-cart, then there was an elderly car, then a horse-drawn waggon and then scores of people. They were going where the ebb and the flow of the war demanded, the flotsam and jetsam. Sometimes they dived to the ditches when an aeroplane flew overhead but mostly they kept on. The convoy stopped and Oakwood heard voices. The language was German. Was it too late to jump out with hands up and be a prisoner of war? The likelihood was that he would get shot out of hand. Refugees irritated every army on the move. You shot a

241

few, mowed a few down with cars but there were so many of
them. Oakwood sensed what was being said—get off the road
and let us through.

The vehicles and people behind scampered to the side of the
road, and two motor cycles bored through, followed by a staff
car. There was a long wait before the army lorries came,
followed by a couple of cavalrymen, their horses sweating and
their helmets awry. Then there were the foot soldiers. They
were not defeated but they were silent as they marched. And
then the convoy went on.

The lorry turned left and stopped. Oakwood got out. The
driver rubbed his first finger and thumb together and Oakwood
gave him two notes, working out that he was giving them
approximately the equivalent of ten English pounds.

'Why did the Germans keep on the road?' Oakwood asked
with curiosity.

The driver stared with incomprehension. 'Why, those are the
comte's vineyards,' he replied with awe. 'The comte he has, you
understand, an arrangement.'

From the way the two men looked at each other, Oakwood
though it advisable not to say any more. The comte had an
arrangement. As with other rich and influential people, he was
easing the burdens of war on himself by using wealth and
power. Oakwood looked about him, back at the slow-moving
line of people and vehicles, forward at the endless fields and
vineyards, seemingly untouched by war. Did the comte have
jurisdiction over the artillery too?

'What do I do now?' Oakwood asked.

The English speaker shrugged his shoulders, and motioned
towards the refugees. 'The English forces are not far away,' he
explained, 'you join the procession. If you wish we have suitable clothes in the lorry.'

Oakwood saw the drift, and produced another note. He
changed into farm labourer's clothes and threw his stained and
muddy uniform into a ditch. As he walked away, he wished that
he had kept his boots; the peasant's sabots caused him to
hobble. When he took his place in the throng no one gave him
more than a passing glance.

After walking for three miles he began to feel that he really
was a refugee. A country girl came to the end of a lane with a

basket and threw small loaves of bread into the crowd, as if she were feeding animals at a zoo, and he grabbed one greedily before being almost knocked over by the surge of the crowd as they swung to the side of the road to avoid another German column. There was a deliberation about the German withdrawal, none of the panic that Oakwood had seen when the British troops were on the retreat at Ypres.

As the rumble of artillery told him that the battle was becoming nearer, he wondered why he was travelling with this rabble. As soon as they got nearer some idle airman would machinegun them. They passed through a small village, and Oakwood slid off into the courtyard of an inn, sitting on a bench and rubbing his bruised ankles. He had money to buy food and shelter and a degree of discomfort was preferable to a possible court martial.

He wondered if his name had appeared in a casualty list as missing believed killed. He could not imagine anyone worrying much either way.

31

They brought Corporal Bullfinch back to the hospital unconscious, with a bullet in his knee and a smashed hand. Sergeant Oakwood was not given access to him and one of the German orderlies whispered to Leonard that Bullfinch was to be interrogated as soon as he regained consciousness. Leonard was sent to clip the grass. While he was doing this Captain Berry-Faulkner sidled up to him.

'What's the news about the corporal, Sergeant?' he asked. 'Don't look up. You're not supposed to speak to me.'

'Pretty bad, sir,' said Leonard, 'the guards aren't taking too kindly to him. They think they might be shipped to the Western Front as they let him escape.'

'I've heard that you're being taken to Golpa,' said Berry-Faulkner. 'It took me five cigarettes to learn that. I don't know if it's any good to find out. It's a coal mine.'

243

'Better a coal mine than a Stalag,' said Leonard heavily.

When he arrived there, crammed in a truck with some Frenchmen, he was not so sure. It was open-cast mining and the prisoners were employed in gangs on a cliff edge, mainly used to move the railway metals as the surface was continually scraped. Leonard was summoned to the commandant's office.

'Read that,' the commandant ordered. He was a stern-faced man with a monocle.

Leonard looked at the notice on the wall of the office:

The State may utilize the labour of prisoners of war, other than officers, according to their rank and aptitude. Their tasks shall not be excessive . . . The Government into whose hands prisoners of war have fallen is bound to maintain them.

'That is the international law,' said the commandant, 'if you accept that, your lot here will not be hard. You will work as a supervisor over the Russians. The Russians do not come within the terms of international law as they are animals. You will be called a director.'

He nodded to the guard and Leonard was led out to a dormitory where he deposited his few possessions, then to a mess-room where he sat down at trestle tables for vegetable stew. He presumed that turnips constituted the main ingredient.

In the babble of sounds he heard one or two English voices, but was unable to pick out a recognizable uniform. Some of the men wore discoloured uniform, others hardly more than rags. But everyone was stained with coal dust, and their hands were grimy; some of the hands were bruised and bloody. A bell sounded, and the men were formed up in columns of two outside the mess-room. It was warm and muggy, and Leonard wanted more than anything a bath. Baths had been easy to get at the hospital.

'You're a new one, aren't you?' asked a voice behind him, 'don't turn round in the march. They don't like it.'

'Oakwood, flying corps,' said Leonard, 'just came in.'

'Did you try to escape?'

'No,' replied Oakwood.

'They're the ones they usually send here,' said the man. 'My name's Johnson, Royal Engineers. Being a sergeant they'll make you a director. It's not what you or I think of as a director.'

Leonard soon found that out. Each man was given an iron crowbar and placed at intervals along a section of the line. At the back stood the director. His job was to chant the signals for each man to place his bar beneath the rail and pull together. It reminded him of books he had read about the chain-gangs in America. The shouting made him hoarse but he was ignored by the guards who were more interested in flicking long hide whips at the Russians. There was little animosity. It was a habit, goading unresponsive cattle.

After two hours Leonard's voice had become hardly more than a whisper, and the man Johnson took over.

'Just fall out,' he said, 'have a smoke if you like. They won't bother you.'

Sometimes Leonard wished that he did smoke. It seemed to soothe the nerves of the men who did.

He felt sorry for the Russians. They worked doggedly, exchanging incomprehensible remarks, occasionally glancing at him. They were leftovers from a part of the war he knew nothing about. Johnson kept going longer and Leonard took over again. The chant was like a memory of distant church parades he had heard at Aldershot.

By the evening his legs felt like lead. One of the Russians fell over with fatigue and a German guard kicked him in the stomach until he climbed to his feet, grinning at Leonard as he did so, as if both belonged to civilization and the Russian did not. At seven the men were marched back to the barracks and more stew was set before them. They lined up at a huge enamel ewer and drew mugs of acorn coffee. Then they were marched back to their dormitories. Leonard heard the turning of the key in the door.

A corner of the dormitory was divided off and here Leonard found a foul-smelling bucket full of ordure and urine. A sheet-metal sluice ran alongside and, his face turned away, Leonard emptied the mess down it and heard it slithering out of sight. As he walked to his bunk, the men looked at him dully. The uniforms, or what was left of them, were those of the French Army. All except one, a sickly British infantryman who lay on his bunk in the corner and looked at Leonard with puzzlement but said nothing. One of the Frenchman said something to Leonard, but it was an incomprehensible dialect that was nothing at all like the French he had learned at night school. So the Frenchman wiggled his finger at his head. The message was clear enough; the Englishman was out of his mind.

The half dozen paraffin lamps were left on until they guttered and went out through lack of fuel. Leonard lay on the bunk on grey unwashed blankets feeling sick. The smell was of stale sweat and coal-dust; the coal-dust seemed sweeter.

Breakfast was a chunk of dark brown bread of the consistency of clay, and a mug of coffee, then the prisoners were marched off to the mines. Leonard could not see Johnson anywhere and when his voice became hoarse one of the German guards took over, motioning to Leonard to do his stint after an hour. As they passed, he gave Leonard half a bar of chocolate and winked.

Leonard lost count of the days. One of the Frenchmen came to him and began to converse haltingly in a broken English. He wanted to find out how the war was going, but Leonard could not help him. He had received one letter from his mother, heavily censored. She was, he thought, too naive to let him know what was happening without appearing to. He was glad to hear that Elizabeth was with them and he wondered what had happened to the letters she had written to him.

The French must be a dirty lot, he considered. It was always he who emptied the slop pail down the chute; they would have let the disgusting mess overflow. The Germans provided newspapers as toilet paper and from these Leonard garnered a little news, though he realized that what he read was in most cases fantasy, doctored hope for the masses. Occasionally the English soldier in his dormitory came over to his bed, and giggled at him.

After about a fortnight the commandant called him to his office. 'There has been some irregularity, Sergeant,' he said, 'you should have been posted with the other sergeants. There has been an administrative error.'

'Might I say something, sir?' asked Leonard.

The commandant looked up from his desk in surprise. 'By all means,' he said politely.

'There is a British soldier in the dormitory who is mad,' Leonard told him. 'He should be in a hospital for the insane.'

'That is where he is, Sergeant,' said the commandant, leaning back and adjusting his monocle; 'this establishment was a lunatic asylum. But I will see to it and he will be transferred. You are right to bring this matter to my notice.'

He was as good as his word. Two Red Cross men appeared in the afternoon and gently led the British soldier away while Leonard packed.

The sergeants were not effusive. One was a South Wales Borderers man who took capture as a personal affront and who was obsessed by the fact that more VCs had been won in the Borderers than in any other line regiment during the war, and that by being captured he had somehow missed out on the glory. Sergeant Brocklebank had his own preoccupations. On account of what he called his gentle birth he had anticipations of being an officer in his regiment, the Oxfordshire and Buckinghamshire Light Infantry. This would enable him to wear a white tie in the officers' mess, the only regiment granted this privilege. This seemed to him to be the summit of man's achievement.

Sergeant Flaherty of the Army Ordnance Corps was more congenial, and the quiet dark-haired airforce sergeant looked a likely companion to play chess with or, failing that, draughts. There were also four French sergeants, one of whom persisted in wearing the plumed helmet of his calling both indoors and outdoors, and a Pole who spoke French but refused to communicate with any of his companions.

'We're not quite certain which lot he was fighting,' said Flaherty as he helped Leonard make up his bed.

'He hates the BBs, that's for certain.'

'The BBs?' asked Leonard.

'The Bolshevik Bastards,' explained Flaherty, 'the Russian prisoners who bring us our grub and clean our billet. When he thinks no one's looking he gives them a kick but we cuff him round the ear when we see it. He doesn't seem to mind.'

'Do we do any work here?' Leonard asked.

'It's on a rota system,' explained Flaherty, 'one of us goes down to the mines and supervises. I don't mind, actually, as all we do is sit in a little hut and have a fag. Do you smoke?'

'No,' replied Leonard.

'Good,' said Flaherty, 'do you fancy making a swap, my chocolates for your fags?'

'What chocolate? What fags?' asked Leonard.

'Red Cross parcels,' said Flaherty, 'we do pretty well.'

'The others don't get them,' said Leonard.

'The guards probably take them,' said Flaherty unconcerned, 'but the commandant behaves very properly with us. Probably because the war's going to end soon and he'll cop it if he comes the old soldier. We got the sheets a fortnight ago. A sign of the times, eh?'

'Is the war going to end soon?' Leonard asked. 'There's nothing about it in the German papers.'

'So one of the guards told me,' said Flaherty, 'if you speak the lingo he'll tell you. Not a bad fellow. I'd rather have him than that Welsh idiot. The stupid bugger wants to earn himself a VC. He's going to try and escape and mess us all up. You're not going to escape, are you? If you do, it's a long way from home.'

Compared with the other dormitory, the sergeants' billet was unimaginable luxury. The sheets were changed regularly and the food was much better, with real bread and what tasted like genuine butter. And there was meat. Probably horse-meat but meat nevertheless. Leonard never wanted to see another turnip as long as he lived. Every week a grey-haired civilian brought in a pile of English novels and took away the previous batch.

'It teaches you to read quickly', said Flaherty, 'and you learn not to start a book on the Friday when he comes on the Saturday. I was never much of a reader, but when you're cooped up it's amazing what you'll do. I like the big buggers, Dickens and a fellow named Trollope. They can keep me going all week. And old Moses—that's what we call him, Moses—he approves of them. He teaches English at the local school. Gives me a big smile when we talk about Trollope. He think it's like that now, grand ladies and everyone lah-de-dah.'

He was right about the undemanding nature of the sergeants' duties. At first Leonard had qualms about descending the mine shaft in the cage, but it was so roomy and extensive below that as he sat in a little wooden hut he became accustomed to it and even to the coal dust that sifted into his clothes and boots. They were mainly Russians at the coal-face, hacking at the seam with their picks and loading on to trucks fixed to an endless chain. Occasionally one collapsed with fatigue and a guard, often accompanied by a wolfhound, ordered the Russian's companions to haul him to his feet. There was little arbitrary cruelty underground of the kind Leonard had seen at the open-cast mine and his scruples at the use of slave labour were not intense.

The time drifted by not unpleasantly. Leonard was taught to play chess and acquired a taste for long Victorian novels. After the privations of the men's dormitory he found unlimited access to a bath a keen pleasure. Every Saturday he had a long chat with the civilian who brought in the books. One day, after Leonard had been in the camp seven weeks, he came but only to collect books from the previous week.

'You are all being moved,' he said. 'This is to be a hospital for wounded soldiers.'

'The commandant should have told us,' the South Wales Borderers sergeant said sullenly.

'He has gone,' said the civilian, 'gone to fight with his regiment.'

Leonard felt his heart sink. What would happen now? He did not have long to wait. He and his companions were paraded outside together with the men from the dormitories and marched to the railway station.

'I should have escaped,' muttered the Welshman to Leonard.

The guards on the station were not the easy-going men Leonard had grown accustomed to; they had fixed bayonets and had the appearance of soldiers who would not hesitate to use them if the occasion offered. Their manner was an affront to Sergeant Brocklebank, who attempted to argue with them. One of the guards took a threatening step towards him and Brocklebank said no more, not even when he was pushed into one of the cattle trucks, alongside some smelly Frenchmen.

'I should have escaped,' repeated the Welsh sergeant. 'I don't like the look of this.'

Leonard looked round for Flaherty but he must have been pushed into one of the other trucks. The stench was awful, far worse than the dormitory. There was a smell of fear.

They changed trains in the dead of night in pitch darkness.

Overhead there was the droning of aircraft engines and the wavering beams of German searchlights. A German officer hurried slackers along with his cane and Leonard winced as he slashed at him as he went by. The prisoners were packed solidly, as if the guards were awarded marks by their skill in cramming as many men as possible into a set area. One man had fallen to the floor and was being crushed. Leonard heard him whimpering, but could do nothing as he was jammed against the next man, his arms numb. He fell into a doze, awakened by the jerking of the truck and the grinding of brakes. The doors were thrown back and the men tottered out, several of them collapsing on to the platform. The light was dazzling and Leonard held his hand to his eyes. The guards were standing about smoking cigarettes and talking. One of the prisoners made a dash along the platform. Casually one of the guards released his Alsatian dog, which caught the man and tore at his thigh. The other guard dogs caught the scent of blood and began to howl. But none of the guards moved until an officer came out of the stationmaster's office, drawing on his gloves.

Sergeant Flaherty edged up to Leonard. 'Christ, that was a rough ride!' he muttered, 'I don't like the look of this, Oaky. I've been a prisoner-of-war for two years, escaped five times, and know the signs. It's always bad when they don't pick on a sergeant-major or senior sergeant to organize things; worse when there are no officers about. They're pigging us all in together. Where are we, do you think?'

'I was listening to them talking,' said Leonard. 'We're at Leipzig.'

'Still a hell of a way from home,' said Flaherty.

Someone yelled at Flaherty.

'What's he saying?' he asked.

'He's telling you to keep quiet,' said Leonard.

The guard came up to him, and punched him in the kidneys, not hard, but not playfully either.

The platform was long, and the few civilians waiting for trains were pushed to the back to let the prisoners through. It was an effort for Leonard to walk, as his legs were still numb. They shambled along, without cohesion, with guards at the rear. There were a few houses near the station and beyond that an open space, in which was set a huge metal shed. Something

250

jutted out of it. It was a Zeppelin, and to the right Leonard could see a number of aircraft sheds. Three aeroplanes of an unknown make stood ready for take-off, and the wind indicator gusted gently. Automatically Leonard took his bearings from the position of the sun. It was about three o'clock and there was a strong wind due west.

Almost absently one of the guards pulled him from the side of Flaherty and flung him into a mob of Frenchmen. One of the Frenchmen was crying, tears making rivulets in his coal-ingrained cheeks. He had had enough and a subdued murmur of anger spread through the French contingent. The guards did not appear to notice anything amiss. The guard dogs had disappeared and now that there was no officer about the soldiers were smoking.

There did not appear to be any signal for the riot that broke out. Afterwards Leonard wondered if it had been hatched up in the cattle truck. As men fought on the platform he saw a train coming in the opposite direction, and dropped down on to the rails, racing across, praying that the pins and needles that had replaced insensibility would not result in his being killed by the train. For a few seconds he was hidden from the guards and the five or six people waiting for their trains watched him politely as he rushed by them and down the steps into a cobbled lane. There was a niche in a wall and he stepped into it, taking off his tunic and throwing it over the wall. A group of workmen came along and he stood aside. They paid him no attention. He was merely another dirty, sweaty factory-worker; the train journey had transformed the neat tidy sergeant into another nondescript.

Unhurriedly he approached the aerodrome, looking through the high wire fence at the nose of the Zeppelin. A number of men were grouped at the entrance. He sensed that they were casual workers, recruited when anything need be done, such as helping to haul the Zeppelin out of the hangar. They were better dressed than he was, with clean shirts. They watched his approach suspiciously, and he walked past them.

His stomach was rumbling with hunger and he stood in a queue at a soup kitchen. Everyone was shabby and depressed. He aroused no particular notice. Wondering what to do, whether it was ridiculous to try to steal a German plane, he strolled down the lane when he saw some washing on a line in a walled yard. Quickly he opened the door and took a selection of likely looking clothes, and was away before anyone noticed.

This must be the slum area of Leipzig, he decided, and where there are slums there are second-hand clothes shops. The man in the shop could not understand why the customer wanted to exchange the perfectly good items which smelled so clean for dusty overalls and a greasy beret, but he was satisfied with the deal. Obviously the man was a foreigner, probably a Hungarian or a Pole.

Happy with his new camouflage, Leonard went back to the aerodrome. He did not wait with the others by the wire-mesh gate, but boldly walked through. Civilian aircraft mechanics were anonymous. He had seen them on every aerodrome where he had been stationed. They moved about unchallenged, walked to aircraft and did things. Hoping that he would come across something he recognized he entered one of the sheds. The worst news would be to see nothing but Gotha bombers. He knew that the Germanische Flugzeugwerke of Leipzig produced aircraft of the general German tractor type, so there might be something for him.

He found a Fokker Parasol Monoplane, with its familiar-looking rotary engine. If pressed, he knew that he could take the engine apart and put it together again, but there was no one in the shed and he climbed up and looked at the instrument panel, acquainting himself with it. It was all typical, key switch, pressure gauges for main and auxiliary tanks, grease pump, while below was the starting magneto, petrol switch, hand pump.

A mechanic came round the corner, looking without much interest at Leonard as he wiped his hands with a rag.

'Trouble with the petrol supply,' said Leonard.

'It wasn't here this morning,' said the mechanic, 'are you from Mokau?'

Leonard was not sure where it was or what it was but knew that he had to account for his uncolloquial German.

'Budapest,' he said. 'I am a Hungarian mechanic.'

'Ah!' said the German, his face lighting up, 'getting out while there's still time. I don't blame you, my friend.'

'Would you give the propeller a swing?' Leonard asked.

252

He hoped that he had used the right word for a propeller and that his memory of an article he had once read in *Flight* was not letting him down. Apparently all was well. The mechanic nodded and Leonard settled himself in the cockpit, reaching for the goggles at his right hand and restraining himself at the last moment. A goggled mechanic would arose suspicion.

Leonard switched on, the mechanic put his weight behind the propeller, stepping back, grinning, as the engine roared to life. Damn, who would remove the chocks from the wheels? The mechanic was saying something. Leonard took the risk and switched off the engine.

'What?' he asked.

'You can fly?' asked the mechanic.

'Oh, yes,' said Leonard.

'I should take it up then,' said the mechanic, 'we often do. Nobody bothers us. They're more interested in the Zeppelin. Hans crashed an Albatross the other day, but walked away from it. Nobody bothered.'

Leonard switched on again. The mechanic swung the propeller and pulled the chocks away from the wheels. Leonard taxied forward gently, not over-revving in his excitement, waved to the other and was out on the field, pulling on the goggles as his eyes began to smart, and seeing if there was any ammunition for the forward-firing machine-gun. There was not.

He swept into the wind and was airborne in the friendly current. The controls were light and responsive, there was petrol enough. He looked down at the railway line. There were three bodies on the platform. He hoped that one was not that of Sergeant Flaherty.

There were more urgent things to think about than Sergeant Flaherty. With a bit of luck there should be some delay before the Germans were alerted and in any event one Fokker monoplane was very much like another. What he had to fear was the advent of a British far-ranging scout. The Parasol Monoplane, particularly one that could do nothing but dodge, was no match for one of the more modern British aircraft. The crosses on his wings made him the most vulnerable thing flying that late afternoon, as the sun dipped behind the cumulus and the ground was tinged with russet.

He decided to keep low, to bemuse German anti-aircraft

253

gunners who might chance their arm at a lone mysterious aircraft of an antique design and to escape any vigilant British flyers. There was no immediate danger yet; that would come when he neared the front and Leipzig was well behind the fighting area, unless events had made his knowledge obsolete and the sudden transfer from the mine to Leipzig meant that the Allies were hammering on the doors of Cologne.

Flying high above him, heading east, was Captain Maddox of the US Army Air Force, flying a Sopwith Camel fitted with the powerful Liberty engine. A row of twenty-four Maltese crosses on the belly of his fuselage indicated that Maddox was no novice. The paint on the last cross was not yet dry. It was said by sceptics that Maddox had chalked up so many because he made the most of the learners and the inexperienced and that he dreamed at night of unarmed reconnaissance planes with the engine missing on one cylinder and the pilot semi-conscious with Schnapps. Maddox did not mind; he did not talk to many people and spent as much time in the air as was consistent with a good night's sleep.

With extra fuel tanks he had a range of four hours instead of the normal two and a half hours. He preferred to fight when he had discarded his extra fuel tank, and it would soon be time to switch over from the auxiliary to the main tank. He loosed off half a dozen rounds from his twin Vickers machine-guns.

It was quiet below. He peered at another anonymous town, and at a train puffing its way across the placid countryside. He supposed he was over Bavaria. He could see the Alps in the distance, the peaks capped with crimson and purple. If he did not find a victim he would strafe a train. He yawned and methodically searched the skies, reaching for his binoculars when something took his eye. Satisfied, he replaced his binoculars; he had found a possible victim, a low-flying Fokker monoplane.

Leonard had already seen the Camel and his heart had jumped. It would be the final irony to be killed by one of his own, maybe some pilot he had nodded to across the sergeant's mess, some likeable officer such as Captain Lewis. He kept his course, hoping that he had not been seen, but the Camel was losing height, coming in against the setting sun. Leonard turned the nose of his Fokker so that he was facing the sun and put on full throttle so that the Camel would overshoot. But

254

Maddox swung in a gentle arc, anticipating the move, for a second getting the tailplane in his sights but losing it as Leonard banked.

'Contour flyers,' muttered Maddox, 'I hate them!'

It meant that he not only had to watch his opponent but the ground as well. He fired a short angry burst, but Leonard watched the tracer going well wide, taking his plane down to a few hundred feet, skimming over whitewashed farms and herds of cows. He approached a lake and went down to zero feet, confident in his ability to judge distances and bullets skimmed across the water as Maddox did likewise. Leonard banked, realizing that his wing-tip was a mere whisker off the water, and the slightest contact could cartwheel him to his death. His mouth was dry, and his hands were ice-cold. The previous pilot had omitted to leave any gloves in the cockpit and the torn-up beret was no substitute. And his bones were frozen.

He realized that he could turn and offer a token menace to the Camel, the pilot of which might be more cautious, but if his bluff was called it would be the end of him. Maddox forced him into a tight circle, confident of his superiority, and Leonard put his nose upwards to gain height. He had seen the Camels in action, though he had never flown one. He knew that they could be tricky in tight turns.

An odd bullet twanged at his wing as he climbed, putting the machine into a half-spin at four thousand feet and encouraging the Camel to follow him. Maddox cursed. The fellow was turning too tight for him. He fired a speculative burst, and Leonard, for the first time, relaxed. Maddox was nowhere near and Leonard knew that this little plane could more than match the bigger Camel in manoeuvrability. Maddox, with a lump in his throat, knew it too. He had found someone who could cope with him and he felt that the Fokker pilot's refusal to fire on him was a taunt, a gesture of contempt towards an inferior flyer. He swung away towards the west and when the Fokker took the same course Maddox had a momentary spasm of apprehension, as if retribution was about to be wreaked on him for his twenty-four victims. Only when he considered that he had at least twenty-five miles an hour on the Fokker did he recover his composure.

The long-range fuel tanks had been jettisoned at the beginning of this shadow boxing, but he still had sufficient fuel for a modest sortie. It was too far from the fighting to strafe artillery or troops, but a train emerged from a cutting, a few carriages and then a dozen goods waggons, covered with tarpaulin. The great advantage of strafing goods was that no matter what they were someone would applaud their destruction. If it was food, the Food Minister would guarantee that the enemy's fighting potential was reduced by the pressures on the civilian population. If it was armament, the War Minister would approve. There was some ambiguity about boots and shoes but Maddox, boiling with anger at the impudence of the Fokker pilot, was in no mind to think of them as he swept to the attack, raking the goods waggons with a full drum.

The train puffed to a halt and Maddox, jamming on a fresh drum of ammunition, turned his guns on the locomotive. He could almost hear the sharp clatter of steel against the metal boiler. It was an empty victory, like potting a stranded whale. Maddox flew off, bored, and the engine driver, perspiration streaming from his brow, sat down and put his hand over his heart. The stoker was crouched in the corner of the cab, blinking. Two German soldiers appeared, one of whom was laughing. He led the engine driver to one of the carriages. The windows were starred with broken glass and the seats splintered. The soldiers pushed open the heavy mahogany door and pointed to the two dead occupants.

One was Lieutenant Scott, late RFC, and the other was Captain Culpeper, formerly with the Royal Warwickshire Regiment. The engine driver looked at them dispassionately then at the two soldiers. Slowly he climbed down on to the embankment and returned to the engine. The one soldier looked at the other and without a word exchanged they began to go through the officers' pockets.

It was a lean haul. In Culpeper's pockets there was a pocketwatch, a diary, a pencil and a wallet containing a few English pounds, some German marks, and some photographs. One of the soldiers picked out a photograph of Mrs Culpeper. He turned up his nose at her and tore it in four, scattering the pieces out of the broken window. The frau was a widow now but from the saucy look she had given the photographer it would not be long before she wedded again.

256

32

The relative failure of their great attacks of March and April 1918 forced the German General Staff to realize that the only means of keeping the initiative in their hands was to launch another offensive elsewhere. Shortly after midnight on the night of 26–27 May a bombardment began along a section of the Western Front. The Battle of the Aisne had begun. At 4.40 am the German infantry went over the top, taking the Allies completely by surprise.

The company of the Royal Warwickshire Regiment, of which Corporal Harry Oakwood had once been a member, had been resting for a month and were now back in the trenches. Oakwood's former officer, Wilcox, had been made up to company commander and, shortly after the forward troops were beginning to absorb the German attack, he received a call from the signals officer, testing the lines. The Second Battle of the Somme had been resolved in the Germans' favour by the artillery's ability to destroy British communications.

The formal part of the test over, the signals officer asked Captain Wilcox if he remembered the chauffeur he once had.

'Indeed I do,' said Wilcox smiling, 'a bit of a ruffian looking back, but he knew his cars.'

'Funny thing's happened,' confessed the signals officer. 'We've just had a rush of refugees through. Thought they were escaping the war and then ran bang into it. One of them was young Oakwood, dressed in mufti. Escaped from the Jerries.'

'Good for him,' said Wilcox enthusiastically. 'I thought he was with the Tank Corps on attachment.'

The signals officer did not add that Corporal Oakwood showed no pleasure at rejoining his old regiment, and that the sharp-eyed Sergeant-Major Jenkins was responsible for his reunion with his comrades.

'I'd know that 'orrible face anywhere,' Jenkins had said, 'even under that stupid cap. Gorblimey, look what he's got on his feet! Bloody clogs!'

Harry Oakwood, recognized, made the best of it. The last couple of days had been a chapter of accidents. The village he had stopped in had been owned in full by the comte, who was friendly towards the Germans. No one would sell Oakwood food, no one would give him shelter, and he had tramped across country until he found a farm. Despite being paid with more of the stolen French money, the farmer had told the Germans and Oakwood had escaped in the nick of time. There was no point in surrendering as a prisoner of war in civilian clothes; the least he could hope for was a painful interrogation and being shot as a spy.

After he had latched on to another refugee exodus he had had to run into the fields as a battery, Allied or enemy, was shelling the road. He had hidden in a wood as there was an eruption of German field-grey, but he must have been in that ambiguous area where one company impinges on another and, with a motley crowd of men, women and children, had escaped into Allied territory, the combatants forbearing to fire on them.

Captain Wilcox managed to get through to the Tank Corps unit and spoke to Captain Bland.

'We lost most of our unit on the Somme,' said Bland. 'We found the blown-up signals van and thought that Oakwood had been killed. What's he doing up that part of the front?'

'Taken prisoner and escaped,' replied Wilcox. 'Shall we send him back to you?'

'If it's his own regiment it would be best for him to remain with them,' said Bland evasively. 'He's no good with the tanks because of his medical classification. Got gassed, you see. I never thought he had it in him to escape.'

'What do you mean by that?' asked Wilcox sharply.

'Oh, nothing,' replied Bland wearily. 'I'm just tired, that's all. I'll arrange to do our end of the paperwork. There's so much transferring and replacing that we can slip him in easy enough, always supposing that you can use him. We'll notify headquarters to have him taken off the missing believed killed.'

'Well, Harry,' said Captain Wilcox, 'you're back in the fold again. I must admit I agree with Captain Bland. I didn't expect you to escape from the Germans. They were after you for looting or something, I daresay. I was a trifle crusty with Bland, but he had you weighed up.'

Harry was indignant, but he saw that there was a twinkle in

258

the officer's eye. Yet he was embarrassed. Captain Wilcox was the only officer he had liked, and it was humiliating to be regarded, even by him, as a skiving ne'er-do-well.

'I've had drivers since you went,' said Wilcox, stretching out his arms and yawning, 'but never one like you. My God, this is a tiring war. I'm off to see the colonel at three. The motor's outside. Just check it over, will you?'

It was a battered Lancia but Harry warmed to his task, and Wilcox found him polishing the headlamps.

'There's no need to make a meal of it,' he said, 'it's not my car. It's C company's. When I want you polishing headlamps I'll tell you. Merely see if there is petrol in the tank and water in the radiator.'

'Yes, sir,' said Harry submissively. There was a bite in Wilcox's voice that he had not heard before. He kicked the running-board angrily. It was always the same with officers—you thought that you had them sold on you, and then they turned. And he had thought Captain Wilcox was a good sort, different from the others.

The colonel looked at the car through the flaps of his tent. He leaned back in his folding chair, drumming his fingers on the trestle table. Suspended from the roof of the tent were the colonel's trophies, consisting mainly of German helmets. Occasionally they jangled, giving out a modest carillon effect. The colonel had small bloodshot eyes and a clipped moustache.

'That's C company's car,' he barked, 'done up like a dog's dinner. Who's the driver? Looks young. Should be fighting. Lost my nephew a week ago. Good man. Sorry to see him go. Derbyshire regiment, can't remember it's damned name. What are you here for, Wilcox?'

'Don't know, sir,' said Wilcox.

'Hmmm, nor do I,' the colonel said, sorting through the papers on his table. 'Oh yes, I know. Another big push on the way. All the way to Berlin and all that. So get your chaps out of sick bay and into their full kit and equipment. You're a good man, Wilcox, good company commander. Don't let them run you. You run them. Get it?'

'I get it, sir,' said Wilcox.

'Got another helmet yesterday,' said the colonel, 'my batman's polishing it up for me. Wish it had a head inside it.

That's my style, Wilcox, that's my style. Frowned upon by Haig and his lot. Namby-pamby fellow.' He looked at Harry again sitting in the staff car. 'Get him off his backside and banging off with his rifle, and that's an order.'

Captain Wilcox was reluctant to let Harry go so easily. 'He's just escaped from a prisoner-of-war camp, sir, rejoined his unit.'

'Knows the ropes then,' grunted the colonel. 'Send him on leave, then. If he rejoined his unit you can trust him. Won't hole up in some back street. Give him stomach for the fight to come. On to Berlin and all that. If you believe all they tell you. I bloody well don't. Do you, Wilcox?'

'Not altogether, sir,' replied Wilcox.

'Nor do I. A few more men and a few less pouffs would help. That's my opinion, anyway. But battle on, eh? All right, Wilcox, off you go. And don't forget what I said about your driver. That's an old man's job, driving you around.'

An interview with the colonel always made Wilcox's head reel. The old man was mad, no doubt about it, but one had to admire him. He took the German helmets himself, went on scouting parties. For a plumed job he had raced across no man's land with a dagger in his hand, screaming at the top of his voice. He got his plumed helmet. And he had a memory like a box file. Harry's days as driver were numbered but Wilcox decided to keep that from him until he had returned from leave. A Harry destined for the front line was a Harry who might not return from leave.

Harry sat in a borrowed car, ill at ease. Then, on an impulse, he headed north. On the outskirts of Birmingham he stopped at a pub and had a large brandy.

'We don't charge soldiers,' said the publican, 'have it on the house.'

'Me as well, Corporal,' said a woman sipping gin.

'Does she mean it?' Harry asked the publican.

'Do you mean it, love?' asked the publican in an undertone.

The woman looked at Harry shrewdly. 'I didn't when I said it,' she said, 'but I don't know now.'

Harry guessed that she was about his age, pretty in a gin-soaked way, wearing good quality clothes.

260

'It depends whether you have a motor,' she said, 'I live in Solihull. Think about it, Corporal, while I do my nose.' She smiled, and left the bar.

'She ain't no angel,' said the publican. 'She's often in here. Always the saloon bar, never the public. Picks up a fellow now and then—if he has a motor. Husband's a prisoner of war, an officer too. Culpeper's the name, Captain Culpeper.'

'An officer's wife, eh?' said Harry reflectively. 'Even if she had a face like a back of a bus I'd take her on then.'

'That's the spirit, young 'un,' said the publican approvingly, 'and take a bottle of Gordon's gin with you, talking of spirits. When she sobers up she gets a bit on the hoity-toity side.'

'Have no fear of that,' said Harry, taking out his hip-flask and filling it carefully.

On the way, Mrs Culpeper spoke of her husband. 'You've no conception of these prisoner-of-war camps. They let them out, you know, they let them out to go into the town. And when a man is locked up for a time, you know what he's like. Any woman's good enough for him. He was worse when he was in a hospital. Mind, Corporal, I have to read between the lines. The censor tries to avoid hurting my feelings, but I know what he's doing when he does his crossing out.'

'I know, dear,' said Harry, feeling her knee experimentally.

She giggled, and he went further.

The way to the bedroom was dotted with her discarded clothing, and picking his way between piles of old newspapers and empty gin bottles Harry fell upon her, as, according to her story, her prisoner-of-war husband fell upon the German fräuleins. She could, he thought, do with a bath, but beggars can't be choosers and he left her house tired but happy.

'Is that your car blocking the driveway, my man?' asked a big fat man.

'It is,' replied Harry amiably.

'Shift it,' said the man, 'my name is Bumpus and I am a councillor. What are you doing here, anyway?' He looked at Harry uneasily.

'It's what I've done that you've got to worry about, old chap,' said Harry, climbing into the car. 'Cheerio.'

He sat in the car without starting it, partly to irritate Councillor Bumpus, partly because he had no plans for the future. In

261

a strange way he was not enjoying this leave. No doubt he would find more lonely women to enjoy but he had discovered, much to his surprise, that the young men he met aroused in him contempt rather than envy. The person he would have liked to have seen most was his brother, but who knew where he was now? Was Leonard dead? He hoped not. And he wondered what had happened to Mary.

Mary, in fact, was going home. Being a postwoman had been tedious and the forestry no better. Planting small trees and sawing down large ones seemed a pointless occupation.

London had not been so big as she had thought. It was a messy place, full of dirt, dust and fumes, and the food queues were more bad-tempered than those in Birmingham. When she got on the train it was as though she was going home, though panic seized her when she got off at New Street station, hearing the familiar Birmingham twang and seeing the chestnut seller outside in Stephenson Place.

The shoe-shop was as bright and neat as ever, with a symmetrical display in the window that she knew her mother had done herself. She waited outside in the arcade until she was certain that there were no customers in the shop. She could see her mother's head above the boxes in the window. Her hair was now white but she did not appear to have changed otherwise. There was a calmness about her that Mary envied.

Although the shop was now empty except for her mother, Mary took a long time to summon up the courage to enter. She shut her eyes and made the plunge. Jane Oakwood turned to stone as she saw who the customer was. The words 'Good morning, madam' froze on her lips.

'Mary . . .' she began.

It was like looking at herself thirty years before.

'I'm back, Mummy,' said Mary reverting to a child's terminology and she broke down and cried, her mother trying to comfort her.

'There, there,' Jane said soothingly, 'come on upstairs. But quietly. Your father's having a nap.'

She realized that the sudden appearance of Mary on the scene would alter their lives; it was absurd that her daughter should live away from home trying to make both ends meet.

Now that everyone was saying the war would be over in a few months what would Mary do then? The soldiers back from the war would get their old jobs back and there would surely be no place for her.

George wondered who was downstairs. They were all shadowy figures, with only his wife a stable comforting presence. When Mary came into the room he thought at first that it was Jane. How much like her mother she had become! He was saddened by the lines that had appeared in her face and the subdued attitude. He remembered how arrogant she had been, how she had flounced out of the house to live with her in-laws, how bitter she had been about the quiet life he and Jane enjoyed. Perhaps enjoy was too strong a word. He pulled himself together for the regular visit of the doctor.

Did Mrs Oakwood realize how her husband had deteriorated, wondered the doctor. There was nothing he could do. The patient had lost the will to live, and it was no good saying that there was no reason why the old man should lie in bed thinking about the past. He had had many old soldiers on his books in the past. They could never get used to the fact that they were no longer needed and never prepared for the future. Other people had hobbies but the old soldiers never.

Pausing only to tell Mrs Oakwood that he would visit George again in another fortnight he scribbled out a prescription that would at least show that he was doing something. He walked through the shop, smiling at the girl behind the counter, and into the arcade, almost bumping into an officer who was looking in the window. Smart and authoritative, there was something about the officer that made him look twice, as if he reminded him of someone. Lined and war-weary, it was difficult to say how old the man was. As he limped forward, the doctor felt a stab of sympathy.

'Good morning, Captain,' he said, 'can I help you at all?'

The officer smiled. 'No thanks,' he said, 'I've come to see Mr Oakwood.'

The doctor hesitated. 'Are you a relative?' he asked.

Captain Bland avoided the question. 'I used to know him,' he said. 'How is he?'

'Not well,' confessed the other, 'he's had a lot of heart trouble, but his condition has worsened over the last few weeks.'

Captain Bland thanked him and went into the shop.

Behind the counter Mary also felt that sensation of half-recognizing a familiar face, shared by Jane when she came down the stairs.

The officer removed his cap. 'I would very much like to see Mr Oakwood,' he said.

Jane looked at his insignia. It was not the Royal Warwickshire Regiment, but the man was probably once one of George's officers.

'He is not well', said Jane, 'but I will ask him if he would like to see you. Have you come a long way?'

'I'm on leave,' said Bland. 'I have rooms in London.'

'I'll see,' said Jane briskly.

'Tell him Captain Bland,' said the officer, 'the young Captain Bland. He'll know what I mean.'

And Jane knew what he meant. The years flooded back to her like the waves during that idyllic holiday in Weston-super-Mare in 1914, and beyond that to Aldershot, when she had learned that an officer's wife had had a son by George. And here was the son. She wanted to grasp his hand and tell him that it did not matter any more, that it was unimportant, that he should have come before.

When Jane went upstairs to tell George she had to use all her self-control to prevent herself from weeping. When she told him of the arrival of the unexpected visitor, he thought for a moment that it was some ghastly joke: Jane had found out at last about him, and this was the final humiliation. But there was no malice in her eyes. Could it be that his illegitimate son had come to see him? With an effort he propped himself up in bed and confusedly tried to tidy his scanty hair and button up the front of his pyjama jacket. His heart beat frantically as he sat up and waited, each pulse sending a thin persistent pain across his chest.

His son limped up the stairs, wondering if he should have come. He had decided to motor up to Birmingham on an impulse and as he pushed open the bedroom door he was glad he had. But was this old man with the blotched face really his father, the man he had met once before on the field of the Battle of Omdurman almost twenty years ago? Silently he crossed the room and took the old man's hand.

264

'You know who I am?' he asked quietly.

George's eyes clouded over with tears. 'Yes,' he said, 'you are my son.'

Clive Bland, MC, sat down by the side of the bed.

'You've been wounded,' said George.

'Twice,' said his son, 'with the tanks. No room for cavalry these days.'

'I remember your horse when we met in Africa,' said George. 'It was a fine creature.'

'You would not have liked this war,' said Bland sadly, 'it was not your kind of war. Thank God it is nearly over.'

'What are you going to do after the war?' George asked. He stopped himself saying 'sir'. It was ridiculous.

Bland sensed the confusion. 'My name is Clive,' he said. 'My mother liked the name. She was reading about Clive of India. After the war? I shall be a soldier still. Perhaps a desk-bound soldier, but a soldier. I shall soon be forty-five, and wars are now for young men.'

They talked for nearly three hours. Clive Bland told his father of his meeting in no man's land with Leonard.

'There's another one of the family following the tradition,' he commented. George glowed with pride. He did not mention Harry, the memory of whom still hurt. And the family; this strangely familiar figure had meant the Oakwoods, not the Blands.

'A family of soldiers,' George said softly. 'There are worse things to life than that. I hope it goes on.'

'If I get married it will,' his son asserted. 'A man is not a man if he is not a soldier. People think that that's old-fashioned. But the Blands, whatever their faults, have taught me that.'

'My grandfather was a drummer-boy against Napoleon, my father was a soldier in the Crimea, and you know what I was. I wonder what the future holds.'

There was a silence.

'You must be tired,' said Bland tenderly, 'but I'm glad I came.'

George took his hand and gripped it. 'You have done an old man a great kindness,' he said, choking. 'Could I give you a small memento?'

'I would appreciate it . . . father,' said Bland gravely.

George reached over and picked up *Soldiers of the Queen*. Bland did not ask what this battered taped-together book was. He only knew that it represented something important in his father's life. He took it without speaking.

'If it means a lot to you it means a lot to me,' he said after a long pause.

In the evening George Oakwood died. There was a smile on his face. Jane sat by the bed, crying, holding the cold hands. It was providential that the last man to see George was not a doctor, a daughter, but an officer. George had gone to his maker knowing that he was not forgotten by the mysterious force to whom he had given the best part of his life—the army.

33

'I've got a choice, Harry,' said Captain Wilcox folding his hands in front of him. 'The colonel wants you back in the front-line, I want you as my driver, but what he says goes unless I want my helmet hanging up in his collection.'

'There's no choice then, sir,' said Harry disconsolately. Returning from leave had been a tiring and depressing business. Most of the men in the train to Dover had appeared to be under armed escort and nobody made jokes.

'The choice is this,' said Wilcox, 'you go into the front-line or you go back to the tanks. If they let you tinker with the engines you're not likely to get your head blown off.'

That had been the worst blow of all, thought Harry, that spot check by the medical board in Calais.

'All out,' the transport sergeant had yelled, 'get your pay-books out. A1s to the left, cripples to the right. Get a move on. That includes you, Corporal.'

'C2, sir,' Harry had told the medical officer, 'gassed twice.'

The officer looked over his glasses, and poked his stethoscope languidly between the buttons of Harry's shirt. 'Lungs as right as rain,' he said, 'provisional A1. Report to your MI room if you feel dicky.'

Harry felt dicky now. 'The tanks then, sir,' he told Wilcox.

'It will help out the orderly room,' said Wilcox. 'We never got your transfer back to me on paper. War Office sent a nasty memorandum.' He waved his hand genially as Harry saluted, and Harry went to the orderly room to collect his movement order.

'Rendezvous at 0700 hours,' said the sergeant. 'Back to the tanks, eh, Corporal?'

'Can't wait, Sarge,' said Harry sardonically. He went to the large wooden hut and found himself a palliasse and a couple of blankets. The cookhouse was a corrugated-iron shack, with three cooks in dirty aprons dealing out a greeny-grey stew. Nobody bothered with transit camps; no generals visited them, no MPs made a fuss about them.

'What do you call this muck?' he asked the cook.

'We call it ragout,' said the cook brightly. 'What do you call it? You might find a bit of rabbit in there. Or on the other hand you might not.'

It was a dry clear evening and as Harry left the cookhouse, feeling sick, he saw Captain Wilcox drive away with an old man in the driving seat. The Wilcoxes of this world did not stay long in transit camps. It would be some requisitioned farmhouse for the captain.

Harry slept badly and woke worse.

'Did you find your rabbit?' asked the cook as he ladled out greasy bacon and eggs. 'Come on, Corp, give us a smile.'

Harry bared his teeth at him.

'That's it,' said the cook, 'the Kitchener spirit. Have a cup of cocoa. It's diabolical, but it's better than the tea . . .'

'Cut out the cackle,' said the orderly sergeant rapping on the lead counter with his stick. 'It's 0640 hours, you buggers haven't shaved yet, and the Tanks don't like dirty unshaven odds and sods. Oi, you, what's your name?'

At first Harry thought the sergeant was talking to him but then realized that it was the burly private next to him.

'Stryker, Sarge,' said the man.

The sergeant's tone altered. 'How old are you, son?'

'Eighteen, Sergeant,' said the man.

'I don't believe it,' said the sergeant, 'you don't shave yet, do you?'

The man coloured. 'No, Sarge,' he gulped. He looked at Harry appealingly. 'Don't tell the others I don't shave,' he said quietly.

'You and me, we seem to be the only Warwickshires,' said Harry. 'Did I hear you say your name was Stryker? My old man had a chum named Stryker. He was a sergeant about the year dot. My old man used to talk about him for hours on end.'

'Died more than forty years ago,' said Private Stryker, 'died in Africa. He was my grandad.'

'That's the bloke,' said Harry. 'You under-age?'

'Does it matter, Corp?' asked the man.

'Not to me, mate,' said Harry.

'Dad hated Grandad,' said Stryker, brooding. 'Grandad never married Grandma, but she took his name. Had to, with Dad on the scene. Dad hated the army. And you know what topped it up? Some sergeant came to the house one day, all done up with shiny boots, just to talk about Grandad. Just to talk about *him* as if he was Napoleon. Dad used to go on alarming about the army. Used to get on my nerves. And Mum's nerves. She left him, you see.'

'It came to that with us,' said Harry, 'but he followed her to Brum from Aldershot. Always on at me to join up, and in the end I did. Look where I am now!'

'You're a corporal,' said Stryker, 'I'd give anything to be a corporal.'

Harry looked at him as if he were mad. 'You mean . . .' he began but shrugged his shoulders realizing that he was wasting his time.

'Dad was so much against the army that I decided I wanted to join,' said Stryker, 'I didn't get on with him, you see. I wouldn't have got on with Grandad, from what I hear. Come on, we'd better go.'

But when they reached the railway station the train had not arrived and the men were fallen out for a smoke. A lieutenant appeared and the sergeant drew the men up at attention.

'Train not in yet, sir,' he reported.

'So I see, Sergeant,' said the lieutenant. 'Are they all for the tanks?'

'Als are, sir,' said the sergeant, 'the rest pioneers and stretcher-bearers.'

'I suppose they're wondering what it's all about,' said the lieutenant.

He turned to the men. They were a mixture, half cavalry and half infantry. Once upon a time, he thought, you could tell a cavalryman by the way his legs bowed. Now it was different. Some of the men in front of him had not seen a horse since they had arrived in France.

'You're privileged to serve with the tanks', he shouted, 'but I'll try and see you're kept in regimental groups. Two Warwickshires, I see, three Durham Light Infantry. You'll be together. Don't forget your pride of regiment. Tanks are the coming service. Any questions?'

A corporal clicked his heels.

'Yes, Corporal?' asked the lieutenant.

'Aren't there enough tanks men to go round, sir?' Harry asked.

This was not an easy one to answer for the lieutenant. He could not tell them that the casualties among the tanks had been higher than anticipated and that scores of men had died horrible deaths fried alive in their burning vehicles or asphyxiated by poison gas which had filtered through the hatches and gun ports. Those who had not been killed had been so battered by their experiences that they had been left vacant-eyed, deaf and stupefied. No one had any conception of the noise inside a tank in battle. He decided to let the corporal, who did not look too happy about the situation, have a half-truth.

'No one realized how many tanks there would be,' he said, 'in the next offensive the British and French—and the Americans as well—will be using hundreds of tanks. Sergeant, have any of these men had experience with tanks?'

The sergeant consulted his list. 'Corporal Oakwood, sir,' he said, 'he was with them when they were attached to the Machine-Gun Corps.'

'A veteran, eh?' said the lieutenant jovially, looking at the NCOs, trying to find one expressing delight. It was a search without success. Tanks were bad news.

The train rumbled into the station. Harry and his comrades in misfortune were bundled into cattle trucks while the senior

269

NCOs and officers occupied the carriages. As morning drew on the heat in the truck became oppressive and one of the men beat a hole in the side of the oblong box with the butt of his rifle. Others joined in until there was an aperture about a yard square. The train puffed past village stations and peasants waiting for their trains stared stolidly at the protruding soldier heads.

'And they're the buggers we're fighting for!' said a private in the Buffs. 'Who's this bloody corporal who's been in tanks? Is he in this bleeding truck?'

'He is,' said Harry. 'I was a tank mechanic. I'm laughing, mate.'

'I've heard that we're to be crew,' said the man from the Buffs. 'They've got civvies to do the repairs.'

Harry sneered. As soon as he saw his old workshop mates they would welcome him back. He was the best mechanic they had and they knew it. But as the men stretched their legs on the platform and as if with one accord went to the station fence and urinated on it, Harry had qualms. He heard the booming of guns in the distance; they were well behind the lines. The huts in the fields were substantial and well built. There was an immaculate parade-ground and dozens of tanks were drawn up as neat as a file of guardsmen. It was so different from the muddle and chaos of his old tank unit.

'Now you've had your pee get into line,' said the sergeant. 'Which bugger smashed that truck?'

He was not very interested and did not pursue it. He would do a roll call, get the men signed for and go back to the transit camp. He led them on to the barrack square and ticked their names off on his nominal roll. The sergeant who took over was one of the old school, nurtured in military traditions, delighted to see such a medley of regiments. His uniform was spotless, his back was like a ramrod.

'The Cauliflowers, the Bengal Tigers, the Bloodsuckers, the Brass-heads,' he said, mouthing the old regimental nicknames with gusto. He looked at his list. 'I'm looking for drivers. Step forward all those men who can drive a car.'

Harry breathed a sigh of relief. It was the same everywhere. Officers needed chauffeurs, men to run them from the mess to meetings, to other units, to boozers and to brothels. For all he knew, he might find another Captain Wilcox to latch on to. He stepped forward smartly.

'Five,' said the sergeant, 'not bad. You will report to Sergeant Cowleaf in number seven hut at 1500 hours. Are you all A1?'

One of them shook his head, and stepped back.

'The rest of you to number six hut after you've collected your blankets and bedding. Gives you all an hour to settle in and get some grub.'

He dismissed the men and uneasily Harry collected his blankets. At least the blankets were clean. But what was he to do with Sergeant Cowleaf? Cowleaf was probably going to quiz them, to find out if they really could drive. It stood to reason that officers' drivers were cushy numbers.

Sergeant Cowleaf proved to be an elderly man with a stoop and a wisp of hair that stuck up at an angle. He had the hard horny hands of a man who had done manual work.

'I'm not going to ask if you can really drive,' he grunted, 'we'll soon find that out and if you can't you'll cop it. Any of you driven lorries or trucks?'

Harry at first kept his hand down. But there might be opportunities for selling goods to Frog farmers, and he might even be able to resume trafficking in petrol. He put his hand up.

'Took your time to think about that, Corporal,' said the sergeant, 'you'll have to have your wits about you now you're with us. Still, you know what it's like to drive big things and how you've got to be extra careful about changing gear. Now, to put no fine a point on it, changing gear in a tank is bloody hard work. That's why you have a second driver. The steering levers need a strong hand to move them, as they're counteracted by strong springs. The clutch-lever and left-foot brake can be bastards. The Mark V tank is better than the Mark IV, but once you've said that, you've said everything.'

Horror gripped Harry and he hardly heard what else the sergeant had to say. He loitered behind and the sergeant grinned at him. It was like looking at a death's head, thought Harry, but the sergeant was merely demonstrating pleasure at having someone so keen.

'I thought I would probably be doing the mechanical work,

271

Sarge,' said Harry, trying to be casual though his heart thumped.

'Mechanics are easier to come by than drivers, my boy,' said the sergeant.

'Captain Bland would vouch for me,' said Harry.

'No doubt he would,' said the sergeant. 'He's on leave at the moment. No, you're a driver, my boy. You'll be able to make it. Once you get the hang of it it's not so bad. I don't like the lads to get cocky. You'll be second driver until you get into the swing of it.'

Getting into a tank was no new experience for Harry. When he was detailed for bringing in repaired tanks he had often taken the controls and knew all about the steering levers, brakes, clutch and gearing. Philosophically he made the best of it. He was the star pupil of Sergeant Cowleaf and as the other tanks stalled, engines shrieking, or ran into each other like dodgems at a fair, Harry's tank was, to Cowleaf, a joy to behold. And as the days went by, Harry began to feel happy at the controls, even feel safe in the monster.

'I'd like to see that lad made up to sergeant,' said Sergeant Cowleaf to his sergeant-major.

'No room on the establishment at the moment,' said the sergeant-major, 'but when the next push comes there'll be a few dead 'uns and he can be made up then. What's his name? I'll put it forward to the adjutant.'

But before anything could be done, the tanks were ordered forward. Harry, promoted to first driver, crouched over his controls, peering through the peep-hole, Private Stryker, the gunner, waited patiently and Lieutenant Bloomenfeld sweated, his stomach rumbling. The second driver checked that his gas mask was intact. The word was that this was the big one and gas would be used by both sides.

Through the night the tanks went at a steady speed, keeping to the roads, stopping frequently at depots for refuelling. The hatches were open and all but Harry were riding outside. The noise of eighty tanks on the move was deafening and as they passed through the villages lights went on and people came out to cheer. It was the first sign of popular enthusiasm Harry had seen for four years.

The tanks began to jog as the roads became shell-marked

272

and the squadron was waved off the road by a group of military policemen to assemble in open country with other tanks in a huge tank park lit by searchlights. The noise of the guns was nearer and the sky was broken by flashes of yellow light. A cookhouse marquee had been erected. The tank crews crowded into it, reaching desperately for their cigarettes and tobacco. Women and girls made tea in large urns, cut sandwiches and washed up the enamel mugs. One elderly lady in gold-rimmed spectacles took the trouble to cut the crusts off her sandwiches and garnished them with tiny sprigs of parsley.

He must be getting old, Harry thought. He looked at the girls without a spark of desire, even a big-breasted one piling rock cakes on to the counter. To his surprise he felt no fear. Somehow the tank gave him a feeling of utter safety, though this was flatly against his experience when he was repairing them. Stryker pushed his way through the crowd to Harry.

'What do you think is happening, Corp?' he asked.

'It's a big one,' said Harry, 'there must be a couple of hundred tanks out there.'

'It's good to be with an old soldier like you,' said Stryker, 'you give me confidence.'

'I've never heard that before,' said Harry, surprised. 'I'll try and get you through. Have you heard where we are?'

'I heard someone say we're near Amiens,' said Stryker.

'I've been there before,' said Harry. He sat down, nursing his mug of tea. He was aware of a quiet satisfaction. He had been through it all. No one could say that Harry Oakwood had not done his bit.

The tanks were on the move again and after ten miles they stopped so that the reserve fuel cans fixed to the sides could be jettisoned. It was a sign that they were nearing the battle area, though the noise of the guns had not got appreciably louder. In one of the leading tanks Major Bland, back from leave, looked at his watch. It was three o'clock. The bombardment would soon begin.

The horizon ahead was just visible in the faint morning light when, suddenly, it became a red sheet of flame. The sound took a second or two to reach the men in the massed tanks and then hit them like thunder. The air seemed to vibrate and the metal sides of the tank acted as a curious modern gong.

'Get started up, Corporal,' ordered Lieutenant Bloomenfeld as a Very light from the leading tanks soared into the sky. The roar of the tank engines momentarily cut out the noise of the bombardment.

Half a mile out Harry narrowly avoided a collision. Another tank driver had tried to change gear on a slope, which was not permissible, faltered backwards and braked just in time. One tank was already in difficulties and Harry selected a more gradual incline, letting the tank have its head. The officer and the second driver were still outside. 'Good work, Corporal!' shouted the officer.

They came up with the reserves, Australians, Scotsmen and Americans. The Americans flicked chewing gum at the officer as the tank trundled by.

'Here!' shouted the lieutenant.

'Come off it, pop,' said an American infantryman, 'if that's the worst that happens to your tin box . . .'

They passed the cavalry, infantrymen resting on the low banks of the muddy road, others trudging on.

'Lid down,' said Bloomenfeld, and it was not before time as odd bits of shrapnel clinked off the tank.

'Gas, sir!' tapped out Harry as he saw the green-grey smoke swirl ahead of him, and he reached for his gas-mask, his hand jolting on the steering lever. The heat began to build up inside the tank and all the crew felt their clothes sticking to them. Stryker, feeling as though he was suffocating, blindly tore off his tunic. 'Take it easy, Stryker,' muttered Harry, but it came out as a mumble under the gas-mask. The smoke disappeared and he could see the tank in front of him. At the edge of his vision, he saw a cavalryman toppled from his horse. He wore a gas-mask, but the horse did not.

Harry took off his gas-mask and the petrol fumes got at his throat.

'Tunics off if you want,' spluttered Bloomenfeld, 'can we open a hatch, driver?'

'Your decision, sir,' said Harry.

'I say we take a chance on it,' said the second driver, 'at least until these bloody fumes disperse. Are you all right, Harry? Want me to take over?'

'I'm all right, cock,' said Harry. 'How about you, sir?'

'I feel as sick as a dog,' admitted Bloomenfeld. 'I feel I ought to tell you that this is my first time in battle.'

'The corp's the old hand, sir,' said Stryker.

The lieutenant nodded, and opened the hatch, pulling on his metal visor, a steel mask padded in leather, the eyes protected by small flat steel bars a sixteenth of an inch apart, with the lower face covered by chain mail. He looked out, aware by the growling low gear that they were ascending a steep hill and were therefore safe from bullets. The tracks slid on old disintegrating trenches, clacking against ancient bones and equipment. A half-buried machine-gun was hurled aside and a system of warning tins strung on barbed wire clattered aimlessly.

'We should strike the road again soon, Corporal,' shouted the officer.

'I should put the lid down when we get to the top,' yelled Harry. 'I don't know what we'll find.'

'All right, driver,' said the officer.

They breasted the hill.

'Seems safe,' said Harry, 'a lot of smoke around. Hold your seats, for we've got more trenches ahead of us.'

The tank bucked and swayed, the crew hanging on to the hand-holds on the side of the tank and Harry felt his eyes watering as he peered through the smoke. The going became smoother.

'We've come to the road,' he said, 'the tank in front's stopped, and the men are getting out.'

Bloomenfeld opened the hatch and climbed out. His bones were aching and there was a bruise the size of a half-crown on the side of his hand. Stryker was bleeding from the nose where a sudden swerve had sent him against the tank wall.

'Can't see a damned thing,' said a sergeant from the tank in front. A captain trotted up.

'Have you got the bridge sections?' he asked Bloomenfeld.

'What's happened?' Bloomenfeld asked.

'We've got to get across a river,' said the captain, 'and the Huns have blown up the bridge.'

'They're on the run then, sir?' asked Harry, climbing out.

'They must be,' said the captain, 'but I don't know.'

He went on to look for the tanks carrying bridge sections, pushing through the reserve infantry making their way forward. A sergeant-major came up.

'We're going on, sir,' he told Bloomenfeld, 'if you'll detail one of your men to act as guide. Visibility is two yards, that's all. Safe as houses. The Boche aren't shelling us.'

'That never occurred to me,' said the lieutenant, marvelling. 'Did it to you, Corporal?'

'It did,' said Harry. 'Could they be hatching something?'

'They're in this black smoke like us, Corporal,' said the sergeant-major. 'I was talking to an artilleryman. They're sending over two of shrapnel to one of smoke.'

The tank ahead began to move off and the second driver acted as guide. As suddenly as it had descended, the pall of smoke lifted and the guide climbed back on to the tank. Through his visor Harry could see the tanks ahead of him. As he increased his speed to match theirs he could see shells bursting in the middle distance. The Germans, he reckoned, had found a range for their artillery that would not involve killing their own men. Obviously the front-line troops had been at close grips. Hurriedly the officer closed all hatches and as the tank went on what sounded like hailstones on a window could be heard. Harry put on his splinter mask in case an odd machine-gun bullet came through his visor.

He passed a blazing tank on his left. One man was lying by its side, his back ash-black, and another was half-in half-out the hatch. Whether he was dead or not Harry did not know. A second tank had been struck on its tracks, which had peeled off like an over-ripe banana skin. He passed infantry, running, or jogging, or sometimes taking it easy. They were not acting like men under incessant machine-gun fire. Wondering how his tank could have become the target of machine-gunners he saw the running men drop to the ground, their arms outstretched, fingers into the mud as if that would help them. For a fraction of a second as the tank breasted an incline he noticed the wings of a German scout, diving and firing on the men.

The second driver began to vomit with the fumes. The lieutenant opened the hatch again, slamming it shut as he saw the German aircraft turning at low level and coming in for another attack. Private Stryker, his hands gripped round the butt of his machine-gun, had not yet fired a shot. He peered out through his peep-hole but there was nothing to shoot at. He saw the old trenches, long deserted, relics of a battle forgotten and deplored and noticed that Harry was more skilful than most in avoiding the shell craters. One of the tanks was tilted at an angle of forty-five degrees and the men were having a hard time of it getting out. The officer was waist-deep in murky water, his mouth opening and shutting, though the shouting could not be heard in the racket of engines, jangling tracks and the crump of shell-fire, which, inconsequential as it seemed, occasionally put paid in a completely arbitrary manner to a tank. Stryker swallowed as a man ran like a flaming torch through the advancing infantry. One of the infantrymen pushed him into a water-filled shell crater, whether in irritation or to save the tank man's life was not clear. A motor-cyclist who had left the road for no very evident purpose was sitting by his upturned machine wondering what to do.

'Jesus!' shouted the second driver. He lay on the floor of the tank in a pool of blood.

'Get him out!' shrieked Stryker, his finger trembling on the trigger.

'Shut up!' shouted the lieutenant, 'control yourself!'

But the second driver screamed until he died. Stryker wiped his arm across his forehead. The edge of his peep-hole was distorted and sheared off white where the bullet had entered, missing him and striking the driver in the chest.

Harry tightened his lips and went on. The gaps between the tanks were becoming wider and the barbed wire he was slicing through was shining and new. There were trenches, but they were trenches full of people, hurling themselves at each other, throwing themselves aside, friend and foe, as the tanks lumbered over them, occasionally crushing someone slow off the mark.

The lieutenant crept across the tank, put his mouth close to Harry's ear. 'We're over no man's land; whatever you do, keep going.'

As he finished speaking the tank rocked sideways, and the hull vibrated and echoed as if struck by a giant hammer. Harry could see the officer's lips moving, but heard nothing. The engine roared but he knew the tracks had been hit. He altered

277

gear and changed the reversing lever. The tank wheeled at an angle and the engine stuttered and stopped.

'We're sitting ducks, Corporal,' said Bloomenfeld, 'let's get out.' He took his revolver from his holster, and pushed up the hatch.

'What do I do, Corp?' asked Stryker, sweating.

'You cover him,' said Harry tersely.

'But I can't see a damn thing,' said Stryker, 'there's something blocking my visor.'

All Harry's philosophy of life indicated to him that he should sit tight, and that the inconvenience and discomfort, not to mention the presence of a corpse, inside the tank were preferable to the dangers outside. Lightning could strike twice and his tank could be hit again, but for every shell there could be a hundred machine-gun bullets and a machine-gun bullet could kill as efficiently as the biggest Jack Johnson. He was therefore surprised when he found he was the one to poke his head and shoulders out of the tank and not Stryker.

'It's an arm,' he said, looking at the object blocking Stryker's vision. 'It's field-grey, so it's not one of ours. I don't know where the officer went. The smoke barrage is coming in again.'

'Is it safe to get out?' asked Stryker.

'Search me,' said Harry, lighting a cigarette, stubbing it out rapidly when he realized that the shell could have damaged the petrol tank. A colourless river trickling through the mud confirmed his fears.

'Let's go!' he shouted back, 'before we go up in flames!'

But go where? They were unarmed. They did not know where they were and, although at present the smoke barrage was preserving their anonymity it would hide the identity of whatever shadowy figures appeared from some direction or other. The only clue was their wrecked tank, but how much did it veer round when it was struck?

Harry knew from experience that soldiers on the advance have the fixed idea that all who appear in front of them are enemies. He recalled the lieutenant shouting in his ear that they were over no man's land. Did he mean past no man's land? Certainly the ground he and Stryker were walking on was not pitted with craters, churned up by tanks and the forward infantry as it was. There was even the occasional tuft of grass, proof if proof was needed that this was not country that had been crossed and recrossed and soaked in the blood of tens of thousands. Maybe the Allies had broken through. If that was the case, it stood to reason that the generals would not follow it up; they would be sitting in their headquarters holding back the reserves, fearful of another catastrophe like the Somme.

He took a chance. 'Let's get on,' he said, 'no sense in going back.'

'That's the spirit, Corp,' said Stryker, his face lighting up, and together, bent low to reduce chance of being hit by a stray bullet, they trotted forward. Somehow it was strangely quiet. The ever-present boom of artillery was remote and even the ominous clack-clack-clack of machine-guns seemed to be in the distance.

Harry felt less sanguine as the smoke increased in intensity and his companion broke out coughing. His foot clinked against something, and bending down he picked up a beer bottle of an unfamiliar shape. He heard voices and put his hand on Stryker's arm to still him. And then the smoke lifted. They were near the rim of a narrow trench, and he could distinctly hear the chug-chug of a mechanical pump. There was barbed wire stretched out but it was limp and half-hearted. Making certain that there were no tin-cans tied to it to give warning of an attack, Harry crawled beneath the loose strands, crunching a wooden box of flowers some enterprising military horticulturalist was growing.

This was ridiculous, he thought. He must be dreaming. Or he might be dead and this was some dark purgatory. But if that were so, would he have a spectral Stryker at his elbow trying to repress his coughs? Still if he was alive he had seen this happen before. The advance had gone on, somehow bypassing a set of trenches. This was evidently a communications trench that had never felt the rigour of battle. As he was weighing up what to do he felt himself slipping. The stupid German buggers, he thought. They had not shored it up with sandbags.

He landed at a crouch, Stryker slithering after him, and heard voices further up the trench. Protected for the present by a sharp angle in the lie of the trench, he looked about him, and spontaneously picked up a peculiar kind of gun. It was big and clumsy and had a tube connected to a black container. It also had a trigger and when half a dozen men, most of them without their helmets, appeared, he shut his eyes and pulled the trigger. Stryker stepped back in amazement as flames licked at the earth.

As if with one accord the men put up their hands. One of them had a rifle which he hurled over the top of the trench and stood embarrassed, grinning. Four more men joined them. Two of them wore cooks' aprons, and one was clutching a radio transmitter and was clearly undecided whether to drop it and risk breaking a toe or put his hands up. Eventually he placed it gently on the ground, his eyes fixed wonderingly on Harry.

Nothing like this had ever happened to Corporal Oakwood before. For the first time he could understand his father.

'If Dad could see me now!' he said aloud, feeling his eyes prickle. He felt a strange affection for these men, these ageing non-combatants.

'Cigaretten?' one of them said hopefully, and when Harry nodded he lowered one hand, unbuttoned his tunic pocket, and reached for a packet of cigarettes, handing it to Harry.

'It's a trick!' hissed Stryker. Harry shook his head stoutly.

'They're old 'uns,' he said, 'they want to go into the pen. Find me a rifle or something, will you? This flamethrower's bloody heavy!'

Forward of Harry and his batch of prisoners Major Bland relaxed for the first time. All the objectives had been taken. He and his tanks, 456 of them, had proved their worth and had broken through. He sat in his tent and examined the reports that were handed to him. Overhead twenty SE5s flew in perfect formation, their control of the air space complete. Prisoners were marched by in their hundreds, their weapons thrown away, some of them capless, some of them smoking, some of them sullen.

'This is splendid,' he said to a sergeant-major who came up to him with a mug of tea, 'if I were a drinking man I would want something stronger.'

'Aye, sir,' said the sergeant-major. He hesitated. 'Promotions in the field, sir,' he began.

'I don't normally approve of them,' said Bland, 'but there will be some in this one. We've smashed the Hindenburg Line.

God knows how but that's what the reports say. Medals as well. I'm not accepting any recommendations at this moment. Have you anyone particular in mind?'

The sergeant-major took off his cap and scratched his head. 'This is a funny one, sir,' he said, 'I don't know whether you ever remember Sergeant-Major Oakwood. Before your time, I expect. I met him during the Boer War. But I've just met his son. "If Dad could see me now!" he said. He's just captured twelve Heinies single-handed, confirmed by a Private Stryker. Took 'em with a flame-thrower . . . is everything all right, sir?'

'That's Harry Oakwood, is it?'

'Don't know his first name, sir,' said the sergeant-major, 'corporal in the Royal Warwicks.'

'By God!' muttered Bland, 'so he *was* related to him!'

The sergeant-major did not catch this and merely said, 'He was with our lot, sir, the tanks.'

'His tank officer will have to be found . . .' began Bland.

'Dead, sir,' said the sergeant-major, 'took off when the tank was hit. I'm sorry, sir, I've taken a bit of a liberty. "Spot of promotion for you here, Corporal," I said to young Oakwood. He looked at me sort of cheeky. "Promotions in the field, Sarge-Major?" he said. "Can you put me up two, so I can be level with my dad?" '

'What did you say to that?' asked Bland, trying to hide his agitation.

'I told him not to be a cocky young whipper-snapper,' said the sergeant-major. He swallowed. 'There was something in his eyes, sir. I'd like to see him in the sergeants' mess. He was one of us. You know what I mean, sir. Not one of your bloody territorials or Kitchener's bloody men but one of us.'

'I know what you mean, Sergeant-Major,' said Bland quietly. Corporal Oakwood, his half-brother Harry, was one of them. At last.

That evening Sergeant Oakwood, Royal Warwickshire Regiment, sewed on his sergeant's stripes. He did it badly for his eyes were blurred with tears.

Epilogue

The world waited for the Armistice. Thousands of men stood in their trenches, their rifles propped against the sandbags. An officer stood tensely, his eyes on his watch, a whistle between his lips, sweat on his brow. He suddenly smiled, realizing the absurdity of it all and spat the whistle out. He and his men would not be going over the top again. Peace was coming.

'Eleven o'clock,' he said quietly to his sergeant-major. Somewhere from afar he thought he heard church bells.

'That's it then, sir?' asked the sergeant-major.

'That's it, thank God!' said the officer grimly.

He climbed out of the trench and looked across the countryside at the craters and the ruined farmhouses. There was the farm where he had lost a platoon on an idiotic patrol. There was the crater that had done for his number two. There was the wreckage of the Fokker monoplane which had crash-landed. He had been surprised to see that sergeant walk away from it—what was his name? Yes, Oakwood, Sergeant Oakwood. He wondered what had happened to him. He hoped he was all right; he was a brave lad.

Leonard stood by his SE5a. His mechanic had just mended a fractured fuel pipe and he was checking it. The mechanic trotted up to him and shook his hand. He did not say anything, for tears were running down his cheek.

'I know,' said Leonard quietly. 'What can you say?'

He patted the engine cowling of his aeroplane as if saying goodbye to a favourite horse, and walked back to the mess, thinking of Elizabeth, of Harry and of his mother. He wondered what they were doing now.

Jane and Elizabeth stood in the empty shop. Jane was crying, and Elizabeth put her arms around her shoulders.

'I don't know why I'm crying,' Jane said, 'both my boys are coming home safe and sound.' She picked up the letter from Harry. It was a different kind of letter from any other she had received from him and it warmed her, not with its content but in its tone. It was from a Harry who had always lurked beneath the surface; there were two sides to him, just as there had been to George. Had she not seen the newspapers she would not have known about his exploits. 'Birmingham hero captures Hun platoon single-handed,' the caption to Harry's photograph had read. A modest Harry—it did not seem possible.

Mary came into the shop. 'All the people are in the streets singing. Well, I suppose that's that.'

Jane did not say anything. Mary had lost a husband, though she did not mention it these days. Thank goodness, Jane thought, Mary was not going to be a professional war-widow.

'I saw Henry in town,' Mary said casually, 'he's asked me out tonight. I think I'll go.'

'He's a nice boy,' said Jane.

'Boy?' said Mary brightly. 'He's forty-two!'

Judy had seen Harry's photograph in the paper as well. 'Bloody cheek!' she had said moodily, and put more lipstick on in preparation for her evening out.

'What is it, Ma?' Harry's son had asked.

'Your dad's a hero,' she had told him.

'Which dad is that?' he had asked slyly. 'Daddy Sid or Daddy Tom?'

She had not answered; it was all too complicated. She had looked for her rouge; it took a lot of time these days preparing to be twenty and full of girlish fun.

Major Clive Bland was preparing to return to England. He had just listened to the colonel's speech in the mess, and it had depressed him; the colonel was calling for a standing army of half a million to combat the menace of Bolshevism. He watched his batman packing for him.

'What are you going to do, Samuels?' he asked.

'Back to the missus, sir,' said Samuels. 'Dunno about a job. A land fit for heroes the papers say. I dunno, though. Beg pardon, sir, what are you doing?'

'Still in the army, Samuels,' said Bland, 'it's my life you see.'

After Samuels had taken Bland's luggage to his car, the major realized that his batman had forgotten to pack what in a curious way had become his most valued possession. He tucked it under his arm and went out. He stumbled and a hand helped him to his feet. He looked at his helper.

'You've dropped something, sir,' said Harry Oakwood, 'it's a book.'

He picked up *Soldiers of the Queen*. The cover was criss-crossed with tape and the spine had been assiduously restitched. Harry looked at it wonderingly. It was such a familiar object that to see it here was bizarre. He looked at the pencil scribbling on the brown tape; *that* had got him into trouble when he was six.

'It was my father's book, sir,' he said. 'I didn't know you knew him.'

'I didn't know *you* knew him, Sergeant,' said Bland ironically. 'I see the resemblance now.' He looked at his half-brother with something like affection. 'Shake hands, Harry,' he said, the Christian name coming naturally, 'you're one of us now. My God, it took you a long time to find out who you were!'

'And what I was,' added Harry. He handed the book over, still puzzled, and looked directly into the officer's eyes. 'Good God!' he breathed.

'You'll have to think about it, Harry,' said Clive Bland softly. He looked at his watch. The boat-train left at five o'clock. It was time to go.